TAM

TAM

THE THREE CHANGELINGS

Guy Winter

Adapted from the screenplay by Guy Winter and Ross Beveridge

inspired by and featuring the poems and songs of Robert Burns

ISBN-13: 9781976088575
ISBN-10: 1976088577

For Hannah, Annabel and Mia-

"I will luve thee still, my Dears,
Till a' the seas gang dry!"

I am a Bard of no regard,
Wi' gentle folks an' a' that;
But Homer-like, the glowrin' byke,
Frae' town to town I draw that.

I never drank the Muses' stank,
Castalia's burn, an' a' that;
But there it streams, an' richly reams,
My Helicon I ca' that.

The Jolly Beggars, Robert Burns

———◆———

Chlanna nan con thigibh a' so 's gheibh sibh feòil!

Sons of dogs, come here and feed on flesh!

War Cry of Clan Cameron

PROLOGUE

———

THE BONFIRE SPAT SOOT AND hissed like a cornered cat. Swirling sheets of rain lashed into it, sending plumes of steam and smoke steepling high above the cliff-top. Tendrils of black and white vapour writhed up together, intertwined, then dispersed into the night sky. The flames twisted and contorted in the gale, bewitching the capering fire-daemons that they flung headlong down into the bay below.

Four dark-cloaked figures stood seawards of the fire, wreathed in shadow. A man and three women, to all appearances, each of them craning their necks forward into the storm. Watching, waiting, eagerly scanning the tempestuous horizon stretched out before them. At length, the man shuffled closer to the cliff-edge. The firelight revealed his terrible deformity, upper back and shoulders hideously hunched and crooked under the cloak.

"It is true then? The word your sisters sent from France?" he said slowly.

He spoke without turning his head, impervious to the elements raging around him. Even so, his voice carried effortlessly to them through the storm, perfectly attuned to the tumult.

"Do you no' feel it- feel it in the air? Through the thunder, lightnin' and rain!" said the woman closest to him. She held her cloak up to shield her face against the downpour, exposing a flash of green material beneath it. "I can hardly breathe for it! And yet it had to be so... For Banquo's accursed seed returns to Scotland this night!"

"Nannie is right! Vile Banquo... Infamous Thane of Lochaber!" shrieked the woman next to her, raising her voice high to vie with the howling of the wind. She adjusted the crimson scarf in her hair, as she continued bitterly: "Too shrewdly did our foremothers prophesy the rise o' his ill-fated race to Macbeth- the wretched Stuart kings!"

"And yet they didnae' divine the future clearly enough..." said the last woman, hair blowing wildly. "For had they seen his descendant, James Stuart, wi' the crowns of England and Scotland newly united atop his pinched, witch-hatin' face, surely they would've found a way to set bloody Macbeth against him sooner!"

"To think that they could've put an end to this, right there and then, on that ancient heath!" cried Red Scarf shrilly, oblivious to the glare that the hunchback had turned on her. "How could they have let Banquo's son, skittish Fleance, flit through their fingers, friendless in Scotland as he was? To live an' sire such hateful heirs, to torment and to hunt us!"

But she had tried the hunchback's stunted patience for too long.

"Cast no doubt now on the divinations of the past, brat!" he snapped, voice cutting like a cat o' nine tails. His ageless, unlined face was suddenly illuminated by a flash of lightning as he whirled around to them, back twitching and lurching with his anger. "Your mothers traced dark paths through many lives of men to find their way. Paths that even now are hidden far too deep for your feebler arts to discern!"

"How d'ye ken that, then?" said Wild Hair, stung by the rebuke.

"Who do you think guided them, you dolt?" he said. Slowly he swivelled his gaze round upon her, uttering a strange, consumptive rattling sound from deep within that made her shudder. "The reek of their nauseating potions? The babble of their cabalistic mumbo-jumbo?" He spat on the ground. "Don't mistake the trinkets and gimcracks of their craft for the graver powers that they paid tribute to!"

He gazed far out to sea once more, momentarily lost in a black reverie of his own. The women recoiled from him, as his lumpen back shifted and squirmed, moving arrythmically with his rasping breathing.

"They knew how to summon those anguished spirits who walk unimpeded down the corridors of time, long barred to men..." he said at last. "They knew that a short season of persecution- even of being hunted- is nothing, to those of us who deal in the currency of centuries!" He gave a harsh, chattering laugh that seemed to echo in his chest. "With my guidance, they saw what you could never imagine! That Macbeth, my pretty Thane of Cawdor, may yet have proved a direr threat to your kind than any mealy-mouthed Stuart... Had I not poisoned his baleful roots, before they could delve their way deeper into Scotland's soil!"

"But he was one of our own!" cried Red Scarf, and then clapped her hand to her unruly mouth.

The hunchback smiled to himself, relishing her disquiet.

"Oh no, my dear- he was only too human!" he said. "That is the flaw in most monsters... Banquo at least had good cause to welcome your ancients' prophecy- the flattering vision of his own heirs as kings of Scotland!" He shrugged his crooked shoulders. "But did I not dispose of them both in accordance with my own designs? And after them, Mary, Henry, Charles and James Stuart in their turn? Did I not transmute the Elector of Hanover into King George the First of Great Britain, in the very face of James Stuart's ancient claims? And will I not deal with all the Jacobite Jameses and Charleses and Henrys that are here, and are yet to come, in the like coin? I was not in jest when I swore to grind the head of the Stuart snake beneath my heel!"

He stared hard into the blackness, eyes gleaming with malice, hunched back leaping. Then he turned once more to the chastened witches behind him. No secret, black and midnight hags, these. Even robed in the darkness of a ghastly night, they were all comely enough, and Nannie herself something more than that- possessed of an ethereal beauty far beyond the rustic charms of her fellows. An intoxicating, even maddening, beauty, thought the hunchback- a beauty such that even the strong ones of this world should not take lightly. And of a certain higher grace too, that perhaps served to soften his tone a little when he spoke again.

"So before you dare dream a word of complaint against Macbeth's ancient trio, those weird, Wayward Sisters, ask yourselves instead what you have done to safeguard their great legacy to you! This wild Scotland, that we severed Charles Stuart's very head from its shoulders to deliver to you! Your birthright..."

"Fear not, Rannoch. What we have, we will hold," said Nannie calmly. "No gods, no masters! So it has been wi' us, these seven hundred years and more. You need not fret about our birthright, for we have forgotten nothin'- no, nor forgiven it either..." She looked into the heart of the bonfire, still raging in the teeth of the storm. "And we would see this whole country set to fire and sword, plunged back into the very darkest days of the Covenant, before we would let it out of our grasp again!"

"Ah, the Covenant!" said Rannoch, savouring the memory. "Hold that darkness to your hearts. For it may yet come to that once more, before this act has played itself out..."

"You have everything you need, sisters- to set it in motion?" Nannie asked the two witches by her side.

Red Scarf nodded eagerly, then paused, momentarily startled by another great thunder-clap.

"Everythin', Nannie!" she said. "All except for- him. For the findin' is easy enough. But no one can get to him..."

"I know how to get to him!" said Nannie fiercely. "Start your fires! When we meet again, you'll find the last precious charm delivered into your hands as though it were- a mere trifle."

"But- but what if his own folk were to come for him first, Nannie?" said Wild Hair nervously, wiping an insistent trickle of rainwater away from one side of her face. "If the fairy folk were to take against us?"

Even as she spoke to Nannie, she kept casting terrified glances towards the brooding hunchback on the cliff-edge.

"That's no' their way!" said Nannie. "They can only shape nature- or steal it. They can't destroy it. And so their power is fadin' away, just as surely as nature is losin' its own grip on this world... For man's one great gift is destruction!" She laughed. "Who now fears a fairy barrow, when a battery of cannon could blast the black rock of Edinburgh Castle itself into dust! All that's left for the fair folk, and their dwindlin' power, is to bequeath it to us. And then be forgotten forever! Well may they call them the still folk then..."

"Oh, don't underestimate the old ones, my dear," said Rannoch. "Their ways were ever subtle beyond the minds of men- yes, and even of witches! They were here before you, and here they will linger, long after you are forgotten. They are lead actors in Scotland's great tragedy, where you are merely spectators- little children on your tiptoes, straining anxiously to see what the next scene will hold! For who among mortals ever dreamed that the taciturn changeling, Macduff, would be the killer to undo Macbeth's dread charm? Even your mothers only saw it through a glass, darkly..."

He threw his head back, and his laugh seemed to roll around his lumpen shoulders and out into the bay, caught up in the thunder, echoed by an unnatural, almost bestial chattering sound from deep within his cloak.

"The old ones knew, though!" said Rannoch. "They knew of old that a man not born of woman would come to serve their turn, if Macbeth were ever to threaten the balance of the three worlds. So they planted Macduff in the human world, and they waited like patience on a monument for his moment to come- just as they always have. As they still do. And they look after their own on this side, too- when they can..."

"So... So whit can we do to foil them, if they do come for him then, my Lord?" asked Wild Hair, fidgetting and adjusting her cloak against another merciless gust of wind. Rannoch scowled at her, and she drew further back from him, repulsed. "The fairy folk... the *mnathan-shìdh?*" she stuttered.

"You dare to bandy words with me, you idiot daughter of Hecate?" he hissed, advancing on her. "And in words of their own foul tongue! How dare you?"

To her horror, the hump on Rannoch's back seemed to swell and leap in time with his rising fury as he approached her. She shuddered in terror as his cloak parted and a ghastly, grinning face appeared next to Rannoch's own thunderous glare. Now there was a second head on his shoulders, horribly assymetric with the first, freakishly shrunken by some arcane, timeless black magic. Lined and wizened, framed in coarse white hair, it was as though it had absorbed all of Rannoch's infinite years of malice and wickedness into itself, leaving him to present his own, unnaturally unaged visage to the world. Wild Hair gazed at it, transfixed by the mocking eyes and bared white teeth, as the gnarled face leered and chattered in wordless malevolence.

"What- what is it?" she whispered.

Rannoch paused, revelling in the power of the lightning as it lit up the corrugated seascape once more. He tasted the salt and iodine in the air, drinking it in like old Falernian wine. The little monkey squatted on his shoulder, head still next to his.

"*He* is a son of the greatest house of men!" said Rannoch. "And even in his present reduced form, he is descended from the Great Order of Friars Minor Capuchin- so show some respect!"

The monkey hissed at Wild Hair, throwing her off balance, and Rannoch seized her cloak, pulled her hard towards him and then gave her a sudden shove, pitching her straight over the edge of the cliff. The wind carried back her hideous screams as they bounced back up the sheer rock-face, before another deadening flurry of rain swept down and drowned them out completely. Red Scarf leaned forward over the precipice in shock to watch her friend's descent, the spell of Rannoch's revelation broken. Too late she twisted back to Rannoch, as he turned towards her.

"No! No!" she screamed. "I'll do better! I'll serve you well!"

"And pigs might fly!" said Rannoch, pushing her heavily between the shoulder-blades. The brutal shove sent her tumbling headlong into the void, and this time there was no sound at all. Nothing but the eery, piercing shrieks of gulls, cutting through the wind like icy diamonds through glass.

"She does have a point though, Rannoch," said Nannie calmly, straightening her own cloak. "What of the *mnathan-shìdh*? You must know that they could yet confound even your designs..."

"Of course I know that!" snarled Rannoch. "Who better than I? But then who now among us can tell what path they will choose- whether they will venture everything for such a cause? Will they really change their policy of centuries, and throw their lot in with men?"

"No' that disgustin' ape of yours, at any rate!" said Nannie sharply.

"Disgusting?" said Rannoch, as the monkey shrieked its disapproval at Nannie. "Why, you are forgetting your poetry, child: 'Of all this numerous progeny was none; So beautiful, so brave, as Absalom'!"

Nannie laughed.

"Beautiful or no', I wish you'd no' let him run free, to terrify my witches like that! They dread you enough as it is, without lettin' that wretched beast scare them all out of their senses..."

"And that, my dear, is just as it should be!" said Rannoch, stroking Absalom's wiry head, as he leaped and gibbered in excitement on his shoulder. "Terror- hate- fear... Those are the ties that truly bind. For fear is always stronger than love, in the end- isn't that right, Absalom?"

He pinched the monkey's ear between the nails of his finger and thumb. Absalom gave a blood-curdling shriek of rage and pain, before scampering off to warm his wrinkled paws in front of the bonfire.

"Love may fade and wither..." said Rannoch. "But if you nourish it properly, fear will last forever!"

He laughed and resumed his restless pacing along the lip of the cliff, now slim and straight-backed without Absalom fidgetting beneath his cloak. He somehow contrived to light a long pipe in the face of the howling wind, the flame of the taper from the bonfire dancing at the end of his fingertips.

"The old ones enter the world of men on their own terms, or not at all," he said. "They are not like you poor witches, doomed to live forever amongst your bitterest foes! Hating all, and hated by all! You were right about one thing, though, Nannie- they still have a great power over nature, and its creatures…"

He puffed on his pipe, and Nannie waited in silence for him to continue. She knew better than to force this tune.

"And so…" he said at last. "And so what we shall work is something so unnatural- so fatal to the old order of things that they represent- that it will shatter it altogether! For I have watched and waited too, and my own gift is to sow discord- yes, and to find a bane. A bane to kill any living thing!"

"And for witches too?" said Nannie drily.

He laughed again.

"Why, you are the brittlest creatures of all, in your own sweet way! With your superhuman powers, and your supernatural frailties… You are like those pathetic, soft-bellied crabs that must use their wits alone to borrow strength and dominion from another creature's shell, are you not?" said Rannoch, and did not wait for an answer. "Do you think I don't know why you and those slovenly sisters of yours brood so on these so-called *mnathan-shìdh*? The still folk, fairies, old ones or fair folk- whatever it is you want to call them!" he said. "It all comes to the same, because for all your airs and graces, all you witches hate them- you always have! You hate them and you fear them. And you are right to do so, my dear! You are the most natural enemies of all. The most ancient. For can they not bend even water to their will?"

This time Nannie did not respond, but stared evenly back at him. He laughed.

"Ah, so you didn't know? Well then, it is so. It is just as you always feared, my pretty! And it is not only my designs that are at stake here. If the old ones choose to take against you in the coming struggle, then they will dash you to pieces, like a seagull cracks a crab. Not even I will be able to protect you- even if I wanted to…"

He turned his back to her in a gesture of dismissal.

"Oh yes, 'too much of water hast thou, poor Ophelia'!" he said. "Too much of water… But for now you have a journey to make, do you not, my dear? You all have your own parts to play in this great game!"

For the first time, Nannie's face seemed to wear a gossamer shroud of care.

"So I must- I must go back to the blind, weak world I came from?" she said. "After all these years away from it? After everythin' I went through to get here?"

"Of course!" said Rannoch, his eyes flashing dangerously. "That is why we took you in the first place. That is the part that is entrusted to you! It was the last, precious vision of those three ancient sisters, now long forgotten in this world…"

"*'Three changelings will come, to shape Scotland; One from the Wayward Sisters, one from the Still Folk, and one from Man',*" recited Nannie.

"Good! You have not quite forgotten everything that I taught you as a child, then…" said Rannoch.

"Oh, I remember!" said Nannie. "But are you still so sure that I am one of the Three?"

"Such mysteries are traced in the sand, not etched in stone…" said Rannoch. "But be sure that I did not wait seven hundred years on a whim! You came from Man, did you not? Born of a human woman, but raised as a witch- you already bestride the two worlds, and there is great power in that."

"An' the others?"

"The second changeling, an old one raised among men, we have hunted since birth- and you now have him at your mercy. The face of the witch-born changeling is still hidden, even from my eyes. Few have left that dread coven- but one who has done so, and somehow lived to master the ways of the old ones, will be a formidable foe…"

"I am ready," said Nannie quietly. "Ready to face whatever risks await us. I will not allow my sufferin' to have been in vain!"

"We will see about that…" said Rannoch. "But don't talk to me again of suffering, child- for I reckon it in millennia, not in the petty lifetimes of men!"

They stood in silence for a moment, until a jagged fork of lightning seemed to rend the very sea and sky asunder. Rannoch watched it with glee, and then he spoke again.

"Fulfill your destiny now, girl, and there shall be witches in Scotland forever! If not, well then…"

He tapped the bowl of the pipe out over the cliff-edge. The falling embers glowed brightly for the blink of an eye, and then the darkness swallowed them. Nannie nodded. She swept her cloak around her, disappearing silently into its black folds, and then leapt off the cliff.

CHAPTER 1

THE BLACK SHIP WAS SLOWLY but surely being battered into submission by the waves, its foredeck completely awash with sea-water. The closer it got to the salvation of the shore, the more the elements conspired to smash it back. The drenched seamen were risking life and limb to execute their captain's screamed orders, but they were already exhausted by the relentless storms of the crossing. All they could do was hold their breath, as suddenly the sea seemed to drop away beneath them. The hoary old Sea of Moyle made one last effort to drag the ship under, pulling at it like the tentacles of an ancient kraken, then spat it out into the safety of the bay.

Within sight of land, the black-painted vessel seemed even darker than the icy fingers of water clawing at it. Then unseen hands sent a dull, cast-iron anchor plummeting down to unseen depths. Finally, after a few lurches against the current, it found equilibrium, ducking and bobbing in time with the waves. Now shadowy figures could be made out on deck through the driving rain. They rolled barrels marked "*Calvados*", "*Vin de Chypre*", "*St. John Commandaria*", "*Cognac*" and "*Vin de Bordeaux*" down a gangplank and onto a bucking tub-boat.

Even the sharp eyes on shore- and up on the cliff-top above it- couldn't have made out the ghost ship's name and port of origin: '*Du Teillay, Nantes*'. There was no golden *fleur-de-lis* to brand this wolf-ship one of Louis XV's ravening pack. Nothing at all, in fact, that could catch the barest glimmer of light. But the secret vessel was already being left behind now, treading water impassively as two files of sailors silently strained at the oars of the longboat, thrashing urgently on through the rain towards *terra firma*.

Seascape rapidly gave way to landfall. The rowers jumped out into the shallows, running the boat up through the breakers. Now the landers scuttled stealthily out from the shelter of the rocks, like crabs at low tide. They swarmed over to help unload the contraband. Some of the smugglers clutched blazing torches with which they neurotically scanned the rocks for waiting Excisemen- or worse. The usual muttered speculations raced around the jumpy shoremen like wild-fire: "What's the cargo the night? What's the crop, boys, what's the crop?"

But there was an unusual sense of unease too, and insistent, nagging questions that were not so familiar in the lonely bay: "Where'n the world is this one from? Why do they row as though the devil himsel' is at their heels?" And over and over again: "Why do the gulls shriek so, tonight?"

Questions, questions, so many more questions than answers- whispered by the whippet-like tubmen, poised to carry off the precious liquor in their oval kegs; growled by the goonish batsmen, armed to the teeth to protect it. This crop was hard to find, harder to land and hardest to keep, and every man jack of them was ready to defend it with his own heart's blood. Or so they swore, for it was easy enough to say so in Sawney's tavern- what with the heady buzz of smuggled liquor coursing through your veins, and your fine new mates boozing, bragging and swaggering away around you! But now it was a cursed, ill-omened night, with devilry in the air and evidence enough on the Crown's Estate to hang a whole legion of landers. Small wonder that the torches themselves fizzed and crackled with tension in the rainstorm, as the tub-boat was run high up onto the shore.

The tubmen rushed in to unload the booze. Time was of the essence. Only this time there was something wrong, a discordant grind of wood on shingle, something about the landing they instinctively mistrusted. They hesitated for a moment, and then reeled back in shock as a young man leapt out onto the beach from under a shaggy blanket.

The wind caught his curly fair hair, accentuating the raffish, devil-may-care air about him. It also caught his travelling coat, lifting it clear of the brace of long Pietro Beretta pistols beneath it. The customised Italian pistol-stocks reflected the firelight back around the beach, red and orange rubies and cairngorms glinting wickedly like cats' eyes. The traveller hurriedly folded his coat back over the traitorous gems, but it was too late- far too late to deceive the unblinking eyes on this shoreline.

"Excise pig!" hissed the nearest tubman. "Cosh him!"

The batsmen instantly converged on the traveller, raising their cudgels menacingly. They were ready to dash his brains out in a heartbeat. They were staking their necks on this rough and tumble smuggling game, and "Cosh first, quiz second" was always the lander's watchword. But this time there were other powers at play too. Before the thuggish batsmen could land a single crushing blow, a group of a dozen shoremen swiftly melted out of the unruly mass of smugglers and rushed to form a close circle around the youth. They faced outwards defiantly, their ranks already prickling and gleaming with the dull glint of forged steel. The smugglers hesitated, watching murderous dirks stealing silently out of the concealment of Highland plaids. The beach was eerily quiet now, as the two groups of men sized each other up. A peal of thunder shattered the silence, taking frayed nerves to breaking point. Then a challenge rang out from the tight knot of Highlanders around the traveller:

"Come on then! C'mon, ya bass!"

"No' so hasty, lads, no' so hasty!" called out the burliest batsman, his two long pistols levelled lazily into their midst, his hooded eyes crinkling with infinite shrewdness. Rivulets of rain ran down the gun-barrels. "Did ye ever feel the slug hit your chest like a hammer?"

"Two shots, fat boy- then we'll rip you!" shouted back one of the Highlanders, rolling the 'r' as he let the pommelled hilt of his dirk roll slowly around the palm of his hand. The lethal blade was perfectly balanced. "Did you ever see your guts opened up like a mackerel?" The Highlander laughed out loud. "Ah've seen smugglers find God when they start bleedin'- sayin' 'Lord Jesus, help me', when they cannae' stop their blood leakin'…"

And then came the first chant, a chorus from the clansmen around him, so quiet that it was almost a whisper. So quiet that you could almost have taken the lilting Gaelic voices for the west wind, kissing the crest of the breaking waves.

"*Creag an Sgairbh*…" they murmured.

There was something beautiful about it, thought the batsman. Something ancient- elemental. And like the broiling sea and the driving rain, it just kept on coming.

"*Creag an Sgairbh, Creag an Sgairbh*…" it built up, lapping relentlessly up the beach with the tide.

The craggy batsman paused for a second. Swagger and bluster he was used to- that was all part of the braggart smuggler's customary stock-in-trade. But this was something else, this was something quite different. Big Eck had never set eyes on the Rock of the Cormorants, implacably rooted in distant Loch Laich, that this ancient war cry of the Stewarts of Appin evoked. His foes could picture it quite clearly, even a hundred and forty miles away. It was the foundation rock of Castle Stalker and the Appin Stewarts' whole dynasty, their pride, their self-respect. Their fighting fury.

"*Creag an Sgairbh! Creag an Sgairbh!*"

"Name o' the Wee Man!" Eck muttered to himself. "This wee stooshie here could turn intae' an absolute bloodbath…"

"*CREAG an Sgairbh! CREAG AN Sgairbh! CREAG AN SGAIRBH!*"

"Jings, these boys are cracked!" blurted out one of the tubmen beside Big Eck. "Run for your lives, lads, whiles ye still can!"

Big Eck clamped a massive restraining hand on the lank neckerchief of his skittish fellow smuggler, and tugged him backwards.

"Keep the heid, boys, just ye keep the heid!" he growled. "Or I'll put a bullet in ye myself, and save these Highlan' laddies the bother!"

Big Eck expertly surveyed the traveller's bristling phalanx of protectors. He gave a low whistle. They were working themselves up into a fury.

Eck's eyes were hardly visible at all now, screwed up with sagacity- and concentration. He knew that just one stray pistol-shot now would send them all off, like a tinder-box.

"Keep the heid, lads, and we'll have all this sorted oot in a wee jiffy!"

But despite the calmness in Eck's voice, the traveller noticed that he was continually shifting his grip on the stocks of his slippery pistols, sausage-like fingers fidgetting on the arched cocking hammers of the flintlocks. They weren't exquisitely worked like the traveller's own, but the worn, notched frizzens of these terrible twins told their own story. They were the tools of a tough trade, and they'd killed more men than the King's Evil- most of them shot in the back, or from behind the discreet cover of a barrel or wagon. Eck wasn't afraid of missing his man-but what would happen after he had hit him? Could a brief volley of pistol-shots and a flurry of cudgels really break a Highland claymore charge, once it got started?

"No' even if it was just a wheen of Highland midges comin' at us..." Big Eck told himself.

He couldn't keep his eyes off the tempered Spanish steel of the Highland dirks. At close quarters like these, in the hands of fighting clansmen the long stabbing daggers were fatal against the most battle-seasoned regular troops- let alone a rabble of bully-boy smugglers. If they got through, his men would literally be disembowelled, eviscerated- mutilated.

"What's the matter, *Sassenach?*" cried the same Highland voice. "Cold feet?"

"They havenae' even bothered to unsling their pistols..." Big Eck thought, then cursed silently to himself, as he saw that the Highlander had followed his tell-tale glance. It was as though they could smell his fear now.

"Lochaber Rules now, fat boy!" said the Highlander. "Cold steel. Because dirks dinnae' jam..."

"Aye, an' they're none the worse for gettin' their heids a wee bit wet, *Calum Mór!*" laughed one of the other Highlanders.

"Are ye no' worried about your own gun-powder gettin' damp, big man?" Callum asked Big Eck. "It's blowin' a hooley oot here… An' if the powder doesnae' spark- well, we'll cut your heart out!"

"Crivvens, what in the wide world've we got oorselves into here?" Eck asked himself.

He shifted his grip on the wet pistols yet again. But this time, to his horror, one of them slipped and clattered noisily down onto the shingle.

"Sons of the Cormorant!" shouted Callum in Gaelic, broadsword held aloft. "On my word!"

They took a pace forward as one, while Eck hastily scrabbled on the ground to pick up his lost pistol, cursing his own clumsiness. He franticly tried to cover them with its twin.

"You want a war here, fat boy? Is that what you want?" shouted Callum. "Well then, come and get it, ya bass! Did you ever hear of how we raided the Campbells of Dunstaffnage? No? For people still talk about the honour and the glory, back home in the village, drinkin' comfortably in the inn. The bard will even sing you sweet songs of it! But let me tell you how that war really was. There were limbs, heads, guts, I mean you've literally hacked folk to pieces back there, man, there are headless trunks left behind you. When you look back, you just can't believe it- what you've done. You're seein' things no man should ever see. Somethin' out of hell, only the priests all seem happy enough when that hell is here on earth. And so you just burn everythin', so that it really is hell that you leave behind you. And that- that's what victory looks like!"

"What does defeat look like then?" Eck couldn't help asking.

"It looks very much the same, *laochain*- only you're no' there to see it!" said Callum. "And do you know what the last thing- the last thing all those bold Campbell warriors ever heard was?"

Big Eck silently shook his head.

"*Creag an Sgairbh*… The Rock of the Cormorants helped them on their way down to join Auld Hornie in hell, right enough!"

Eck loved his crop as much as he loved anything on God's earth, but he wasn't sanguine enough about his prospects in the next world to leave this one. Not just yet. Still the Stewarts made no move to advance, content to stand their ground, defying the smugglers to take a step closer. After what seemed an eternity, Big Eck made his calculation. He wiped the great beads of perspiration from his forehead with the back of his hand and slowly slid his pistols back into his broad leather belt. He held his hands up deliberately to show that he no longer held a weapon, smirking horribly at the traveller all the while, like a great, gnarly Carrick crocodile. The leathery folds of skin on his face obscured his eyes as he smiled.

"There's nae' bother here, Your Honour!" he said. "We came doon tae' the beach for a wee dram and a blether- we've a drop or two to hand, as ye can see! Perhaps ye'll stop and take a dram wi' us yourselves?"

The other batsmen breathed a sigh of relief as they took their lead from Big Eck, lowering their cudgels and backing off warily. But without taking their eyes off the Highlanders for a second, the traveller noted.

"We'll leave ye to it then, Your Worship!" said Big Eck. "This wee crop of oors will no' carry itself to Ayr!"

The traveller saw that the longboat had already been stripped of contraband by the locust-like landers, and the tubmen were melting out into the night with their heavy casks.

"A fine gentleman!" thought Big Eck, touching his forelock to the traveller. "But who can he be?"

A snippet of information like this might be worth more than an anker of Geneva gin- in the right market. And Eck knew his way around every market in Scotland: Cattle, contraband, cadavers- the blacker, the better, for there would be more brass in it.

In the light of the Highlanders' torches, the traveller looked younger than his commanding, gallus swagger in the shadows had suggested. He was undoubtedly good-looking, boasting an incongruous touch of Continental sophistication- and, Big Eck noted, showing unmistakable signs of repeated medicinal applications of the ship's rum.

"I'm no' askin' any questions, mind…" said Big Eck. "For it's considered a discourtesy in this part of Ayrshire! But if youse fine gentlemen are any dearer friends of Sleekit King Georgie than we are ourselves; well then, see me, I'm a big fat Dutchman, *ja?*"

Now the traveller threw back his head and laughed merrily. Even in such pressing need of a shave and a good hot bath, it was plain enough that he was cast from a different mould than the rough men of their hands now surrounding him. For this was Charles Edward Louis John Casimir Sylvester Severino Maria Stuart- Prince of the Royal Blood, Knight of the Most Noble Order of the Garter and rightful heir to the three kingdoms of the British Isles.

The Prince stooped down to pick up a handful of coarse Culzean sand, before kissing it and then scattering it into the gusting wind. The ring of Highlanders around him, bearded faces lit up by the tubmen's flaming torches, dropped to their knees before him as one. The professional smugglers facing them stared in astonishment. They bent their heads to no one but the hangman in Ayr, and that unwillingly enough.

The Highlanders gazed at the Prince enthralled, impervious to the relentless rain drenching their plaids and bonnets. Yet to Big Eck's practised ear, there was nothing of the Highlands or of the Old Tongue in Charles Edward's own voice, when he murmured to himself in English, almost under his breath:

"And so- the Great Game begins..."

Callum and another man stepped out from the knot of Highlanders. As a leader of men himself, Big Eck could easily discern that both of them were imbued with leadership too- in their own ways. The first, Malcolm, looked around him nervously, running skinny fingers through scanty grey locks. His kilted plaid hung loose on spindly shanks. He bowed low to the Prince, with the courtly stiffness of a previous generation.

"A pretty night for your homecoming, Your Highness!"

"Better one such night of summer in Scotland, than one hundred years of sunny exile in Rome, my noble cousin!" rejoined the Prince gallantly, gesturing Malcolm to rise.

Callum was about the Prince's own age, slim and light on his feet, but exuding a physical power and agility that served to emphasise Macolm's own fragility. A born swordsman, thought Big Eck, as Callum shaped to bow, then thought better of it and wrapped the Prince in a warm bear-hug. With a mouth on him, too- for he was the one who had faced him down on the beach. And if Eck recalled correctly, had threatened to gut him like a mackerel into the bargain- not something a smuggler was likely to forget in a hurry.

"Aye, he's a killin' gentleman this one, right enough!" Eck muttered to himself. "It takes one to know one, so they say…"

"You shoulda' seen the winter, *co-oghan*!" said Callum to the Prince. "You're lucky to be here at all, mind- for Auld Hornie himself's against us the night!"

"So the devil really is an Englishman!" laughed the Prince, hugging Callum back before disengaging and nonchalantly brushing the rain off his sleeve.

"Och, it's worse than that, man- he's a Campbell!" said Callum. "And he's emptyin' the clan bath-tub out on us the night…"

"Worse luck for me then, my friend," said the Prince. "To return on the one day of the year when those bastard sons of Diarmid bathe them-selves!" The Highlanders roared their approval. "But don't worry your great shaggy head about a drop or two of water, *amico mio*- they say that he who was born to be hanged, will never be drowned!"

"And amen to that!" said Big Eck to himself.

"We must make haste, my Lord!" cried Malcolm, fidgetting impa-tiently in the rain. "We are vulnerable to the Usurper King's troops here, wedged in between these treacherous cliffs and the sea!"

Callum trotted over to a screen of wind-blasted gorse bushes by the edge of the bay. He returned holding the halters of two stalwart country horses. The Prince patted their faces and spoke softly to them in Italian, before swinging himself elegantly up onto the taller of the two. Callum helped Malcolm to clamber awkwardly up onto the other horse, making a mounting block with his knee, before boosting him bodily up onto its back.

"I trust it will not prove so challenging to set my father back on his throne, Chevalier!" said Charles Edward, smirking.

He surveyed the fire-drenched bay from his vantage point on the horse, shielding his pale eyes against the driving rain.

"Those fires up there on the cliff- I suppose they are to guide the ships safely into land? What enlightenment!" said the Prince.

"It's blacker business than that..." said Callum, before Malcolm could silence him with a furious glare. The young man turned his eyes quizzically to Malcolm.

"What is it then, Chevalier? Who lights them?"

Malcolm seemed to hesitate before replying.

"The Lord Lieutenant's men, Sire- some of them..." he said at last. "Traitorous swine- they watch this coast day and night, on London's orders. At the personal behest of the Usurper himself, so they say..."

"But more than that by- ship-wreckers!" broke in Callum.

Malcolm scowled at Callum as the Prince raised an arch, interrogative eyebrow.

"Ghouls! Scavengers- they use the beacons to lure unwary sailors onto the treacherous rocks below," said Malcolm. "When the vessels are broken and lost, the wretches plunder the cargo and loot the stricken crew- down to their very corpses..."

The Prince crossed himself piously.

"*Dio mio*! But this is monstrous, my friends! To think that this- this ship-wrecking- should be happening in my kingdom, and before my very eyes! And no one stops them? We'll soon see about that, when my father is restored to the throne!"

Malcolm and Callum looked at each other.

"Folk with the knowledge say that it is the local witches who light the pyres, my Lord..." said Callum.

"Witches, by God!" said the Prince.

"Aye, *bana-bhuidsichean*... Witches! Your great-grandfather hated them," said Callum. "An' they say that snatchin' innocent souls somehow gives them- strange powers- over mortal men."

"Go on, *mon brave*!" said the Prince.

Callum shook his head. "What can I tell you? Things are different in the Lowlands! You couldnae' say for sure whether our own fairy-folk of Appin are for good or ill, for they are no' such as to be judged by the priest's straight yard-stick." He instinctively touched the steel of his dirk, as though to ward off any evil spirits his words might invoke. "Though they too have been known to lift children for their own purposes; and to leave their own queer brood behind them, as fairy changelings in their place. The mind of the fair folk is no' for the likes of us to read- it shifts like the cloud over the black pool itself, and you would be as well trying to predict it." Callum paused and looked around the bay. "But whatever a man may believe in his own heart- any fool can see that somethin's no' canny here! An' how could it be, with no rightful king seated in Scotland, and the Stone of Destiny carried away to London? Did you ever see a fire burn like that, and in such a gale as this one? For I never did!"

The other Highlanders muttered assent, crossing themselves.

"There's a precious lot o' seagulls oot the night, *Calum Mór...*" said one of the Highlanders.

"Well, what of it, man?" said Malcolm. "We're right by the sea here, in case you hadn't noticed!"

"Aye, but seagulls don't fly at night, Malcolm..." said Callum quietly. "It's no' natural. For that's the form the sea-witches of the West Coast take, when they go abroad in the world..."

"Enough! Hold your tongue now, sir! Hold your tongue, I say!" snapped Malcolm irritably. He looked apologetically at the Prince. "As I had the honour to report to you in my letters, Sire- this kind of feeble-minded superstition is only too rife here."

He looked up at the bonfire on the cliff above them. Again, the Prince followed his gaze. For the first time he could see that it was only one of a long line of beacons, running all the way up the Carrick coast-line: Dunure, Lagg, Ayr, Prestwick, Troon, Ardrossan, Largs. The fires blazed as far as the naked eye could see, and far beyond; as though marking the boundary of an unseen kingdom.

"But the truth is- these are evil times in Scotland..." said Malcolm. "For all his superstitious clap-trap, Callum was right about one thing: This old country of ours needs your father, King James, like startled sheep need their shepherd! Without him, well..."

Together they peered at the roaring bonfire. For an instant a cloaked figure appeared, silhouetted against it, black against fire. Then the flames flared up all around it, fresh sheets of rain burning up into a dense haze, shrouding it from view again. A huge seagull soared out of the billowing cloud of smoke and steam, screeched and then wheeled around in a low arc above the heads of the men on the beach, heading inland. Suddenly the demented screaming of gulls filled the bay.

"Without him- uncanny things hold sway here..." said Malcolm.

"*Figlio di buona donna!*" said the Prince. He patted his horse's neck until the shrieking of the gulls subsided, whispering soft, soothing words to it in his sonorous Italian. "Truly this poor country of mine rests upon the razor's edge..." He gave spur to his horse impetuously. "*Avanti, avanti tutta!*" he shouted. "The last one to Ayr is Fatty Cumberland!"

Malcolm bumped and rolled in his saddle as his horse started off after the Prince's.

"*Tiugainn!*" shouted Callum to his clansmen, and they bounded after him on foot behind the riders, like a pack of ravenous hunting dogs at their heels.

"Fine fellows, these clansmen of yours, Chevalier!" shouted the Prince to Malcolm as they rode, watching the Highlanders course through the rough ground behind them. "Relentless! With ten thousand men like them, I could sack the twin cities of Hell and Inveraray themselves, let alone sleek, fat London! And they say there are thirty thousand of them in the Highlands, even allowing for Campbells... What an avenging army!"

He kissed his fingers and held them up into the night sky, letting the wind rush through them.

"You know a good inn in Ayr, cousin?" he shouted back to Callum. "For all this sea air has given me a rare thirst!"

"The Jolly Beggars' Inn is the place for us, Cherlie!" cried Callum with gusto. "The best beer, ballads and brawls this side o' the Stirling Bridge!"

"Then the Jolly Beggars' it is!" shouted the Prince, drawing one of his jewelled pistols and shooting it into the night air. "Jolly Beggars', ho!"

The Highlanders raced after him. Behind them, out in the foaming sea, twin files of rowers propelled the empty long-boat back out into the gloom. The beach was deserted now, save for a lone figure standing in the long shadows that fringed it. He waved amiably at the Highlanders' retreating backs.

"The Jolly Beggars', eh? Godspeed you then, my Lord!" called Big Eck softly. "Oh aye, I'll be seein' you, Your Worship! An' maybe no' at the point of a dirk next time, either..."

———

CHAPTER 2

THE SEAGULL'S DARK-TIPPED WINGS RIPPLED effortlessly, speeding it over moor and field towards a tiny square of light in the distance. Watching it master the unruly gusts and squalls of wind with minute corrections of its flight feathers, feeling it savour all the unholy glee of its own velocity, you would stake your very soul that its ruling element was the air. But as it skimmed over an inky loch, torpidly stirred by a gurgling burn, for an instant the reflection that flashed back showed no gull.

For the burns and rivers are the borders between our world and theirs. Beneath it all, they are the creatures of water, and running water alone they cannot deceive.

As swiftly as a snowflake melting into a stream, the glimmer of truth had passed, and the loch was left far behind. The howling wind swept after the seagull, distorting the reflection out of all recognition and leaving nothing but ebbing ripples of doubt behind it.

Already the flyer was a bird once more, hurtling at break-neck speed towards the glimmer of light ahead. It dipped and swerved to avoid the wind-blasted trees, walls and dikes in its way, and then banked into the wind, arresting its head-long flight. The seagull leaned into a neat, three-pace landing and planted its feet firmly back on the earth. It strutted purposefully up to the casement window of a whitewashed stone building, nodding knowingly as it went. There was nothing visible to betray the fact, but to folk for miles around, this was simply known as Mungo's Inn. The snug tavern was as much a landmark in the area as the local church and, except on the interminably glum, grey Sabbath days, far better-frequented by the parishioners.

The gull hopped up onto the sill of the window and peered in. To its surprise, a shaggy Highland Cow stared straight back at it. The seagull tilted its head from side to side, and the cow followed suit, the dense fringe of hair overhanging its eyes wiping the condensation off the glass so that the gull could see in. The seagull nodded in satisfaction, and the cow stooped its head back down to the floor below, contentedly lapping at a pool of spilt beer. Its proud Highland horns framed the courtly scene unfolding inside the cosy inn.

"May I have the pleasure of the next dance? Unless, of course, *mademoiselle* has already engaged herself for it?" asked the gentleman gallantly, bowing down almost to the floor. "I trust that you have not already bestowed so precious a boon elsewhere- although, i'faith, there must be many humble suitors for so fair a hand!"

"Nah, ye'll dae' for me, Souter Johnnie!" said the young lady, flinging her arms around his neck. She took a hearty swig of her ale over his shoulder, smacking her lips with relish.

Without further ado, they joined another couple in a strenuous but shambolic foursome reel around the cramped front parlour of Mungo's Inn. The two men were in their early thirties, just about young enough for the exertion, but quite old enough to know better. Their dancing-partners were pretty but tousle-haired, wild both in appearance and manners.

Kirkton Jean and Hielan' Mary were their names and, like Mungo himself and the Highland Cow, they were local celebrities too in their own way. They could certainly boast at least one unique charm- they were the only girls in the room. Indeed, this was the most excitement Mungo's Inn had seen since Lord Kilmarnock himself had stopped there to take a glass of small ale during the Jacobite Rebellion of 1715, thirty years before. Mungo claimed still to have the glass the rebellious peer had drunk from, even if he couldn't be absolutely sure which one it was. The drinkers in the inn were already concocting their own versions of how Jean and Mary had unexpectedly appeared from nowhere out of the wind and rain: drenched, dishevelled but exhilarated by the elements- and coquettishly demanding to be invited in and stood drinks by anyone who was man enough. The animated locals were only too aware that it could be another thirty years before anything so dramatic happened again there.

The dancers span round in dizzying figures of eight and vertiginous elbow turns, faces flushed, ale sloshing out of tankards onto nearby drinkers.

"Ye're supposed to present the right shoulder in a reel of four, Tam!" shouted Souter Johnnie, as the two men careered into each other at full speed, sending another plume of beer flying high above their heads. "Any fool knows that!"

"The other right shoulder, ya big dummy!" said Johnnie impatiently, as there was another bone-shuddering collision on the very next circuit. "Jings, the gentlemen should always end up back to back!"

Irresistibly attracted by the prospect of beer, and exhibiting a surprising turn of pace, the Highland Cow shuffled over to hoover up the spillage. The dancers completed another hearty but abominably arrhythmic setting step, bringing dust and debris cascading down from the ceiling, and then clumsily linked arms behind each other's backs. The intricate grip for the Tulloch turn was far beyond their co-ordination at this stage of intoxication, and the manoeuvre was executed more in hope than expectation- but all the same, it offered a gratifying level of primal physical contact.

"Now the ladies end facin' each other!" shouted Johnnie. "The ladies, Tam, ya eejit! Wi' their backs to their own partners!"

The Highland Cow slily nuzzled closer into the dance, dipping its huge head into the midst of the reel to get at another puddle of ale. Completely engrossed in the Souter's bewildering instructions, Tam promptly tripped over it, tumbling right over its neck. The Tulloch grip ensured that his partner, Kirkton Jean, was dragged down after him like a sack of potatoes. She screamed, clutched desperately at Johnnie and

Mary in a vain attempt to save herself, and pulled the others down in a chaotic heap on top of Tam. The Highland Cow gave a bellow of annoyance, sending the seagull hopping backwards on the window-sill outside, only to be swiftly placated by a stream of foaming ale from Hielan' Mary's fallen tankard.

"Is this what you meant by endin' up back to back, Souter?" shrieked Hielan' Mary. She giggled uncontrollably, as she tried to extricate herself from Johnnie's clutches and retie the bright red scarf in her hair.

"It's Tammie, he's got two left shoulders, I tell you!" said Johnnie.

Over at the cramped bar of the inn, the rotund, rosy-nosed landlord himself and pub regular Hosea Goldie studied the mangled wreckage of the reel with interest. Mungo's rich claret colouring and overwhelming geniality was in stark contrast to the sourness of Goldie's own sallow, pinched face. He seemed to have been left out on the moor too long, until the elements had drained every last physical and moral pigment from his bony frame.

"Did I no' bar that bloody animal from this inn?" said Mungo, as the dust settled.

"Och, there's no restrainin' it!" said Goldie ruefully. "It's got some kind of sixth sense when it comes tae' beer… It's no' natural, I tell ye, ye willnae' see anythin' about beasts drinkin' ale in the Good Book. Even they Gadarene Swine would draw the line at that, an' they wis capable of jist aboot anythin'!"

"Does the cow no' have a name, like any good Christian?" said Mungo.

"Aye- we call him King Billy!" said Goldie. "On account of his bein' orange, ye see…"

Mungo nodded slowly, considering this.

"They're all orange though, aren't they, Hosea?"

"Oh, aye," said Goldie. "Orange. It's in the breedin' o' them, Highland Coos, ye see…"

"Aye, that's what I thought… Well, orange or no', it lowers the tone!" said Mungo, spitting on the floor reflectively.

The dancers unhurriedly disentangled themselves, and Mungo shook his head indulgently as Tam and Souter Johnnie took the opportunity to steal illicit kisses and cuddles from the girls. Hielan' Mary put her arms around Johnnie's neck playfully and began to sing raucously:

"A Highland lad my love was born,
The Lowland laws he held in scorn;
But he still was faithful to his clan,
My gallant, braw Johnnie Highlandman!"

"Speakin' of the tone of the place… I'd certainly no' want to be in Tam O'Shanter's dancing brogues when he gets home to his good wife the night, I can tell ye that!" said Mungo, nodding over towards Tam.

"If it even is tonight, Mungo! But oh, aye, he's in for a good dose of fire and brimstone, right enough!" said Goldie, taking a deep swig of ale from his tankard. "An' did ye see the state of yon Kirkton Jean and Mary when they came in, like a pair of bolts frae' the blue? They looked as though they'd been dragged through a hedge backwards! And maybe they had been, if ye ken what I mean… It's just no' respectable!" He passed his beer-mug to Mungo for a refill, before continuing. "Indeed I'm surprised at you, Mungo McGillivray, playin' fast and loose with the good name o' your auld father's inn here like this! No' to mention those of us who frequent it… How'd they even get here, arrivin' on a filthy night like this, without so much as a pony between them?"

"Och, it's a free house, Hosea!" said Mungo. "We're no' livin' in the times o' the Covenant anymore… Ask nae' questions, an' you'll hear nae' lies!"

Mungo paused, as another rowdy burst of Hielan' Mary's song rang around the inn:

"Sing hey! My braw John Highlandman!
Sing ho! My braw John Highlandman!

There's not a lad in all the lan',
Is a match for my braw Johnnie Highlandman!"

"It'll be a bitter harvest for me if the missus comes to hear of it, mind you…" said Mungo.

"Right enough, Mungo!" said Goldie happily. "An' dinnae' say I didnae' tell ye so! On the bright side, this is another smokin' peat on the tormentin' fires o' hell for young Master O'Shanter. So it's no' all bad news!"

Oblivious to Goldie's dire predictions for their future prospects, Tam and Souter Johnnie cheerfully struggled back to their feet. They hauled Kirkton Jean and Hielan' Mary upright after them, like stevedores loading sacks of New Cumnock coal in Ayr Harbour.

"Ups-a-daisy, my fair ladies, you're the belles o' this ball!" said Johnnie. He was the village cobbler, stockier and darker both of hair and complexion than Tam, and by far the jauntier and more cocksure of the two. "Those glasses look awful empty though, eh? Even the bonniest flowers need waterin'! Can you excuse us for a moment, my dears?"

"Nae' bother, laddie!" said Kirkton Jean, patting at her hopelessly unkempt hair. "Ah need to powder my nose, anyway!"

"The minutes will pass as hoors, hen!" said Johnnie suavely, as the two girls made their way to the door of the inn. He turned to Tam. "See's a hand at the bar, Tammie- we need to talk about your dancing technique! I think King Billy the Coo' could teach you a thing or two aboot dancin'… They say we Highlanders take in dance wi' our mother's milk, an' Billy's certainly a Highlander!"

"And so am I, Johnnie," said Tam. "By birth, if no' by address…"

"Aye, right enough," said Johnnie. "Well, you must have skipped your breakfast that day then!"

As Tam obediently followed him to the bar, Johnnie draped his arm around his shoulders conspiratorially.

"There's actually somethin' else I've been meanin' to talk to you about, Tam lad…" said Johnnie.

Tam brushed his mop of sandy hair away from his eyes, and fixed the open beam of his blue eyes on Johnnie.

"Is that a fact? What's on your mind then, Johnnie?" he said. "It's no' like you to be so shy o' speakin' your mind!"

For one so naturally brash and glib as Souter Johnnie, he seemed curiously abashed by Tam's candour.

"So, eh, Jeanie was askin' why you don't walk her home one of these nights?" said Johnnie. "She's awful lonely, livin' all alone out there by the Auld Kirk as she does- a nice sociable lass like that!"

"Sociable! That's one word for it, right enough," said Tam.

"So you'll see her home then? Good man, good man," said Johnnie hurriedly.

"No!" said Tam impatiently. "It's market-day tomorrow, an' I've to sell the white colt. I'm far enough behind on the rent already, you know that, Souter!"

"Aye, an' your carriage'll turn into a pumpkin at midnight, eh, Cinders?" said Johnnie mockingly.

"You'll be needin' a hand with your own stall too, eh?" said Tam, eager to change the subject. "Grease the wheels of sacred commerce, an' a' that?"

"Don't you worry about my stall, wee man- my shoes sell themselves!" said Johnnie.

"Aye, an' if they could only learn to stitch themselves too, they'd be doin' a better trade as souters than they are as shoes!"

Tam lifted his own foot up to demonstrate Johnnie's handiwork. The shoes were hideous in their sheer asymmetry, shaggy, uneven animal hide haphazardly stitched together at apparently random points.

"These are the worst yet, I tell you," said Tam. "No wonder King Billy was showin' me up- he's got better dancin' slippers!"

Johnnie surreptitiously studied his own wildly unshapely shoes.

"Well, well, jist hearken to you!" he said drily. "You stick to muckin' out byres, Farmer O'Shanter, an' leave the world o' high fashion to me! I'm no' takin' artistic direction from someone who spends all day wi' his hand up a sheep's arse!"

"Less of it from you, Jimmy Shoe!" said Tam. "The only difference is that with me that's business, no' pleasure..."

"An' what about Jeanie's pleasure?" said Johnnie slily.

Tam fell silent for a moment, suddenly sobered up.

"If ye must know, Johnnie, I'm, eh, I'm takin' Wee Tam wi' me to market tomorrow," he said. "He's been needin' a new suit of clothes, and the missus thinks the trip'll be good for him. You know, with- how he is..."

"Fair enough, fair enough- just thought I'd mention it," said Johnnie. "You can lead a horse to water, but you cannae' make it gargle, eh?"

"Why're you so set on matchmakin' anyway?" asked Tam. "I thought you were quite the carefree young bachelor?"

"Och, that's just my philanthropic nature for you, I suppose..." said Johnnie evasively.

"Is that a fact?"

"And, eh, somethin' Mary said... Somethin' about her no' comin' back to the cottage with me if it meant leavin' Jeanie alone..."

"Philanthropic, aye!" said Tam, putting a fatherly arm around Johnnie's shoulder. "Have you no' seen the state of Kirkton Jean the night, Johnnie? She's got a heid like a hedgehog, an' she's three sheets to the wind! Gie' her a thimbleful more beer, an' she'll be fast asleep under the straw in Mungo's byre! I dinnae' think there's much risk o' her playin' the gooseberry tonight..."

"You may be onto somethin' here, Tam!" said Johnnie. "I'll be right with you..."

He hurried back to the girls.

"John- were you no' gettin' the beers in?" said Tam. "Och, c'mon, Souter..."

Tam shrugged in resignation. He continued on his way to the bar, where Mungo was awaiting him expectantly. He'd broached a new keg of ale specially, when he'd heard that Tam and Johnnie were out on a toot tonight. The way things were going, it was looking like a pretty sound investment. But as Tam passed the door of the inn, it suddenly burst open, lurching back alarmingly on rickety, rusting hinges. The wind rushed in, carrying a cloaked figure with it. The gale outside sent shadows dancing like hobgoblins around the snug room, and the dark cloak swirling around the new arrival.

CHAPTER 3

——————

A BLAST OF WIND SPLATTERED tallow over tarnished candlesticks. The inn regulars swivelled and spun on their stools. They gaped at the doorway, jaws as loose as the door itself, left swinging unattended in the wild wind. All eyes were fixed for a moment on the strange new-comer in the doorway, then averted by the unblinking, quizzical gaze that he directed straight back at them. Even the fire seemed to cower cravenly down in the hearth in his presence.

The grave-faced, dark figure strutted slowly into the inn. He was swathed in a bat-like, black cloak which trailed behind him, emitting unpredictable squawks and screeches as he hobbled over the rough floor. The eery sounds set the drinkers' strained nerves jangling further, and they shuddered and crossed themselves as he passed them.

"He took in damnation wi' his mother's milk, that yin!" said Goldie at the bar, at the same time artfully inclining his drinking-mug towards Mungo for another refill. "In good old King James' day, it would've been straight up onto the stake wi' a notorious witch like that! A wee splash 'ay oil on the wood, spark it all up, an' nae' questions asked... At least no' before a few demons had been toasted out of him!" He leaned towards the new-comer, his pinched face lined with ill-will. "Will you no' have the decency to shut the door behind you, ya jakey bass?" he cried. "At least dae' us poor humans that wee courtesy! For no' all of us are so accustomed as you to sleepin' in ditches, byres- and witches' covens!"

The spell finally broken, there was a ripple of ill-natured sniggering from the drinkers around the inn. They were still embarrassed at having been so disconcerted by the new arrival, and only too willing to revenge themselves on him through Goldie's spite.

The new-comer nodded slowly, apparently in recognition of Goldie's words. He turned awkwardly to close the door behind him, but tripped on the uneven floor of the inn and started to fall to the ground. Tam lunged over to him, just about managing to catch him mid-fall and set him back on his unsteady feet. As he regathered his wits, Tam put his hand on his shoulder in silent greeting, and then stepped over to shut the door himself. Even as he was doing so, Tam sensed an unfamiliar presence outside. He stood holding the door open, as if in a trance.

For a moment Tam stared out into the darkness, and then his senses were scrambled by the appearance from nowhere, right in front of him, of a bewitchingly beautiful young woman. Her outfit alone was enough to force the air from his lungs. A dark cloak over a daringly sheer, green silk shift that no woman in the village would have dared to wear- not even as a night-gown. They would have called it a cutty sark, to be fashioned from chaste linen and worn beneath the modesty of their capacious woollen dresses. But this was like no cutty sark Tam had ever seen- or even dreamed of. He stood transfixed before her, frozen in her calm gaze. Her eyes were the colour of that deep green silk.

"May I come in, Tam?" said Nannie, inclining her head slightly towards him, in what seemed to Tam a gesture of the most sublime grace imaginable. But he couldn't find the words to answer. He was lost in a vision of shimmering dark hair, of red lips and ethereally perfect white skin.

"Why, it's Merry Andrew!" said Souter Johnnie, hurrying over to greet the new-comer inside the inn. "And you've even brought your bagpipes with you! Gonna' gie' us a wee tune, Andy?"

Merry Andrew still didn't utter a word, but he nodded slowly. A hint of a smile seemed to creep across his dark face, as Johnnie clapped him on the back in welcome. As he passed Goldie, Johnnie called back warningly over his shoulder.

"Just you make sure you behave yourself wi' our guest this time, Farmer Goldie! Or you'll have me to reckon with…"

The Souter turned back to Merry Andrew.

"It's good to see you, Andy- an' Hosea here was just tellin' us how he owed you a drink! Quite a coincidence- a cup o' kindness, for the sake of auld lang syne, ye might say!"

"Eh? Me? Aye, eh- a…" stuttered Goldie, fumbling for a small coin and rapping it on the bar. "Small… glass of gin for our friend here. And I hope it chokes him!" he added under his breath.

It seemed more likely to choke Goldie himself, as Mungo poured out an eye-watering slug of neat gin and set it down in front of Merry Andrew with a flourish. Merry Andrew downed it in one and, without any further warning, whirled around and broke into song:

"Sir Wisdom's a fool when in drink;
Sir Knave is a fool in a session;
He's there an apprentice I think,
But I am a fool by profession!

My grannie she bought me a book,
An' I held away to the school;
I fear I my talent mistook,
But what will ye hae' of a fool?

Poor Andrew that tumbles for sport;
Let nobody name with a jeer;
There's even, I'm told, in the court
A jester called the premier!"

Johnnie passed Merry Andrew another glass of gin. He paused to dispose of it summarily, before continuing:

"Observed ye yon Reverend lad;
Make faces to tickle the mob?"

Merry Andrew stopped between lines, to grimace horribly around the inn.

"He rails at our mountebank squad,
It's rivalship just in the job!

And now my conclusion I'll tell,
For by God my mouth is bone dry!"

He paused again and placed the empty gin glass upside down on his head, apparently for effect- though not a flicker of revelry crossed his grave face- before concluding:

"The man that's a fool for himself,
Good Lord, he's far dafter than I!"

Ironic cheers and slow hand-claps rang out all around the inn at the end of this impromptu performance, until they were silenced abruptly by a threatening look from Souter Johnnie. Johnnie himself applauded sincerely and heartily, accompanied by Mungo.

"Bravo, bravo!" said Mungo. "Good for business, havin' a wee bit o' entertainment thrown in like that!"

Johnnie glared at Goldie, cowing him into joining in half-heartedly with the applause. Merry Andrew looked around unmoved, before stooping, slightly stiffly, into an elegant bow and then shuffling off into the corner of the inn with another brimming glass of gin.

"Just oor luck to have a village idiot who thinks he's Scotland's own Billy-bloody-Shakespeare!" grumbled Goldie. "Jakeyspeare, more like! Ah'm more of a Ben Jonson or, eh, Kit Marlowe man myself..."

Mungo tilted the gin bottle invitingly towards Johnnie.

"Och, I really shouldn't..." said Johnnie. "Thanks for lookin' out for Merry Andrew though, Mungo. I appreciate your kindness!"

Mungo nodded over to the corner of the inn.

"Poor Andrew- looks like his troubles are no' over just yet..."

Johnnie turned, just in time to see Merry Andrew stumbling again. This time it was straight into a bull-necked local farmer, Rab Scott, who shoved him back hard, clearly spoiling for a fight. Even the most peaceable character could feel as quarrelous as the weasel after half a dozen pints of Mungo's celebrated heavy ale, and Scott was already well into his seventh.

"Poor Andrew?" muttered Goldie. "There's nothin' wrong wi' that wee scunner- nothin' that a good blaze, wi' himself staked out on top o' it, wouldnae' sort out! Old King James kent how to deal wi' witches, an' no mistakin': Torture first, an' ask questions later! Man, he's limpin' on a different leg this week... He's nae' more crippled than I am, I tell ye!"

He put up his puny fists, miming a complex sequence of punches.

"Banjo him, Rab! Show him the haymaker!" he shouted. "The Scotts o' Culroy have always been bonny fighters! An' ah dinnae' agree wi' the lads who're sayin' you're the end o' the family line!"

"Which bass said that!" roared Scott, giving Merry Andrew another mighty shove. "I'll kill him!"

"Aye, wi' you it's more your sense of decency that's crippled, eh, Farmer Goldie?" said Johnnie.

He winced as Scott drew back his own massive fist, winding up to punch Merry Andrew into next week. Johnnie couldn't watch, but at the critical moment Andrew briefly postponed the inevitable by deftly jabbing Scott in the crotch with the bass drone of his pipes. As the farmer doubled up in agony, Merry Andrew poked him in the eye with the bagpipe blow-stick, and then cracked him hard over the back of the head with the drones. The pipes almost drowned out Scott's roar of fury, as he swung again at Andrew with all his might. Almost. His hand crumpled into the bag, compressing it and making the pipes wail shrilly with the impact.

"Christ, the ancient war-cry of the Scotts o' Culroy! Better pour me that dram, after all…" said Johnnie. "Dutch courage, eh?"

He seized a glass of gin from Mungo and drained it hurriedly, before rushing over to Merry Andrew. He looked around for his old ally Tam as he went, but Tam was nowhere to be seen. In fact, he was completely oblivious to Merry Andrew's plight, lost in a world all of his own, standing with Nannie outside the door of the inn. At that moment, he couldn't even have said that it was a world of his own- it seemed so intoxicating, so strange and so new.

"So you're no' goin' to ask me in then, Tam?" said Nannie.

"You don't seem to me like someone who would need to wait for an invitation!" said Tam.

"You'd be surprised!" she said with a laugh. "We all have our weaknesses."

"That's true enough…" said Tam ruefully.

"Quite a show you put on for us tonight though!" said Nannie. "I wouldn't have taken you for a dancer…"

"Glad you enjoyed it!" said Tam. "I must have missed the encores…"

"Aren't you the prima donna, Tam!" she laughed. "Next time I'll bring a bouquet along with me!"

"So you'll be comin' back here then?" he said quickly.

"If you like!" she said. "For I know the way well enough…"

Tam laughed in relief, though he wasn't quite sure why- or even what she meant by it. The important thing was to see her again, whatever the cost.

"A wee bit o' appreciation certainly wouldnae' go amiss!" he said. "The only plaudits I get around here are the anonymous letters to my wife, tellin' her exactly why and when I'm headin' to hell in a handcart…"

Nannie raised an eyebrow archly.

"Now then, let me see…" she said. "That means someone who can write- which certainly narrows it down around here! But then what do you care, Tam? You of all people shouldn't be afraid to make your own rules!"

"Well, I did try that…" said Tam. "But it turns out my rules are just no' so strict as everyone else's!"

"And what are you so afraid will happen if you were to- break them?" said Nannie, with a smile.

"Och, you know, roastin' in hell for all eternity!" said Tam. "Missin' the last boat to paradise, an' a' that… You can get an update on eternal torment every Sunday in the Kirk- for the good Minister serves up more hell than heaven around here, I can tell you that! For a man of God, he seems a damn sight keener on the Devil's hoose than he is on our good Lord's…"

Nannie smiled, and put her hand over Tam's. Even that gossamer light touch was enough to send a tingle of agitation running through his body.

"Oh, I know all about that…" she said. "But then perhaps he's right not to beguile his poor, mortal sheep with foolish day-dreams of a paradise to come in the future! You should always be careful when someone promises you joy in another life, Tam- for they usually want to steal it from you in this one. Break your back in the fields to make the landlord fat, an' you'll get your reward in heaven. Work like a slave for a lazy husband, an' you'll have eternal life stretched out ahead of you! But what kind o' life? For if it's just more o' the same, then they can keep it, an' be damned to hell!"

Tam stared at her in amazement.

"But then I think you know all about that already, don't you, Tam?" she said quietly. "That's why you drain every last drop of pleasure that you can find in this life, isn't it?"

She leant in closer towards him. He could hardly breathe now in anticipation. But anticipation of what?

"No gods, no masters, Tam!" she breathed. "That's the only way we can truly be free. All you wanted was to numb the pain of life. But now you know that pleasures are like poppies spread- you seize the flower, and its bloom is shed..."

She raised her hand to Tam's face slowly, cupping it, and Tam closed his eyes.

"Do I know you?" he murmured. "There's somethin'- somethin' so familiar about you... Almost as though you were- but it can't be! An' how- how do you know my name?"

"Oh, I know much more about you than that, Tam O'Shanter," she said. "What you're really like. What you really want from life..."

She stroked Tam's face and began to sing quietly:

"A fig for those by law protected!
Liberty's a glorious feast!
Courts for cowards were erected,
Churches built to please the priest!

What is title, what is treasure,
What is reputation's care?
If we lead a life of pleasure,
'Tis no matter how or where!"

"Sing with me, Tam!" she said. "For it is the song in your heart too, I know it! You just need to shut out the voices from outside, and listen to it..."

And she was singing louder now:

"Life is all a variorum,
We regard not how it goes!
Let them cant about decorum,
Who have character to lose!

30

A fig for those by law protected!
Liberty's a glorious feast!
Courts for cowards were erected,
Churches built to please the priest!"

Tam listened, captivated, craving more- but he couldn't utter a sound, even to beg for it. All too soon, the bitter-sweet voice fell silent. He opened his eyes, but she had disappeared. Tam looked around desperately. There was nothing to be seen outside now but the dark void of the moor. Somehow he could feel in his heart that she was gone- and it left a dark void there too.

"What's the matter wi' you, Tam O'Shanter?" he scolded himself. "You're gettin' a wee bit old for love at first sight, aren't you? If that's even what it was…"

He turned back towards the door of the inn. But before he could open it and go back in, another man was violently propelled through the doorway and bundled straight into him, knocking him off his feet.

"Johnnie!" said Tam.

He was still struggling back upright when he was smashed out of the way again by Scott, bowling out of the inn in hot pursuit of the Souter. The burly farmer had blood in his eyes- quite literally, after his close encounter with Merry Andrew's bagpipes. He pinioned Tam effortlessly against the door-frame as he passed, with a weighty elbow into the midriff. Tam doubled over, momentarily winded, and could do nothing but stagger around blindly for a moment. He was just sucking the air back into his crumpled lungs when he was jostled, knocked over and finally brushed out of the way a third time, by a flood of the other drinkers from Mungo's Inn. The entire population of Alloway seemed to be congregating outside, enthralled by the prospect of a scrap.

"This bloody village!" gasped Tam, picking himself up and following them, as soon as he could breathe again. "'Rustic labour' isnae' the half of it! C'mon now, boys, what're you up to? Johnnie! Johnnie!"

CHAPTER 4

———

"JUST LOOK AT THE SORRY state of you two, you pair o' scare-crows!" said Nannie, laughing aloud as the three witches hurried away from Mungo's Inn together. "Your hair, Jeanie! Or is it Aunt Sally? I've seen less tangled brambles! By the great Lady Hecate, what a shambles... No wonder I had to get involved myself. Wi' an appearance like that, you could hardly have charmed a drunken tinker fiddler on market day, let alone Tam O'Shanter himself!"

"Well, jist hearken to you, Madame Nannie!" said Hielan' Mary, adjusting her red scarf with dignity. "Tam O'Shanter himself, is it now? You were supposed to be doin' your own job, no' whisperin' sweet nothin's to Tammie! We had it well in hand back there!"

"Aye!" said Kirkton Jean indignantly.

"I played my part with the Souter tae' perfection, though I say it myself!" said Mary. "Bewitched he was, poor laddie, pure bewitched- I a'most felt sorry for him! For he did his level best to persuade Tammie to come out to the Auld Kirk, I heard him tryin'... He'd hae' carried him out there on his own back, by the time I was done with him! No' that I'm blamin' Jeanie for her part in the piece, mind you..."

"An' flyin' plays havoc wi' the hair!" said Kirkton Jean, patting her coiffure defensively.

"Your other fancy man, yon Rannoch, didnae' help matters much either, Nannie!" said Hielan' Mary. "Fancy throwin' us off the cliff like that- what a cheek! I was halfway down before I'd even gathered my wits enough to transform. That water was rushin' up on me like naebody's business!"

"Aye!" said Kirkton Jean. "An' it was cold, I tell ye! It's alright for some- Nannie here gets a fine, silk cutty sark. Jeanie an' Mary get the fright o' our lives from Rannoch, an' that disgustin' monkey creature o' his!"

"An' then a shove in the back off the highest cliff in Ayrshire, jist for good luck!" chimed in Hielan' Mary.

"You poor fools!" said Nannie, stopping in her tracks and catching their wrists in her hands, so hard that they winced and cried out in pain. "Can't you see this is no school-yard game we're playin'? No' any more! This is about survival- for all of us. For all of our kind. Great forces are about to clash together, an' gettin' caught between them means- oblivi- on. The humans have fire, to roast us alive if they catch us. The fairy-folk control the water. An' Rannoch controls the magic that is our life-blood. So forgive me if I hurt your feelin's a wee bit!"

"You're hurtin' my arm!" said Kirkton Jean, clutching at her wrist.

"Oh, am I, dear?" said Nannie. "I am sorry! If Rannoch had seen your efforts back there, the next time you fell off a cliff, you wouldnae' be able to shift shape at all- until you hit the bottom. D'you no' think that might hurt even more?"

"You really think he'd- he'd actually kill us, Nannie?" said Mary, with a shudder. "We're a' on the same side here, are we no'?"

Nannie laughed grimly.

"Rannoch is on Rannoch's side, an' ye would do well to remember that!" she said. "The stakes are far higher here than your wounded pride. Do you really think he would hesitate for a second to destroy us, any of us, if we fail him in this? Even now, I see in his eyes that he might yet change allegiance, if we can't find the third changeling in time... You only survived your last encounter with him because you still have your parts to play!"

"So what do we do now then, Nannie?" said Hielan' Mary.

"We must watch now for the fairy-folk- for the *mnathan-shìdh*," said Nannie. "They are abroad at last, and they are much more deadly to us than Rannoch's ridiculous pet- than anything in this world, alive or dead, except for Rannoch himself. An' they are reachin' out to find us, even now..."

"Is that what Rannoch told you?" said Kirkton Jean, her eyes wide. "Back on the cliff top? He wanted to warn you about the still folk?"

"I need no warnin' from him, Jean- I can feel it!" said Nannie impatiently. "I can feel them sensin' for us, wherever we go now. That is what it means to have a foot in both worlds. To be a changeling..."

"Who are they?" said Hielan' Mary nervously. "Tam?"

"Of course!" said Nannie. "Tam we know about, we have long known about. But now I feel the two Watchers in his shadow, always with him, stalkin' him wherever he travels in the human world. They will never rest. For the first time it all makes sense- how he seemed to escape from us..."

"You were right- we were too careless!" said Kirkton Jean ruefully.

"That's what we were supposed to think," said Nannie. "But now I know that he was snatched from our very grasp! An' by someone with far greater power than I ever suspected. I should have known, even then! He could never have done it alone- not yet, anyway. But in time..."

"So how do we root out these accursed Watchers?" said Hielan' Mary.

"They will be the last people we expect," said Nannie. "For that is always the way of the still folk. And yet we must find them- before they find us. Before they ruin everythin' we've worked for. We must stay close to Tam now."

"An' the third changeling, Nannie?" said Hielan' Mary. "Whit aboot the third changeling?"

"Just shut up an' follow me, sisters- for now we fly again!" said Nannie, swirling her cloak around her. "An' to the devil wi' our hair! No gods, no masters!"

"No gods, no masters!" said Mary and Jean, as they disappeared into their own cloaks.

CHAPTER 5

—————

"THERE'S BRASS IN THIS, WULLIE, just you watch!" said Big Eck, packing a long clay pipe with baccy as they walked slowly over the cobbles of Ayr. "There always is in a time o' upheaval- just so long as ye dinnae' get up-heaved yoursel'! I can smell it in the wind…"

He rolled the fine Virginia tobacco between his fingers, drinking in the aroma. Even over Ayr's own distinctive scent, concentrated by the narrow streets of the old town, it was a rare treat for the senses.

"For just who could afford a passage across the Moyle, in a fine French privateer like that?" continued Eck. "One of the fastest vessels on the Seven Seas, I'd reckon… And you'd want a craft like that to carry ye, if you knew you'd have Admiral Byng and the whole King's Navy on your arse, as soon as you put your nose oot o' Brest or La Rochelle! For yon Byng is no slouch himself, no' when HMS Gibraltar is fully-rigged, wi' an extra tot of rum for all hands if ye can pass The Lizard by day-break!" Eck smiled, and studied the pipe carefully. "I dinnae' care who you are, this little sea voyage would've been an expensive high-jink, if ever there wis' one!" he said.

Finally satisfied with the compacting of the tobacco, Eck nodded to Wullie, who lit a taper from the rough shag tobacco he was smoking himelf and held it out to Eck. Eck drew deeply on his pipe. The baccy flared up and then glowered red, like a malevolent, all-seeing Cyclops.

"So aye, there's somethin' in this, Wullie, right enough!" he said. "It's Scotia's history in the makin'. History- and a wee bit o' brass to be made along the way too! An' after all, whit certainties are there really in this life, if no' for history and brass: the names we leave behind us, an' the gold we need to gild them?"

"Some name ye're goin' to leave behind you, eh, Eck?" said Wullie. "The richest smuggler on the Carrick coast!"

Eck looked at him, for once unsure of himself.

"The richest..." He paused. "Aye. Aye, I s'pose I've spent all my life chasin' the gold part..."

"An' no one's chased it harder than you, Eck!" said Wullie enthusiastically. "Nor caught it mair often!"

"I always thought there'd be time to make a name for mysel', once we'd enough gold..." said Eck.

"Right enough, Eck!" said Wullie. "Ye can never really have enough gold though, can ye? So- where're we headed for then?" he said.

Eck puffed at his pipe thoughtfully, exhaled, and let the spreading tendrils of smoke point the way.

"For the Jolly Beggars' Inn on the High Street, Wullie!" he said. "A wee birdie told me that's where we'll find our fine travellin' gentleman, and his Highland friends... An' if I cannae' wheedle a story out of a Highlander inside an inn, wi' the price of a drink in my pocket, well then I'm no' the man I thought I was, that's all!"

CHAPTER 6

———

A BAYING CROWD INSTANTLY FORMED around Souter Johnnie and Farmer Scott, feet sinking into the swampy field outside Mungo's Inn.

"C'mon, lads, let me through!" said Tam. "I've got tae' speak to the Souter! It's urgent!"

He tried to slip through the throng, but no one wanted to lose their vantage point for this scrap. It was the local sporting event of the year.

"Let me through! Och, come on!" complained Tam. "Where did you all come from, anyway? There's no' this many folk in the whole village! It's like the Glasgow Fair oot here!"

"You just wait your turn like everyone else, Young Tam O'Shanter!" said Farmer Goldie sanctimoniously. "He's tryin' to break it up, lads!" he added. "He's desperate to save that scunner Souter Johnnie from his just deserts- they're thick as thieves, ye know…"

The ranks of spectators closed irretrievably in front of Tam. Tam and Johnnie were well-known cronies, and the last thing these blood-thirsty spectators wanted was for a promising brawl to be broken up pre-maturely. There would be talk of nothing else for weeks to come, in the poky cottages of Alloway, Minishant and Culroy, and even as far afield as Dalrymple and Maybole. It was proving to be a memorable night for the district.

"Well, he'll get what's comin' to him, dinnae' worry about that!" shouted Goldie. "Stick one on him, Rab! I'm right behind ye! They dinnae' call ye the Culroy Killer for nothing, lad! Ahoy, the Culroy Killer! Kill him! Kill him!"

"Keep your guard up, Johnnie!" shouted Tam, suddenly alarmed for the Souter's well-being. "C'mon Souter Johnnie! C'mon the Alloway Alligator!"

Tam could just about make out the sturdy form of Scott through the forest of spectators. The Culroy Killer was slugging wildly, throwing punches like confetti. Johnnie was somewhat unconvincingly trying to duck and weave out of the way.

"Dinnae' turn your back on him like that, man!" shouted Tam anxiously. "Watch him! Keep both eyes on him! An' gie' him the old Carrick Cross! But block that counter punch!"

Pinned back by Scott's onslaught, giving up both weight and reach to the brawny farmer, Johnnie was quickly confirming Tam's suspicion that he was more adept in the amatory arts than the martial ones.

"The Carrick Cross, Johnnie!" Tam shouted. "Remember the old Carrick Cross!"

Tam was wracking his brains for something- anything- more to inspire Johnnie to victory, when suddenly he heard the voice again. At first it was just a silvery tinkle of sound, the words barely distinguishable. Tam followed it, hardly knowing why- or where he was going.

"Tam!" shouted Johnnie desperately. "Which one was the Carrick Cross, again? The rear hand or the lead hand? An' where dae' I put my feet, man?"

But Tam was beyond the fight now, beyond Johnnie, beyond Alloway- and everything and everyone in it. His head full of the mysterious Cutty Sark, he stumbled around blindly in the mud as he tried to trace the source of the voice, face turned up to the heavens. As he approached the door of Mungo's Inn, he could make out the words of the song for the first time:

"I'm o'er young, I'm o'er young,
I'm o'er young to marry yet;
I'm o'er young, 'twad be a sin
To take me frae' my mammy yet!"

"I know that song… I've heard it before!" said Tam. "But where? An' when? My mother would never have sung a Lowland song like that at home… So where? Was it at Tarbolton School? Who are you? Where are you?" he asked out loud. "It almost sounds as though you're- above me!"

But the voice just carried on regardless:

"Full loud an' shrill the frosty wind
Blows thro' the leafless timber, sir;
But if ye come this gate again;
I'll aulder be by summer, sir!"

"Who are you?" said Tam. "I want to see you now! I cannae' wait till summer!"

This time there was just a peal of laughter, and then the enchanting voice fell silent.

CHAPTER 7

———

"Banjo him, Rab!" shouted Goldie, baying for blood, as Scott rained blows down on the struggling Souter. Johnnie was still dodging and ducking as many of the farmer's wild haymakers as possible, but some of them were getting through, and the effort of parrying and blocking them was wearing him out quickly now.

"He's wide open to the uppercut!" yelled Goldie. "He's beggin' for it! Smash his face in! Pagger him, the Culroy Killer!"

"Really, Hosea?" protested Johnnie, between gasps for air. "We've been neighbours for fifteen years!"

But as the Souter looked over to Goldie reproachfully, Scott took full advantage of his distraction by swinging his right fist up towards his chin. The mighty uppercut crashed straight through Johnnie's erratic guard. It crunched painfully into the Souter's jaw, sending him spinning and tumbling down into the wet mud.

"Aye, that's the one!" gloated Goldie. "Spot on, son! Now get the boot into him, Rab Scott! Gie' him a shoein'! Shoe him good and proper! For he's a cobbler, d'ye see?" He guffawed, then shuddered as the rain-water soaked through his Souter Johnnie-fabricated footwear. "It's mair than he's ever done for us, when you come tae' think of it! Shoe 'im!"

"Cheers, Hosea!" muttered Johnnie, rubbing his throbbing jaw. He somehow managed to struggle back to his feet, but he knew he couldn't take much more of this punishment. He shook his head, in a vain attempt to drive away the kaleidoscope of spectral bodies dancing around his head. "Now, if I could just see him! An' I think ah'm hearin' things, man… Was someone- singin'- oot here?"

"Ye'll be as deaf as the Ailsa Craig, by the time Scotty here is done wi' you!" said Goldie triumphantly. "Pride o' Culroy! He's gonna' skelp ye, son! He's givin' it laldy the night!"

"Where's Tam?" asked Johnnie, looking around wildly in his disorientation. "Tam O'Shanter! I need you! Tammie!"

"Ye've got him now, Rab lad!" said Goldie with satisfaction. "He doesnae' ken up from doon! Are ye comin', or are ye goin', Souter Johnnie? See ya' later, Alloway Alligator! The 'Dalrymple Dentist' will have a' your teeth oot in a wee jiffy now! Lights oot, Sunny Jim, lights oot!"

Scott bellowed in triumph, sensing blood. He wound up his hamlike fist for the knock-out blow, and then rushed square onto his quarry, yelling with rage.

"What was it you said, Tam lad?" Johnnie muttered to himself. "The counter punch? Och, where are you Tam? You'd ken what to do now!"

And then on plunged Farmer Scott, swinging with both fists. Knees bent against the weight of the charge, Johnnie shaped to jab at him with his right fist and then pivoted his weight onto his left foot. Then he swung his left hand around with all his might. The change of angle threw Scott off balance, and sent Souter Johnnie's left fist arcing right around the farmer's doughty guard. Almost tumbling into the sucker punch already with the momentum of his own attack, Scott caught it squarely on the jaw, sending his head snapping back with the impact.

"Crivvens, that's no'- that's no' the Carrick Cross?" said Goldie, his face falling.

"Right enough! It never fails…" said Amos McIntosh next to him. "Well, well- so the Souter is a southpaw! Why, ah've no seen that particular move from a lefty since the 'Auchendrane Blood-drainer' stuck one on the 'Tarbolton Thunderbolt', durin' the 'Maybole Mayhem'! An' that was back in 1699! Aye, nick-names was longer back then, Hosea…"

Scott's sturdy frame shuddered as he absorbed the mighty blow and then, almost in slow motion, he crashed heavily down to the ground in a dishevelled heap.

"No!" shouted Goldie. "C'mon, Rab! Scotty! Up wi' you, lad! Up, an' at him! What's wrong wi' him, Amos?"

"Well, I'd say as he is oot for the coont, Hosea," said Amos solemnly. "Oot cold. Awa' wi' the fairies!"

"Alright, alright, I get the picture, Amos!" said Goldie impatiently. He scuttled up to the prone form of Scott, and started ineffectually trying to haul the big man back to his feet. "C'mon, Rab! Never say die! Back up on your feet wi' you, and straight back at the scunner! Culroy Killer, ahoy!"

For so embittered a man as Farmer Goldie, this was the very height of wishful thinking. With the amount of Mungo's 'Seventy Shilling' strong ale and home-distilled whisky that the Culroy Killer had taken on board in the course of the evening, it was highly unlikely that he'd be getting up from a blow like that any time before the Sabbath day- not without the aid of a stout carter, and a pair of dray horses to help him.

"Och, come on, Scotty, you big jessie boy, you!" Goldie shouted.

In his vexation, he didn't even notice Souter Johnnie walking towards him purposefully.

"Are ye goin' to let yoursel' be beat by any old tinker cobbler off the street?" screamed Goldie.

"How's the Culroy Kitten doin' then?" asked Johnnie, approaching Goldie menacingly. "Are you ready to take his place yet, 'Terror' Goldie? For there's a tinker cobbler here, wi' a shoein' ready just for you!"

Goldie slunk furtively back to the bar, suddenly unaccountably anxious to avoid Johnnie for a while. Fortunately for him, the other spectators thronged around Johnnie whilst he made his get-away, clapping the dazed Souter heartily on the back in congratulation.

"It's as though you never doubted me for a moment, eh, lads?" said Johnnie. "No' for a minute, eh? Where's Tam though? Was he no' watchin' that wee stooshie? Dinnae' tell me he missed my Carrick Cross, after all that!" He looked around again. "An' where's Andrew himself, if it comes to that?"

But Tam and Merry Andrew were nowhere to be seen on the victorious field of battle. All that Souter Johnnie received by way of an answer were the haunting notes of a bagpipe pibroch, drifting back down the Valley of Doon to Mungo's Inn. He understood the message well enough, though.

"Aye, farewell, Merry Andrew!" the Souter called into the night sky, as the music slowly died away into the distance. "Fare ye well, my friend, whoever you may be!"

———

CHAPTER 8

TAM LINGERED ALONE OUTSIDE THE door of Mungo's Inn, desperately scanning the moor for any trace of Nannie. It was too dark to see much but, in his distracted state, he didn't know what else to do with himself.

"Christ, it's as black as the Earl of Hell's waistcoat!" he muttered.

Suddenly, for the blink of an eye, he thought he could just make out a fleeting shape on the horizon. He stared after it, until long after his eyes lost focus.

"Och, it was probably just an owl…" he said, and pushed his way back through into the pub.

"C'mon on in, an' have a drink on the hoose, Tammie!" said Mungo jovially, as Tam approached the bar. "This wee fight o' the Souter's is a gift from the gods, I tell ye! A good brawl gives an inn a wee touch of distinction- a certain *ginny-sais quoi*, if ye ken what I mean?"

Tam clapped his hand to his head.

"Christ, there was a pagger back there, wasn't there? How could I jist have left Johnnie to it like that? What happened, Mungo? Is the Souter alright?"

"Fit as a fiddle!" said Mungo. "Och, young Rab Scott landed him a good one on his chin, right enough, but he just bounced up and gave him the auld Carrick Cross!"

"Thank God he's alright!" said Tam. "I never would have forgiven myself, for leavin' him like that…"

"It's certainly no' like you to miss a stooshie, lad!" said Mungo.

"Aye… Listen, Mungo, that lassie who I was just- who just spoke to me. Do ye… Well, d'ye ken her or no'?" said Tam.

"Kirkton Jean?" said Mungo. "I certainly dinnae' ken her in the biblical sense, Tam! I'm a happily married man, as ye well know…"

"No' her, man!" said Tam. "The, eh… the beautiful one. The lass in the green cutty sark. The Cutty Sark!"

Mungo poured himself an enormous slug of whisky, blinked as the pungent fumes of the home-distilled spirit temporarily blurred his eyesight, and then saw it off like a stalwart.

"A lass in a cutty sark?" he said. "Stuff and nonsense, son, it's your imagination runnin' wild! There'll be no lassies gallivantin' around this inn in their under-garments, green or otherwise, I assure you o' that!"

"Who is she, Mungo?" repeated Tam hopelessly. "I need to know!"

Goldie slunk back up to the bar, ears flapping, and signalled to Mungo to pour him a whisky.

"Who's she? The cat's mother?" said Goldie unpleasantly. "Who might you be talkin' about then, Tam O'Shanter? There's no' many 'shes' around here! I just hope you've no' been pesterin' Mungo's missus, ye young rascal, ye!"

"Pesterin' who, Tam O'Shanter?" said stout ginger matron, Morag McGillivray, appearing behind the bar. She glared short-sightedly at Tam. Goldie rubbed his hands together in satisfaction, drank off his whisky and then sat back to watch the show.

"Dinnae' ye be takin' my name in vain, d'ye hear me?" said Mrs McGillivray fiercely.

"Eh, ah, sorry, Mistress McGillivray…" muttered Tam. "Just a case of, eh, mistaken identity…"

"Mistaken whit, son? Speak up!"

"Sorry…" mumbled Tam again. He stumbled away from the bar, writhing in confusion and embarrassment.

"Come back, lad!" said Mungo. "Ye're no' in any state to ride home! Come an' sit wi' us for a while! Och, he's away an' gone…"

Mungo turned back to his wife and Goldie, tilting his hand to mime reckless drinking. Mistress McGillivray sniffed and withdrew from the room in disapproval, sweeping her capacious skirts up as she went.

"The man's in the horrors!" said Mungo. "And as for you, Hosea- pleased with yourself, are ye? You know the mistress has no' been herself since our Colin- disappeared..."

"Disappeared nothin', Mungo!" said Goldie irritably. "He was snatched by those damn' witches! They're up to their old tricks again, same as they ever were. You know it, I know it- but still we have to put up wi' that Merry Andrew, walkin' aboot free an' untortured, as though he owned the bloody place! Souter Johnnie should be ashamed of him- self... For Wee Colin wasn't the first one either, no' by a long chalk- though ye'd sometimes think it, to hear folk around here talk!"

Mungo sighed and shook his head.

"I'm sorry, Hosea. Poor Wee Anne! She's never far away from your mind even now, is she? She was a such a lovely lassie... But run an' fetch Souter Johnnie, will you? I'm worried about Tam O'Shanter. I've never seen him like this before, for all his drinkin' and his womanisin'! He seems, well- half-bewitched, himself..."

"I'm surprised ye've the heart to worry about a feckless rascal like that Tam O'Shanter, when ye've Colin an' your own worries in mind!" said Goldie.

"Aye, well, we're sometimes better to do what we can to remedy the sorrows before us in the here and now, than to dwell on the pain of the past..." said Mungo. "Run an' fetch Souter Johnnie, won't you, Hosea? He'll have forgotten all about that wee fight by now! An' besides, I've to mind the bar- I'm no' havin' the folk around here helpin' themselves to my ale, it'd be the ruin o' me in five minutes!"

"It's your new friend Merry Andrew you should be speakin' to, if it's missin' bairns you want to talk about!" grumbled Goldie. He paused to dispatch the brimming mug of whisky that Mungo had diplomatically poured out for him. "He could tell ye a thing or two about these bloody witches an' their midnight deeds, I'll wager! Ye saw him, lordin' it up in that black cloak of his… Cock o' the walk, he thinks himsel'! It makes me sick tae' see him! If we could only get some good old-fashioned thumb-screws onto that wee scunner, and gie' them a twist and a twist and a twist, we'd find out what really happened soon enough! To Colin, and to Wee Anne too, if it comes tae' that… Och, the old king had some sound notions when it came to his sort, right enough! The only good witch is a deid witch. An' the only thing better than one deid witch is two deid witches! An' I ken just where to start, Mungo… Merry Andrew!"

"Aye, aye, we've no time for all that again just now, Hosea…" said Mungo wearily.

"Och, alright then!" said Goldie, getting up reluctantly to go and look for Souter Johnnie. "A twist and a twist and a twist!" he muttered to himself.

CHAPTER 9

———◆———

"So it's you yourself, sir! Fancy meetin' you again, Your Worship!" said
Big Eck in feigned surprise, artfully contriving to bump into the Prince
at the long bar of the Jolly Beggars' Inn. "An' here at the Jolly Beggars'!
For I thought you'd be lodgin' up at the Castle, so I did! Forgive me, an'
my shockin' clumsiness! An' you a person of such clear distinction! It's
me, my Lord- Big Eck. Eck MacIver, Esquire, frae' the seaside- at your
service. An' you'll mind my associate Wullie here too, of the very same
address. Your humble servants, my Lord!"

Eck gave a pretty bow, which Wullie awkwardly tried to follow him
in.

"D'ye like coincidences then, big man?" said Callum, tapping the hilt
of his dirk. "For it's a strange thing, but I've noticed it before- the man
who goes lookin' for trouble, is as like as not to find it…"

"Ah, Callum, relax, *ragazzo mio*, relax!" said the Prince, taking a deep
draught of ale. "Men who are looking for trouble are precisely what I
am looking for myself! Men of wrath, like this Big Eck jackanapes, this
great hulking rogue here! No offence intended, of course, my friend…"
He toasted Big Eck with his beer mug, draining the ale to the last drop.
"Here's to rascals! Here's to men of deed, and here's to men of anger!
Fie upon weedy political milksops and men such as sleep a-nights, I will
have none of them! Why, Master MacIver, you will find that many of my
most trusted allies in this venture of mine are either looking for trouble-
or running away from it!"

"An' who might they be then, Your Worship?" said Eck, ignoring Callum's warning glance.

"Bring me another flagon of this vile substance first, my friend," said the Prince, "And then perhaps we shall talk a little more!"

"Of course, my Lord!" said Eck. "But I think I can dae' ye a wee bit better than that, on a special occasion like this one! What would you say to a drop of *vino*- or to a bumper o' the finest French claret, to be more precise?"

The Prince held his hand theatrically to his brow.

"Ah, do not jest with me, *mon ami*!" he said. "For it will be the death of me, I swear it! What would I not give! I asked that rustic dolt behind the bar for a dozen bottles of best Bordeaux, and he had the effrontery to serve me this slop... Beer may be good enough for a German valet like the Elector of Hanover, but gentlemen drink claret!"

Big Eck smiled, crocodile eyes once again disappearing from the face of the earth.

"It's a grand thing we should have, eh, chanced upon one another like this then, Your Eminence- for I happen to be in the wine trade myself! An' I have a cask of my own finest Saint-Émilion stowed in the cellar here for, eh, safe-keepin'..."

"Then broach it, my friend, broach it at once, and you shall hear all!" said the Prince.

CHAPTER 10

—————

TAM TRUDGED STOICALLY THROUGH THE churned-up quagmire of mud outside Mungo's Inn.

"It's like wadin' through treacle!" he thought. "Or even worse- like wadin' through the muddle in your own head, Tam O'Shanter..."

He swung open the rickety door to Mungo's stable, the thoughts whirling in his mind like the deranged bats who inhabited the byre. Tam cursed as he walked straight through a thick screen of cob-webs. He lit the ancient lantern dangling down from the ceiling, and then petted and fussed over his beloved mare, Meg. She nuzzled his face, instinctively sensing his disquiet.

"There, there, girl- calm down!" murmured Tam. "Though, God knows, it's me who needs to calm down the night!"

Even the Arctic gusts of wind sweeping through the byre couldn't clear his mind of cutty sarks now.

"What's the matter with you, Tam lad?" he muttered to himself. "Why can't you get her out of your poor, empty head? It's no' as if this is the first time you've been close to such a- such an indiscretion... Or even as if you were really close to it this time, however much you'd love to flatter yourself! What in the world would she want with a penniless yokel like you- a girl like that? And you'll probably never see her again anyway, thank the Lord..."

Meg fretted and whinnied, sensing Tam's agitation, anxious to get him safely home and out of harm's way.

"How could you see her again, even if you wanted to, ye big dummy?" Tam asked himself, but even as he did so, he knew that he had an ulterior motive. He wanted to find an answer. He paused and caught his breath, as a sudden flood of hope washed over him.

"But then didn't she say herself that she knows the way to Mungo's well enough? Was she just jokin' with me? Messin' with my heid, for some cruel reason! Or is she maybe friends with someone who lives nearby? And then she seemed so familiar… But who could it be, around here? Who would wear a cutty sark like that- who in Alloway or Culroy would even know someone who did! An' where would ye buy such a thing- in Glasgow? Edinburgh? London, even? But if she was serious- if she does know someone from one o' the villages- then she'll maybe be back in Mungo's one of these nights! If you can only get out again, Tam… But when? Tomorrow? Or the next night, maybe! But even then, what would you do- what could you possibly say? To someone like her? And what if it was only for that one moment in time where you connected, an' this was your big chance, an' you fluffed your lines… Just stood there like a great daft Highland Cow! An' now it's gone forever, an' even if you do see her, she'd just laugh at you- at your crazy day-dream…"

Meg looked on anxiously, as Tam smote his own forehead in an agony of frustration and self-disgust. She had carried him into and out of many a drunken escapade, but she had never seen him like this before.

"But then maybe she'll be in Ayr on market day?" said Tam to himself, his hopes somehow reviving again. "For the rest of the world an' his wife certainly will be! There'll be so many people around that you can barely think- just no' the one person you really want to, really need to, see! And yet you didnae' need to see her. Even a few hours ago, you didnae' need to see her at all… Christ, if only you could get back to that place- to that peace. But then to think of goin' back to that emptiness, too! For what was there to live for, back then, if ye'd only known? Whereas now there may be pain- but it's her… It's something of her."

Distraught, torn between a burning compulsion to give up everything for the Cutty Sark and a fervent wish never to see her again, Tam didn't even look up as Souter Johnnie walked quietly into the stable. Johnnie stooped under the low roof, patted Meg's face and gently took the reins out of Tam's hand.

"So here you are then, Judas O'Shanter!" said Johnnie, rubbing his chin gingerly. The adrenalin was wearing off now, and his bruises throbbed with pain. "Thanks for your support in that wee stramash back there- I couldnae' have done it without you!"

"I'm sorry, Johnnie!" said Tam, suddenly contrite. "I don't know what came over me, man! I never should have left you like that- after all these years that you've watched my back! Mine and my family's. It was unforgiveable…"

"Och, dinnae' fret about it now, Tammie!" said Johnnie, instantly mollified. "I'm still alive and kickin', aren't I? An' after all, it was your tip to throw the old Carrick Cross that did the trick back there…"

But Tam's attention had already strayed back to the Cutty Sark.

"Did you see her, Johnnie?" asked Tam. "You must have!"

"Who, Tam?" said Johnnie. "I wasnae' seein' quite straight the whole time, I must admit…"

"That girl- the Cutty Sark! What's the matter with everyone?" said Tam furiously. "What's the matter with me?"

"What's got into your heid, Tam?" asked Johnnie gently. "You're no' yourself, man!"

"Into my heid is right…" said Tam, rubbing his temples again, as though he could squeeze out the torment like a bee-sting- and somehow stop it pumping poison into his head. "She was- she was like nothin' I've ever seen, Johnnie! I mean, like nothin' in this world. It was like fallin' in love- or maybe fallin' off a cliff. Bein' hypnotised- or drugged…"

Johnnie shook his head ruefully.

"So this is what obsession looks like! But Tam- there was no one there but Jeanie and Mary, I swear it to you! I was there wi' you the whole time. An' d'ye really think I'd have missed a gorgeous lassie, prancin' aboot Mungo's Inn in silky underwear? A cutty sark, by jingo!"

He sighed wistfully, then winced as the movement made the tender area around his jaw twinge again.

"There was no one there but local folk, Tam..." continued Johnnie calmly. "For who else would come out to a tiny back-water like this? Somewhere in the middle of nowhere- no' a city, nor yet the Highlands. Just- nowhere... This is the very last place anythin' would ever happen- anythin' that really meant somethin' to anyone!"

Tam blinked.

"Merry Andrew was here, Johnnie..." he said quietly.

"Andy!" laughed Johnnie. "He's a good lad- an' harmless enough, whatever Hosea Goldie might like to think- but he's no' exactly a man o' the world!"

"I think that's what she was tryin' to tell me back there, Souter," Tam said. "That's it's no' all about high an' mighty folk- that it does matter, what you and I think- how we feel!"

Johnnie shook Tam's shoulder gently.

"Tam, for the last time- there was no one there!" he said. "Just like last night. Just like every other night that there's ever been at Mungo's Inn. No one!" The Souter could feel himself growing suddenly exasperated, and he wasn't quite sure why. "I'm sorry, Tam! I'm just so sick of bein'- of no' countin' for anything!" he said. "So really I should be the first to sympathise with you- with this feelin' you seem to have, that there has to be somethin' bigger out there for us... Well, I believe in you, Tam, whatever form that takes! I s'pose I have to believe that too!"

"I saw her, Johnnie- I talked to her," said Tam. "She- she touched my face..."

"So who was it then, Tammie? You must have seen her before, somewhere, surely?" said Johnnie. "I mean, Mungo's Inn is no' exactly aboundin' wi' the romantic mysteries of decadent Paris, wi' a dusky, exotic beauty around every corner, is it? This is rural Ayrshire, man! King Billy is probably the most sophisticated creature in the whole village. At least he knows how to take what he wants in life..."

Tam started at the expression.

"That's just what she said, Johnnie! About what I want from life!"

Johnnie smiled.

"That's probably what all this is really about then, isn't it, Tammie?" he said kindly. "It's no surprisin' that you're wonderin' what this is all about- at this time in our lives! I'm no different! Because look at us!" He gestured at the murky interior of the stable with disgust. "Let's face it, we've got nowhere since our folks left the Highlands! They moved down here for a better life- to gie' us the chance to make somethin' of ourselves- and we're spendin' the best years of our lives standin' in a byre, knee-deep in cow slurry! At least, I hope that's what it is... Our lives mean nothin', Tam. I mean, literally nothin', for we're surrounded by massive great pagans, wi' nothin' better to do than try an' knock the heid off an honest tradesman after they've had a few beers!" He winked at Tam. "No' that any o' that would bother you, of course, for you'd be showin' a clean pair of heels at the first sign o' trouble..."

"Souter..." said Tam, but Johnnie nipped his apology in the bud.

"Och, I'm just sayin'- life has no' exactly turned out as we planned it, has it? No' for either o' us!" said Johnnie. "So I for one dinnae' blame you if you're hearin' voices from a mysterious lassie, and you cannae' even tell me who she was! Frankly, I'd be glad o' the distraction myself..."

"I don't know who she was!" said Tam desperately. "That's what I've been tryin' to ask everyone- to tell everyone. Ye've all gone mad- or I have mysel'! An' I suppose that's more likely, when you come to think o' it. It's only that she did remind me a wee bit of... She reminded me of..."

"Of who, Tam?" said Souter Johnnie, taking Tam by the shoulders and staring earnestly into his eyes. "Of who?"

"But how could it be, Johnnie?" said Tam hopelessly. "She was just a girl!"

"Who, Tam? For God's sake, who're you talkin' about? C'mon, man, spit it out!" said Johnnie.

"Well, you remember Hosea's wee girl, Souter- Anne was her name..." said Tam uncertainly.

"Wee Anne Goldie?" said Johnnie, staring at Tam in astonishment. "Nannie Dee, we used to call her, when we were bairns? Tam, she was taken- what, twenty years ago? And Hosea was right there in the inn tonight! Stirrin' it up good and proper at that, I might add…"

"I don't think he saw her though …" said Tam.

"Really? After everythin' that he and Cathy went through, wi' Wee Nannie disappearin' like that, he just didnae' see her? I think he might've noticed, if his long-lost daughter had just come strollin' back in from out of the blue yonder, don't you, Tam?"

"Aye, you're right, Johnnie…" said Tam. "Of course you're right! But then she'd have changed so much in that time, we all have!"

"It broke him, Tam, you know it did," said Johnnie quietly. "So, change or no change, he'd hardly just have missed it, if she'd suddenly turned up again under his very nose at Mungo's Inn, would he?"

Tam fell silent for a moment.

"I don't know what to tell you, Johnnie," he said eventually. "You're right- but then I can only tell you what I saw. She had changed, an' I can't say whether even a father's eyes would have seen through- through what she's become now. There was somethin' different about her- somethin' a thousand miles from this village! The wee bit scraps of lives that we struggle through here… It was like steppin' into a completely different world for a moment. An' it seemed to last forever, an' no time- all at once. It was a world wi' just me and her in it. And I- I didn't want to come back, Johnnie."

CHAPTER 11

"SO YOU DECIDED AGAINST THE Eriskay landin' in the end then, eh, Cherlie boy?" said Callum, dipping his mug into the open cask of Eck's claret. "Didnae' fancy the cold, eh? Well, I dinnae' blame you! There's nothin' up there in the Outer Hebrides but sleet, wet sheep and teuchters- an' it wouldnae' have done that fancy Parisian hair-style o' yours a bit o' good!"

He took a deep swig of ruby Bordeaux and swung his brogues up onto the table. Tongues had been wagging pretty freely in the Jolly Beggars, ever since Wullie had rolled the aged barrel of Saint-Émilion out into the front room and crudely staved in its top with a hatchet. The Prince had pouted slightly at the barbarity with which such a noble barrel had been broached, but since then the wine had disappeared as quickly as if he'd staved in the bottom of the cask too. And Big Eck wasn't missing a precious word of this loose talk. He could hardly believe his good fortune at the rich Jacobite prize that seemed to have fallen out of the stormy sky, and landed straight in his lap. But Eck was no believer in divine providence. He made his own luck. He went through the motions of matching the others mug for mug of wine as they drank, but he hardly swallowed a drop himself. There was a time for drinking, and a time for listening. For something told Big Eck that he would have gold enough to buy all the fine wine in Bordeaux, if his theory about this fine traveller was proved right.

"There's been talk of nothin' else these past few weeks, amongst the rebel… I mean, amongst our true brothers o' the white cockade!" said Big Eck. "Eriskay, Eriskay, Eriskay- but then here are the cream o' the Jacobite generals! In the flesh an' in the pink, an' right here in jolly auld Ayr!" He held his wine out symbolically over the untouched jug of water on the table. "The King!" he said, with a great wink. "By which I'm really referrin' tae' the 'King Over the Water', of course!"

The Prince clapped his hands.

"Very good, my dear Eck!" he said. "I'm delighted to see that you are as ingenious as you are loyal!"

"Oh, aye!" said Big Eck. "No' a drink do I take, but I toast Good King James wi' it! Wullie here will tell you himself."

"Right enough, Eck!" said Wullie dutifully. "He does that! It's the 'King Over the Water', until we're a' feelin' seasick…"

"I only wish we could toast ye all by name!" said Eck cunningly. "For 'tis an honour beyond dreamin' to be at the heart o' the King's plans…"

"Ha- well, yes and no, my friends!" said the Prince, waving his own mug in the vague direction of the wine. Callum took it from his hand and filled it liberally. "Ah, thank'ee, Callum, you are a true kinsman indeed! Eriskay was very much part of my master plan. Devised, I may say, in the face of my royal father's most assiduous 'assistance'…"

"But ye changed your mind?" said Eck.

"Not so hasty, my dear Eck, not so hasty!" said the Prince. "A part of my plan- but I did not say which part! For I have already received word from the Chevalier's sources that the fair French frigate *Doutelle* did indeed land in some such godforsaken spot in the Outer Hebrides, not five days ago!"

"But empty, then?" probed Big Eck.

"Again I say- both yes and no!" said the Prince with a complacent chuckle. "Not quite empty, for it was bearing some, how shall I say it, some truly indispensable Jacobites! It was dispatched amid great ceremony, with some splendidly weasel words from my most musteline French agents- spread all around the ports of Belle-Île, Dunkirk, Nantes and Brest. All the better to confound and confuse my enemies further! Oh, and to let my own sleek ship, *Du Teillay*, slip straight through Admiral Byng's net, of course..."

"A decoy, eh?" said Big Eck. "You're a canny lad, my Lord, beggin' your pardon! For this is the last place they'd have looked for you to land alone! Here in the Lowlands, miles from your clansmen, an' wi' two garrisons o' redcoats in the neighbourhood..."

"Only my own kinsmen of Clan Stewart were made privy to the secret!" said the Prince. "I knew that they would never breach my confidence, not for all the Usurper's gold..."

"No' for all the gold in Christendom!" said Callum. "I like it! Who says you're no Highlander, eh, Cherlie?"

"No one who craves my favour, you may be sure of that, Callum!" cried the Prince fervently. "For do we not share a surname?"

"We bear a royal name!" broke in Malcolm staunchly.

"None nobler in all of Europe, *cugino mio*!" said the Prince.

So it was Charlie Stuart, then! Charles Edward Stuart... Big Eck could have hugged himself with glee. Exiled Jacobite gentry were worth their weight in gold. Everyone knew that the Prime Minister, the Duke of Newcastle, had dispatched his shadowy agents from London to Scotland's great ports, Leith, Gourock, Greenock, Port Glasgow and Montrose. There they lurked in tavern and warehouse, purses laden with bribe and reward, all a-twitter at the threat of the House of Stuart's long-feared return. Eck had done some brisk business with them already, and no questions asked. And now the Old Pretender's son and heir himself had landed at Culzean! Even Eck could hardly comprehend what that information might be worth. But he was pretty confident that he could find out.

"So who is up there in the Hebrides then, Your Highness?" said Big Eck. "All the great Jacobite lords o' the land?"

The Prince laughed, taking a great swig of claret as though it were Highland spring water.

"Great lords..." he smirked. "Well, perhaps we must wait to see how history will judge them! Friends of the king, but not necessarily of his Prince of Wales, shall we say... These 'Seven Men of Moidart', as I hear that they have taken to calling themselves, with suitable modesty!"

"They've a great name, at any rate!" laughed Callum. "An' they say that is half the battle, in a long campaign..."

"Oh, they are my most trusted generals and counsellors- my royal arse!" said the Prince. "The Seven Sisters, I prefer to call them!"

"An' who might they be, then?" said Big Eck, drawing another sidelong look from Callum. "These famous Seven Men o' Moidart?"

Callum stepped swiftly across towards the Prince and whispered a few words in his ear, before springing back to his seat. The Prince laughed, nodded and then studied Big Eck's face for a moment, a droll smile playing across his lips.

"What say you to a friendly contest, Eck, *mon ami*?" said the Prince innocently. "To a little sporting wager? And, you might even say, to a token of good faith?"

"Whit do you mean, my Lord?" said Eck cautiously.

The Prince smiled enigmatically, and then topped Big Eck's mug of wine right up to the brim.

"Let me explain what I have in mind, *ragazzo*... I will tell you the name of one member of my bold Seven for each bumper of wine that you pledge to our white cockade!"

Big Eck gulped and looked at the brimming mug.

"Ha, 'tis a crackin' jest, my Lord! I salute your noble wit! But I'd hate tae' deplete your royal supplies, just for the sake of a high-jink- an' me havin' drunk more than my fair share already..."

Callum leaned meaningfully in towards Big Eck.

"There's plenty more where that came from, Cap'n Blackbeard!" he said, pushing the mug over to Eck. "Besides, ye've hardly taken a drop all night… I do hate to see a big chap like you jist blowin' on his wine like this- an' so does Royal Cherlie. So drink, man! Drink!"

Big Eck looked around him, but there was no way out. The Highlanders were drumming the hilts of their dirks on the tables of the inn, and chanting "Drink! Drink! Drink!". Slowly to start with, but the rhythm was getting quicker and quicker. For Eck it was uncomfortably evocative of their war-cry, back on Culzean Beach.

"An' if I see one drop spilled…" said Callum, drumming the hilt of his own dirk on the table right in front of Big Eck. "Your own claret will follow it onto the floor, big man! So drink! Drink!"

Eck decided to make a virtue of necessity. Beaming genially around the room, he raised the mug to his lips.

"The King Over the Water, then!" he cried, taking a draught of wine.

"All of it, ya bampot!" shouted Callum.

Eck took a deep breath, and then drained the rest of the huge mug of wine, to cheers from the Highlanders.

"Well then!" said the Prince, clapping his hands gleefully. "A bargain is a bargain! And so, Man of Moidart Number One: A shrivelled up old banker, one Aeneas MacDonald- you may as well call him Judas MacDonald, for his surpassing love of freshly-minted silver pieces!" the Prince added maliciously. "Old 'Anus' is back in Scotland to protect his precious financial investment in this great venture of mine, but in reality is as unwilling a traveller as you ever saw dragged kicking and screaming down a leaping Belle-Île gang-plank… And I may confess to you that I was sorely tempted to deliver the final kick to his nether regions myself, as I waved him off! *Ma foi*, the very convict conscripts in Louis *le bien aimé*'s Atlantic Fleet serve their esteemed king more graciously than this Scottish Shylock serves my father! He might have put some of his beloved gold behind us as a speculation, but that's precisely where he wishes to remain- behind us! And more specifically, as far from the Elector of Hanover's cowardly English dragoons as he can possibly manage… No ornament to heroic Clan Donald him, believe me!"

"They always were a funny bunch, the MacDonalds," said Callum. "As proud as Lucifer himsel', wi' every one of them thinkin' himsel' the Lord of the Isles… But then they fight like the devil on pay day- so long as they're on the right flank of the King of Scots, as is their ancient honour! And they do hate the Campbells with a passion… So they cannae' be all bad, in my book!"

"They have reason enough to hate the perfidious Campbells of Argyll and Breadalbane, after the atrocities of the Massacre of Glencoe…" said Malcolm solemnly.

"Mort Ghlinne Comhann…" breathed Callum, visibly moved.

"Och, come on!" said Big Eck. "That's ancient history now, lads! When did it even happen?"

"1692," said Callum. "The thirteenth of February, 1692. Early in the mornin'."

"You see!" said Big Eck. "Mair than fifty years ago! I was but a babe in arms. Ancient history, man!"

"It will no' be forgotten so quickly as that, in our lands of Argyll and Lochaber," said Callum quietly. "No' when 1892 comes around- no, nor yet 2092! For we have long memories in the high country. Sons live to avenge father- aye, and neighbour to avenge neighbour. An' murder under trust is the worst of all crimes, by our laws."

"Crivvens, come now!" said Big Eck. "Leave a' that to the lawyers and the royal commissions, laddie! Ye have to let the past bury its dead and move on, chaps, or ye'll be forever broodin' over your wrongs!"

"Is that a fact?" said Callum. "Perhaps you dinna' mind the story right then, big man! For the Campbells were invited into the MacDonald country as guests. And so they were still guests when that fateful mornin' came, an' they blocked all the passes in an' oot o' Glen Coe. They were still guests when the order went out among them, to put all MacDonalds under seventy to the sword, be they armed or no'. They were guests when they shot and bayonetted their gentle hosts in their own homes, an' in their own glen! The Campbells breached the ancient Highland code of hospitality that day, and that can never be made right- no' wi' any words or royal commission!"

"Bravo, cousin!" said the Prince with gusto. "Never trust a Campbell! Not until you have your foot on his throat, or his shaggy head upon your castle gates!"

"But it was war, chaps!" protested Big Eck. "Dinnae' be cryin' over spilt milk now, bully-boys, for ye cannae' make an omelette withoot breakin' a few eggs!"

"It was women and children!" said Callum, rising to his feet, hand on the hilt of his dirk. He slammed the table top in front of Big Eck with his other fist, making the mugs and glasses leap and tremble. "It was our neighbours!"

———

CHAPTER 12

"Now listen, Tam lad," said Johnnie, looking around the byre with exaggerated caution before he spoke. "I didnae' follow you all the way out here, just to stand in a great steamin' pile of horse manure an' watch you go all starry-eyed over this mysterious Cutty Sark of yours! Bigger things are afoot in the world than your wee schoolboy infatuation! Have you heard what they're sayin' in the town? That he- that the Prince Over the Water- landed in Ayrshire tonight!"

"Young Cherlie?" cried Tam in amazement. "Cherlie Stuart, you say, Souter?"

"Hist, man, no' so loud!" hissed Johnnie. "They say that the Duke o' Newcastle has his spies everywhere in Scotland! Though that is a wee bit hard to imagine, in the case of this particular byre... But aye, Prince Cherlie himself!"

"How did ye come to hear of it, Johnnie?" said Tam, excited in spite of himself.

"From Auld Amos McIntosh, of all people!" said Johnnie eagerly. "He had it from a tipsy Highlander in the Jolly Beggars' Inn last night..."

Tam raised an eyebrow.

"So the Prince Over the Water is in Ayr, is he, Johnnie?" he said sceptically. "A strange choice o' headquarters, when you consider the history and geography o' Scotland! But I suppose it makes sense, if he's taken a wee fancy to the ale at the Jolly Beggars'..."

"Listen to me, Tam!" said Johnnie impatiently. "Amos was stayin' in town overnight, and he ran into a Highland laddie at the Jolly Beggars'. Naturally enough, this Highlander was after the price o' a drink- an' said he had a piece of information well worth all the ale in Ayrshire! Well, of course Amos bought him a mug of beer right away- ye know what an auld gossip he is! An' so they got to talkin', an' after a drop more ale Amos asked him what the great secret was, and then this Highlander told him straight out that he and his clansmen were down to meet Royal Charlie! He was landin' in a booze smugglers' boat from France. Arrivin' the next night! An' just down at Culzean Bay, a coupla' miles from here at most, as you know! So it's this very night, if ye can believe it!"

Johnnie could hardly speak for excitement now. He grabbed Tam's shoulders and shook him bodily.

"D'ye no' see what this means, Tam- that Scotia's exiled prince is returnin' at last! And this time to claim back the throne for his royal father! It's finally happenin'... Somethin' big is finally happenin' here! I just cannae' believe it! After all these years..."

"Some night for it!" said Tam sympathetically. "You'd think one more day of exile would no' make much difference, after all these years! I cannae' believe it's really so grim over there in France, that you'd no' wait another day or two for a clear night to return on..."

"Aye, but there's his safety to think of as well, ye see!" said Johnnie eagerly. "Timin' and secrecy are of the very essence, in such a clandestine operation..."

"I'd say a wee bit o' the element of surprise has already been lost, if half his men are on the swally wi' Amos McIntosh in the Jolly Beggars'!" said Tam. Johnnie ignored him.

"Otherwise I suppose he'd be landin' in Leith- just by Edinburgh. Or in Port Glasgow," continued Johnnie. "But alas, there are plenty of folk who like it just fine without the rightful king around! Even here in the village. You must have seen- must have felt- that there are things afoot in this poor land that should never have seen the honest light of day. Unnatural things..."

Tam nodded slowly.

"They're strange days we're livin' through, right enough, Johnnie," he said. "The barley's withered on its stalk in the back field, and yet we've had rain enough for a year. Sometimes the land- speaks to us. In its joy- an' in its sufferin'…"

"The land? Oh aye, the land, right enough!" said Johnnie. The conversation was getting a little esoteric for him, at this time of night. "Well, we cannae' haver out here all night, Tammie! Let's talk in the mornin', lad. For it's goin' to be some day in Ayr tomorrow, I can tell you that! Such a day as we've never seen, these thirty years past! Finally, it's our turn- to play our part in Scotland's great story! To right some ancient wrongs…"

"What's gonnae' happen now then, Johnnie?" said Tam.

"Why, we'll join him, of course!" said Johnnie. "We'll rally to the famous white banner of the Stuarts! Now away wi' you, and get yourself ready for market day tomorrow. An' send my love to Katie- for soon we'll be makin' her and Wee Tam proud!"

Tam took the reins back from Johnnie, still lost in thought. He led Meg out of the byre and swung himself up onto her back. Market day, of course- and that might mean seeing the Cutty Sark again! He had forgotten about her for- what, all of five minutes- in the excitement of the Souter's news from Ayr. But now she had recaptured his imagination again, and in a way that no prince or king in Europe could have done.

"Thank you, Johnnie!" he said at last. "Kate'll be right glad o' that."

The rain was still lashing down outside, and Johnnie pulled a blue woollen bonnet out from the pocket of his coat and clapped it onto Tam's head against the wild elements.

"Thank you, brother!" said Tam, leaning down out of the saddle to hug Johnnie close.

"Och, c'mon, Tam, ye auld softy, I'll be seein' ye tomorrow!" said Johnnie.

He was laughing, but he still hugged Tam tightly back.

"Awa' wi' the both of you, then!" said Johnnie, patting Meg farewell and giving Tam a great shove. "Make sure you see him home safely, Meg! Until tomorrow- tomorrow, an' the greatest day in Scotland's history!"

"Until tomorrow!" shouted Tam, spurring Meg into a brisk trot.

"But what will tomorrow bring us all, girl?" he asked Meg, as she started to canter and they sped into the darkness. "An' who will it be great for?"

CHAPTER 13

"STEADY ON NOW, LADDIE, STEADY on!" said Big Eck, backing away from Callum. The Highlander was advancing upon him with murder in his eye. "Just wait a wee minute now, son! Ye've accepted my hospitality! Hospitality!" said Big Eck. Nonetheless he prudently picked up a bar-stool to hold Callum off with. "Just think o' the Highland code! Ye din-nae' want to be like yin o' they perfidious Campbells, do ye? Ye've had aboot a gallon of my vino, by the auld Winchester Standards, Johnny Highlander! Ye surely cannae' dirk a man after that kind o' hospitality, can ye?" He gulped, as Callum swiped the bar-stool out of his hands and it clattered heavily onto the floor. "'Course you can't! More vino for the man, Wullie! A wee bit o' hospitality wouldnae' go amiss now! C'mon now, let's sing together!" said Eck desperately. "Hospitable, like! Altogether now:

"Should auld acquaintance be forgot,
And never brought to mind?
Should auld acquaintance be forgot,
And auld lang syne?

For auld lang syne, my jo,
for auld lang syne!
We'll tak' a cup o' kindness yet,
for auld lang syne..."

There was a tense pause, whilst Eck crooned his song in a slightly tremulous baritone. Wullie hurriedly refilled Callum's mug with wine.

"Och, I wass just makin' a point!" said Callum, finally backing off and sitting down again. "Here's to you, Big Eck- for auld lang syne, then! *Tapadh leat!*"

Wullie gave an audible sigh of relief as Big Eck and Callum clanked their drinking mugs together by way of truce, and then the Prince sealed it with a royal toast. Callum took another deep draught of wine to cool his blood, before continuing.

"But how would it be, Big Eck, if we were just to walk down the Ayr High Street oot there, and dirk every man, woman and child under seventy who crossed our path? Would that be war too? It'd be easy enough- for how long would it take the redcoats to get here from Irvine? The point is that we wouldnae' do it. For there's a difference between war and peace!" said Callum, seeing off the rest of his wine. "There's a difference between these Campbell dogs of Clan Diarmid, and men of honour- Highland gentlemen!"

"Right enough, Mister Stewart…" said Wullie, thinking of his own sprawling family, snug in a slum tenement of Ayr. "Here's tae' men o' honour!" He raised his mug to Callum, who clanked it with his own.

"An' who else is up there in Eriskay then, Your Highness?" said Big Eck off-handedly.

After his narrow reprieve on the Glencoe question, he was eager to press on with the business at hand- not to get bogged down in a litany of ancient clan grudges. Especially if there was a danger of being drawn into them himself, by these ever-touchy Highlanders.

"Ha!" said the Prince. "Next, there is a trio of bibulous Irishmen, fire-eaters who are almost ready to tear the Usurper apart with their bare hands- when the old port is travelling around the table, that is!"

"They sound like valuable allies of the cause!" said Big Eck, thinking of the three rich bounties on their heads.

"If they hit the Hanoverian lines as hard as they hit the Madeira bottle, then we would all be in London by next week!" said the Prince. "But then they fall strangely silent- until they have wet their feeble lips with the first stoup of wine the next morning... 'Bottle Jacobites', as I like to call them! But speaking of which, my good Wullie, pray bring us three brimming bumpers for Eck here to pay for the names of another three of my Seven Men: Sir Thomas Sheridan, Sir John MacDonald and the most Reverend George Kelly!"

"Drink! Drink! Drink!" chanted the Highlanders, as Wullie brought up the bumpers of claret, and Big Eck forced them down with the utmost reluctance, coughing and spluttering.

"Bravo!" said the Prince. "Yes, fine travelling companions for a prince, these toping geriatrics! Indeed, the only really useful man on that luckless ship is my dear Colonel O'Sullivan..." He nodded towards Wullie. "Another drink for Eck, my man... No jibbing now, old fellow! Down in one! Try to keep it down, for it is the finest Saint-Émilion! Yes, yes, this O'Sullivan of mine is another prize mountebank, and as Irish as *delirium tremens* itself, of course! But he at least has a few real campaigns in the tipsy piquets of Beloved Louis' Irish Brigade behind him. He has even seen military action, in the ancient bandit country of Corsica no less! And after all, are these sausage-loving Hanoverian Usurpers any less outlaws and criminals than the commonest of Corsican *banditti*, Chevalier?"

"No, indeed!" said Malcolm devoutly.

"And so is this O'Sullivan to be ra' general of yer royal army then, Your Highness?" asked Big Eck, slurring his words slightly now.

"*Sei matto*, Big Eck!" exclaimed the Prince, spitting out a mouthful of the precious wine. "*Sei un bel matto!* John William O'Sullivan is a commoner, for God's sake! My father would lose his mind- what little is left of it- were he ever to hear of such a thing! No, Adjutant is more the role I have in mind for the good Colonel O'Sullivan..."

"Is tha' the lot, then, Your Highness?" interrupted Big Eck, who was rapidly losing count- both of Men of Moidart and of the bumpers of claret he had consumed.

"*Dio mio*, no!" laughed the Prince. "I would not have you forget Sir Francis Strickland, the sole representative of my fine English Jacobites- another bumper, Wullie, to refresh Eck's failing memory!"

"D'you think he'll be able to raise the English Jacobites for you, Cherlie?" asked Callum eagerly, as Big Eck reluctantly swilled down the latest instalment of wine. "We could use all the help we can get from them- or at least their gold- in the great struggle before us!"

"I certainly hope so, or I shall have endured his pompous utterances through many interminable dinners for nothing!" said the Prince. "*Ma foi*, the man is the most perfidious of courtiers! A pompous ass, who takes an hour to request the salt if it be from one of his betters! Which, of course, is everyone in Parisian society, since everyone knows that the English have no breeding to speak of, and the gentleman in question is not even a *duc...*"

He stood up and pointed dramatically through the window of the inn, down towards Alloway, Minishant, Maybole and beyond it- the South.

"My dear Callum, London town- my father's ancient capital- lies in faraway England!" he cried. "Why would I be here in Scotland at all, if my English supporters had shown me a glimmer of the same love that you and my beloved Highlanders have so faithfully rendered me? If they had cherished the white cockade so lovingly in their hearts? No, my friend, let me at once do for my English Jacobites all that they have ever done for me..."

The Prince raised his mug and took another great gulp of wine.

"Drink their good health, by God! To the English Jacobites!"

He dashed the mug onto the floor, where it smashed into pieces.

"The English Jacobites!" roared the Highlanders, bellowing with laughter and draining their own mugs.

Malcolm mimed participation in the toast for the sake of appearances, but he wasn't even pretending to smile this time. Without material assistance from the Jacobite party in England, this jaunt to Ayrshire could all turn out to have been an extremely expensive mistake. The wily Chevalier knew from 1715 that failed rebellion meant losing your liberty, your head- or even worse, your land and estates.

"And which o' the great houses of England have been the first to declare themselves for your father, Your Highness?" he asked.

The Prince scowled at so blunt- and so inconvenient- a question.

"You forget yourself, Chevalier!" he said haughtily. "I am in the midst of a wager with my friend Eck here…" He turned back to Eck and solemnly passed him another huge mug of wine. Eck accepted it without much enthusiasm, lolling back in his seat. "The last of the Secret Seven is another fine old Caledonian fossil, by the name of Murray, Marquis of Tullibardine! Second Duke of Atholl- though he has a good deal of fighting to do, before he can reclaim that particular title from his own Hanoverian usurper! The noble Duke at least was 'out' in the 1715 rising, and so he may be said to compensate with gallantry what he lacks in physical vigour… His younger brother, Lord George Murray, already has some name as a general, and may prove an asset to our cause…"

"Oh aye, I remember the bonny Duke of Atholl well enough, Your Highness!" said Malcolm. "The flower of the royal army! A credit to the white cockade! He was certainly out in the '15!"

"By all means, Chevalier- if by that one means 'out to pasture'!" said the Prince acidly. "For I very much suspect that he was already somewhat past his best as an *homme de guerre*, even thirty years ago… What I need for my own royal army is more men like Eck here- bold men of their hands! Not these doddering old veterans of 1715… No offence intended, of course, Chevalier!"

Malcolm bowed respectfully.

"And so now you have met them all- my brave Seven Men of Moidart!" said the Prince ironically. "What do you make of them, Eck? Do you wonder that I was so easily able to dispense with their company?"

But Big Eck was already fast asleep, slumped beneath the table. The tribute of wine for the Seventh Man of Moidart had proved too much, even for his doughty constitution. The Prince's secrets were safe with him, unless the Duke of Newcastle's sinister spies could decipher snores as well as words. If they could have done, they would have heard something that would have amazed them, and Wullie- and even Eck himself. For the first time in his life, he was dreaming of something other than Cousin Jacky and Holland gin, making hard cash and salting it away. He was dreaming of the Prince dubbing him MacIver, Marquess of Carrick. He was dreaming of a legacy.

"These smugglers have no stamina!" said the Prince, as the clock struck twelve. "We cannot leave Ayr until tomorrow at the earliest. And I for one will be damned if I miss my last opportunity to sup on a decent wine before we go!"

"Perhaps you will be anyway, my fine prince!" said a voice from the doorway. "Damned, that is!" The words were spoken quietly enough, almost in a whisper, but somehow they reached every man's ears over the din and hubbub of the inn anyway- carried on the draught, like spider's silk. The banter and chatter stopped dead in an instant, and beneath the table Big Eck stirred uneasily, rubbed his eyes and sat up.

"I beg your pardon, my good man?" said the Prince. "What the devil do you mean by speaking to me like that? And why do you slink and skulk in the darkness, like a Hanoverian spy in the night?"

There was a cold laugh from the doorway.

"Your good man?"

"It's just a figure of speech, pal," said Callum, standing up and padding softly to the doorway. "If the cap doesnae' fit ye, then dinnae' put it on!" He unsheathed his dirk. "We can maybe fit ye up for some windin' clothes, if they'd suit ye better!"

Big Eck's head cleared like the fog lifting from the Clyde, as he felt the first tell-tale beads of sweat forming on his palms. He knocked over a mug deliberately, to hide the click as he cocked a long pistol under the table.

"By the prickin' o' my thumbs, somethin' wicked this way comes..." Eck muttered to himself. "There's some dangerous lads in this wee tea-party of ours now, right enough! Ye're playin' with the big boys here, Eck MacIver, make no mistake aboot that! Ye'll have to look lively, if you dinnae' want to lose your marquess' coronet, before it's even settled on your ugly great heid..."

"May I join you, Charles Edward?" said the voice insistently. "May we come in out of the rain? May we cross the threshold? For it is midnight now, and we two have much to speak of. Matters of high politics, matters of life- and death. And what is much more than any of them- matters of power!"

There was an echoing animal howl from outside.

"That's no' a human voice!" muttered Big Eck.

"It's no' canny, Eck..." said Wullie nervously.

"What'n the world was that noise?" said Callum. "And who's 'we', anyway, *laochain*? Speak your names, like good Christians, before I come an' find out for myself!"

"Why, just myself," came back the voice. "I go by the name of Rannoch here. Oh, and Absalom, of course. Only have a care of Absalom, Highlander, for he's in an evil temper tonight! And he has a fearful bite, the little brute... Well might the poet have called him 'warlike Absalom'!"

CHAPTER 14

———

TAM AND MEG SPED ACROSS the black moor, running away from Mungo's Inn, the Cutty Sark and all the endless tumult inside Tam's own head. Meg was skittish, struggling to settle into any kind of regular stride.

"What's wrong, lass?" ask Tam soothingly. "It's no' like you to pull on the bit like that!"

He spurred her on again, and she gamely plunged on over the swampy turf. Suddenly there was a gust of wind over Tam's head, causing him to duck, and Meg to shy wildly off course.

"What in the world?" said Tam, holding his bonnet onto his head as a freak rush of air tugged hard at it.

Suddenly a silvery voice seemed to echo all around him.

"Tam! Tam O'Shanter!"

Now Tam jerked hard on the reins and wheeled Meg around in a circle, peering myopically into the darkness, trying in vain to trace the origin of the sound. As if on cue, the words "Tam O'Shanter!" rang out again, only this time it was in the harsher tones of his wife, Kate, in her wrath.

Meg reared up at the sound of the familiar voice, startled and disoriented at hearing it so far from home.

"Kate?" cried Tam. "Kate, is it you? Have you been with me all this time?"

"Which way is the wind blowin', Tam O'Shanter?" asked the voice mockingly. "Which way will it blow you?"

Now it was laced with silver again. Or rather quicksilver- mercurial, suddenly changeable, an infinite weight of sadness lying beneath it. Then there was a peal of laughter, sweeter than honey but riddled deep with bitterness. Or was it longing? And for whom- or what? Now Tam had abandoned all faith in his senses and just leant back in the saddle, completely in thrall to the voice, looking vainly all around him for the source of his bewitchment. Silence, aching silence. Then, as if out of nowhere, a huge white seagull swooped down just over his head, screeching demonically.

"Christ!" shouted Tam, as two more seagulls swept after it, screaming and hissing at him.

Meg bucked and bolted uncontrollably away from the sharp beaks and the unfamiliar noise so close to her pricked ears, and Tam struggled to stay in his saddle. Suddenly he felt bony fingers scrabbling at his neck, clutching at him, pulling him off Meg's back, but when he cursed and grabbed at them, horrified, the sensation ceased as abruptly as it had set in. Meg turned around in alarm, but once more there was nothing there.

"Easy girl, easy!" shouted Tam, wrestling Meg steady and then sliding off her back onto the ground. He held her reins and patted her face gently.

"Who are you?" he shouted out into the darkness. "Are you out there? Or just inside my head?"

But this time no answer came back.

"Is it really you, Nannie?" shouted Tam desperately. "Who are you, Cutty Sark? Tell me who you are! Cutty Sark!"

"No gods, no masters!" came back the voice, but it was already drifting away on the wind.

"Cutty Sark!" screamed Tam. "Tell me! I'm beggin' you!"

"Where are you, Tam O'Shanter?" called Kate's voice. "Where are you?"

"Kate?" shouted Tam.

A final peal of laughter echoed back and was immediately swallowed up by the silence, leaving Tam stranded, alone with Meg, in the midst of a raging torment of confusion.

For the first time in a lifetime of journeys across the lonely moor, Tam had the sensation of complete isolation there. Since boyhood it had felt like his home straight, leading him safely back to the comforting old bridge over the River Doon, the Brig o' Doon, by which his family's croft nestled. Part of his own domain. Now the moor seemed to belong to something far more rooted in the land itself- to something far older. He had never felt so from his own folk, from Kate and Wee Tam. And inside he could feel the terrible longing growing, a craving for a girl he didn't even know. Unless it really was Anne Goldie, thought Tam. But then how could it be? And did he even know Nannie Goldie? Where in the world could she have been, these twenty long years? And who could possibly have raised her- into the beautiful, sophisticated sylph he had encountered at Mungo's Inn? For whoever this was, this devastating, disorienting force of nature that Tam had just encountered, she far surpasses anyone in the neighbourhood for grace and elegance- that at least was clear. And wasn't Johnnie right- wouldn't Goldie have known, have somehow sensed her presence- if it was really her? After all the long years he had waited for her. Nannie Goldie! Could it be her, after all?

Tam tried to shut the questions out of his head, but they were not as easy to shoo away as the mad bats in Mungo's byre. Tam shook his head, as though trying to dislodge them physically, and then swung himself back up onto Meg's back.

"C'mon, girl, we can't stay out here in the pourin' rain all night!" he cried. "We'll be just fine, once we reach the Brig o' Doon!"

But even if he made it to the sanctuary of the Auld Brig, how could he ever hope to ease the torment inside his own head? Was it even a sanctuary now? For however fast he rode, he would still carry that along with him- inside him. The rain lashed down harder than ever, running down his face in maddening rivulets. He pulled Johnnie's bonnet further down over his brow and rode hell for leather on into the blackness. He was hardly conscious of making for home at all now- he only wanted to lose himself in the blackness of the night, to find forgiving oblivion in any guise, even at the cost of a broken neck. Perhaps ideally that way.

Suddenly he pulled up again, at the hint of a voice carrying on the wind.

"No gods, no masters!"

Was it her voice again? Or just the wind itself, playing the cruellest of tricks with his fevered mind? Either way the words seemed unspeakably distant, horribly detached from him now. When all he wanted, all he craved, all he feared, was to be with her.

"If it's just the drink talkin'- then why is it getting louder and louder, the further I get from the Inn?" Tam asked himself. "And whose voice is it? Her's? Kate's? My own?"

Now they were galloping madly, desperately, heedlessly across the moor, the onrushing wind somehow helping to drive the voices out of Tam's head- most of all his own. But you have to ride perilously fast to escape that. And as fast as he thought he was riding away from their world, the truth was that he had never been closer to it than at that moment- or further away from the material world of men, the mundane daily struggle of feeding, clothing and sheltering himself and his family that had preoccupied him for longer than he could remember. For during that frantic ride, for the first time Tam was completely consumed by the elements to which he had so recklessly entrusted himself and his loyal mare. Love, hate, anger, fear, desire. And the elements that set us free can so easily enslave us in their turn. Fire, earth, air, aether- and water. Witches.

Utterly lost to those wild elements, giving Meg her head, Tam sat up in his saddle with a start as they finally clattered onto the comfortingly cranked stone span of the bridge. The Brig o' Doon! The familiar ring of iron horse-shoe on cobbles chimed with the peaceful gurgle of the Water of Doon to break the spell, and bring Tam blinking back into the everyday world. He stared around him as they trotted over the narrow bridge and out of the trance, safely back down onto Alloway side. Tam sighed as he recognised the outline of his own modest byre through the darkness. And in that sigh was such a mixture of relief and despair as long centuries could never have separated out.

"We rode though hell- to get back to this?" said Tam, looking at the simple homestead. "But then this is our life, I s'pose! And we're safe home now, thank God... So just where would I be without you, eh, lass?" he said, rubbing Meg's velvet muzzle. "At least one of us remembered the way back home- from wherever it is we've been tonight!"

He slipped off her back as they approached the byre, led her inside and then carefully rubbed her soaking coat down with an old horse-blanket. There was solace in being back across the Auld Brig, back on his own side, back home. But there was also a nagging sense of loss. Tam wasn't ready to ask himself yet whether that would ever leave him.

"Christ! For a moment there, I really thought we were lost forever this time, girl!" he murmured, as he helped Meg to a generous bundle of hay.

He stroked her nose one last time, then gently pulled the rickety door of the byre closed behind him. He paused outside his own humble croft, just a few steps away, to wring out his sodden bonnet.

"Time's up, Tam," he muttered to himself. "Last chance to get your head together, before you face the music..."

The water trickled steadily out of the misshapen lump of wool onto the soggy ground. Shaking the rain off his clothes as best he could, Tam gingerly opened the door of the croft. A flood of freezing water crashed into him, soaking him from top to toe. He gasped as the shock of the cold water left him winded for the second time that night.

"No' again!" spluttered Tam.

Inside the door a handsome woman, wearing a tightly-buttoned night-gown and tighter-buttoned lips, tucked an empty metal bucket neatly back behind the door.

"Caught in the rain, were ye, Tam?" said his wife, Kate. "What a shame! It's really no' the time of year to be out gallivantin' at all times o' night now, is it? You could catch your death!"

Tam followed her mutely into the one-roomed cottage. Kate led him to the side of a tiny bed where a small boy, eight years old but slight for his age, writhed in the fearsome grip of a nightmare. Tam looked helplessly at his son, Wee Tam. Lost in uneasy sleep, stranded alone with his fears, he looked no different from any other scared young child.

"Aye, look on!" said Kate bitterly. "Look well, Tam! This is what's been happenin' to your family, forgotten back here, whilst you've been takin' your sinful pleasures elsewhere…"

For the first time, Tam suddenly felt chilled to the bone. He would have done anything to take all this suffering onto his own shoulders, to spare Wee Tam even one second of his pain- and Kate hers. But that is not the way of such things. Instead he shared it in silence, crouched at Wee Tam's bedside, straining to follow the boy's agitated dreams. And he shuddered along with him through every tortuous twist of the nightmare.

CHAPTER 15

———————

MUNGO'S SON COLIN STRIDES ACROSS *the moor, brandishing a long stick like a sword. He is the same age as Wee Tam, but taller, stockier, red-headed and chock-full of bravado. Wee Tam follows him meekly enough at first, but he is becoming increasingly anxious. It is early evening, the gathering mist swallowing the sunlight quickly now. Soon it will be dark on the moor. Wee Tam puts his hand on Colin's shoulder to restrain him, trying to pull him back as they approach the ford on a narrow stream, but Colin shakes it off impatiently.*

"We're nearly there now!" says Colin. "Last one across the burn is a big jessie boy!"

Wee Tam looks in horror at the stream. He can't explain why, but he knows that they shouldn't cross the water. It is the kind of moment when he feels somehow-older- than Colin and the other boys in the village.

"C'mon, Tam!" shouts Colin impatiently. "You're no' a jessie boy, are ye?"

Wee Tam shakes his head, but he doesn't care whether or not he's a jessie boy. All he knows is that he doesn't want to cross that stream. Colin runs down to it and fords the narrow burn, jumping onto the great stepping stones tipped into it by local farmers in time immemorial, then shouts out as his foot lands on a slippery rock. He twists his ankle, and tumbles straight down to the ground on the other side, screaming in pain. His face is a picture of agony, as he clutches at his ankle.

"Tam!" he shouts. "My foot! My foot!"

Wee Tam gulps down his fear and forces himself to jump over the stream. His need to help Colin is even greater than his fear of crossing. When he reaches

Colin, the red-haired boy cries out. Tam bends down towards him, terrified that he has hurt himself badly. Colin gives another loud shriek, but this time of laughter. He bounds nimbly up to his feet, and rubs Tam's head, ruffling his sandy hair mercilessly.

"Fooled ye!" he said gleefully. "You are a jessie, Tam, a big jessie boy, no' wantin' to cross a wee stream like that! Och, dinnae' look at me like that, ye can see it's alright now! C'mon! We're across!"

Tam looks back at the stream. He still feels that they shouldn't have crossed it, more strongly than he has ever felt anything in his life. But Colin is right- he's across it now, and there's no going back. They walk on in silence, picking their way through a sparse copse of trees.

"This is Kirk Wood..." says Colin. "Just like I told you! It's years since anyone has been here after dark. Any human soul, that is... For the Cat Sìth roams here! A giant black cat- you'll ken it by the white spot on its chest. It's no really a cat at all, ye see, Tammie. It's a witch!"

Even Colin is a little intimidated by that knowledge, although he is as desperate to bluff his way through it as any eight-year-old boy could be.

"It can turn itself into a cat nine times, an' after that it will be stuck in a witch's form forever!"

Tam himself is terrified, wide-eyed. He isn't particularly scared of seeing a black cat, but for some reason the thought of witches terrifies him now. And he is transfixed by the sombre Gothic ruins of the Auld Kirk and the desolate church-yard surrounding it, which are now looming large through the trees before them. Was the stone always so black, he wonders. To him it feels more like a fortress, an ancient stronghold, than any place of worship. But is it to keep us out, or to hold something else in, Wee Tam asks himself.

"Well, c'mon then!" says Colin, impatiently, pulling him by the arm.

It's as though he's using my fear to drive himself on, thinks Tam. He trudges after Colin, but as his misgivings grow he is dragging his heels, following him ever more reluctantly.

"What in the world will Malky Scott have to say when we tell him about this?" says Colin. "He was too frightened tae' throw a stone at Merry Andrew, even when his old man told him to! But then he doesnae' have- this..."

He pulls out a tiny pocket-knife and slashes the air violently with it. Wee Tam shies away from the bright blade.

This reaction seems to spur Colin on even further, and he immediately starts prising open the gate in the crumbling wall of the kirkyard with the small knife. This gate is iron, horribly rusty and worked all over with hideous gargoyles. The very decay of the metal accentuates the terror of the spectacle for Wee Tam. Age has eaten away at the physical form of the gargoyles, but never diminished the force of their malevolence. That is more vivid than ever to him, a life force animating the cold metal, despite all the unrecorded years that have slipped by since some unknown hand wrought them. It seems to Wee Tam that everything about them has been forgotten, save for the deep evil that they embody. Who could ever have imagined something like this, wonders Wee Tam, and from what ghastly models were they working? What horrors had they seen in this world- or another?

A great, metal cat looms out of the chest of one particularly grotesque gargoyle. It almost seems to be hissing at them under its black paint.

"The Cat Sìth!" gloats Colin. "I told ye, Tam! It's comin' straight oot o' the witch! An' it wants to eat ye alive…"

He seizes Tam's hand and pushes it towards the cat. Tam pulls away violently, unable to look the witch-cat in the eye- or to touch the metal itself. It strikes him now, for the first time, how much he hates the feel, even the scent, of metal- how he always has.

What is it about me, wonder Wee Tam. Am I really so different from the other boys? He takes another step back from the gargoyles, but Colin is actually inside the kirkyard now, holding the gate open for him, urging him to follow. Tam stands staring at another gargoyle, a bald-pated, goblin-like figure with stumpy wings folded behind him and an infinitely cruel leer etched into his face. It looks a wee bit like Farmer Goldie, thinks Tam. Could it really be him? Is he a witch too?

"Come in, little one! Come in!" it seems to hiss to Tam. As though it knows him.

"It doesnae' count if you dinnae' come in, Tammie!" yells Colin, unconsciously echoing the gargoyle's voice in Tam's head. Colin himself takes another bold step towards the kirk and then spins dramatically around on his heels, covering his eyes, a showman to the last.

"I'm gonnae' count tae' ten, and you better be in here with me by the time I'm done countin'! One, two, three..."

Wee Tam jogs to catch up with him, but just as he is about to cross the threshold of the kirkyard, the gate slams shut in front of him, separating him from Colin.

"Four, five, six..." counts Colin aloud.

Shocked, Wee Tam peers through the bars of the gate. Colin still has his hands over his eyes as he counts down, "Seven, eight..."

Only now Tam can see skinny white hands clutching at Colin's face and clothes, as he stares in horror through the metalwork of the gate.

"Nine- ready or not!" shouts Colin. "Ugh, get off, Tam!" says Colin in irritation. "What are you doin'? You're- you're hurtin' me now, Tam! And what's happened to your hands, they're- they're freezin'! Ten! Ten! Time's up, Tam! Ten!"

Colin's eyes flash open. Time is up. He screams uncontrollably, as he sees that it isn't Tam who is holding him at all. Wee Tam yanks at the gate to get to him, but now it won't budge in either direction. He reaches through the bars towards Colin. There is a low growl, like something unspeakably ancient awakening, and the gate itself seems to come to life, rusty ironwork writhing like the tentacles of some hideous sea-monster. The Cat Sìth hisses and yowls. The gargoyle's cold iron eyes swivel towards Tam, and its clawed metal hand seizes his wrist. It is as cold as ice, but instantly retreats from him on contact, as though scalded by the warm blood coursing through his veins. There is a hiss of pain and alarm- and surprise, Tam somehow realises. He tries the gate again. This time it opens, shrinking from his touch, the gargoyle leering impotently after him as Wee Tam takes Colin's arm and pulls him out of the kirkyard after him.

"Whit's happenin', Tam?" says Colin, face white, in shock. "I'm scared! I want to go home!"

But Tam just takes his hand and leads him into a headlong flight with him, back through Kirk Wood. They run as fast as they can, wending a desperate path between the spindly trees, dodging roots and branches as they flee. Thorns clutch at their clothes, but they just keep on running. Exhausted and out of breath, they don't pause until they reach the very edge of Kirk Wood, where they turn back and peer through the trees with wide eyes.

"Faces!" *whispers Colin in breathless gasps.* "Under the cloaks. I saw them, Tam! I saw them!"

Suddenly a pale hand reaches out around a tree and grabs his collar, and a dark-cloaked figure looms out from behind them. Colin holds out his pocket-knife to defend them, but the cloaked figure just slaps the feeble blade out of his trembling hand. Now he holds up a pocket bible, but this too is knocked away and falls to the ground, as the cloaked figure seizes him in a vice-like grip. Wee Tam takes Colin's hand, but the cloaked figure starts to drag Colin away and he is gradually losing his grip.

"Tam!" *shouts Colin in terror, as their hands are prised apart.* "Help me!"

Two more cloaked figures emerge from the Kirk Wood, running straight towards Wee Tam.

"Run, Tam, run!" *shouts Colin. Tam can sense his hope ebbing away.* "Save yourself now! Go an' get help! Go to ma' father's inn! Just go, Tammie!"

The first cloaked figure strikes Colin hard across the face, the thin, white fingers leaving long red weals behind them. He falls to the ground, whimpering.

Wee Tam hesitates for a moment, then runs across the moor, looking back over his shoulder as he flees for his life.

"Tell them, Tam!" *shouts Colin behind him.* "Tell them what's happenin'!" *And then there is silence.*

The second and third cloaked figures are chasing hard after Wee Tam now, their longer legs eating up the distance between them. Wee Tam sprints and sprints, choking back his sobs as he runs. He can feel his pursuers close behind him, closer and closer, panting like hunting dogs as they run him down. Somehow Tam knows what they are- he can sense it. And there is something else too, an inhuman chattering and shrieking that chills his blood.

Tam franticly picks his way through the big stones leading down to the stream and is shaping to leap back across it, when suddenly he feels sharp nails digging hard into his shoulder. A hand closes painfully on his shoulder-blade, pulling him back, and then another one around his ankle. He looks down to see the howling face of a monkey, teeth bared at him, and then up at the black cloaked figure looming large over both of them. He closes his eyes in horror, and then the usually gentle burn gives a roar and rises up from its bed. The fingers loosen on his shoulder and ankle as a torrent of foaming water surges down the bed of the stream. Wee Tam knows that if he is to escape, it is now or never. He takes a deep breath and leaps straight through the wall of water. To his amazement he passes effortlessly through the surging current and lands on the other side of the stream. He scurries to a huge boulder on the far side of the water, then peers cautiously out from behind it. There is a sheer screen of water rising up from the burn, through which he can just about make out the shape of three human-like figures. They are wearing dark cloaks, but their faces are completely obscured by the rushing water, a smaller figure capering by their side.

"Witches!" thinks Tam. "An' that monkey..."

For the first time he is aware of another dark figure, right next to him behind the boulder, who nods slowly in confirmation, as though he can read Tam's thoughts. Somehow Tam knows- he just knows- that he is not one of the witches, that he means him no harm. The man nods again. He is holding one hand aloft, and suddenly Tam realises that it is him who is controlling the stream, lifting it from its bed to bar the way to the witches.

"But why- why didn't you save Colin, too?" wonders Wee Tam.

Merry Andrew shrugs his shoulders, without relaxing his control of the water for a moment.

"It was no' for you to interfere in that?" thinks Wee Tam.

Merry Andrew nods again. He looks sad though, thinks Tam- as if he feels Colin's loss too. Merry Andrew inclines his head behind them, back towards Wee Tam's home, still holding up the burn.

Wee Tam just about manages to raise his hand to Merry Andrew in thanks, blinking back his tears, and then he runs as fast as he can back across the moor, back home to his mother. He only stops once, up on the crest of the hill, to look back down towards the stream. It is flowing as placidly as ever. There is no sign of Merry Andrew, of the witches and their hideous monkey- or of Colin.

CHAPTER 16

SUDDENLY WEE TAM'S EYES FLASHED wide open. Kate and Tam started back in surprise, before Kate instinctively leaned forward and stroked his pale face. She kissed his forehead, and then pulled the blankets up over him. He sighed, closed his eyes and sank back down into sleep. The wind whistled through the draughty cottage, sending the candle-light dancing into eerie shapes.

"Still nursin' your wee boy, eh?" said Tam.

"Aye, an' nursin' my wrath- to keep it warm for you, Tam O'Shanter, ye bletherin', blusterin', drunken blellum!" Kate hissed.

She sniffed at Tam's shirt-front and then wrinkled up her nose in disguest.

"Cheap whisky... or is that your friend John Davidson's cologne? The good Souter will find it warm enough where he ends up in the next life too, I don't doubt!"

She gave Wee Tam a final kiss before disappearing behind the threadbare curtain that separated the marital bed from the rest of the croft, without a backward glance at Tam. Tam stood for a moment watching Wee Tam, still dripping gently on the floor from his latest drenching, then kissed his forehead too and followed Kate. But just as he opened the curtain, a heavy black book flew out from behind it, hitting him on the head and laying him flat out on the floor. Tam lay for a second, gently groaning, as he tried to make out the title, printed in austere letters:

*"INSTITUTES OF THE CHRISTIAN RELIGION. JOHN CALVIN.
TRAD. HENRY BEVERIDGE ESQ. 1599."*

Tam groaned.

"Buggered by Calvin…" he said, resting his head on the floor. "Now I ken how the Pope feels!"

"See that you gie' that a read, before ye slip into your swine-like sleep tonight!" Kate whispered from behind the curtain. "And there's no need for any of your popery, neither, Tam O'Shanter! This is a Presbyterian house, whatever vile idolatry you an' that family of yours may have practised up there in the Highlan's!"

"Can I no' come in and sleep in the bed, love?" said Tam hopefully.

"I'll see you in the mornin', and no' a moment before!" said Kate furiously. "An' if you forget to buy Tam's new suit tomorrow- well, sleepin' down on the floor there will seem like a night in Holyrood Palace! For you'll be sleepin' in the byre with your precious Meg until ye've mended your ways, I can tell you that for nothin'!"

Tam closed his eyes in resignation, but there was nothing he could do to shut out the unruly thoughts reeling around behind them. After a few minutes of tossing and turning on the bare floor, he heard a shuffling sound from the corner of the room. He opened his eyes in alarm, only to see Wee Tam climbing out of his own bed and creeping across the floor towards him. He lay down next to Tam, carefully covering them both with his blanket against the chill of the night. Tam's dog, Bran, padded up towards them and wriggled down under the blanket next to Tam.

"Night, lads…" said Tam.

Suddenly Wee Tam pushed Tam away from him, writhing and kicking.

"What is it, son? Are ye havin' another bad dream?" asked Tam anxiously.

Then he noticed that the big iron key to the croft, slung from a chain around his neck, had come free from his clothes and touched Wee

Tam's skin. Tam hurriedly took it off and hung it from a nail on the wall of the cottage.

"Sorry, son!" he said, as he lay down next to Wee Tam again. Wee Tam nestled his head against his father's chest.

"But listen, Tam... Promise me you won't react like that- you know, to metal- in front of folk from the village, eh?"

Wee Tam looked back at him inquiringly.

"Och, it's fine to do it in front of me, or your mother," said Tam. "And it's a load of old nonsense anyway! But they do say that- that fairy changelings are afraid of iron. It's cobblers of course, absolute bobbins, but in troubled times people will always cling to the old beliefs..." Tam paused, and ruffled Wee Tam's hair affectionately. "So you can see why- why it'd be as well just no' to show them that you dinnae' like the stuff? It can lead to needless trouble, that's all I'm sayin'. When I was a lad up there in the Highlands, the people in the village once... Well, they..." Tam stopped, as he saw that Wee Tam was drifting off to sleep, reassured already by the removal of the metal and the soothing presence of his father. "Well, listen to me haverin' away to myself! This no time for my nonsense. Sleep, lad, sleep- it doesnae' matter now..."

Tam put his arms around Wee Tam and Bran, breathing in time with the unhurried rhythm of their sleep. Somehow the line between watching their sleep and entering his own blurred, and he started to drift off himself, until he heard a sudden hiss.

"Open your eyes, Tam O'Shanter! Open your eyes! No gods, no masters!"

Tam's eyes flashed open again, and he stared wildly around the tiny croft. There was no one there. Wee Tam and Bran slept on, oblivious. But it had to be her, it just had to be. The Cutty Sark! And at his own croft! Did that mean that he would see her again? And was that the merciful blessing he had been praying devoutly for, or the curse that all his instincts warned him against? Was he just afraid of happiness- of freedom- or of losing everything else?

"Are you in my house? Or my head? Or in my nightmare, Cutty Sark?" Tam asked desperately. "For I havenae' known a moment's peace since I first set eyes on you!"

But again there was no answer. Now he lay awake, eyes wide open in the darkness. In his mind, he ran feverishly through a million scenarios, hopes and fears. In his confusion, it was almost impossible to distinguish which was which. But what he couldn't see was the cloaked figure, silently watching him, Wee Tam and Bran through the tiny window of the croft. Or the eyes underneath the cloak, dark, unblinking and old beyond human reckoning.

———

CHAPTER 17

THE GREAT TRESTLE TABLE IN the back room of the Jolly Beggars' Inn was vaguely set for breakfast, with a scattering of clean dishes and utensils nestling in between the mass of broken glass, mugs and bottle stubs from the night before. Some unknown hand had thrust a razor-sharp *sgian dubh* deep into the wood, a couple of feet down from the head of the table. It jutted menacingly out of the dark pine like a squat, Gaelic Excalibur.

"Whoe'er shall draw this blade from the wood, will be King of Scotland!" said Rannoch, as the Prince sat down in state at the head of the table. "But then you, my dear Charles Edward, are already amply wreathed in regal splendour!"

Two files of Highlanders straggled down the table beside Malcolm on the Prince's right and Callum on his left, arranged by Callum in an approximately descending order of social precedence and presentability of appearance. Standards were fairly low by the time you got to the opposite end of the table.

"*Et maintenant*, please report without further ado on the exact location and state of battle-readiness of our royal breakfast, Chevalier!" said Charles Edward impatiently to Malcolm.

The mere mention of food caused several of the more dishevelled Highlanders to blanche visibly. Malcolm goggled back uncertainly at the Prince.

"You dare to question my orders, man?" said the Prince. "Are you not commissioned Quartermaster General of my father's army, by royal appointment? An army cannot march on wine and song alone, Chevalier!"

"Well then, Callum?" said Malcolm. "What are you waitin' for? Where is your prince's breakfast?"

Callum sprang to his feet and set off into the front room of the inn to investigate, tucking his dirk into his stocking purposefully as he went.

"All this brave talk of armies and regiments!" said Rannoch with a smile, looking at the breakfast table. The Prince and Malcolm had painstakingly marked out a makeshift map of Britain, complete with wine-stain lochs, cork towns, snowy drifts of spilt salt, beer-mug city walls and bottle citadels. "Sieges and battles! Honour and glory... Fitting toys for boys, my friends! Why, if that bottle of claret really was Edinburgh Castle, I do believe that you would reduce it to rubble in an instant!"

To Malcolm's horror, Rannoch opened his cloak and released Absalom out onto the table, where the monkey leapt and played.

"Absalom never was much of a strategist!" said Rannoch.

The little ape licked up the long line of salt that marked out the Great Glen, and then knocked the mug marking Carlisle over with a contemptuous swipe of his tail, all in his haste to get to a plump sugar-plum on the bottom right corner of the map.

"Ah, so you have targetted London!" said Rannoch, stroking Absalom's head. "Perhaps I underestimated your grasp of tactics all those centuries ago, after all..."

Malcolm toiled in the monkey's wake, picking up the wreckage of Carlisle and stemming the spillage with the ragged cloth that marked the Grampian Mountains.

"But it is all folly and vanity too..." said Rannoch. "Just like a monkey's dance! For the hearts and minds of men are where this great war of yours will be fought, Charles Edward! Where it will be fought and won- or lost..."

"But, my dear Rannoch- surely you do not expect this egregious Usurper to fall head over heels in love with me, and hand back my father's throne with a gallant apology?" said the Prince, laughing.

"Not the Usurper- but his subjects!" said Rannoch. "You will never field an army strong enough to subdue England's doughty yokels to your wills- not by force alone! There will be no second New Model Army, forged out of iron and will-power, to force Hanoverian London to its knees..."

"Perhaps not, but we have a few stout Ironsides of our own, do we not, Chevalier?" said the Prince. "There are still loyal clansmen in the Highlands, who are bold enough to take all of Scotland by the sword!"

Absalom howled scornfully, and Rannoch nodded his head.

"Ah yes, Scotland- but stands Scotland where it did?" he said.

"We can raise five thousand clansmen!" said Malcolm proudly.

"Five thousand!" said Rannoch. "Do you know how many men the Duke of Cumberland fielded at the Battle of Fontenoy, Chevalier? Fifty thousand! And Maurice de Saxe opposed them with even more! This was none of your petty Scottish skirmishes, at the Stirling Bridge or Bannockburn... The world is moving on apace, outside the rocky glens of Badenoch and Lochaber!"

"Ahem!" said Callum, bearing a huge steaming platter before him. "Your Highness, my Lords, clansmen and, eh, smugglers: Breakfast is served!"

He set the dish down in front of the expectant Prince, and lifted the lid off with an extravagant flourish. Charles Edward peered in with enthusiasm, only to be confronted with the flabby, congealing face of an unappetising mess of porridge. For a moment, prince and porridge stared expressionlessly at each other.

"An oat can look at a king, eh, Charles Edward?" said Rannoch with a sly smile.

The Highlanders muttered in approbation as they drank in the porridge's stolid, oaty aroma. Callum set a rough wooden bowl in front of the Prince and then slopped a generous helping into it.

"Fit for a king, eh, Cherlie?" he said.

Charles Edward raised an eyebrow dubiously.

"What is this, my friends?" he whispered.

"Porridge, Your Highness..." said Malcolm apologetically, glaring at Callum.

"Chief of Scotia's food!" said Callum.

The Prince winced, as another cloud of dense porridge vapour wafted towards him.

"Did you really think such skinkin' ware good enough for the heir to the three thrones of England, Scotland and Ireland, Callum?" hissed Malcolm.

"Right ye are, Chevalier..." said Callum, deftly stooping to pick up a bottle from underneath the table. He sprinkled the dregs onto the Prince's bowl, with the air of a master chef putting the final touches to a sublime gastronomic creation. "*Et voilà*, eh, lads?"

Malcolm rolled his eyes in despair.

"Oh, that'll make all the difference..." he muttered.

Even adorned with whisky, the Prince surveyed his breakfast with genteel revulsion, and prepared to banish the bowl from his presence- but then he noticed that the Highlanders, gripping their own spoons like daggers, were watching intently to see how their leader would tackle his porridge. In their minds at least, there was no hint of irony to porridge's chiefdom of Scottish cuisine. The Prince swallowed.

"*Ma foi!*" he muttered under his breath. "It seems that porridge is the politeness of princes in this benighted land..."

"Hearts and minds, Charles Edward..." said Rannoch, leaning towards the Prince. "Hearts and minds! Louis XV can afford to impress the wretched serfs of France by his splendour- you must teach the free men of Britain to love you, by becoming a man of the people! Leave no stone unturned to win their simple hearts- whatever horrors you may find beneath that stone..."

"By God, Rannoch, I believe that you are right!" said the Prince. "Will you not say grace to the Holy Father, before I sup on this, ah, sumptuous fare, Callum, my boy?" he said.

"Eh- right you are, Cherlie..." said Callum, clearing his throat.

"Some hae' meat and cannae' eat,
And some wad' eat that want it,

But we hae' meat and we can eat,
Sae' let the Lord be thankit!"

"Amen, amen, fee fi fo fum, I smell the blood of an Englishman..." said the Prince. "And now: *Bon appetit, mes braves!*"

He reached out to the *sgian dubh* embedded in the table, drew it effortlessly out of the wood and then used its blade to scoop a respectable portion of the porridge into his mouth.

"*Figlio di puttana!*" he shouted, banging the hilt of the *sgian dubh* on the table. "Now I know why you rascals don't fear death! Who can stop an army that can thrive on this!"

The Prince sat back down at the table, and kissed his fingers in extravagant appreciation. The Highlanders cheered raucously, enraptured by his showmanship, and banged their spoons thunderously on the table.

"Callum, prepare my Royal Guard!" cried the Prince. "It is time to win the hearts and minds of this town!"

One of the slumbering Highlanders at the far end of the table finally gave up the ghost, and collapsed down onto the floor with a heavy clatter.

"I have the very men for ye, Cherlie!" said Callum. "Nothin' but the Flower of Scotland here!"

He dragged the inert Highlander to his feet.

"*Na bean ris a chat!*" grumbled the Highlander, struggling against Callum's grip in an attempt to return to his slumbers. "*Na bean ris a chat!* Touch not the cat, ya bam!"

"The Clan of the Cats, Your Highness..." Callum explained apologetically to the Prince. "Nuts to a man, and touchy with it- but they're handy fighters in a scrap!"

"They are the right men for me then, by God!" proclaimed the Prince. "For a scrap is precisely what lies before us all- my Cameron dogs and my Chattan cats alike! And the sooner it comes, the happier I shall be!"

The Highlanders cheered again, drumming the hilts of their dirks on the table, sending Absalom scurrying back into the folds of Rannoch's cloak.

"Aye, we're up for that!" said Callum. "C'mon, lads, and let's get tooled up!"

The Highlanders wolfed down the rest of the porridge, wound their plaids around them and rapidly assembled a remarkable array of weaponry, from dirks and broadswords to antique muskets and Lochaber axes. They lined the draughty corridor of the Jolly Beggars' Inn, shouting and cheering as the Prince, Malcolm and Callum led them running out onto Ayr High Street.

"Hearts and minds!" shouted the Prince.

CHAPTER 18

MORNING HAD BROKEN IN TAM'S cottage- but so too had Tam's hangover, like a great black wave smashing onto a desolate, desiccated shore. Tam blinked his eyes in the painful glimmer of the morning. It took him a moment to get his bearings from the unfamiliar vantage point of the floor. The somewhat unfamiliar vantage point of the floor, Tam had to admit to himself. He looked around him for Wee Tam, but found only Bran. The dog stirred, then turned around to lick his master's face.

"Ughh... I appreciate the sentiment, but no' now, Bran!" Tam protested. "No' now, boy, I'm just no' up to it!"

Tam tried to sit upright, but even that modest movement sent stabs of pain into his temples, and he subsided back down. He lay still for a moment, regathering his forces for a fresh sortie into the land of the living. He could just about make out the table in the corner of the croft, at which Kate and Wee Tam were eating breakfast in grave silence. Noticing that Tam was awake, Wee Tam smiled down at his father, but Kate pointedly ignored him.

Tam got up gingerly, each movement sending a shiver of exquisite agony through his throbbing head. He stood for a moment to steady himself, then manfully strode over and tried to give Kate a peck on the cheek. It was more in hope than expectation. Just as well, for Kate shied away from him, as though from a mildly toxic but essentially contemptible insect. Still without looking at him, she slid a wooden bowl across the table.

"Eat, Tam!" she said.

"Cold porridge, eh?" said Tam. "Champion stuff!"

He grimaced at the sight of the grey, glue-like mess stuck to the bottom of the bowl, but then picked up a spoon anyway. He wasn't quite sure yet what he was going to do with the cloying porridge, but this was clearly no time to show any sign of weakness.

"It could do wi' a drop of whisky to warm its cockles a wee bit, eh, love?" said Tam hopefully. "It's as cold as the grave!"

"Is that a fact? Well, the minister finished up the last of the whisky when he called round last night," said Kate.

"Typical man o' God!" said Tam, but Kate didn't deign to rise to the bait.

"Speakin' o' which," she continued, opening a well-thumbed Bible. "You'll be glad to hear that you're just in time for today's scripture class... Ah- Methuselah!" she read with relish. "Wi' God's good grace he lived to 969!"

"He was a babe in arms next to this porridge then, eh, hen?" said Tam, winking at Wee Tam in a vain attempt to lighten the mood. "He must've been in short trousers when you made this stuff!"

Kate snatched the bowl back, with a face like thunder, and stalked back over to the stove.

"Forget young Methuselah, son!" whispered Tam conspiratorially to Wee Tam. "Today's real lesson is how to sell a lame colt at Ayr market. There's no flies on the horse-dealers there, I can tell you- for they'd milk them, if there were!"

"What're you two gossipin' about?" asked Kate suspiciously.

"Scripture, hen!" said Tam. "The wages o' sin, an' when's pay-day..."

A ghost of a smile flickered across Wee Tam's face.

"Well! Satan has made you pretty glib, hasn't he?" said Kate severely. "You ken fine that we're still on the Old Testament in this house..."

"Right enough!" said Tam, feeling his head for the bump where Calvin's Institutes had clocked him. "But that's enough betterin' ourselves for one day! The bairn should be out in the fresh air. He seems to thrive on it- an' it's no' healthy for him to be cooped up in here all day..."

Tam ruffled Wee Tam's hair, but Kate immediately grabbed him by the shoulder and straightened it severely.

"Should you no' be out there yourself, Tam O'Shanter? The land-lord's man called for the back rent again last night."

"Aye, we'll gie' the soil a wee turnin' over before we head off to market…" said Tam quickly.

"Just you see that you do!" said Kate sternly. "For crops don't just grow themselves: no' in this life."

"No' in any life, Katie!" said Tam. "If there's one thing I'm sure of, it's that."

"Well, whatever the state of the harvest in heaven- or wherever it is that you end up- you'll need to work a sight more diligently than you usually do today, if you're to get that ploughin' finished in time to get off to market!" said Kate. "Sloth is no' one of the seven deadly sins for nothing, Tam O'Shanter! But then why exclude that one from your repertoire, eh?" she added sarcastically.

"Alright, alright, I'm goin', I'm goin'!" said Tam, lacing up his work-boots.

"An' you look after my wee boy in Ayr, you hear me?" shouted Kate after Tam. Tam stood up and wrapped his arms round her. She stiffened and pushed him away. "You hear me?" she said pointedly.

Tam nodded, and then stepped out over the threshold of the house. He blinked in the brightness of the morning, as he walked gingerly across to the byre.

"Morning, old girl!" said Tam, patting Meg's face affectionately. "I hope you slept better than me, for there's no peace for the wicked! Or for the wicked man's horse either, I'm sorry to tell ye…"

Meg gave a long whinny of greeting, as Tam gently harnessed her to the long-handled plough that she shared the ramshackle shelter with. They trod the familiar path out into Tam's narrow field companionably, Meg pulling the plough carefully behind her so that it wasn't damaged on the doorway of the byre. Wee Tam was already scurrying along in front of her, plucking the biggest stones out of the way of the plough with nimble fingers and tossing them into a big bushel, as Tam set the plough's sock to the furrow.

These stray stones were the bane of the Ayrshire ploughman's life-sending the plough leaping off course in his hands, bumping the heavy wooden handles into his face when he wasn't paying attention or, worst of all, cracking the precious iron cladding of the ploughshare. The largest would have to be dug out, or even smashed into more manageable pieces with the heavy-headed sledgehammer back in the byre. Ploughing was back-breaking work for both man and beast, even without these unwanted geological obstacles. But Wee Tam had an almost sixth sense for when a stone was small enough to ping harmlessly out of the way on contact with the plough or when, iceberg-like, its true menace was concealed beneath the top-soil. He knew Tam and Meg's pace so well that he could nip in to remove rocks, without breaking their stride. And rhythm was everything, the only way to conserve energy, equipment, livestock- and the livelihood itself.

"You're a wee man o' the land, son!" said Tam proudly. "A natural!"

Wee Tam grinned shyly. He was still far too small to wield the mighty sledgehammer himself, but he was adept at spotting a fault-line in a seemingly impregnable boulder that might allow it to be splintered with a few taps of the sharp chisel, rather than obliterated with brute force. He really was worth another ploughman, Tam thought, as he stopped to mop his forehead for the first time. The alcohol was seeping steadily out of his pores, so that he could almost smell the haze of whisky fumes around him. It wasn't enough to deter the clouds of biting midges swarming around his face though. If anything, they seemed to relish it, thought Tam.

"Well, they are Scottish midges, I s'pose..." said Tam, as he slapped at them. "We shouldnae' grudge them their dram! But oh, to be a Campbell on a day like this- for they say that even the midges will no' lower themselves to sup on Campbell blood!"

Wee Tam sniggered. He had been raised on the ancient, bloody rivalries of the Highland clans at his father's knee.

"We're no different from any of the poor beasts that gather their own wee stores o' food for the winter really, son," said Tam. "No different at all... Except that we have the wit to dread the future, as well as to suffer in the present! That God o' your mother's..." he went on, looking at his blistered hands. "He's a miserly bastard alright, it seems to me!"

He paused for a moment, just listening.

"But you hear it, don't you, Tam? You know what Johnnie and the rest o' them town gadgies will never understand! I see it in your eyes- that you hear it. When the land whispers..."

Wee Tam stared back at him.

"Aye, you know what it's tryin' to say," said Tam, rubbing his son's head. "But you're no' tellin'..."

Something like a flicker of acquiescence might have skated across Wee Tam's face, but even Tam couldn't be sure.

"Speak no evil, eh?" he said. "Aye, that's always been your way, son." He slapped at his face again. "An' these midges! Whoever heard of midgies in March?"

He looked at Wee Tam curiously.

"But they don't touch- you. You're no' a Campbell, are ye, lad?"

Wee Tam shook his head vigorously.

"You sure?"

Wee Tam gave a glimmer of smile.

"The whole bloody world's gone topsy-turvy!" said Tam. "Well, come on then, Meg, old girl. We've a long road to travel together, we three..."

They ploughed on in silence in a long, straight line over the crest of the hill. Suddenly Wee Tam stooped in front of the plough. He put his hand down to retrieve the stone as usual, but left it there too long, so that Tam had to pull Meg up sharply to avoid crushing his arm beneath the heavy ploughshare. Still Wee Tam stood staring at the stone, before kneeling down to examine it more closely.

"What is it, son?" said Tam, running round to the front of the plough in concern. "Are you alright? You normally nip out long before the plough could ever get close to ye!"

By way of answer, Wee Tam just held up the stone. It didn't differ in size and colour from any of the thousands of fragments of Ayrshire andesite that the farmers found in fields, all along the length of the Carrick coast. But there was something different about this stone. It was beautifully carved into a smooth almond shape. The shape of an eye. Tam stared at it, then turned quickly to Wee Tam.

"Have you seen anyone watchin' us, son?"

Wee Tam just looked back at him.

"This is important!" said Tam. "If you didnae' see it- did you feel it?"

This time Wee Tam nodded slowly.

"I knew it!" said Tam. "I felt it too… But whoever it was- they would have had to know that we were comin' this way! That we would find it in this very furrow! They'd have to know our every move…"

He looked around the hillside. There was no one to be seen, except for the two of them and Meg. But Wee Tam held up the stone again.

"Aye, I know, son," said Tam. "They're watchin' us even now…"

CHAPTER 19

———

OLD AYR WAS SEETHING WITH bargains, brawls, shaggy livestock, shaggier farmers and casual thieving. A typical market day, in other words. The whole of South Ayrshire had poured into the Market Square with all of their portable wares, worldly wealth and wickedness. Tam, Meg, Wee Tam and Souter Johnnie were in the thick of it, carrying a long pole from which a motley crew of Johnnie's shoes dangled by their spindly laces. The reeking brogues jerked freakishly, like horrifically decomposed corpses on a swinging gibbet, as they bumped along. Passers-by screwed up their faces in horror at the smell of the imperfectly tanned leather. Wee Tam led a limping white colt along after them. He petted it, gently encouraging it to greater exertions, rather than administering a vicious, medieval blow of the type being rained down on less fortunate creatures all around the market. Johnnie was in exuberant spirits, singing his market song aloud as they walked:

> "O, rattlin', roarin' Willie,
> O, he held away to the fair!
> An' for to sell his fiddle an' buy some other ware:
> But partin' wi' his fiddle, the salt tear blinded his eye,
> An' rattlin', roarin', Willie,
> Ye're welcome home to me!"

"Bit like sellin' your colt, eh, Tam?" said Johnnie.

"Aye, except that's certainly no' welcome home!" said Tam.

"Right enough!" said Johnnie jovially. "Sing along now, boys!"

"O, Willie, come sell your fiddle,
O sell your fiddle sae' fine!
O Willie, come sell your fiddle,
An' buy a pint o' wine!
If I should sell my fiddle,
The world would think I was mad,
For many a rantin' day
My fiddle an' I have had!"

"Altogether now!" cried Johnnie, as he and Tam swung the pole in time with their own raucous singing, and Wee Tam smiled in delight at their clowning.

"As I came by Crochallan,
I had a crafty look inside,
Rattlin', roarin' Willie was sittin' at the table end,
Sittin' there among old friends,
An' among good company!
Rattlin', roarin', Willie,
Ye're welcome home to me!"

Distracted by their antics, Wee Tam bumped straight into a burly butcher in full professional regalia, with a wicked meat-cleaver swinging free from his belt. After a hearty liquid lunch at the Jolly Beggars' Inn, he was up for a scrap with anyone, regardless of age or gender. He scowled at Wee Tam.

"You away wi' the fairies, son?" he asked aggressively.

"Aye- the tooth fairy! You expectin' a visit, pal?" said Johnnie, dropping his end of the pole in his haste to square up to the red-faced butcher. The unleashed shoes cascaded down the pole onto Tam, who hastily batted them away from his face. Suddenly the crowd opened up in front of them.

"Och, no' all this again!" groaned Tam. "Jist you remember the Carrick Cross, Johnnie!"

But this time it was not the enticing prospect of a brawl that was transfixing the crowd. Not far from where they stood in the Market Square, a dark figure swirled its black cloak around itself, first disappearing mysteriously in the billowing folds, then looming alarmingly back out from them. The crowd shrank away from it, and even the belligerent butcher cowered back behind a wagon.

"A witch! A witch!" shouted the stall-holders.

"What'n the world?" said Tam, gaping at the figure in black. He grabbed Wee Tam close to his chest, as the remaining shoes tumbled down to the ground, unheeded. "Here! Here, in broad daylight?"

CHAPTER 20

———

THE BEST PLACE TO HIDE may be in plain sight, but the second best place is Ayr on market day, thought Big Eck, as he lumbered down the High Street from the Jolly Beggars' Inn towards the Town Hall. Here he was perfectly concealed from prying eyes by the throngs of farmers, merchants and shoppers pouring into town over the Brig of Ayr, and the Town Hall itself was a humming hive of activity. Everyone was selling something, Big Eck thought, as he saw two yokels and a boy carrying a long pole strung with grotesque fur parcels- even if it wasn't always completely clear what it was they were selling. Big Eck himself didn't need any paraphernalia for his own wares this time- they were all neatly stowed away inside his head.

The Sheriff of Ayr had his usual seat at Loudoun Castle, out of town beyond Kilmarnock, but Big Eck knew from personal experience that as the representative of the king's justice in Ayrshire, he could always be found in his grand office at the Town Hall on market days. There would be a mob of petitioners, pursuers, defenders and the ubiquitous lawyers laying siege to it today. Eck had no idea exactly how much of Ayr's criminal activity was carried out on market days, but his best guess was that with the honourable exception of smuggling, it was pretty close to one hundred per cent.

A red-faced butcher, reeking of ale and incipient violence, careered bodily into Eck. He seemed momentarily minded to make something of it, but Eck just tapped the butts of the pistols in his belt meaningfully.

The butcher started at the sight of them, and then scurried off into the crowd, headed for the Market Square as quickly as his sturdy legs would carry him.

"Business before pleasure today, MacIver," muttered Eck to himself, as he maintained his course for the Town Hall.

Eck wasn't usually one to hurry himself, and certainly not when there were no Excisemen on his heels- but with the reward he would shortly be claiming from a grateful Government buzzing through his head like a great swarm of golden sterling bees, he was fairly bustling along by the time he stepped up off the High Street. He hopped onto the stairs that ran up to the door of the Town Hall. Some men might have been weighed down by the burden of such valuable information, but not Eck- it gave him a new skip in his step. He was walking on sunshine, as he sung merrily to himself:

"Bonny lassie, will ye go?
Will ye go, will ye go?
Bonny lassie, will ye go?
To the birks of Aberfeldy!"

That might have been why he crashed down so heavily when the blunt shaft of the Lochaber axe swung from out of nowhere, taking his legs neatly out from underneath him.

"Bonny lassie, will ye go…"

Eck never even saw it coming. He just toppled head over heels back down the steps to the High Street. Before he could even sprawl out on the pavement, unseen hands had dragged him upright in a grip of iron, a coarse tartan plaid was bundled over his head and a dirk jabbed up against his gizzard.

"No' wi' you, smuggler!" said Callum. "You're lifted, pal!"

Big Eck struggled against his unseen captors, trying to free his head from the smothering plaid.

"Easy does it, big man!" whispered Callum in his ear. "Easy! We ha-venae' followed you all the way down the High Street in broad daylight, jist to let you go now!"

"Whit do you want?" gasped Big Eck, struggling for breath. "Would it help if I- if I told ye I was thinkin' o' joinin' Royal Cherlie's army?"

Callum laughed.

"Oh, I wanted to believe that you could make a real contribution to the cause- because Cherlie seemed to want it..." he whispered. "But in my heart of hearts, I think I always knew that- I'd have to kill you."

He pressed the dirk even further into Eck's side, cutting through the wool of his outer waistcoat.

"Well, never order a soldier to do somethin' you wouldnae' do your-self, eh?" Callum said.

Suddenly the hideous realisation struck Eck that the vibrant streets of Ayr on market day would now provide the perfect cover for something else too. Cutting his throat in a side street, and disposing of his body, along with all the other lumber being hauled through the town and dumped in the harbour or river- for fair reasons or foul. Aye, there's always a rub, thought Eck. But there was no time to brood on it long, for then there was a shuddering blow from somewhere out of the darkness, and everything went dark.

CHAPTER 21

THE BLACK CLOAK SWIRLED LIKE a kaleidoscope, changing the picture instantly.

"Why, it's Andy!" laughed Souter Johnnie, clapping Tam on the shoulder. "It's only Merry Andrew, Tam! Calm yourself, man! It's our old friend! He's earnin' himself a copper or two on market day, just the same as ourselves!"

"Right enough..." muttered Tam.

Now he could see that it was Merry Andrew alright, leaping and capering to entertain the mob, pulling ghostly, other-worldly faces when his pale face came out into view from behind the dark screen of his cloak. Then Merry Andrew caught Wee Tam's glance and paused, face frozen, his eyes locked on Wee Tam's. Time seemed to stand still as they mutely read each other's faces. Merry Andrew slowly turned to stare directly at the pugnacious butcher, back out from behind his wagon, and then started to sing:

"The man that's a fool for himself,
Good lord, he's far dafter than I!"

Visibly disconcerted, the burly butcher couldn't hold Andrew's gaze. He looked away, humiliated, then stared sheepishly at his feet. Merry Andrew gave a deep bow to the crowd, who bellowed with laughter. The butcher fled in embarrassment, roughly pushing his way back out through the crowd, without another glance at Wee Tam. Johnnie stared at Tam, astonished.

"You sure Wee Tam can't speak?" he said.

Tam shrugged.

"Maybe some things aren't meant for us to understand, Johnnie..."

"They seemed to understand each other right enough, though!" said Johnnie. "Him an' Andy... It was almost as though they could- could speak! An' without a word passin' between them. I've never seen anything like it! Although there were tales enough about it, back in the Highlands. Tales of..."

"I know those tales too, Souter," said Tam quietly, as Wee Tam pulled at his sleeve.

"What is it, son?" Tam asked.

Wee Tam pointed anxiously at Johnnie's stock-in-trade, scattered all over the muddy ground. One hairy shoe had been picked up, gnawed at and then discarded by a passing prize hog. Several others had been ground into the dirt by passers-by and livestock.

"C'mon, c'mon, pick them up, lads!" said Johnnie in alarm. "Pick them all up, before anyone makes off with them! That's valuable merchandise right there, goin' a-beggin'!"

Tam looked at Wee Tam, raising an eyebrow at this remote contingency. Wee Tam's eyes laughed back at him, but for the Souter's sake they both scrabbled around in the mud anyway, gathering up all the scattered shoes that were not already savaged beyond recognition. The survivors swung from their pole, like martyred marionettes.

"Look at them, they're in fine fettle, they're none the worse for a wee roll in the mud!" said Tam encouragingly to Johnnie.

Johnnie looked at him suspiciously, ready to refute any potential slight to his cobbling prowess, but Tam just gazed innocently back at him.

"C'mon, lads, there's the perfect pitch for Souter Johnnie's Super Shoes, just over there!" said Johnnie, studying the Market Square with a practiced eye.

He trotted briskly up to one of the vacant stalls, leaving the rest of the party trailing along after him, laden down with all the shoes.

"Oh aye, we'll mint it here, laddies!" he said enthusiastically. "The ideal position, jist between the cattle market and the Jolly Beggars' Inn..."

"An' down-wind of the food stalls..." said Tam, but Johnnie studiously ignored him.

"For the farmer-boys will all have cash tae' burn from the cattle sale– an' they'll certainly no' be wantin' to spend all day arguin' with the lady wife aboot the cost o' her new shoes, when they could get into the Jolly Beggars' to spend the rest of it!"

"You're surely no' tellin' me those shoes are intended for ladies?" said Tam incredulously, but Johnnie just held one of them up to the passers-by.

"Roll up, Ladies and Gentlemen, roll up!" he cried. "Souter Johnnie's Super Shoes! An' just try sayin' *that* three times quickly after a dram! Well, ye dinnae' need to, for Souter Johnnie's famous footwear emporium needs nae' introduction... Specially imported from Paris, London and Kilmarnock! Impeccable taste, wi' an unbreakable lace! Here for one day only! Roll up, roll up, for it's too good to miss, an' they're walkin' themselves oot the door!"

CHAPTER 22

———

DARKNESS. NO, NOT QUITE THAT. More like a deep brown, in the flickering candle-light. Aged wood. Old, and curved. A ship's hold? Too still. A coffin? Pull yourself together, Eck, man! No, of course not- it was a barrel. Barrels, more like. The first impressions pieced themselves together hazily through the mist, as Eck's eyes slowly refocussed, re-aligning painfully with his poor bruised brain. And then the next images to solidify into fixed pictures were all words. "*Vin de Chypre*". "*St. John Commandaria*". "*Calvados*". "*Cognac*". The elegant French of contraband booze! To Eck, that was as good as a Government map. He recognised the order of those cherished names, the syntax of smuggling. He knew exactly where they were now. The cellar at the Jolly Beggars' Inn. In Eck's own private corner of it, to be precise, safe behind a dummy wall, leased and constructed at his considerable expense. He had paid for this place out of his own pocket, had risked his life to bring these barrels to safety here, had used them as the bait to catch a prince, and now they were going to kill him right here in front of them. The cheeky wee bastards! Eck could almost have smiled to himself, if his head hadn't been throbbing so very hard. It was ironic too that he had been coshed himself, and so hard that he felt like throwing up, rather than administering the punishment to someone else- but that was nothing to smile about. That could damage his reputation, for the Carrick coastline talked. If he managed to get out of this alive, of course. Well, he would cross that bridge if he got to it.

"So ye brought me back to ma' own cellar then, lads?" he croaked, as soon as he could muster the moisture in his mouth to move his lips a little. "Well, ye've got some nerve, I'll give ye that!"

"Aye!" said Callum. "We're kinda' the- paramilitary- authority in this town today, if ye ken what I mean? Our leader is the monarch of all he surveys... And as for you- you're convicted o' high treason, pal!"

"So why am I still alive then, son?" said Eck.

"For now..." said Callum, contemplating the barrels.

Eck decided to hold his tongue for a while.

"Ye know a wee bit about us, I think, Eck?" said Callum eventually. "About us Highlanders, and our ways?"

"Aye..." said Eck. "My auld man was a MacIver. He moved here off the boats one fine day, and married a Lowland girl."

"A MacIver of Inverary?" said Callum keenly. "A MacIver Campbell?"

"No, no!" said Big Eck, hastily. That was not a family tree that was likely to prove fruitful- or long-lived- in this company. "MacIvers of Lewis!"

"Of Lewis, eh..." said Callum thoughtfully. "Aye- MacKenzies by another name, I suppose. Well, perhaps that does make things easier..."

"I can help you, Callum!" said Big Eck, ready to clutch at any straw. "I can help Prince Cherlie! Just say the word, son- for I can be much more use to ye alive than deid!"

Callum knelt down next to him.

"That's why it maybe helps that you've a bit o' Highland blood in your veins..." he said.

He seized Eck's hand, and held his dirk to it. Eck shrank back, but Callum held him fast, in a vice-like grip. Eck was a big man, but this was a different kind of strength.

"Steady, man!" said Callum. "You're just goin' to swear- swear on this blade- that ye'll no' betray Prince Cherlie for a second time. For you know that if you break such an oath, on the blade of a dirk..."

"Aye, if I break the oath, this'll be the blade that kills me!" said Eck. "Right enough then, Callum, I swear it! I'll no' fail the Prince a second time. I took a shine to the lad from the first, you musta' seen that! I wanted to help him! Besides, I still want that marquisate..."

"Ye what?" said Callum.

"Eh, nothin'!" said Eck. "Musta' been that wee knock on the heid..."

"I'm findin' this whole loyalty routine a bit hard to reconcile wi' your wee visit to the Sheriff of Ayr!" said Callum. "What was that, then- a social call?"

"It- it just seemed too good an opportunity to miss!" said Eck. "Think of the reward, son! I couldae' hung up my pistols, and taken up golfin' at Troon! Old habits die hard in this business... You cannae' spend forty years o' your life smugglin' liquor and shootin' Excisemen, an' then turn into Saint Columba overnight!"

Callum raised an eyebrow, and Eck shook his head sadly.

"Dinnae' hate the player, man, hate the game!" said Big Eck. "This is what they call a second chance, I suppose. So it shall be, then- loyalty to the Prince, an' the House of Stuart! An' let this very dirk cut me down, if I ever break my oath!"

Callum nodded.

"So it shall be, Master MacIver of Lewis!" he said. "We could spend many more words on it, without takin' the matter any further. An' lest you think me too trustin'- you should know that this'll make it easier to deal wi' you, if we were ever minded to! For this is a sacred oath. Nowhere on God's earth is safe for you, if you break it now! Not holy ground, nor yet a royal palace. For neither divine mercy nor royal pardon can spare an oath-breaker. That's the ancient law. I would strike you down in front of King James himself, or the Pope in Rome, an' no' heed a word of mercy from either of them- no' even if they came to me on bended knee, and begged me to spare you!"

"I know it," said Eck solemnly. "So what exactly is it you want me to dae' then, son? Dinnae' be shy now!"

———————

CHAPTER 23

"TELL ME ONE THING, SOUTER," said Tam, studying the shoes with morbid fascination, as they hung limply from their laces like obese spiders. "Just tell me, because I'd like to know: How on earth do ye plan to sell any o' those things? And who in the world to? You shouldnae' feel under pressure to make shoes, just because you're called 'Souter Johnnie', man..."

"I'm called 'Souter' because ah'm a master cobbler, ye dafty!" said Johnnie. "An' let me explain somethin' else to you, Farmer O'Shanter- to sell a shoe, ye just need to feel the soul of the shoe, if you ken what I mean?"

"The sole of the shoe?" said Tam.

"No, man!" said Johnnie. "The heart an' soul!"

"Well, there's one over here that does seem to have some kinda' internal organs attached to it," said Tam. "But I couldnae' say for sure if it's heart or no'..."

Tam and Johnnie quickly set up the stall, hanging the pole from which the shoes were slung between the sturdy posts on each side of it. Actually selling any of them seemed likely to prove a significantly less simple task. Wee Tam did his best to arrange the many singleton shoes into pairs. He worked hard, trying to distract himself from the uncomfortable sensation that they were being watched. It was a daunting task, for the truth was that very few of Johnnie's masterpieces bore any resemblance to each other- or indeed to most people's wildest dreams of what could constitute a shoe. Wee Tam looked at his father in exasperation, as he tried unsuccessfully to find a twin for another freakish misfit. Tam just laughed, and tousled his son's hair affectionately. He was under no illusions about his friend's craftsmanship, but at the same time long experience did suggest that Souter Johnnie would find a way to muddle through- one way or another.

"Dinnae' worry, Tam lad- Johnnie's the living proof that you can fool some of the people, all of the time!" he said reassuringly. "Just listen to that patter of his… He can keep it up a' day! And very possibly he will…"

He nodded over to the front of the stall, where Johnnie had already slipped into his best salesman mode, projecting his voice out to the multitude now swarming through the Market Square.

"Finest footwear in all South Ayrshire!" he shouted, displaying a hideously deformed specimen to the passing shoppers, who looked on in varying degrees of horror, fascination and amusement.

"Hand-crafted from the hides o' happy Highland Coos, for the comfort o' your feet, and the delectation o' your senses!"

"Whit aboot the comfort an' delectation 'ay oor noses though, son?" shouted back a red-faced lady of a certain age, swathed in a black cloak and freshly emerged from the Jolly Beggars' Inn on the High Street. This was Doxy Mary, even in her early fifties still the proud possessor of a reputation as racy as the crimson network of veins on her nose- and a good deal more dangerous. She was already suitably refreshed after a long morning in the tavern. "'Cause they pure reek, man, they're a danger tae' the public health!"

There was a roar of laughter from the crowd, but Johnnie just carried on regardless. Inspired by his example, Tam patted his own somnolent white colt, in a vain attempt to buck it up a little. There was absolutely no reaction, so Tam surreptitiously pricked it in the fetlocks with his pocket-knife. It barely stirred.

"Really? Still nothin'?" said Tam, under his breath. Wee Tam frowned at him, and if anything the horse's spirits seemed to slump still further at this inhumane treatment. "I ken how you feel, boy…" said Tam to the colt.

"Roll up, roll up!" shouted Johnnie. "Catch me while ye can! For these shoes were made for walkin'! I'm soon to be a shoemaker by royal appointment, an' I'll no' have time for the likes o' you commoners then!"

"Where's your warrant o' royal appointment then, son?" asked Doxy Mary. "London's just doon the road!"

"It's in the post frae' Good King James Stuart in Rome, hen!" retorted Souter Johnnie. "We've no' truck wi' the Elector of Hanover at this establishment! Royal shoes for royal Stuart feet, an' Usurpers no' served at any price! Aye, that's right, Ladies and Gentlemen," he cried, warming to his theme. "Ah'm souter by exclusive appointment tae' His Royal Highness Prince Cherlie! Pride o' the House of Shoe-art! Ye see what I did there, Ladies?"

"Gonnae' put they things on royalty, darlin'? Ye're braver than ye look then!" shouted Doxy Mary. "They've hung better men than you for less! Ah'm in the fashion business mysel', an' that's treason pure and simple, son, there's no other word for it! Ye can read all aboot it twice a week in *The Edinburgh Gazette*, if ye dinnae' believe me!"

She leaned towards the stall and pushed at one of the shoes. It swung gently to and fro on its laces.

"Aye, ye'll swing just like Dick Turpin in your deid rat puppet show there!" crowed Doxy Mary.

"That's no' Dick Turpin!" said Johnnie indignantly. "An' it's certainly no' a deid rat! It's a luxury gentleman's brogue, as any fool would know!" He was determined not be thrown off his stride, come what may. But privately he had to admit to himself that with Doxy Mary in full voice, this was proving an even tougher crowd than usual. "The most divine shoes since Jesus' sandals!" he continued gamely.

"Jesus' sandals? That's nothing, laddie!" shouted Doxy Mary, pointing at Tam and his feeble colt. "Yer pal here's got his donkey an' all! It's lookin' its age, mind! Whit's seventeen hundred and forty-five in donkey years, then? Why, ah've seen deid dogs wi' more get up an' go than that thing!"

This time Johnnie did deign to crack a smile.

"What are you laughin' aboot, Souter?" hissed Tam. "You didnae' think it quite so exquisitely amusin' when she was baggin' on those shoes of yours! How'm I supposed to sell the wretched beast, wi' every drunken auld witch in the market pokin' fun at it in public?"

"There's nae' such thing as bad publicity, Tam!" said Johnnie under his breath, steeling himself to resume his own sales pitch. "The only thing worse than bein' talked aboot, is no' bein' talked aboot! An' besides, you dinnae' want to provoke Doxy Mary- for you know what they say about her… You'll be turned intae' a donkey yourself!"

"For the last time, it's no' a bloody donkey, Souter!" said Tam, but Johnnie had already assumed his public persona once more.

"If they were good enough for Him," he proclaimed. "O, shoes of God, begotten of the Souter…"

"Och, it's horses for courses!" yelled Mary gleefully. "You'd needa' bit of ventilation in the deserts o' Palestine, wouldn't ye? Awfu' hot in Jeroosalem, so they say! But I wouldnae' fancy those raggedy auld things so much on the Auld Mauchline road- what ye need in these parts is a wee bit 'ay protection from the elements, son!"

There was another ripple of laughter. The crowd had built up steadily during the course of Mary's repartee. But not all of them were shoe-shoppers. Wee Tam thought he saw another cloaked figure, watching them through the crowd. He tried to make out the face under the hood, but the more he stared at it, the more it seemed to melt away out of sight. He shuddered, and clung tightly to Tam. Even Johnnie was getting a little deflated now, shoulders slouching as the relentless heckling ground down his usually irrepressible patter.

"By the good Saints Crispin an' Crispinian, Patron Saints o' Shoemakers!" declaimed Johnnie, holding the shoe out in front of him reverently, like a sacred religious icon.

"It was Saint Cretin who made that one, right enough, love!" shouted back Doxy Mary. "An' he was havin' an off day, at that!"

Johnnie looked helplessly round at Tam and Wee Tam, momentarily stumped. This time Tam couldn't help but smirk himself.

"Pass us the shoe, then, Johnnie..." said Tam, stepping forward.

Johnnie passed him the demonstration shoe, now open to fresh inspiration from any source. Tam brandished it under his colt's nose. The glum horse bucked and whinnied in olfactory protest, rearing up on its spindly hind legs and even kicking its front legs spiritedly- almost like a real stallion. The crowd roared with laughter. Tam beamed round at them, gratified at the vigour of its response.

"See that, Ladies and Gentleman! The beast is just sublime! Anyone can see that it's in tip-top condition! Tip-top! Full 'ay animal vitality!"

"Crivvens, it's a miracle!" shouted Doxy Mary, miming a faint. "Yon nag is back from the knacker's yard, no less! Jist one whiff of the Souter's handiwork was enough to bring it back from the deid, like Wee Lazarus o' Bethany! I saw it wi' my ain eyes, lad! You're like a donkey necromancer, Souter!"

"Cheers, Tam- that was all I needed..." sighed Johnnie.

"Those shoes are like swine before pearls, I tell ye!" crowed Doxy Mary triumphantly. "Swine before pearls!"

Tiring of the sport, she swigged deeply from a hip-flask and began to sing, beating time on the ground with her broomstick:

"I once was a maid, tho' I cannot tell when,
And still my delight is in proper young men!
Some one of a troop of dragoons was my daddy,
No wonder I'm fond of a sodger laddie!"

The crowd whistled and hollered its approval at this bawdy tale, and Doxy Mary beamed and gave a ladylike curtsey.

"The first of my loves was a swaggerin' blade,
To rattle the thundering drum was his trade;

His leg was so tight, and his cheek was so ruddy,
Transported I was with my sodger laddie!"

"More! More!" yelled the mob.

"But the godly old chaplain left him in the lurch;
The sword I forsook for the sake of the church:
He ventured the soul, and I risked the body,
'Twas then I proved false to my sodger laddie!"

"The sly old dog!" shouted a neighbouring cheesemonger, and Mary put her hand on her ample hip coquettishly, and gave him a lascivious wink.

"Full soon I grew sick of my sanctified sot,
The regiment at large for a husband I got;
From the gilded spontoon to the fife I was ready,
I asked no more but a sodger laddie!"

Suddenly Wee Tam spotted the cloaked figure again. It moved in and out of view, as the crowd swayed and shifted to the rhythm of Doxy Mary's song. But it was always staring, staring intently at them from under its dark hood. He grabbed his father's arm, but like everyone else Tam was engrossed in Doxy Mary's rowdy performance. Wee Tam pulled at his hand, but by the time Tam turned to him, the mysterious watcher had disappeared into the crowd again. Wee Tam shook his head in frustration- and fear.

"Don't look at me like that, son!" said Tam, misunderstanding the look in Wee Tam's eyes. "I was just tryin' to pep the beast up a wee bit- he was as glum as MacFarlane the priest, when it's time for last orders in Mungo's Inn! We'll no' sell it in a month of market-days at this rate! An' will it even make it through another round-trip to market an' back?"

"Shhh! Shut it, Souter!" the cheesemonger hissed at Tam, brandishing a long cheese-cutter at him threateningly, as Doxy Mary wound herself up to belt out another verse:

"And now I have lived- I know not how long!
And still I can join in a cup and a song;
But whilst with both hands I can hold the glass steady,
Here's to thee, my hero, my sodger laddie!"

The crowd whooped and applauded Doxy Mary, as the cheesemonger wolf-whistled.

"Souter!" said Tam indignantly. "What do you take me for?"

He took the opportunity to give the apathetic colt another nauseating nostril-full of raw bull-hide shoe leather. It reared up briefly, and then subsided straight back down into a slough of despond.

"Sheer animal vitality!" said Tam to the watching shoppers, determined to leave no stone unturned in his efforts to sell it.

"Oh aye, you'd need an extra bolt on the stable-door for that one!" called a caustic new voice from the back of the crowd. "He's a real wild child! Down, boy, down! Sit yourself down, eh, Pegasus lad! Hold him back, Bellerophon, ya bam!"

Tam scanned the crowd for this unwelcome addition to the sales process. The voice seemed only too familiar. Then he caught sight of a huge shaggy beast, straining on its rope to get at the wares of a nearby ale-stall. Its motivation certainly put the white colt to shame.

"King Billy!" said Tam. "All hail the Prince of Orange!"

"Hosea Goldie..." hissed Souter Johnnie. "What's that wee bam doin' here?"

"I imagine he's earnin' himself a copper or two on market day, Souter, just the same as ourselves!" said Tam.

It was indeed the sallow-faced farmer, with the Highland Cow nominally in tow behind him. It was wearing an ancient halter, draped so casually around its neck that it looked more like an elderly toper's cravat than any form of active restraint. Doxy Mary cackled in delight at the arrival of an ally- especially one with such apparently profound reserves of sarcasm.

"Puir beast, the reek of the Souter's mink cemetery there will be the death o' it!" continued Goldie, warming to his malicious theme. "Take mercy on it, lads, for we're all God's creatures!"

"You should practice what you preach then, Farmer Goldie!" said Johnnie, fighting spirit aroused by the sight of his old adversary. "That poor coo' of yours is as drunk as auld Doxy Mary over there! If it were no' so much prettier than her, there'd be no tellin' the difference!"

"Come here and say that, ya bawbag!" said Doxy Mary furiously.

"Johnnie..." said Tam warningly. "Dinnae' bandy words wi' a witch, man!"

But Souter Johnnie's blood was up. He pointed down at Goldie's feet.

"An' it looks like you could do wi' some new shoes yourself, Farmer Goldie! Or d'ye prefer to go bare-foot- like your mother?"

Even before he had said it, Johnnie was regretting the jibe. Goldie flushed beetroot and stormed off, the Highland Cow reluctantly following him, casting languishing glances back at the ale stall.

"You leave my poor auld mother out of this, John Davidson!" Goldie shouted back over his shoulder, suddenly close to tears.

"She's, she's no' been herself! Ye're no different frae' the folk in our old village..."

"Wait, Hosea... Come back!" said Johnnie repentantly. "I'm sorry!"

"Bein' a wee bit different doesnae' make someone a... You know..." said Goldie, dragging the Highland Cow along behind him. "Real witches are child-stealers- murderers!"

Tam and Wee Tam looked away, unwilling to be complicit in this particular insult. Even Doxy Mary was struck silent, and shrunk away through the crowd.

"C'mon, Tam- I was just... well, you heard what he was sayin' himself!" said Johnnie. "The gloves were off, man! He could damage my livelihood wi' that kind of public defamation! Besides, I never actually said she was a witch, like anyone else in the village would have..."

Disappointed at the apparent end to the verbal sparring, the crowd quickly evaporated away in search of ale, brighter baubles and more promising distractions.

They weren't long in coming. Before Johnnie could justify himself further, there was a huge roar of raucous applause, drowning out all conversation in the town centre and causing even the sluggish colt to startle and rear up on its hind legs.

"Christ, Johnnie, what is it this time?" asked Tam.

"I don't know, Tam! But I'm going to find out!" said Johnnie.

CHAPTER 24

DISTRACTED BY THE BELLOWS OF the crowd, Johnnie didn't even notice the arrival of an ageless, dark-cloaked man at the edge of the stall. Somehow he sensed it though- and so did Wee Tam. It was the same figure he had seen before, watching them so intently through the market throng. Wee Tam shuddered and clung to Tam's arm even harder, as the stranger approached Johnnie purposefully. Tam looked at his son curiously, and then at the new arrival. He was learning to trust Wee Tam's instincts- almost more than he did his own, Tam thought ruefully.

"Well, well- you've a bit of devil about you, don't you, Souter Johnnie!" said the interloper.

He seemed to be telling rather than asking.

"Do I know you, pal?" said Johnnie.

"Ha! Perhaps better than you think…"

"Let me put it another way then- what's your name?"

"I go by Rannoch here, Souter."

"That's a curious name for an Englishman! For I know Rannoch Moor well enough- but I don't know you."

"True, true- but what's so much more important is that I know you, Souter! And when you do come to know me better, you'll find that I'm certainly no Englishman!"

"Where are you from, then?"

"Lots of different places..." said Rannoch with a smile. "You could say that I'm a man of the world... But besides, the point is that I know someone else- someone who you desperately do want to meet."

"And who might that be, then, Mr Moor?" said Johnnie, torn between his growing curiosity and his irritation at Rannoch's knowing tone. It seemed to hint at a wisdom of a wider world that Johnnie was suddenly uncomfortably conscious of lacking himself.

"Can't you guess?" said Rannoch teasingly.

"Better give me a clue..." said Johnnie.

"Oh, he's a man of many names."

"Aren't we all?"

"True, true enough! A very palpable hit, my dear Johnnie! Souter. John Davidson. Even you have a few. And as for me, I have a name in every language! But you'll know all of his already, I'll wager..."

"Go on then, Rannoch!" said Johnnie. "I'm losin' my patience with this game!"

"Prince Regent. Pretender. Young Chevalier. Prince from Over the Water... Need I go on any further?"

"Cherlie? You really mean Prince Cherlie?"

Rannoch clapped his hands together slowly.

"Oh, yes!" he said. "The man of the moment. All Europe will be talking of no one else before the month is out, believe you me! The porky Duke of Cumberland will be quite green with envy. Which, of course, means everything to young Charles Edward..."

"Royal Cherlie!" said Johnnie, in a reverie. "He's really here then?"

"Indeed he is! But watch your tongue here..." said Rannoch. "You could swing by the neck, just for uttering that name on this side of the Stirling Bridge! Human life seems to be held very cheap in times like these... I sometimes wonder if I'm not the only one who really cares, after all!" He laughed to himself, as Johnnie stared at him curiously. "But that's enough idle chatter. Let's take a walk now, you and I!"

"An' why would I want to go anywhere with you?" said Johnnie, irritated again by Rannoch's blithe assurance.

"Because, my dear Souter, for all your ridiculous bluster, you really do want to make a difference, don't you?" said Rannoch. "To be something- something more than yourself. More than this place. Is that not right, Master Cobbler?"

Johnnie looked at him in surprise. For Rannoch was right.

"What makes you say that?"

Rannoch laughed again.

"That is my gift- one of them!" he said. "I know what people really want…"

"And Tam? What about Tam?" asked Souter Johnnie.

"Aye, what about Tam?" said Tam, hearing his name spoken to this stranger.

"Oh, he hasn't quite made up his mind which side he's on yet," said Rannoch, smiling crookedly at Tam. "What he wants… Or what he plans to do about it. Have you now, Farmer O'Shanter?"

"I plan to sell this colt!" said Tam stubbornly.

"Well then!" said Rannoch. "I'll take it!"

Without waiting for an answer, Rannoch took the reins of the colt from Tam. He brought out a leather bag and poured a stream of silver coins into Tam's instinctively outstretched hands. Rannoch laughed and led Johnnie away, holding him by the crook of his arm, the colt's reins in his other hand.

"Do I have my name printed on my forehead?" Tam asked Wee Tam, looking in amazement at the coins in his hands. "An' Johnnie too, for that matter! Suddenly all the world seems to ken exactly who we are. But surely- we're nobody? Just the same as we ever were?"

Wee Tam shrank back from the coins in his father's hands, looking at them in horror- and inquiry.

"Thirty shillin's…" said Tam. "Thirty pieces of silver…"

Wee Tam pointed after the departing Rannoch in alarm.

"Aye, I see them," said Tam. "I see where they're goin', Tam. But where are they leadin' us?"

They watched helplessly as Rannoch and Souter Johnnie dissolved into the crowd.

"There seem to be a lot of new folk in our lives all of a sudden, don't there, son?" said Tam. "An' I'm no' sure that they all mean us well!"

Wee Tam shook his head.

"How about tryin' to sell some of these bloody shoes then, son?" said Tam. "We can hardly make a worse hash of it than the Souter did himself, can we?"

Wee Tam shook his head.

"Well then! 'O'Shanter and Son- Wholesale Souters'. It's got kinda' a ring to it, does it no', Tammie? 'Tam O'Souter and Son'!"

Wee Tam smiled up at his father, and then innocently displayed the Souter's wares to some passing shoppers. They shied away from it and gave the stall a wide berth, muttering crossly to each other.

CHAPTER 25

———◆———

KATE AND HER SEWING CIRCLE were hard at their needle-work, in the spotless front room of Kate and Tam's croft. They worked as quickly as they could, to be sure of catching every minute of daylight and save on precious tallow. Even grim John Calvin, back up on his shelf, looked on approvingly.

"I've been meanin' to talk to Tam about it for months," said Kate, as she darned one of Wee Tam's threadbare stockings for the umpteenth time. "About us movin' to Glasgow, I mean. Tam could find a steady job there- make a wee bit more money. He's neat enough with his hands when he puts his mind to it, so I'm sure there would be opportunities enough for him- in a mill or a factory. Wi' a steady wage for the first time, we could build a better life for ourselves. For Wee Tam. He could be educated. Maybe even find some cure for his- his affliction- some day..."

There was a murmur of assent from the other women. Ayr was a prosperous enough little town- for those with the good fortune to have been born prosperous. There was small chance for anyone else to improve their lot in life. But in bustling Glasgow- well, anything was possible!

"But whit about your own affliction, Kate, love?" said Mrs McGillivray, studying her own stitching intently as she spoke.

"And what do you mean by that, Morag?" said Kate.

"I mean that good-for-nothin' husband of yours, of course!" said Mrs McGillivray bluntly. "Whit do you think? That Tam O'Shanter is the talk of three villages with his high-jinks! You should have seen him carryin' on in the inn last night! It was a disgrace to the establishment! Bringin' the place into disrepute…"

"A disgrace to the establishment?" said Elspeth Scott indignantly. "Really, Morag McGillivray? I'm sure I don't know how the place could have any less repute than it did already! Do you know that my poor Rab was assaulted by John Davidson on your premises, just last night!"

"Ah'm certainly aware that he made almost as much of a fool of himsel' as Tam O'Shanter did, if that's what ye mean, Elspeth!" said Mrs McGillivray, bristling. "Ye should no' let him oot at all, if he cannae' hold his ale like a Christian gentleman! It doesnae' reflect much credit on you as a wife, I'm afraid to say…"

"Is that a fact?" said Mrs Scott, even more incensed by this. "I'll have you know they had to carry him back home to me- and it wasnae' even the beer this time! His puir eye is swollen up somethin' terrible! I'm sorry to have to say it, really I am, but it's nothin' better than a- than a common ale-house, that you and Mungo are runnin' there, Morag!"

"An ale-house!" said Mrs McGillivray with disgust. "Lawks-a-mussy, to think that I'd live to hear Mungo's Inn called a common ale-house! And by a radge Culroy Scott, no less! Good for nothin' but drinkin' an' brawlin', an' it seems your husband cannae' even manage that! I had the story straight from Mungo's own lips. Your Rab was playin' the bully- as he always has, ever since we were bairns ourselves… From all Mungo could tell me, he drank far more than he could take, picked a fight wi' a feeble cripple, and then got a well-deserved drubbin' from the Souter for his pains!"

"A feeble cripple!" said Cathy Goldie. "Merry Andrew is in league wi' the witches! He's the one who took our Wee Colin! He ought to be burned at the stake, no' protected…"

"Poor Colin!" said Katie gently. "But you don't know for sure that Andrew was involved in that, Cathy," said Kate. "Innocent until proven guilty, they say…"

"Hosea is convinced of it!" said Mrs Goldie. "An' that's good enough for me. He told me how shamefully the Souter treated Rab, too! It was not at all honourable to trick him so!"

Mrs McGillivray snorted loudly.

"What was he to do- let himself get knocked black an' blue by that great bully Rab Scott! I dinnae' often have cause tae' speak up for John Davidson, as ye know, for he's a rogue, a rascal and a reprobate, just like Tam O'Shanter, but…"

"I'll thank you not to talk about my Tam that way again, Morag McGillivray!" said Kate sharply. "An' in his own house. Beer-sellers should no' be tale-tellers… Let's no' forget that it's you and Mungo who provide all this vile ale and whisky, that gets Tam and John Davidson- aye, and Rab and Hosea and all of them- into such a wretched state o' drunkenness in the first place! We've no such liquors in this house, I assure ye!"

"I'm sorry, Kate, dear," said Mrs McGillivray, with unaccustomed gentleness. "I didnae' mean to add to your worries… I'd like tae' help, if I can. I can speak to Mungo about no' servin' Tam in the inn, if we're contributin' to your woes."

"Oh, don't worry, Morag," said Kate, patting her hand. "I know as well as you do that he'd just find another inn to go to!" She sighed. "At least you and Mungo are there to keep an eye on him at Mungo's Inn. And Lord knows that Tam's no angel! But for all his faults, his heart's in the right place- and he always comes home in the end."

CHAPTER 26

———

THE GREAT TRADING COMPANY OF O'Shanter and Son was still waiting for its maiden sale an hour later, when Johnnie returned at a canter. He bounded up to the stall and enfolded both of the Tams in an emotional embrace.

"Away wi' you, ya big dafty!" said Tam fondly. "What's got into you? These shoes have got more brains in them than you do! Which might actually be part of the problem... Surely ye've no' been in the inn already? Without me?"

"It's finally happenin', boys!" said Johnnie breathlessly. "It's finally happenin'!"

"You've sold a pair?" said Tam. "Cause we certainly havenae'! They're a drug on the market, man... They say the customer doesn't know what's good for him, but he seems to ken alright what's good for his feet!"

"He's musterin' the Lowland Jacobites, Tam!" said Johnnie. "That's what's goin' on here! A grand muster of the Lowlands, to follow him up to Glenfinnan, near Loch nan Uamh. To join the royal army he's assemblin' there! The very opposite of what the Duke o' Newcastle will be expectin', sat down there in London! After all these years, it's finally happenin'! And under our very noses! Can you believe it, Tammie?"

"He'll be raisin' the Highland clans then, Johnnie?" said Tam, intrigued in spite of himself.

"Yes, Yes!" cried Johnnie. "Such a raisin' as there's never been! The MacGregors are out..."

"Och, they'd be oot for the raisin' 'ay a cake!" said Tam. "They've hardly been back in since the 1715 raisin'... There's a fine line between bein' a loyal Jacobite, and plain old-fashioned banditry, wi' those MacGregors!"

"Glenbucket's Gordons," continued Johnnie. "Clan Donald, of course- the best part of it. And Donald Cameron of Lochiel, with nine hundred of his bonniest Camerons! There's even talk of Lord Lovat's Frasers coming out, if you can believe it..."

"Simon the Fox, eh? There must be brass in this rebellion business after all, for the wily MacShimidh to be interested in it!" said Tam with interest. "The son of Shimi doesnae' stir his great carcase, just for the sake of the exercise..."

"I always told you we'd go back to the Highlands together one day, Tam!" said Johnnie, almost beside himself with excitement. "Ever since we were boys!"

"Aye, so you did- you did that," said Tam sadly. "But I never thought it would be to fight anybody..."

"To fight our enemies, Tam- the enemies of our true king!" cried Johnnie.

"There'll be clans out for the government too, Johnnie- and no' just Campbells, either," said Tam. "The MacKays and Sutherlands will never fight for King James, nor for any Stuart king. An' as for the Grants, there's no tellin' what they will do... Kinsmen fighting kinsmen- that's what civil war means. The poor man never wins a war..."

"We'll see, aye, we'll see about all that soon enough!" said Johnnie. "Just you remember that the Highland clans are bound to the House of Stuart by ancient oaths, Tam! But even if it were just me and Charlie- I'd follow him to hell and back, if we only had a piper to keep the time!"

"So where is he now, then?" said Tam prosaically.

"He's, eh, he's just on the other side of the Market Square, if ye can believe it!" cried Johnnie. "He's really here, Tam!"

"Well, we'll keep you company that far at least!" said Tam.

Wee Tam pressed his face into Tam's shirt, anxious and agitated. Tam rested his hand on his shoulder reassuringly.

The Ayr rumour mill was clearly working at its usual frenetic rate, for already a huge crowd was surging past them, bound for the High Street side of Market Square. Johnnie impatiently plunged into it, shoving and squirming his way onward, leaving Tam and Wee Tam to follow him as best they could. Rannoch glided serenely after them, ghosting through the mob as though it wasn't even there. Even by the febrile standards of the average market day, the atmosphere was feverish, hyperactive, close to boiling over with excitement- and aggression. As Tam and Wee Tam waded through the slow-moving human treacle all around them, try as he might, Tam couldn't silence a nagging voice in his own head. And deep down, he knew that that voice was the Cutty Sark's.

"Which way will the wind blow you, Tam O'Shanter?" it breathed. "Have you made your mind up yet?"

"Just what that Rannoch character of Johnnie's said too…" Tam muttered to himself. "Strange how all these Johnny-come-latelies seem to be piping the same tune!"

But it was one thing to see that- to feel it- and quite another thing to be able to resist the Cutty Sark. Even as he murmured the words, even in the safety of broad daylight, Tam knew that he might not have the strength to do that- not if she were to appear again, in maddening person. He put his hand on Wee Tam's head, as though reaching out for a charm against bewitchment, wondering all the while if even his love for his son would be enough to ward off the Cutty Sark. What would he do- if he was to be put to the final test? At least that would mean seeing her again…

Trapped in his own head with such tormenting thoughts, Tam was almost relieved when there was a sudden swell of noise from the other side of the Market Square. A flurry of whispers rushed through the crowd: "The Prince! The Prince! Prince Cherlie has come at last! Lang life to King James! Scotland forever!"

Wee Tam looked up at Tam inquisitively, but Tam shook his head.

"I cannae' see anythin' either, son! Wait- wait a minute, though- someone's comin'..."

The crowd rippled like a wave as the Prince's escort of Highlanders pushed an unwieldy ale wagon into a strategic vantage point at the neck of the Market Square, with precious little regard for the life and limbs of the Lowlanders scurrying all around them. The nearest townsfolk were left to dive out of its way and scramble for safety over the accumulated detritus at the edge of the Market Square as best they could. Oblivious to the mortal danger that the heavy cart's reckless arrival posed to the good burghers of Ayr, the Prince jumped nimbly up onto it to address the crowd.

"My beloved Ayr!" he shouted. "Old Ayr, whom no town surpasses- for honest men, and bonny lasses! You deserve your reputation well, my honest men!"

The crowd screamed its approbation of these flattering sentiments.

"And as for you bonny lasses- well, my dears, perhaps we must discuss that further in private..."

The young ladies of Ayr shrieked in excitement. This was rather different fare from the dry speeches usually served up to them by the Provost of South Ayrshire and venerable Sheriff of Ayr. Neither of those august municipal officers was known for their flirtatious tone in public speaking- and they would have received short shrift if they'd tried it.

"My dear subjects!" continued the Prince. "For twenty long years I have tasted the bitterest punishment of all: Exile from Scotland!"

The crowd roared its sympathy, and Johnnie roared along with them. Tam just looked on in silence- but he noticed that Rannoch had somehow reappeared, right next to Johnnie.

"Look at him, whisperin', whisperin', whisperin' away into Johnnie's ear!" he said to Wee Tam. "No good ever came of that kind of whisper, believe you me! That Rannoch scunner would do better to take a leaf out of your own book, son..."

"But I would risk anything- would brave death or damnation..." de- claimed the Prince heroically.

"Be careful what you wish for!" whispered Rannoch, under his breath. But this time the whisper was not for Johnnie's ears.

"... For just one minute in the land of my fathers!"

As the crowd cheered again, Callum passed a fire-brand up to the Prince, who held it aloft dramatically. On the end of it, a wooden cross burned brightly against the grey sky.

"The fiery cross!" breathed Johnnie. "It's the fiery cross, Tam! When you meet it, you must follow your chief, or have your house and land set to the flame!"

The crowd bayed their approval, as the Prince brandished the fiery cross towards all four corners of the Market Square, in the old fashion.

"Follow me!" shouted the Prince. "Follow me! For now nothing on this earth can prevent me from realising my destiny: From regaining my father's crown!"

The crowd was transfixed. But suddenly a fleet-footed figure appeared as if from nowhere, screeching and darting between people's legs, upsetting baskets of fruit and vegetables, startling horses and cattle, scampering over stalls and spreading chaos and confusion throughout the crowd.

"The Usurper's dragoons!" shouted Malcolm in a panic. "The redcoats are come! Flee for your lives! Flee!"

"What'n the world!" said Johnnie. "It's no' human!"

"It's the devil himsel'!" shouted Farmer Goldie, who had somehow appeared near them in the crowd, King Billy in tow. "Nothin' on this earth could stop him, yon prince said! Well, that's no' from this earth, believe me! It's no' canny!"

"An' the wee bugger bit me!" cried the cheesemonger, swinging wildly at Absalom with his cheese-cutter. "Ah'll gie' you mayhem, ya bass!"

Rannoch just threw back his head and laughed, revelling in the havoc that his pet was wreaking. To Tam's horror, the little monkey streaked straight towards Wee Tam, as if seeking him out in fellowship. Wee Tam reached out to it, hardly knowing what he was doing, but at the last second it shied away from him and ran up to Rannoch. He opened his cloak quickly, and it leapt up onto his shoulder, looking curiously at Wee Tam all the while. Tam stared back at him in astonishment.

"Birds of a feather flock together, eh, Rannoch?" said Tam.

Absalom's wizened face loomed back at him from out of the gap in the cloak, now baring his teeth and hissing aggressively. Terrified, Wee Tam shrank back from him. The Highlanders around the Prince crossed themselves and stared anxiously after the furry interloper.

"It's the very worst of omens for the fiery cross to meet a beast in its path!" said Tam. "Any Highlander knows that! Unless the creature be seized at once, and put to the sword without delay..."

Rannoch glared at him, and the little ape shrieked in rage. Wee Tam's face crumpled in pain. He held Tam's arms tightly, as though to restrain him from carrying out so harsh a sentence.

"Och, I'm no' goin' to harm the creature, son!" said Tam. "What do you take me for?"

"Behold, my friends, how even now the Usurper and his perfidious agents- both human and simian- are moving heaven and earth, to banish me from my homeland!" shouted the Prince, desperate to lighten the mood. "They have even enlisted their fellow monkeys to support their hopeless cause! And by my faith, the perky appearance of that little fellow puts the Elector of Hanover's own fat chops to shame!"

The crowd laughed. King George could not count on much active support from the people of Ayr, however willing they might prove to leave their comfortable seaside town and actually fight for the Stuarts.

"Tomorrow I leave for the Highlands to form an army- an army of patriots!" shouted the Prince. "Will you come with me to Glenfinnan? Will you be part of that army?"

There was a moment of hush, and then a voice rang out from the crowd.

"Whit's the pay, then, pet?"

"I don't believe it!" said Johnnie, gritting his teeth in frustration. "It's only that bloody Doxy Mary again! What's she doin' here? She's got some lip on her!"

The Prince made an imperious gesture with his hand, and two Highlanders rolled out a heavy barrel marked *"VIN DE BORDEAUX"*.

Callum cracked it open with a swing of his broadsword, and the crowd gasped as they saw the unmistakable glimmer of gold from the French *louis d'or* inside it. They seemed to like what they saw.

"Will you fight for your true king- for truth itself?"

"Yeeeessssssss!" roared the crowd, as one.

"Yes!" echoed Johnnie, turning to Tam, his face lit up as though with religious enlightenment. "I know you'll no' refuse the call now, Tam!"

"Follow me to battle!" shouted the Prince, drawing a huge cheer from the crowd.

"To glory!"

An even louder roar reverberated through the narrow streets of Ayr.

"And to the Jolly Beggars' Inn!"

This time there was a truly deafening din.

"Tonight we drink like true soldiers of fortune," shouted the Prince. "As though tomorrow will never come!"

"Oh, the day of reckoning always comes eventually..." muttered Rannoch.

"We'll follow you, Prince Charlie!" yelled Johnnie ecstatically. "Me and Tam O'Shanter! We'll follow you to the ends o' the earth!"

"We'll follow you as far as the pub, anyhow..." Tam whispered to Wee Tam.

Wee Tam smiled faintly, but it wasn't enough to clear away the worry etched deep into his face.

CHAPTER 27

"Oʜ!" sʜᴏᴜᴛᴇᴅ Kᴀᴛᴇ, ᴄʀʏɪɴɢ ᴏᴜᴛ in pain and shock.

"What's the matter, Kate, love?" said Mrs McGillivray, worried.

Kate had pricked her finger with her needle. She quickly held it up to her mouth, but it was too late. A livid crimson stain spread slowly across the chest of Wee Tam's best white shirt. Kate held it up to the light, staring at it in horror.

"Crivvens, that's no' like you, lass!" said Mrs McGillivray. "Ye're normally such a neat seamstress... But ye'll be alright, Sleepin' Beauty! Quick, put some cold water on the shirt..."

"No' a drop o' hot water, mind you, or it'll bond it to the fabric forever!" said Cathy Goldie.

"An' I've a wee bit o' good vinegar back in the inn, that'll maybe take the last o' the colour out..." said Mrs McGillivray.

"It's awfu' bad luck, Morag..." Kate said, her voice trembling. "Just look at his wee shirt!"

"Ye make your own luck in this life, Kate lass!" said Mrs McGillivray stoutly. "Jist like you were sayin' before! Ye cannae' dwell on the bad things that happen, or they'll consume you easily enough, believe you me... So don't wait for the luck to find you- you go oot there, and you grab it wherever you can find it!"

"You're right, Morag!" said Kate, sluicing cold water onto the shirt, in the cramped kitchen area of the croft. "You're a good friend!"

"Is it comin' out, Katie?" asked Elspeth Scott.

"Aye, no' too bad, thank you Elspeth!" said Kate, all her old strength flooding back into her as she rinsed out the little shirt. "I think it'll be alright, you know!"

"An' what about you, Katie? What are you goin' to do?" said Mrs McGillivray gently.

"I'm goin' to do it! For I just know Tam would take us to Glasgow if I asked him to, Morag!" said Kate. "For me- for me and Wee Tam! Somethin' has to change in our lives, and soon, for this way of livin' is killin' the both of us. You and Mungo, Elspeth and Rab, Cathy and Hosea- you all have your own places here. The inn, your farms- each other. But somehow me and Tam- we just don't seem to have found our own places in the world. We have Wee Tam, the great blessin' of our lives, who came to us when we least expected it- an' yet..." She held the shirt up, and peered at the fading mark. "We're stood at a great cross-roads in our life together, an' even though I don't know exactly which way we'll go yet, I do know that life will never be quite the same again. That it can't be..."

"But what if Tam has already chosen his way, Kate, love?" said Morag gently. "For I wouldnae' cause you more pain for all the gold in the world, but I have to tell ye that he seems as set on the road to perdition as any man I ever met! There's drink, and there are loose women, an' there's wickedness enough in Glasgow too, you know- there is everywhere. Everywhere that a man carries it in his own heart!"

"Aye! The devil kens his way aboot the city, as well as the village..." said Cathy Goldie.

"I know you mean me nothin' but good, girls," said Kate. "But you're wrong about Tam this time! He's made some bad decisions in his life, he'd be the first to admit it- but he'll make the right one this time. I can feel it in my heart!"

And so she could- or was it just wishful thinking again, Kate asked herself. She wiped the blur of tears out of her eyes.

"I didnae' mean to upset you, Kate, dear," said Mrs McGillivray. "Och, I shouldnae' be takin' out my own troubles on you..."

"Oh, Morag!" said Kate. "You must be worried sick about poor wee Colin, we all are! And you're right that Tam needs to mend his ways, of course you are. He can do it though- I just know he can."

"I hope ye're right, Kate!" said Mrs McGillivray, taking Kate's hand affectionately. "I'm sure I do wish you all the happiness in the world, for ye deserve it! An' now, gie' us a wee song, pet- I think we could all do with a wee bit o' cheerin' up!"

"Right enough!" said Elspeth Scott. "We shouldnae' let those bampots o' husbands get us down like this!"

"Very well!" said Kate. "Though I warn you, I'm in the mood for a sad one today..."

And the women sewed on in silence, as Kate sung her haunting song:

"Farewell, old Carrick's hills and dales,
Her healthy moors and winding vales;
The scenes where wretched Fancy roves,
Pursuin' past, unhappy loves!

Farewell, my friends! Farewell, my foes!
My peace with these, my love with those:
The burstin' tears my heart declare-
Farewell, the bonny banks of Ayr!
Farewell, to the bonny banks of Ayr!"

Even Mrs McGillivray had to wipe a great tear from her eye this time.

CHAPTER 28

———◆———

"FOLLOW ME!" SHOUTED THE PRINCE once more, seizing Callum's broadsword and saluting the hysterical crowd.

The good folk of Ayr waved ancient cutlasses, pitchforks, brooms, pokers, walking-sticks and whatever else they happened to have to hand back at him. The Prince leapt off the cart with a flourish, landing on both feet like an agile tom-cat. He ran along the front of the crowd, rattling his sword against their makeshift weapons, rousing them into a frenzy. Souter Johnnie pulled an antique Highland dirk out from under his jacket and thrust it into the air. Wee Tam shrank from the steel blade, as though scalded. Rannoch stared at him intently, fascinated by his reaction.

"For God's sake put that thing away, Souter!" said Tam, pulling at Johnnie's arm. "Put it away, man, before someone sees it!"

Johnnie resisted him, brandishing it with even greater ostentation.

"It's my auld father's dirk, Tam!" he shouted.

"Aye, I know what it is!" said Tam. "But do you no' see- there's no way back now! This crowd is hoachin' with government men, it has to be! I'm surprised the redcoats are no' here already!"

"Then let them come- let them come, and look to their own blades!" said Johnnie fiercely. "I've chosen my road. I swear it now- on the blade of my dirk!"

He held the dirk to the palm of his hand, tracing the thinnest of red lines of blood on his skin.

"I'll follow my prince- wherever fortune leads him!" he said fiercely. "Or let this very blade be the death o' me!"

Tam shook his head sadly.

"It leads him to crown or coffin, Johnnie," he said. "We know that much already... For there's nae' middle road to London from Scotland-there never has been."

Johnnie shook Tam's arm off him and pushed his way through to the front of the crowd. Callum moved to block his path to the Prince, but Johnnie showed him his dirk.

"Campbell?" said Callum.

"Wash your mouth out, man!" said Johnnie. "My mother was a Stewart!"

"On you go then, cousin!" said Callum with a smile, letting him through. Johnnie clambered up onto the wagon alongside the Prince. He looked across at him, and gulped nervously. He suddenly realised that he hadn't completely thought this through.

"Good people o' Ayr!" shouted Johnnie. "I'm no' a prince- nor even a clan chieftain. I'm just a common man. I'm one of you- I'm plain Souter Johnnie from Alloway!"

"Aye, we ken you well enough, Souter!" shouted Doxy Mary. "Back to stitchin' your wee booties, ya bawbag, an' leave the grown-ups tae' talk amongst oorselves!"

"For too long, we've been content jist to argue amongst ourselves, to live under the thumb o' the redcoats and accept tyrannous rule from abroad!" cried Johnnie, ignoring her. "But no more! This is what we've been waitin' for, these thirty long years! Now sing with me- sing for Prince Charlie! For King James! And for Scotland!"

"Christ, Johnnie, what'n the world are you up to now..." said Tam, holding his head in his hands. But Johnnie was already singing, head held high, dirk aloft, singing by himself in the great Market Square:

"Scots, wha' hae' wi' Wallace bled,
Scots, wham Bruce has often led;

Welcome to your gory bed,
Or to victory!"

Johnnie looked around the crowd, ignoring the blank faces staring back at him. But as he started the second verse, another voice joined him. To his amazement, it was Big Eck. And then another. Merry Andrew. The three of them sang together:

"Now's the day, and now's the hour;
See the front o' battle lour;
See approach proud Edward's power—
Chains and slavery!"

Now the Highlanders were singing along too, stumbling over the unfamiliar Lowland tongue, but led along stoutly by Callum, his own dirk held high:

"Wha' will be a traitor knave?
Wha' can fill a coward's grave!
Wha' sae' base as be a slave?
Let him turn and flee!"

Suddenly the whole square seemed to be bawling out the words:

"Wha' for Scotland's king and law,
Freedom's sword will strongly draw,
Free man stand, or free man fa',
Let him follow me!"

"Let him follow me!" echoed the Prince, striking a noble pose, and the crowd roared again as they launched into another verse together:

"By oppression's woes and pains!
By your sons in servile chains!
We will drain our dearest veins,
But they shall be free!"

"Free! Only death will set you free, you poor fools!" said Rannoch to himself, looking around at the mass of singers, grown men and women with tears rolling down their cheeks. "Freedom is a rich man's toy... You wouldn't know what to with it, not if I served it up to you on a silver platter!" He watched Big Eck, crying like a baby in the midst of the crowd. "And as for you, my jolly smuggler!" he said scornfully. "You probably never shed a tear for anything in your life, besides a lost cargo..." He watched as the whole square was transported by emotion. "And yet- and yet perhaps there is something to be said for a cause that can inspire such passion!"

And so Rannoch too sang along with them:

"Lay the proud usurpers low!
Tyrants fall in every foe!
Liberty's in every blow!
Let us do- or die!"

"Lay the proud usurper low!" repeated the Prince, swiping the air with a murderous cut of the broadsword, that came perilously close to decapitating a nearby Highlander. He acknowledged the crowd's cheers with an elegant bow.

"This is fantastic, Chevalier!" he whispered to Malcolm. "They're lapping all this nonsense up- so let's get them into the Jolly Beggars' and ply them with ale *pronto*, before the spell wears off! *Pronto, pronto, ragazzo!*"

"Really, Your Highness?" said Malcolm. "To the inn? You do know that we don't have much time..."

"Come now, Chevalier!" said the Prince impatiently. "Look around you, man! You remember what my good friend Rannoch said about hearts and minds? Well, I see a Royal Ayrshire regiment taking shape right here! And you know how much you Scots love a touch of drama... *Avanti, avanti tutta!* And make sure you grant a royal audience to that 'Stupid Johnnie' character- or whatever it is that he calls himself! For whatever his game may be, Stupid Johnnie could prove extremely useful to us here in the Lowlands. Be it as recruiting sergeant; or as martyr when my Uncle George finds out exactly what we've been up to here..."

CHAPTER 29

"C'MON, HURRY UP, YE LAZY laggards!" Johnnie shouted back to the Tams. "It's goin' to take us a very long time to get to the Highlands at this rate! What're ye waitin' for? Shake a leg!" He himself was wading manfully through the mob as it surged to the inn. "C'mon, we're gettin' left way behind here, Tammie! The Prince'll be on his second pint by now! Can you no' see that this is the opportunity of a lifetime? It'll no' be so easy to join up wi' him, once he's reached the Highlands an' the battle lines are being drawn up!"

"I don't know about that, Johnnie…" muttered Tam. "It's normally easy enough to join an army that's aboot to be cut to ribbons! It's the leavin' it that tends to be the hard part…"

"What's that you're sayin', Tam?" shouted Johnnie. "I cannae' hear you back there!"

"Eh, nothin', Souter!" said Tam, shouting himself now. "Just that I cannae' go home withoot a new suit for Wee Tam this time! You remember the trouble I had with Kate last time! She'll have my guts for garters, an' no mistakin'!"

Johnnie cursed under his breath, but nevertheless even he seemed to accept the gravity of the situation. He stopped and plunged back through the crowd towards them, scanning the stalls all around for inspiration.

"Bullseye!" he shouted, shepherding the reluctant Tams to a shabby-looking second-hand clothing stall. "Bob's your uncle, lads! A' the finest Parisian fashions here! Now hurry up and pick somethin' out, for we've to get to the Jolly Beggars withoot further delay! Rannoch's waitin' for us!"

The stallholder stared at them in amazement- and recognition.

"Rannoch, did ye say, son?" she said.

"Aye!" said Johnnie, looking at her curiously. "What's it to you, hen? He a friend of yours? D'ye know him?"

She picked up her cloak and wrapped it around herself, anxiously preparing to leave.

"By reputation, that's all..." she muttered.

Johnnie laid his hand gently on her shoulder.

"What's the matter, love?" said Johnnie. "Somewhere else you have to be? There's nae' need to rush off, for we were kind of hopin' you could sell us a new suit o' clothes for the bairn here? I mean, what wi' you bein' the proprietress of a fashion empire, an' all! Ye're no' your usual chirpy self now, I notice... You no' got a song for us this time?"

"Er- no, son..." said Doxy Mary. "Nae' offence intended in that wee matter of the shoes, eh? It was jist a bit of banter between friends!"

"Och, it's a' forgotten now!" said Souter Johnnie. His professional pride as a souter had quickly been overtaken by his desire to buy some kind- any kind- of garment for Wee Tam, and catch up with the Prince and Rannoch at the Jolly Beggars' Inn as soon as possible. "Water under the bridge, ye might say!"

Doxy Mary seemed to wince at the expression, but she submitted to the inevitable.

"Right enough then, son!" she said, forcing a smile. "Whit can I offer such a fine young gentleman?"

"Here you go then, Tam- what'll it be?" said Johnnie, gesturing to Doxy Mary's wares complacently, with the air of a benevolent genie rolling back the stone from Aladdin's Cave. The clothes were a curious mixture of bizarre, anachronistic relics from an altogether different era, and horrendously ill-assembled, rustic smocks and gowns.

"And be quick, will you, pal? Nae' man can tether time nor tide!" added Johnnie anxiously.

Tam sifted nervously through the outlandish apparel.

"Ah've got to admit that I personally am no' too up on all this, eh, infant sartorial elegance business..." he said doubtfully. "Can you no' give us a hand with this, Johnnie? As Wee Tam's godfather, an' all? Sort 'ay a role model, ye might say?"

Johnnie took another impatient look at the now emptying street in front of them, and then picked up the first thing that came to hand: A sack-like, moth-eaten tunic, hopelessly out of date even for rural Ayrshire. He held it up against Wee Tam, studying the effect with a practiced eye.

"Ah- just the job..." said Souter Johnnie, with an air of professional satisfaction.

Wee Tam himself frowned, shaking his head hard.

"Maybe they've one in your size, if you like it so much!" said Tam. "It looks like a bloody dress, man- it goes down to his ankles!"

"Aye, well you do want some room for growth when it comes to bairns..." said Johnnie judiciously. "How much for this one then, love?" he asked Doxy Mary, holding the garment up in all its hideousness.

"Er, a penny?" said Mary uncertainly.

"An' what if we throw in his own wee togs? Finest homespun, that!" said Johnnie, indicating Wee Tam's much patched clothes. "Quality never goes oot of fashion, eh?"

Doxy Mary gave them a cursory glance.

"Och, there's nae' market for cast-offs these days..." she said. "I couldnae' give those away, son!"

"Oh really?" said Johnnie, picking another ancient smock up off the stall. "What are these, then- *prêt à porter*?"

"I could maybe run to tuppence for the trade-in then, son!" said Doxy Mary hurriedly. "Seein' as how I'm in a rush, an' you're in the trade yourself- in a manner of speakin'..." She held out the tunic. "Shall we make the trade, then, lads?"

"There'll be a dram or two out of the change, at that price, Tam!" said Johnnie. "A nice wee bit o' business!"

Suddenly energised, Tam helped the reluctant Wee Tam out of his clothes and into the tunic. It looked ridiculous, hanging down like a night-gown. Wee Tam squirmed with embarrassment, holding his hands out to Tam in a silent appeal for mercy.

"Are you sure it, eh, suits him, Johnnie?" Tam asked uncertainly. "You don't see, eh- anythin'- like that, these days... Come to think of it, I don't even recall anyone wearin' anything like that when we were bairns ourselves! Maybe in biblical times..."

"What're you haverin' about now, Tam?" said Johnnie, looking increasingly impatiently towards the inn. "This suit was made for him, any fool can see that! Fits him like a glove!" He winked at Doxy Mary. "It's as though you were expectin' him! You've the second sight, love- its no' canny!"

"Now why would you say a thing like that, son?" said Mary anxiously. "Ah'm just an ordinary clothes-seller! What do you mean by it?"

"By what?" said Johnnie carelessly. "Och, it doesn't matter... C'mon, lads, you've had time enough to browse! It's only a suit of clothes he's lookin' for, no' a wife! Let's make like a Campbell in church, and get oot of here!"

To the Souter's irritation, Tam and Wee Tam were clowning about with antiquated hats, breeches and doublets from Doxy Mary's stall. Wee Tam draped himself in a sinister dark cloak and swirled it around him like Merry Andrew. Doxy Mary started in alarm, and seized the cloak back out of his hands.

"There's nothin' to concern you here, lads!" she said anxiously.

She hurriedly packed up the stall and handed Tam a grubby coin.

"Aren't you forgettin' something, hen?" said Johnnie. "His old clothes?"

"Aye, right enough, sonny," said Doxy Mary, taking the small bundle of clothes and depositing them carelessly on top of the stall. "Now farewell to youse all! I've to be off post haste, the now... I think I left a, er, pot boilin' at home..."

"Hubble bubble, toil and trouble, eh?" said Johnnie, giving her a wink.

Doxy Mary blanched and picked up her broomstick.

"A wee bit early for spring-cleanin', isn't it?" said Johnnie jovially, enjoying her discomfiture after the torrid time she had given him at his own stall.

Doxy Mary stared at him in horror. She grabbed an armful of her wares, apparently at random, and then bustled off through the Market Square.

"No' an especially shrewd businesswoman!" commented Johnnie. "What the devil's got into everyone today?"

"Did someone mention my name?" said Rannoch, suddenly appearing behind Johnnie. "I do hope so... But my dear Souter Johnnie, what are you doing here? Aren't you coming to see our- our mutual friend? History is in the making tonight! You have a date with destiny..."

"A what? But aye, we're comin' alright, Rannoch!" said Johnnie. "Tam here just had a wee errand to run first..."

"Did he now?" said Rannoch, raising a dark eyebrow. "Quite a time to choose for it! But never mind, never mind- follow me, chaps, and we may just catch him in time!"

Johnnie and the Tams hurried after Rannoch, as he glided down the now-deserted street. Finally they reached the rough, whitewashed exterior of the Jolly Beggars' Inn, from which snatches of shouting and singing were already leaking enticingly out into the evening.

"Come quickly," said Rannoch. "Let's get a good spot at the bar! He hasn't arrived yet..."

"Where is he then?" said Johnnie. "We just saw him in the Market Square! He was only about fifty yards away then!"

Rannoch laughed.

"Oh, he has taken a turn around the block with his precious Highlanders- just to allow the expectation to build a little, you understand! I'm starting to realise that he really is quite the showman... This prince of yours never makes an ordinary entrance when a dramatic one will do! Nor says one word when a hundred will do, if it comes to that..."

Wee Tam looked warily at Rannoch, but he followed the others as they bundled into the bustling inn after him. The atmosphere was feverish inside, full of shouted whispers and palpable expectation. Many of the men were sporting the white cockade of the Jacobite cause, flaunting tartan and make-shift weapons. Big Eck was already firmly moored at the bar, and Rannoch led the Tams and Johnnie up to him.

"Let me present some new friends of mine, Eck..." said Rannoch. "The Tam O'Shanters, Senior and Junior, and Souter Johnnie of Alloway!"

"Pleased to meet ye, chaps!" said Big Eck, extending his great paw jovially. "I saw ye back there in the Market Square! Ye seemed like likely lads, right enough! Pull up a beer!"

Wee Tam looked anxiously up at Tam, who just shrugged his shoulders and accepted a foaming tankard of ale from Eck.

They clanked mugs convivially.

"The King Over the Water!" toasted Big Eck, and Johnnie clapped him on the back.

Suddenly, without turning his head, Rannoch whispered to Johnnie. "And here he comes..."

"How do you know?" said Johnnie.

"Trust me..." said Rannoch, with a smile.

Johnnie and Big Eck turned round, just in time to see the double doors of the inn swing wide open.

CHAPTER 30

———

"The net is closin' swiftly now…" said Nannie. "But on whom, I wonder?"

She strode quickly down the claustrophobic side streets of Ayr, her face hooded close. Kirkton Jean and Hielan' Mary, also hooded, were scurrying to keep pace with her, anxiously straining to catch her words as she skipped over cobbles and through tunnel-like closes.

"We nearly have him!" Nannie said. "But beware of the *mnathan-shìdh* now, sisters… For I feel the hand of the fair folk upon him too! They will never give up. We must find them out, and quickly, before they can discover our own designs!"

"Can you make out the face of the third changeling yet, Nannie?" said Hielan' Mary, already out of breath from the exertion of keeping up with the fleet-footed Cutty Sark, voice shuddering as she tripped over the cobble-stones. "An' the Watchers?"

"A number of shadows have taken shape around Tam now…" said Nannie, deep in thought. "This John Davidson, 'Souter Johnnie' as they call him, we know to be nothin' but a rustic fool, a simple buffoon- and beyond anythin' human! Though he stays so close to Tam…"

"Aye, I think I can vouch for that right enough, Nannie!" said Mary. "The good Souter is no fairy!"

"What troubles me more is this Eck McIver character…" said Nannie. "Where did he spring from? When even the ship-wreckers deny all knowledge of him! And yet here he appears, on centre stage, in the guise of a low Carrick smuggler! The way he trailed Charles Edward from the beach suggests that he possesses a cunnin' far beyond the or-dinary, whatever he may pretend. Somethin' much more akin to the subtlety of the still folk, than to man's bludgeon-like methods..."

"An' he rarely strays from the side of Banquo's heir now!" said Hielan' Mary eagerly.

"He has his own role to play, of that there can be no doubt..." said Nannie. "But what will it be? And when will he make his move?"

"'They will be the last people we expect...'" muttered Kirkton Jean breathlessly. "That's what ye said yourself, isn't it?"

"We certainly didnae' expect this Highlander- Callum Stewart!" said Hielan' Mary. "He even speaks in the tongue of the fair folk! I've heard him at it..."

"That's Gaelic, you idiot!" said Nannie. "Half the country speaks it. An' besides, Callum behaves just like a man- with steel, and with hasty action! They have changed their ways much, if that is how they now come amongst humans. For their numbers are now too few to give them any hope o' winnin' through force alone..."

"What of Merry Andrew then, Nannie?" said Kirkton Jean, between gasps for breath.

"Oh, of Andrew I am almost certain!" said Nannie, pausing for a mo-ment in a shadowy alley-way, to the relief of the panting Kirkton Jean and Hielan' Mary. "He is a changeling- yes, an' a Watcher too! I can feel great power flowin' around him... Greater than I ever suspected as a child, when he limped around the place, a poor misfit among men- pitied and ridiculed by all! There was always talk of a renegade from our own num-bers, one born of a witch but taken in by the still folk- an' who better to watch over a changeling of their own? For it must be one who can live in or around men, and the fairies have always hated that." She started pacing through the narrow streets again, as though suddenly reminded of the urgency of their mission. "But that knowledge alone is nothin' to us, without knowin' the identity of the second Watcher as well!" she said.

"Whit aboot this Farmer Goldie?" said Hielan' Mary. "He keeps showin' up, wherever Tam goes! He pretends a great hatred of Merry

Andrew, but in his heart he too has one foot in the other world... And a way wi' animals, wi' that great Hielan' Cow which travels aboot wi' him- which was ever a sign o' the *mnathan-shìdh*! He has a great sadness in his eyes."

"Hosea Goldie? He is my own birth father, you fool!" said Nannie impatiently. "Have you learned nothin'? Sensed nothin'? Thank God that I am a changeling, and not wrought of the same lumpen clay as you clods! Farmer Goldie's heart casts out to the other world, for it alone can tell him the truth- that he has lost me to it..."

"Your father, Nannie!" said Kirkton Jean in surprise. "But you... Did you..."

"Surely you knew that I was taken from the village- when I was but a girl?" said Nannie.

"Aye, but..." stuttered Kirkton Jean. "That village?"

"You knew your parents then, dear?" said Hielan' Mary.

"Aye, I knew them! Of course I knew them!" said Nannie. "An' Rannoch's very plan depends upon it bein' the same village."

"How, Nannie?" said Kirkton Jean.

"That is not yet clear..." said Nannie. "And yet he has seen that much."

"But is he no' worried that ye might... That ye might go back there one day?" said Hielan' Mary nervously. "Return to them? To your own folk, I mean? To Hosea and Cathy Goldie- your, your parents?"

"My own folk- my parents- my family... Those words have no meanin' for me now!" said Nannie scornfully. "Do you think it was for nothin' that I passed all those years in desolate caves, stranded on wind-swept islands in the middle of nowhere? With old women who could offer me sisterhood- in time- but none of a mother's love? With only study and prophecies, an' interminable spells and incantations, to fill the long winter nights? For months- for years- I hated every minute of it. I begged each day to be returned to my lost family. I pined for my home every night, and I cursed those who had stolen me away from it. But over time I came to discover through their teachin' a world far beyond the sleepy existence of this Goldie and his wife- of Mungo McGillivray and all their small-minded neighbours! A world of spirits and elements- of power-beyond their wildest imagination! A world where a woman's life could mean somethin' more! Somethin' more than a headlong rush into the prison of marriage. Somethin' more than skivvyin' for a selfish, ignorant clod o' a husband day after day, until your precious fire slowly dwindles into resignation…"

"Amen to that!" said Hielan' Mary.

"I was changed forever," said Nannie. "As anyone would have been! The choice in those years was to be changed, or to be broken. That is what it means to be a changeling! A changeling from the world of men… An' you must know that whilst some poor souls wandered deranged around those islands, unable to comprehend the sheer enormity of what they were bein' shown- of what was bein' offered to them- I embraced my destiny! So don't ask me now about my parents, or about returnin'. There is no goin' back! Just be sure when I tell you that this Goldie is no' the second Watcher…"

"'They will be the last people we expect'…" repeated Kirkton Jean. "It is just the kind o' thing they would do!"

Nannie scowled at her, her beautiful green eyes flashing danger-ously, and Kirkton Jean averted her eyes submissively.

"Who then, Nannie?" Hielan' Mary asked. "Mungo himself? Mrs McGillivray, wi' that famous temper of hers? Amos McIntosh? It surely cannae' be Kate O'Shanter- or that brutish oaf, Farmer Scott?"

"The search must go on!" Nannie said firmly.

"We will watch them more closely than ever- all o' them!" said Kirkton Jean.

"Good!" said Nannie. "An' do you know where Tam and Souter Johnnie are headed for tonight?"

"Oh aye…" said Hielan' Mary. "They've made no secret o' that, at least! To the Jolly Beggars' Inn! Where Banquo's heir and Big Eck are carousin' even now, an' have been all day and all night…"

"These fools of men are nothin' if no' predictable!" said Nannie scornfully. "Can they no' manage to stay sober for a few hours at a time, wi' Scotland's whole fate in the balance? It's almost too easy to confound them... But let us go there too, then! It is time at last for the whole cast to come together- for better or for worse, everyone will soon be seen as they are. So do brush your hair, Jean, dear!"

"Whit's wrong wi' my hair?" said Kirkton Jean irritably.

"Och, nothin' more than usual!" said Nannie, passing her a wooden-handled hair-brush. "But the great crisis is upon us now, and we must fight with every weapon that we have within our grasp- be it brush, dagger or magic! We must protect our world, our possibilities, from the limitations that these short-sighted, self-interested fools would impose upon them! We must smite our enemies, whether they come to us in the guise of innocent babes, or as graspin' princes! We must spare no atrocity or cruelty- we must look our own destruction in the eye, an' hug it to ourselves, as though it were our dearest friend!" She threw her dark head back, sending a ripple of silvery laughter pealing down the narrow street. "An' besides, you want to look your very best at the end of days, don't you?"

"Aye, I do that!" said Kirkton Jean resolutely, struggling to force the brush through her tangled hair. "No gods, no masters!"

"No gods, no masters!" repeated Nannie.

They stopped outside the back door of the Jolly Beggars' Inn. Nannie bunched her slender white hand into a fist, and rapped it hard against the dark wood.

"May we come in?" she cried. "Let us in!" she shouted, more insistently. And finally the heavy door swung open. "You invite us in, of your own free will?"

CHAPTER 31

———◆———

PRINCE CHARLES EDWARD STUART STRUTTED into the front room of the Jolly Beggars' Inn like a preening prizefighter, holding Callum's broadsword across his chest. The Highlanders instantly fanned out on either side of him to clear his path, bringing him right up to where Johnnie, Rannoch, Big Eck and the Tams were standing at the bar. There was a moment of awed silence at the sight of the Prince, followed by a wave of rapturous applause that set the glasses and bottles in the inn shuddering and clinking. Whilst Malcolm ordered a sneaky pint for himself, the Prince set a regal hand on the bar and turned to the assembled drinkers.

"My friends!" he cried. "I told you we would meet again soon! For today in the Market Square, we pledged ourselves to fight together. But tonight we do something far nobler: We drink together!"

The Prince grabbed the brimming pint pot out of Malcolm's hands, just as the Chevalier was raising it to his own thin lips.

"*Slàinte mhath! Slàinte mhór!*" he shouted, and quaffed the beer in one great gulp.

"Cherlie! Cherlie! Cherlie!" roared the drinkers around him until the rafters shook, ringing with his name. "Wha'll be king but Cherlie! Wha'll be king but Cherlie!"

"So you know the Old Tongue then, my Lord?" said Souter Johnnie excitedly. "The Gaelic?"

"Oh, I am blessed with a gift for all languages, my lad!" said the Prince complacently. "It is the greatest gift I have, except for drinking and riding! And besides, I know the three most important words in any language: 'It's my round'!"

These magic words sparked a frenzied rush to the bar, and the Prince himself was hoisted up onto the sturdy shoulders of some grateful Ayrshire farmers.

"I have found the way to your stout rustic hearts, have I not, *mes braves*?" said the Prince, waving affably at the crowd. "Tonight you drink on the Treasury!" He extended a royal index finger towards Malcolm. "Just apply to my father's trusted Quartermaster General here for whatever you need!"

Malcolm was immediately swamped by eager drinkers, determined not to miss the opportunity of a lifetime.

"I'll need receipts for all these... these beverages..." he said helplessly, as the drinkers settled down to their work with gusto.

"*Slàinte!*" said Johnnie to Callum, next to him at the bar, as he emptied another of Malcolm's hard-earned pints down his gullet.

"*Do dheagh shlàinte!*" said Callum companionably, following suit. "Where are you boys from then?" he asked, in his lilting English.

"Och, just down the road in Alloway," said Johnnie. "They call me Souter Johnnie!" He pointed to Tam. "And this is my old friend Tam O'Shanter, and his wee lad- o' the same name. This is..." Johnnie turned to introduce Rannoch too, but he had disappeared. "Never mind!" said Johnnie. "He's a bit of a scunner anyway, between us... And last, but no' least, Big Eck!"

"Aye, Eck and I already acquainted, are we no'?" said Callum, nodding to Big Eck. "I'm Callum Stewart, of Appin," he said, shaking hands with Tam and Johnnie. "You must be an Irishman with a name like that, *laochain*?" he said to Tam. "From the other side? *Èireannach*?"

"No, no," said Tam. "My old man was from the Highlands. Crianlarich way... We moved south when I was just a bairn. Souter Johnnie too."

"Is that a fact?" said Callum. "Well, you're virtually a neighbour then! Though there's no O'Shanters in Appin, that I know of..."

"Have you checked the inns?" said Johnnie. "For there'll usually be an O'Shanter or two at the bar, havin' a wee chat wi' the landlord's daughter when they think there's no one watchin'!"

"Stop you, Souter!" said Tam, covering Wee Tam's ears with his hands. It must have been too late though, for Wee Tam was already blushing crimson.

"That'll be it then, we've never tried the inns..." said Callum with a wink. "We'll maybe pop in and see, next time we're back home!"

"There, ah, there seems to be an auld chap over there, tryin' to get your attention, Callum!" said Tam.

Malcolm had climbed gingerly onto the bar and cupped his hands around his mouth.

"Callum! Callum Stewart!" he cried, looking around the inn impatiently. "Where are you? Your Prince demands music, without delay!"

"Crivvens, he'll do himself a mischief!" said Callum. "What does he want now?"

"He says the Prince is wantin' music!" said Tam.

"Music! An' where am I to find a band now?" said Callum wearily.

"If you're lookin' for pipers and fiddlers, I'd start near the bar and work oot the way..." said Tam. "Look, over there in the corner!"

Tam pointed over to a dissolute rabble of drinkers. A few of them were clutching misshapen sacks with pipes protruding from them, that were just about identifiable as bagpipes. "They've been on the sauce for a while already, I'd say!" said Tam. "But if you're quick, you may yet get a couple of tunes oot of them, before they pass oot completely..."

"Pipers, eh!" said Callum. "You cannae' live with them, and ye cannae' go to war without them... *Mar sin leat*, boys!"

"See you later!" said Johnnie.

As Callum hurried across to corral the musicians together into some kind of band, a gigantic Highlander stumbled straight into Souter Johnnie, and then squared up to him aggressively. Johnnie couldn't help but notice that he was clutching a broken table leg, with a long rusty nail protruding from the end of it.

"*Oidhche mhath*, Lowlander!" growled the big Highlander. "Are you on our side in the bar fight or no'?"

"Er- aye?" said Johnnie, playing for time.

"Top man!" said the Highlander, clapping him on the back. "Where're you from, *laochain*?"

"Just doon the road..." said Johnnie cautiously. "How about yourselves?"

"I'm from Dunoon, man! Argyll!" said the Highlander. "But I had to leave Dunoon, ken?"

"Is that right?" said Johnnie. "And why was that, then?"

"'Cause everyone in Dunoon is crazy, man! Crazy!" said the Highlander. "It's all they Maclachlans they have there!"

"Right enough!" said Johnnie, laughing. "I can see why you would-nae' have fitted in..." He held out his hand. "The name's John Davidson-Souter Johnnie, they call me."

"Put it there then, Souter Johnnie!" said the Highlander, crush-ing Johnnie's hand in his huge mitt. "Maclachlan's my name- Gregor Maclachlan!"

"Aye, of course it is..." said Johnnie.

"An' this is Ruaridh Stewart," said Gregor, nodding towards his com-panion. "Cousin to *Calum Mór*, who you've already met..."

They shook hands cordially.

"Listen, Gregor, rather than the actual, er, fightin', what do you two lads say to a friendly wager in the line of drinkin'?" said Johnnie.

"Johnnie..." said Tam warningly, but it was already too late.

"So what exactly did ye have in mind then, Souter-boy?" said Gregor with interest.

"D'you want to choose the game?" said Johnnie.

"You hum it, an' I'll play it, son!" said Gregor.

Johnnie picked up a mug brimming with whisky, knocked it back and then nonchalantly added it to a long line of empties on the bar. Tam applauded, whilst Wee Tam looked on in concern. He knew what was coming next.

"Like water off a duck's back, boys! You cannae' flood a desert!" crowed Johnnie.

Gregor filled up three mugs of whisky.

"Maybe no'..." he said. "But you can shoot the duck!"

Gregor licked his lips appreciatively.

"Here's tae' us..." he growled, downing the first mug.

"Wha's like us..." he continued, as he chased it down with the second.

"There's no' many..." he said, and tilted the third mug towards his mouth. But before he could drain it, he blacked out and slumped face down on the bar. He rolled over onto his back, somehow still holding the mug upright.

"An' they're a' deid!" said Tam. "Ye've got them on the run now, Johnnie-boy! C'mon the Souter! Alloway Alligator forever!"

Johnnie plucked the mug from Gregor's prone hand and swigged it back with a certain swagger.

"Waste not, want not, laddies!" he said, bowing low. "When you're used to drinkin' Auld Mungo's moonshine, this stuff goes down like Strathpeffer spring water!"

There was a burst of applause from behind them. Johnnie and Tam turned around in surprise, to see the Prince watching the contest with a professional eye, Rannoch at his side.

"*Bravo! Bravo!*" said Charles Edward, clapping. "The tide goes out when this one starts drinking! I have frequented every drinking den of Montmartre and the Marais, but never have I seen the like of this before!" He joined them at the bar. "But now you must drink three mugs to beat my bonny Highlander, *n'est-ce pas, mon brave?*" he said to Tam. "Can you find it within you? Now that the battle has reached its very *crescendo?*"

Tam stepped forward uncertainly, then grabbed the whole bottle from the bar and swigged deeply at it until he had drained it completely. Suddenly his legs gave way underneath him. He collapsed, hit the ground and then bounced straight back up grinning, still clutching the bottle in his hand. He placed it in the row of empties and then swayed back to his post, next to Wee Tam.

"Incredible!" said the Prince, clapping him on the back. "*Bravo, bravo, ragazzo!*" He clicked his fingers impatiently for another bottle of whisky to be passed out from behind the bar.

"*Corragio, cugino mio!*" said the Prince to Ruaridh. "The stakes are raised again, cousin, and even your Prince cannot help you now! You must put your faith in God alone… God or the devil!"

Rannoch produced a bottle of whisky from nowhere, and pushed it along the bar towards Ruaridh.

"*Et maintenant- fais ton jeu*, Ruaridh!" said the Prince. "And this time, you must do- well, I don't know, something truly insane, *hein*? Drink responsibly!"

Ruaridh looked at the bottle of whisky long and hard, but without much enthusiasm. He tried ineffectually to rouse Gregor, then gave it up as a bad job and started to drag his huge inert frame away, bumping him along over the debris-strewn floor.

The Prince cleared his throat discreetly.

"And the forfeit, my friend?" he said. "Surely this was not merely a sportsman's bet? We Stewarts must pay our debts, when we can!"

Ruaridh scowled back at his liege lord through beetling brows, before rummaging in Gregor's plaid and then throwing a small bag of coins back onto the bar.

"Take it oot o' that, lads!" he said. "Ye won it fair and square! But be sure an' watch your backs if ye see Gregor in the mornin', for he'll be after gettin' his silver back, by hook or by crook… An' sometimes he's no' as particular as he ought to be whether it's at play, or on the point of his dirk!"

"*Tapadh leat!*" said Souter Johnnie, rapping the coins on the bar. "Whisky all round, landlord!"

CHAPTER 32

—————

"*MON COEUR VOLAGE, DIT ELLE*," sung the Prince sentimentally, as he relieved himself with absolute abandon outside the back of the Jolly Beggars' Inn.

"*N'est pas pour vous, garçon!*" he continued lustily, warming to his theme.

"*Est pour un homme de guerre, qui a barbe au menton!*"

Tam shuffled out, intent on similar business, just as the Prince hit the chorus with everything he had.

"*Lon! Lon! Laridon!*"

Concentrating on his own affairs, Tam didn't even notice the last hope of the House of Stuart, until he was forced to take evasive action from the Prince's royal arc. Charles Edward gave a Gallic shrug, then burst into another boisterous round of the refrain.

"*Lon, Lon, Laridon!*"

"Jings, speakin' in tongues already! You've had it, pal!" said Tam sympathetically. "Believe me, I've been there... Load'ay bollocks this rebellion stuff though, eh? Rich man's problems... I've a family tae' feed, me!"

"Of course it is, my friend!" said the Prince. "But then I too have a family. And all I have is my claim to the throne, and the shirt on my back!"

"Eh sorry, your Worship... I didnae' see you there!" said Tam apologetically.

"Don't be sorry, Tam! You can speak your mind to me, *ragazzo*," said the Prince. "The truth is that I envy you! A man with a home and family, who tills the land- and who belongs to it. Look at me today: an exile, a prince without a crown, without a pot to pee in, eh?"

"I thought there was a Privy Council to take care of all that side of things…" said Tam. "But you seem to be making a decent stab of it yourself, Your Highness!"

"A wandering prince must learn to be resourceful!" said the Prince. "For now, I am as poor as a soap salesman in Campbell country… But tomorrow, my friend- well, who knows what tomorrow may bring! I must hold onto my hope as a miser cherishes his gold- for when that is gone, I am doomed forever…"

"Ye put a pretty brave face on it, back there in the Market Square!" said Tam.

"The wine helps, *mon brave!*" said Charles Edward. "However I feel behind the mask- hope, excitement, disappointment, despair- I cannot let it slip for a moment! For what can a Pretender do, but pretend to the last?"

"Do you no' sometimes wish you could just give it all up?" said Tam. "Jist marry some nice wee lass, maybe wi' a wee bit of her own money, and settle down? Raise a couple of princelings- or whatever they would be. Arch-dukes, maybe?"

"As well ask the fish if he wishes he could fly, *ragazzo!*" said the Prince. "Unless he is the, how do you say, the flying fish?"

"Right…" said Tam.

"You see, Tam, my point is: We are what we are. The fly is the fly, and the fish is the fish. And the flying fish, he is the flying fish!"

"And what if we dinnae' ken what we are yet?" said Tam.

"Then we must just assume the greatest destiny we can, until we are proved to the contrary!" said Charles Edward. "Look at me- will I be doomed to roam the world looking for a kingdom worthy of my breeding, or will I lord it over all Europe, as King of England? The difference is stark, *n'est-ce pas?* It is a cliff-edge- on which a man could go mad, if he peered over it for too long!" He took a great swig of ale from his tankard. "No, I must roll the dice like all of you- whether it be a drinking game, or a game of thrones that we play! I must throw them with all my strength, and not even watch where they fall... *Faites vos jeux*, gentlemen! What will you play for? Well, Tam? What does your own heart most desire? For no one will just bring it to you on a silver platter, believe me! Even a prince cannot hope for that..."

"Sometimes I just want to leave it all behind- go travellin' or somethin', you know?" said Tam.

"And where would you go, *mon ami*?" said the Prince.

"Och, I don't know!" said Tam. "Arran, maybe?"

The Prince put his arm around Tam's shoulder.

"So far away?" he said. "Well, perhaps we'll go there together some day, Tam! Although if I lose this great game of mine, I will need to flee further than the Isle of Arran before I can escape my dear cousin's wrath! But what are you laughing about, my friend?"

"I was just thinkin' about somethin' my wife said to me, Your Highness..." said Tam. "She told me that I'd learn to mend my ways, if only I kept better company!"

The Prince clapped him on the back.

"You are keeping the noblest company in all of Europe now, my friend!" he said. "But now let us make the noblest journey of them all- to the bar..."

They made their way back inside the Jolly Beggars' Inn, arm in arm.

"Now join in with me, *mon brave*," said the Prince. "*Qui port chapeau a plume, soulier a rouge talon!*"

"*Lon! Lon! Laridon!*" sang the Prince and Tam together.

"Ah! There he is! Wherever have you been, Your Highness?" cried Malcolm. "Callum has been looking for you everywhere! We have much work to do... Your standing amongst the working men of Ayr has soared since your, eh, noble exploits at the bar. But I feel that we must now take advantage of your popularity with the- ahem- fairer sex..."

"Why, I have been in my Privy Council, Chevalier!" said the Prince, winking at Tam.

Malcolm raised an eyebrow, but tapped his crystal whisky tumbler daintily with a spoon anyway. "Ahem! I pray silence for the Prince, gentlemen!"

"After me, Tam!" bawled the Prince. "*Qui joue de la flute, aussi du violon!*"

"A-hem! Gentlemen! Gentlemen!" croaked Malcolm again.

"*Lon! Lon! Laridon!*"

No one seemed to be paying Malcolm the slightest attention, so he irritably tugged at Callum's sleeve, shouting at him over the bedlam.

"Oh, won't you shut these peasants up, for God's sake, Callum!"

Callum shrugged his shoulders.

"I don't care how you do it, nephew, just do as I ask!" snapped Malcolm.

Callum shrugged again, took a long dag pistol out of his plaid and fired it straight up into the roof. A huge chunk of plaster collapsed down into the middle of the room, smashing those glasses and tables that were still in one piece, sending nearby revellers scrambling for cover and covering Malcolm's thin hair in a dusting of white powder. Prostrate on the floor where Ruaridh had left him, Gregor's shock of dark hair looked like a powdered periwig, sprinkled with fallen plaster. Cracks were spreading alarmingly around the gaping hole in the ceiling, sending hairline fractures to all corners of the roof and threatening to bring the whole thing crashing down on their heads.

The music abruptly stopped, and the Highlanders all around whipped murderous dirks and daggers out of stockings and sleeves.

"Oh, brilliant, Callum, just brilliant!" Malcolm spluttered, through a mouthful of plaster dust.

He tapped the glass again. This time the noise was deafening, in the tense, tinderbox atmosphere of the inn.

"Gentlemen!" cried Malcolm. "Put your weapons away, and join me in a loyal toast to our glorious leader: Prince Charles Edward Stuart!"

A roar of "Cherlie! Cherlie! Cherlie!" erupted around the bar.

"Let the royal waltz begin!" Malcolm ordered the band.

The half-cut musicians stared at one another, bemused, sucking on the chanters of their bagpipes and tapping fiddle-sticks absent-mindedly on their shoulders.

"Just play somethin'- anythin'- wi' a foreign name, ya dummies!" hissed Callum.

The band struck up a faltering tune.

"And who will have the great- the signal- honour of taking His Highness' hand for the first dance?" said Malcolm in a wheedling tone.

There was an awkward pause. There were no obvious candidates, for the good ladies of Ayr were not likely to hazard their reputations by entering a parlour of such notorious ill repute. Malcolm was searching increasingly anxiously for any presentable female of dancing age, when gradually an excited murmur began to buzz and grow around the room. The crowd melted away, to reveal a young lady who had appeared at the back of the inn, facing the Prince across the room. She made no answer to Malcolm's invitation, other than dancing mesmerically towards the delighted Charles Edward. She didn't need any words. The flickering candle-light played across her ebony-dark hair, and flirted with the green glimmer of her eyes- and the silk of her outfit. All eyes were on her, especially the Prince's. The Prince's, and Tam's, for he had recognized her instantly.

"The Cutty Sark..." breathed Tam, as the Prince gave a courtly bow, and then started the elaborate setting steps of a mincing French dance. For a moment Nannie seemed to be mimicking his movements, but gradually the enthralled drinkers could see that she was dancing traditional Scottish setting steps of her own- at once simpler and more graceful than the Prince's contrived, Versailles manoeuvres. They bayed their approval.

"Good lass!" shouted Tam. "Weel done, Cutty Sark!"

Now she was untying the Prince's Italian silk neck-cloth seductively, pulling it slowly across his face as she danced backwards away from his outstretched hands.

"What does she see in him?" said Tam, suddenly inexplicably-humiliatingly-jealous.

"Well, he's much richer than you…" said Ruaridh, standing next to him. "He's far better lookin' than you…"

"An' he's the heir to three kingdoms!" said Souter Johnnie.

"Alright, alright, lads!" said Tam, shaking his head in shame and vexation.

"You naughty girl!" said the Prince ecstatically. "*Ooh la la*! Come to Charlie, *ma chérie*! For we have much to discuss…"

But that did not seem to be her intention. Instead, she retreated slowly away from the enraptured Prince, still holding his neck-cloth mockingly between thumb and forefinger. The Prince held out his hands to her imploringly, as she finally twisted the silk around her wrist and then danced back towards the door.

"*Ma foi*! The little *coquette*!" said Charles Edward admiringly.

"You, missy!" said Malcolm. "You there, in the green cutty sark! Cutty Sark! Will you not come back, you saucy wench? Will ye no' dance a fair French waltz with His Royal Highness? With your future king!"

"Future king!" laughed the Cutty Sark. "Don't be so quick to take the future's gifts for granted, old man! For your time will soon be over!"

The tinkling laughter reverberated through Tam's head, taking him straight back to the moor near his croft, the wind blasting his face.

"I have no king!" cried Nannie, making an elegant Strathspey setting step. "No lord, an' no husband! An' I would rather dance alone to a good Scottish tune, than dance a step shackled to any foreign prince in Europe!"

"Foreign prince?" said Charles Edward.

"Old man?" said Malcolm.

"Dance, Cutty Sark!" shouted the Highlanders. "Dance!"

Nannie seized a pewter tankard from a nearby Highlander, drained it in a gulp and then began to smash it against a bowing beam on the roof. She chanted as she danced:

"*A fig for those by law protected!*
Liberty's a glorious feast!

Courts for cowards were erected,
Churches built to please the priest!"

"Silence!" shouted Malcolm, incensed. "Have you no shame, ye impudent hussy? Have ye no decency?"

But now the Highlanders had taken up her rhythm, stamping and beating their own tankards against the walls, the ceiling and the heads of anyone foolish enough to get in the way. Malcolm covered his ears, whilst at the back of the room Rannoch looked on, hunchbacked once more, smiling laconically as he smoked a long pipe. The Cutty Sark whirled around in a dizzying dance, then paused to sing once more:

"What is title, what is treasure,
What is reputation's care?
If we lead a life of pleasure,
'Tis no matter how or where!"

"Now sing with me, sons of Scotland!" she shouted.

The Highlanders bellowed out the chorus with her:

"A fig for those by law protected!
Liberty's a glorious feast!
Courts for cowards were erected,
Churches built to please the priest!"

The Cutty Sark laughed out loud in pure exhilaration, took another one of the phalanx of tankards being thrust at her from all sides, drained it and threw it back over her shoulder. It smashed a bearded Highlander in the face, but he just gawped after her in admiration.

"No gods, no masters!" she cried. She laughed that haunting laugh once more, span on her heel and then disappeared back into the crowd, leaving the Prince stranded helplessly on the dance-floor. He laughed aloud at the sheer indignity of his position, before shrugging and kissing his fingers.

"Easy come, easy go! But what a woman, by God! I find that I begin to love this new land of mine more and more!"

He held his hands up in the air, playing to the crowd.

"Does no one have a drink for their forsaken prince, in his hour of need?"

"Oh, your hour of need is still to come, my bonny prince…" murmured Rannoch to himself. "Let it not find you wanting!"

Johnnie sprang forward, fresh pint in hand.

"For Scotland's one true king!" he said, proffering it to the Prince in tribute. "I'd die for you, my Lord!"

The Prince clapped him on the back.

"*Grazie, ragazzo!* Here's to dying as king- or dying young!"

He gulped down the drink.

"Never mix women and drinking, Stupid Johnnie!" he said. "Or is it the other way round? Now, *Maestro,* music! But none of your foreign muck, this time! A reel or Strathspey, by God! A Scots dance, on pain of your lives! Dance with me, Johnnie! Dance, and sing!"

Johnnie spun the Prince round in a wild Tulloch turn, singing at the top of his voice:

"*'Twas on a Monday mornin',*
Right early in the year,
That Charlie came to our town,
The young Chevalier!

As he was walkin' up the street,
The city for to view,
O there he spied a bonny lass
The window lookin' through!

Sae light's he jumped up the stair,
And tirl'd at the pin;
And wha sae ready as hersel'
To let the laddie in!"

"*Encore!*" shouted the Prince. "*Encore!* This is more like it, Stupid Johnnie!"

Encouraged by the praise, Johnnie filled his lungs and belted out the next verse:

> "*He set his Jenny on his knee,*
> *All in his Highland dress;*
> *For brawly weel he ken'd the way*
> *To please a bonny lass!*"

"Will this infernal caterwauling go on all night?" said Malcolm. "We have much more important business at hand!"

But his voice was drowned out as the Highlanders ripped into the chorus:

> "*An' Charlie, he's my darlin',*
> *My darlin', my darlin',*
> *Charlie, he's my darlin',*
> *The young Chevalier!*"

"Oh, I'd make yourself comfortable, Chevalier," said Callum to Malcolm. "For this could be a long night!" Callum joined in the singing, as the chorus brought the house down once more:

> "*An' Charlie, he's my darlin',*
> *My darlin', my darlin',*
> *Charlie, he's my darlin',*
> *The young Chevalier!*"

CHAPTER 33

———◆———

"HEADS!" SHOUTED RUARIDH, AS A beer mug arced through the air. Revellers scattered in all directions, and the tankard smashed harmlessly down onto Gregor's head, ale splashing all around.

"Scots artillery!" said Tam, hurrying Wee Tam into a quiet alcove. It was partitioned from the main body of the inn by a wooden screen, and still remained relatively free from open swordplay and broken glass.

"You're worried, aren't you, son?" said Tam, rubbing Wee Tam's head. "I can see it. What's on your mind? You think I'm goin' away to war with Souter Johnnie, an' his fine new friends here? Or 'Stupid Johnnie', as he seems to be called now! To fight for Prince Cherlie. Well- do you think I should?" He looked into Wee Tam's eyes. Wee Tam just looked trustingly back at him. He had more faith in Tam than his adoptive father did in himself, Tam thought. They might not have been related by blood, but you wouldn't have known it. They both shared the same frank, open countenance, that some people in the village found so unnerving. But not as disturbing as they found Wee Tam's silence. Why was everyone so obsessed with constant chatter, Tam wondered. Wouldn't Alloway, and the wider world too, be a better place for a few more folk thinking more than they spoke?

"Does a man have a responsibility to fight for his rightful king?" he said at last. "For there's no doubt that's what Prince Cherlie is… An' that's what Johnnie- what everyone here- seems to be sayin'. Even Callum, who's really the most sensible o' the lot of them! But then he's

171

a soldier. A warrior. He doesnae' know any other way. Whilst me, I'm just a farmer..." He looked at Wee Tam again. If there was an answer in his deep eyes now, it was more than Tam could do to discern it. "An' a father. So what comes first? What comes first, Tammie?"

Another peal of raucous singing echoed over the partition and around the alcove.

"Well, perhaps that's enough thinkin' for one night!" said Tam, ruffling Wee Tam's hair again. "We'll no' be leavin' the night, anyway! An' I'm sure this rebellion o' theirs can wait till the mornin'!"

Tam sang along with the other revellers, as he span Wee Tam around in a haphazard reel. Wee Tam smiled at Tam's clowning, but immediately assumed his normal grave expression when someone swept into the alcove, with a tell-tale shimmer of green silk.

"May I cut in?" the Cutty Sark asked Wee Tam, curtseying demurely. Wee Tam looked at her in alarm, instinctively cowering back behind Tam.

"It's my prerogative..." said Tam.

Nannie looked at him questioningly. Again he found himself almost unable to think- to breathe- in her intoxicating presence.

"He's leadin' the dance..." Tam said.

"Well then, my lady?" Nannie asked Tam, laughing.

"It's hard to dance with the devil on your back..." said Tam.

"What?" said Nannie, startled by his words. "What do you mean, Tam?"

"I'm no' really sure..." said Tam. "Just a feelin'... But you go on ahead, an' we'll maybe catch you up..."

"I'm no' fallin' for that one!" said Nannie, regaining her composure almost as quickly as it had deserted her. But to Tam's relief- and his despair- they were interrupted.

"Tam O'Shanter!" cried Hielan' Mary, bundling into the alcove. "So here ye are! Ah've been lookin' for you everywhere! Jeanie's quite beside herself, wantin' to see you! Come wi' me, this instant!"

"Mary- what are you doin' here?" said Tam, bewildered. "I cannae' come wi' you- I've got Wee Tam wi' me, an' I've to look after him the night…"

"Och, I can mind him for you, nae' bother!" said Mary impatiently. "Just you go and find Jeanie!"

"An' who might this Jeanie be, when she's at home?" said Nannie.

"You're quite the Highland Don Juan, aren't ye, Tam O'Shanter!" said Mary to Tam, looking the Cutty Sark up and down as though she had never seen her before in her life. "Just you make sure that Jeanie doesnae' catch you wi' your fancy woman here- whoever she may be- because she is the jealous type!"

Nannie raised an eyebrow.

"Well, well- what has the cat dragged in here, then?" she said, playing her own part in the charade. "Have ye come to mop the floor, dearie? So wise of you to wear those old rags for the job!"

"Och, c'mon now, ladies…" said Tam helplessly, trying to cover Wee Tam's ears.

"Nae' need tae' unleash the dog o' war, Tam!" said Mary. "I meant it as a compliment! Besides, we're tired of bein' the only sluts in the village…"

"No need to fret, we'll do our best to find a young buck for you, dearie!" said Nannie condescendingly. "Just you be patient, for they're no' quite so particular once they've had a drink or two…"

"Aye, I can see that!" said Mary with spirit.

"C'mon now, ladies, never mind a' that now!" said Tam, consumed with confusion. Wee Tam was beside himself with embarrassment. "I just want to speak to, eh…"

"Nannie!" said the Cutty Sark.

"Eh?" said Tam, his head spinning.

"That's my name, Tam! But then I think you knew that already, didn't you?" said the Cutty Sark, smiling.

"Ooh, Nannie, is it?" said Hielan' Mary. "La-di-dah! Well then, my fine Nannie, ye're welcome to him!" she said with dignity.

"Nannie- Nannie Goldie?" stuttered Tam.

"Nannie Goldie! Yes, that's the name- the name I used to go by..." said the Cutty Sark. "Many years ago! Before I left all of this behind me. Before I became- what I am today..."

"An' what are you now?" said Tam.

He looked at Wee Tam, who was staring at Nannie in shock, as though he had seen a ghost.

"What do you think, Tam?" said the Cutty Sark with a smile. "Let your heart tell you! If it dares to, even now!"

"I could certainly tell ye what ye are!" said Hielan' Mary, as she flounced out of the alcove.

"Wait- Mary..." said Tam, catching her arm. "Will you no' look after the bairn for a mo', sweetheart? I must speak to Nannie! For Hosea's sake, if nothin' else... He's been waitin' so long for her to come back!"

Wee Tam looked at Tam in silent horror, shaking his head, but Tam could hardly focus on him- or on anything except Nannie. His mind was reeling more furiously than the whirling dancers in the inn, infatuation, shock and whisky kindling a raging fire in his head.

"You entrust him to me, Tam?" said Hielan' Mary.

"Aye, of course, love!" said Tam. "I just need a minute wi' Nannie here. She's Hosea Goldie's lost daughter, Mary!"

"Is that a fact?" said Mary, without much interest. "Farmer Goldie from Mungo's Inn? That's a turn-up for the books! Well then, I'll keep an eye on the bairn for you, Tam, just this once- but you make sure you come an' find Jeanie when you're done here, like I said! Ye great ladies' man, ye! Come along wi' you now, son, come along wi' Mary..." she said, as she bustled Wee Tam out of the alcove. He looked back at Tam imploringly, but it was all just a blur to Tam.

"Alone at last!" said Nannie. "I didn't expect to find you here..."

"Aye, you did," said Tam.

"Well- perhaps you're right!" said Nannie, laughing. "An' is that so wrong, then?"

"I'm no' sure yet..." said Tam. "That kind of depends on... Well, what're you doing here, Nannie?"

"Here in this inn?" she said, teasingly.

"Back here with us!" cried Tam. "An' after all these years! None of it makes any sense! I can hardly even believe it's you, except that- except somehow I know it is. An' does your father even know you're here? Have you been to see him?"

"He's no' my father anymore, Tam," said Nannie quietly. "I told you- I left all of this behind me a long time ago!"

"Aye- so you said," said Tam, more confused than ever. "But you're here now. You're back with us!"

She put her hand up to his face.

"I'm here for you, Tam!" she said. "To take you with me! Can't you feel that?"

Tam could feel everything- and nothing. His senses were turning cartwheels in his head. He pushed her hand away, trying to clear his crazed thoughts in some way, any way possible.

"For me?" he said. "But what is it- about me?"

"It's everythin' about you, Tam! You and this curious old country of ours... It's what I see in you. You're- you're part of it."

"Salt of the earth, eh?" said Tam.

"But you are, Tam, you understand it! You feel it. We're standin' at a crossroad- and I want to know which way you're goin' to go."

Tam gave a start at the familiar words.

"Was that- was that really you, Nannie?" he said. "Who spoke to me out on the moor? In my croft? But the words came- from out of the sky..."

"Your heart has a voice too, Tam," Nannie said gently. "You just need to listen to it. I can help you find your own way!"

"So which way do you want me to go?" he said desperately.

"I want to tear down these rulers and their rules- and return to the old freedoms. The old Scotland! And I think that's what you want too."

Tam rubbed his temples feverishly.

"Look, I'm no' what you'd call a... a pious man," he said. "But I do have certain principles. Beliefs."

"And what is it that you believe in, Tam?" said the Cutty Sark, smiling. "In life? In love? In happiness? You don't even know what they really are, none of you do! You've been deceived, by the greatest trick of them all! Here you live, like fabricated ships in a bottle. You can see the elements around you, but you can't feel them- can't even touch them..." She put her hand on his cheek again, and this time he didn't move it away. "There's a king, and a law, and a church, and they tell you exactly who you are, what you want- what you can have, and what you can dream of! But they're just part of the deception, can't you see? They're just an illusion, a child's play-thing, ready to be washed away like sand-castles on the beach when the tide comes in. Man-made institutions can never hold out against the real world forever. Against our world. Love it, hate it, desire it, fear it- but you can't escape it!"

Tam stared at her, fascinated, as though seeing her through all her beauty for the first time.

"How- how did you get this way?" he said.

"I broke the bottle, Tam!" she said. "I was taken from it. And at first I was scared too. I was no different from you- I was just wee Nannie Goldie!" She laughed. "A human child... How funny it sounds now! To think that I might have lived my whole life in blindness, wallowin' in that tiny village of yours... I might have got married- I might have married you, Tam!"

"If only!" said Tam. But even then he could hardly conceive of such a parallel universe. "So what are you now- a Jacobite? A rebel?"

"A rebel!" She laughed scornfully. "These so-called rebels of yours have their own king for us too! The only change they want tae' make is one rich, in-bred fool for another! But of course you know that already, don't you, Tam? They don't even dare to show their Old Pretender to us, the would-be King James Stuart, for they know how ill-equipped he is to win the people's hearts! He too is an illusion, and a sad one at that."

She laughed again, and gestured through the little window in the partition towards the Prince, still holding extravagant court at the bar.

"Instead they send us this ludicrous princeling! They think his pretty face and Continental posin' will be enough to woo Scotland to his cause! But can you really imagine that vain peacock rulin' this country- rulin' any country?"

Even in the midst of his turmoil, Tam felt ridiculously relieved that she held the Prince in such low regard.

"Well, at least he has somethin' of the loveable rogue about him!" said Nannie, giving Tam another stab of jealousy. "It would all be quite amusin', were it not for the sinister truth behind it... For they have a religion for us too, you know! An old one, as they think it. Like children, who can't imagine a time before their own short lives began. Poor Scotland- stuck between the devil and the deep blue sea..."

"I'm startin' to see which one you prefer..." said Tam.

"Oh, don't play the simpleton, Tam!" she said. "There's a bit of both in all us, you of all people must have accepted that long ago! An' all I know is that when I lose myself in the dark places in my heart I feel- alive..."

Tam stared at her anxiously.

"But what if one day- there're only dark places left?" he said.

"It's no' easy to forget everything you know- to open your eyes to your own soul," she said.

"But if you do?" he insisted.

Nannie put out her other hand slowly, and stroked his face.

"Then you're free! You're born again. Changed. Like me, Tam!"

She turned away from him.

"It takes time to understand- I know that. But everythin' you know about the spiritual world- everythin' you have been taught- it's all a lie!"

"But why?" said Tam.

"Because they want to hide the great truth from you, of course!" she cried. "That life is simpler- freer- at the extremes of existence. For once you get there, you can never be controlled again! You will never serve their turn- will never let them limit you again, with promises of a better world, if you'll just know your place in this one! An' those are the places we inhabit, Tam- the unexplained edges of the world. Far beyond the world of men."

"Until you fall off?" said Tam.

She turned back to him and gazed right through him, with something more than curiosity.

"Are you afraid of heights, Tam?" she said. "Or just reachin' them?"

Despite himself, Tam felt himself falling deeper under her spell. He swayed towards her, taking her in his arms, drawn by some irresistible impulse- not even sure what he planned to do.

"There are no limits, Tam!" she said. "No gods, no masters!"

Suddenly Tam awoke from his trance, as though he had been dashed into the depths of the Sea of Moyle itself.

"It was you!" he cried. "It was you, all along! You're- you're a witch!"

Nannie laughed, pulled away and slipped out of the alcove. Tam tried to follow her, only to find someone blocking his path, looming over him like a great, dark shadow.

CHAPTER 34

—◆—

"OCH, C'MON, KING BILLY, YE dozy ox!" said Farmer Goldie, pulling vainly at the big Highland Cow's halter. They were ambling down Ayr High Street, headed for home-just like any other market day. "Come along wi' ye, ye great dafty! Have ye no' caused me enough trouble for one day already? I could've had a pretty price for you at market, if you'd no' made such a beast o' yourself- ransackin' the ale stall like that!"

Billy just bellowed and strained even harder on his halter.

"Aye, you may well say so, William!" said Goldie bitterly. "Two whole shillin's worth o' beer ye put away, and after market closin' too- they would probably jist have thrown it away, if you hadnae' robbed them in broad daylight like that!"

King Billy lowed repentantly, but Goldie was not to be so easily mollified.

"Na na, ye made a regular exhibition o' the both of us carryin' on like that! As though we dinnae' ken how to behave ourselves in public in Alloway! An' d'ye think I don't know where ye want to go now?"

Man and beast looked up at the sign of the Jolly Beggars' Inn.

"Help ma' boab, is Mungo's Inn no' good enough for you any more, Billy?" said Goldie, in despair. "Ye think ye must be gallivantin' away to Ayr, and drinkin' in a fancy, up-town gin-palace like this? Well, I'm no' havin' it, William! It's as simple as that!"

But suddenly Farmer Goldie was uncomfortably aware that he and King Billy were no longer alone. He looked around, to see a black-cloaked figure watching them in silence.

"Who- who are you, sir?" said Goldie nervously. "Make yoursel' known, if ye please!"

The cloaked figure didn't say a word, but simply pushed back the hood of his cloak by way of answer.

"Merry Andrew!" Goldie murmured in horror. "Whit- whit do you want wi' me?"

Again Merry Andrew did not reply. He took a step closer to Goldie, and extended a pale hand towards the Jolly Beggars' Inn.

Goldie took a deep breath, nodded and swung open the front doors of the inn. King Billy needed no second invitation. He trotted gleefully into the inn, followed by his reluctant owner and finally by Merry Andrew himself.

"What's that ye've got wi' you there, sir?" said the doorkeeper to Goldie, as they passed the threshold of the outer door.

"Whit's the matter wi' you, son?" said Goldie. "Ye no' seen a coo' before? You city boys, I ask ye!"

King Billy still had a halter around his neck but, with the intoxicating scent of ale in his nostrils, he accelerated hard in the direction of the bar, dragging Goldie along behind him at a rate of knots. Goldie tugged back ineffectually on the rope, but he was no match for King Billy's weight- or his visceral thirst for beer. Thrown off balance, Goldie careered straight into a slim figure in a dark cloak, who was just leaving the inn at the head of a small group of travellers.

"My apologies, miss..." he muttered, letting go of the halter. King Billy quietly disappeared into the interior of the inn, in search of his usual tipple.

"Pray do not trouble yourself, sir..." said the leader of the group, refastening her cloak. But Goldie was already scrutinising the company.

"Now wait just a minute!" he said. "Is that no'- Tam O'Shanter? Wee Tam! What are you doin' here without your parents, son? Where's Tam

Senior? An' who are these people you're out with? What is goin' on here, Ma'am?" said Goldie, reaching out to Wee Tam. Wee Tam eagerly seized Goldie's hand in his, almost sobbing with relief. "No one's goin' anywhere, until someone tells me whit's goin' on here!" said Goldie defiantly. "I'm a friend o' the family, an' I'll no' stand by and see any harm come to this poor wee lad!"

Nannie didn't speak, but just let her cloak fall open, pushing back the hood from her dark hair. Goldie stared at her in shock- in disbelief.

"Nannie…" gasped Goldie, letting Wee Tam's hand drop. Hielan' Mary immediately took a tight grip on it herself.

"Is it really you, my darlin' girl?" said Goldie. "After all these years, is it really you?"

His sallow cheeks were ridged with tears.

"Yes, father," said Nannie. "It's your Nannie- what remains of her. I'm back."

———————

CHAPTER 35

"Leaving so soon, my dear Farmer O'Shanter?" said Rannoch, as Tam tried to brush past him. Tam didn't answer. He tried again to slip by Rannoch, but this time Rannoch took him firmly by the elbow and led him back into the alcove.

"One of those nights, eh?" said Rannoch, laughing as he offered Tam a glass. Tam looked at it suspiciously, before waving it away.

"No, I'm alright, pal- I had one earlier," he said. "Where's Souter Johnnie?"

"He's swearing allegiance to his Prince, of course!" said Rannoch. "It seems that you two have- different- views on that particular subject..."

"It didnae' seem that way till you turned up- an' started turnin' him into a fanatic!" said Tam.

"But then sometimes there is no middle road- didn't you say so yourself, Farmer O'Shanter? So the question is- which way are you going to go?"

Tam stared at Rannoch.

"Tick, tock, tick, tock..." said Rannoch, offering the glass to Tam once more.

This time Tam took it from him, but without taking a sip he poured it out onto the floor in front of Rannoch.

"You know somethin', Rannoch- if that even is your name..." said Tam. "You're no' the first person tae' ask me that tonight. But I'll tell you the answer- right after you tell me who you really are!"

They stared at each other in silence for a moment, the hunch on Rannoch's back shifting and squirming.

"Aye, I didnae' think so!" said Tam. "So if you'll excuse me, I'm goin' to find my friend…"

Tam stumbled off into the main room of the inn. Rannoch watched him impassively for a moment, and then followed him.

Tam stormed up to Johnnie at the bar, head buzzing with booze and confusion, doubt and whisky obscuring his mind with swirling copper and steel clouds. Tam recklessly brushed aside the group of unruly Highlanders clustered around the Souter, determined to have it out with him, but before he could start speaking he was pulled back again by a sharp tug at his sleeve.

"Tick, tock…" said Rannoch, smirking. "You can't sit on the fence forever, Master O'Shanter…"

But even as he spoke, he was looking over Tam's shoulder into the great cracked mirror that hung precariously above the bar of the inn. Tam shrugged him off angrily, but Rannoch just pulled at his coat again. This time Tam gave him a hard shove away. Rannoch, still watching the mirror, smirked again and then suddenly let Tam go, moving round the bar to stand next to Johnnie.

The reflection in the mirror could have been a still life painting, thought Rannoch, as Goldie and his long-lost daughter stood face to face in the doorway of the Jolly Beggars' Inn.

"When were ye goin' to come an' see your mother and me?" said Goldie eventually.

"Soon, father," said Nannie. "But there's somethin' I have to do first. Somethin' important!"

"But what is it?" said Goldie. "What could possibly be so important that it couldnae' wait, after all these lost years? After all this sorrow! And wi' Wee Tam?"

Nannie kissed her father's brow. He closed his eyes.

"Just give me one night, father- after all these years. You have to trust me. You have to give me this gift. For this is somethin' I need to do."

"An' then you can come home?" said Goldie desperately.

"Aye, father," she said. "Then I will be at home forever."

"Very well, then…" said Goldie, his shoulders slumping.

Hielan' Mary and Kirkton Jean swept Wee Tam past him and out onto the High Street, rushing over the cobbles.

"When will I see you again, Nannie?" said Goldie.

"I cannot see that yet, father," said Nannie. "But you should know that I never wanted to leave you- you or Mother! They took me- they took me against my will. They took me at the Auld Kirk, and they changed me."

"I knew it!" said Goldie, the tears streaming down his face.

"I always knew it! That you never meant to leave us! And we've never stopped lovin' you, Nannie, no' for one day! Why, when I tell your mother that I've seen you… She's kept believin' in you, through these lonely, these heart-breakin' years! That you'd come back at last."

Now Nannie wiped a tear from her own eye with her cloak. She tried to hide it, but another instantly took its place.

"Don't think badly of me, father!" she said. "Whatever you should come to hear of me, don't think badly of me! For I have seen things- I have lived a life- that none of you can hope to understand! But one day- one day, all this may come to make sense to you. An' part of me will always be your Wee Nannie! Wee Anne Goldie."

Goldie nodded, stupefied by emotion- and by hope.

"I believe you, Nannie!" he said. "You're a good girl, you always were- you're our precious Nannie! You've come back to us once, and you'll come back to us again, wherever ye've been- whatever ye've done!"

But as Rannoch watched her in the mirror behind the bar of the inn, he saw that she cast only the barest reflection in it. The changeling from the world of Man had but little purchase on it now, and even that could not long survive the meeting of the three changelings. Nannie wrapped her cloak around her again, and disappeared into the night.

CHAPTER 36

———◆———

"WELL THEN, SOUTER JOHNNIE!" SAID Tam.

"Well then!" said Johnnie belligerently. "You heard the man- it's decision time, Tam!"

"You too?" said Tam. "Did he put you up to this? Is that what this is all about?"

"It's no' like that, Tam!" said Johnnie. "The question is: Are you for us- or against us?

"Who's us, then?" said Tam. "'Cause I can see two of you, for a start..."

"It's a simple enough question!" said the Souter angrily.

"You think?" said Tam, rubbing his eyes. "Because it seems to me that if the whole country is ready to rip itself apart over it, there must be at least two sides to the story! Take this Rannoch fellow of yours- the one thing that's clear as day about him, is that he has his own agenda! You're no' tellin' me that a scunner like that is willin' to risk his sly old neck for Royal Cherlie?"

"For the last time, Tam, this is no' about Rannoch!" shouted Souter Johnnie. "It's about you and me. About old allegiances- old loyalties. So just tell me where you stand- you owe me that at least!"

"Owe you, Johnnie?" said Tam, tears welling up in his eyes. "Since when were there ever debts between us two?"

Johnnie thumped his fist down on the bar.

"Since you gave up on everythin' we ever believed in- your Highland roots; your Jacobite creed; and your Catholic faith! You're nothin' but a turncoat, Tam- a Hanover rat- a rotten Hanover rat!"

"I'm a what?" said Tam. "I'm no' wastin' my time with this nonsense!"

He pushed Johnnie away from him, heart-broken, and headed straight for the bar to drown his sorrows.

"Tam!" said Johnnie, already repentant. But before he could go after him, Rannoch put a restraining hand on his shoulder.

"Leave him, Johnnie!" hissed Rannoch. "Leave him to stew in his own juices for a while! For we have far more important things to discuss now..."

"Like what?" said Johnnie, curious in spite of himself.

"I'm glad you ask..." said Rannoch with a smile. "For a start, the Prince has been asking me about supplies for his Royal Army. Between the two of us, it seems that I'm to replace old Malcolm Stewart as the Royal Quartermaster General. A new broom, and all that..."

"Never mind the brooms, Rannoch!" said Johnnie eagerly. "He'll be needin' shoes!"

"Indeed- shoes and boots, and in vast numbers! And there is talk of a lucrative supply contract- for someone with the right political convictions, of course... I have a little capital that I could put up to support such a venture- it's perfect, a chance to do our part for the dear, darling Prince, and to make our own fortunes into the bargain! Think of it, my dear Johnnie," said Rannoch, pouring Johnnie another brimming glass of whisky. "You can make a difference, make a fortune, and escape from the wretched obscurity of Alloway forever! By the time you come back here, you'll be a duke! Lord John Davidson of Alloway..."

"An' what about Tam?" said Johnnie, hesitating for a moment.

"He wants no part in greatness, Johnnie- can't you see that?" said Rannoch. "I know fear when I see it, and he's desperately afraid- afraid of what Scotland can become. Of what you can become! He's holding you back now, just as he's held you back for all these years... The truth is that some people have no stomach for glory- or for what it takes to achieve it!"

"Then let's drink- to glory!" cried Johnnie, his eyes shining.

"To glory!" said Rannoch. "Why not? It has always served me well enough…"

CHAPTER 37

———◆———

THE BAND'S RANKS WERE BEING decimated, like the *Gardes Françaises* at the Battle of Fontenoy. Only this time it was shots of whisky rather than grape-shot that were doing all the damage. Unaccustomed to the traditional Highland tribute of whisky for the piper, one by one the heroic Lowland bards tumbled off their stools, blind drunk and temporarily tone deaf. For a while the last fiddler fought a desperate rearguard action, John Barleycorn inspiring him to greater heights of virtuosity, but finally even he could take no more. His bow fell silent, and he fell asleep where he sat.

"*Ma foi!*" shouted the Prince from the bar, each arm around a local lovely. "If music be the food of love, then play on! My kingdom for another song, *mes braves!*"

Even as he spoke, there was a swelling ripple of sound from the corner of the inn. The Prince looked around in astonishment, as a lone piper skirled his pipes and then ripped into a rousing tune. The wild, magical music swirled around the room, kindling with the booze to madden the drinkers.

"*C'est magnifique!*" shouted the Prince, in ecstasies as he saw the party reigniting, and the spirits of his troops soaring before his eyes. "You may name your own reward, *Maestro!* What is your name, *amico mio?*" he shouted to the piper.

The new musician didn't answer, his cheeks puffed out with exertion. Instead he redoubled his efforts, filling the room with sound, until it seemed that the throbbing walls must burst asunder- or the very roof of the inn fly off, to release the pressure. The candle-light pranced around the room in a crazy reel of will-o'-the-wisps, distorted by the clouds of dust melting down from the ceiling like Hebridean mist. The Highlanders looked at each other in wild surmise, then started smashing tankards against the walls in time with the swirling strains of music, sending ale cascading up into the air, spattering the ceiling and soaking the revellers' hair and plaids.

"*Bravo, bravo, Maestro!*" cried the Prince.

The piper smiled, squeezing the bag of the pipes harder, and then really let rip. Johnnie stared in amazement, as he was almost deafened by the din. To him, the piper needed no introduction. It was Merry Andrew. But before he or the Prince could say another word, the inn erupted in mad, anarchic dancing. The Highlanders were leaping up and down on the dance-floor like madmen, careering into each other like rutting stags. Ruaridh was mounted on King Billy's back, riding the great ox around the room, bowling other revellers over like skittles. Absalom the monkey swung from the lanterns above their heads, shrieking wildly, pulling hair and biting undefended ears whenever the opportunity presented itself. The Prince shrugged his shoulders, and then joined the insane reel with a vengeance, climbing up onto the bar and throwing himself off it, only to be caught in the arms of his adoring subjects and hoisted back up again.

"Restore me to my throne, Ayr!" he cried. "Lift me up where I belong!"

CHAPTER 38

———◆———

FARMER GOLDIE STOOD ALONE OUTSIDE the Jolly Beggars' Inn, looking out into the darkness after his long-lost daughter.

"Nannie! Oh, my poor Nannie..." he moaned quietly. The pain of her abduction all those long years ago washed over him like a flood. But this time there was a new torment too- one that he wasn't even ready to face up to yet. Suddenly Goldie cried out and clasped his head in his hands.

"What have you done, Hosea Goldie?" he shouted. "What have you done?"

He ran back into the inn, searching desperately for Tam, seizing King Billy's halter rope along the way.

"Tam! Tam O'Shanter! Where are you, son?" he bawled, and ran straight into Ruaridh Stewart, now dismounted and dancing manically to the hypnotic bagpipe music.

Ruaridh grabbed Goldie by the collar and lifted him right off his feet, pulling him into the direct glare of his wild, staring eyes. Goldie shuddered in terror, involuntarily closing his own eyes.

"Open your eyes, Lowlander!" roared Ruaridh, shaking him like a rag doll.

Goldie gulped. With the utmost unwillingness, he forced his eyes open, only to see Ruaridh's face melt into a beatific grin.

"Music tae' go insane to, eh, pal!" yelled Ruaridh over the din, setting him back down and giving him a monstrous clap across the shoulders. "Ah haven't felt this good since Auld King James came over in 1715!"

Goldie reeled forward from the blow, coughing and spluttering. He smiled nervously at Ruaridh and then shuffled onwards, only to tread on the most sensitive part of Gregor, still prostrate on the ground after his disastrous drinking contest with Souter Johnnie.

Gregor bellowed in pain and lashed out with his brogued foot, sending Goldie flying into a table laden with mugs and glasses. With the halter rope still in Goldie's hand, King Billy was jerked around in an arc, knocking over dozens of dancers as he went. The rope itself performed a clean sweep of the neighbouring tables, sending bottles crashing and beer splashing everywhere. King Billy careered around the inn like a hairy juggernaut, gleefully lapping up the spillage on all sides. Intent on finding more ale, he accidentally caught the breeks of one of the dancers on the tip of one of his horns, sending him toppling down onto Gregor on the floor.

The chain reaction went full circle as Gregor instinctively threw out a boot again, this time provoking a violent brawl as the recipient collided heavily with Ruaridh. Ruaridh hit him with the closest thing that came to hand, which happened to be Absalom, hanging by his tail from a lantern. The little monkey yelped and spat with rage as Ruaridh seized his tail and swung him with all his might into the face of the offending party. In the ensuing confusion Highlanders, Lowlanders and monkey alike indiscriminately assaulted and bit everyone who came close enough. Goldie cowered on the floor beside the prone form of Gregor, terrified by the simian shrieks and splintering tables, chairs and bottles all around him. Absalom leapt up onto Ruaridh's head, grabbing tufts of unruly red hair in his gnarled little fists, and bit his ear viciously. Duly revenged, he nimbly jumped up onto the iron candleholder above them, chattering with glee. Ruaridh roared in pain and anger, and swung his broadsword recklessly at Absalom. Absalom sprung back down to the floor and Ruaridh missed him by inches, smashing the heavy sword into the ironwork, literally sending sparks flying through the smoky interior of the inn.

"*Iosa Crìosd*!" said Callum. "Naked steel in an inn? This'll no' do at all!"

He picked up a chair and neatly broke it over Ruaridh's back, laying him out cold. Ruaridh dropped onto the floor like a sack of potatoes, collapsing right on top of Farmer Goldie, pinning him inextricably in place between himself and Gregor.

"Tam! Tam O'Shanter! Help! Help me!" cried Goldie despairingly, as revellers flooded in from all sides of the bar to take their own parts in the conflict. "There's somethin' I must tell ye!" Broken chair-legs and bottles clattered together just above his head. Absalom gloated over his fallen foe, Ruaridh, pointing and leaping up and down next to him, until King Billy hove into view and caught Absalom's waistcoat with a horn, pitching the monkey right across the room. He landed at the feet of a group of stalwart Ayrshire farm labourers, who examined him curiously, with a mixture of fascination and horror.

"What'n Kilmarnock Fair are you then, sir?" said the boldest labourer, prodding the furry chest suspiciously with his finger. "Some kinda' foreigner?"

Over in the far corner of the inn, an old soldier clad in ragged scarlet regimentals dozed on in a shabby armchair. Sodger Jo was serenely oblivious to the tumult raging all around him, until he suddenly copped a flying pint-pot straight on the head. Revived by the ale trickling down his face into the corner of his mouth, Sodger Jo sat bolt upright, magically energised. He struggled awkwardly to his feet and then jostled through the crowd, purloining a beer-mug with practised ease as he went.

He dragged himself up onto the bar, sending bottles flying everywhere, and then smashed his tankard against the ceiling. Dark Scots ale poured down from the bar like black rain.

For a moment Sodger Jo simply stood staring defiantly at the revellers, blood-shot eyes blinking, slowly beating his tankard against the ceiling. Then Merry Andrew caught sight of him, and stopped piping. Sodger Jo began to sway to the rhythm of his own drumming and, without any further preamble, he roared straight into song:

> *"I am a Son of Mars, who have been in many wars,*
> *And show my cuts and scars wherever I come!"*

Here Sodger Jo pulled up his shirt, revealing a much-scarred torso, to cheers from the revellers- although whether the wounds were from His Majesty's wars or tavern brawls was the subject of much conjecture. The one thing that everyone in the market agreed upon was that only a silver bullet could kill him.

> *"This here for a Wench, and that other in a trench,*
> *When welcomin' the French at the sound of a drum!"*

The Highlanders stopped brawling, yelled their approval and then started dancing maniacally to Sodger Jo's song. The beer was flying like sea-spray, King Billy the Highland Cow raising merry hell as he followed the long slicks of ale on the floor, drinking them up greedily, tripping over and barging into dancers and bystanders alike. Tables and chairs were smashed like matchsticks in the maelstrom, Billy himself sending heavy furniture flying with shakes of his great shaggy head. And still Sodger Jo sang on:

> *"My 'prenticeship I passed, where my leader breathed his last,*
> *When the bloody die was cast at the field of Blenheim!*
> *And I served out my trade when the gallant game was played;*
> *And the Moro low was laid at the sound of the drum!"*

The crowd roared again. Propped up against a beam in the corner of the inn, Tam had achieved his objective of drowning his sorrows so successfully that he could hardly stand up. He watched Sodger Jo, singing his heart out up on the bar. Tam smiled crookedly, revelling in the carnage.

"Ah'd forgotten what freedom sounds like…" he muttered to himself.

But then Johnnie spotted him and made his way through the crowd towards him.

"We're goin' to war, Tam- for death or glory!" he shouted excitedly.

"I never asked for either!" said Tam, slurring his words. "This war's nothin' to do with me and mine. It's for rich men to get richer- lords to get more titles. Well, it's no' in my name!"

Johnnie shook his head, the joy of the moment ebbing away for him.

"So you'll just stand by then, Tam?" he said. "You'll desert your prince, in the very moment when he's thrown himself on the mercy of his people?"

"I've nothin' against the lad!" said Tam. "I told him so myself. But you should look before you leap! He understands it well enough himself, so I'm no' sure how you dinnae'- he's his livin' to earn, and I've got mine. And if you know what's good for you, you'll stay here and earn yours too, Souter Johnnie!"

"I've never heard of any good comin' to a man from abandonin' his honour!" said Johnnie bitterly. "But maybe you'll tell me aboot that at the end of all this, eh?"

"Aye, an' I just hope we both live to see the day…" said Tam. "For there's many a pretty fellow who'll no' come back from this war alive, and they'll no' all be English!"

"So that's what this is really about, is it, Tam?" said Johnnie scornfully. "Rannoch was right! You're afraid of greatness- an' feared to risk your precious neck! I should'ae known! I s'pose I just expected better from you, after all these years…"

Before Tam could answer, Rannoch appeared, proffering more drinks to Tam and Johnnie.

"Drown the quarrel, eh, lads?" he said.

"This is between friends, Rannoch!" said Tam sharply. "Who asked you to poke your neb in, anyway?"

"Oh, I never go anywhere uninvited…" said Rannoch.

"Is that right?" said Tam. "Then why don't you just keep your advice- and your drink- to yourself?"

"And here was me thinking you were a man of peace, Farmer O'Shanter!" said Rannoch slily.

"What d'you mean by that?" said Tam.

"Well, you're no' exactly wearin' your courage on your sleeve tonight, are you?" said Johnnie.

"Sometimes it takes more courage to do your real duty- to stay with your family- than just be blown any way the wind blows…" said Tam.

"And which way does it blow?" said Rannoch.

Tam looked at him.

"Ye keep askin' me that, Rannoch- and I've asked you: Who are you? Tell me now, for I'll no' ask you a third time!"

Tam squared up to Rannoch, who laughed mirthlessly.

"You might not have to, my friend!"

Before Souter Johnnie could intervene, the crowd roared again as Sodger Jo half-hopped, half-hobbled along the top of the bar and then burst into another stirring verse of his song:

"What tho' with hoary locks, I must stand the winter shocks,
Beneath the woods and rocks oftentimes for a home!
When the tother bag I sell and the tother bottle tell,
I could meet a troop of hell at the sound of a drum!"

Song over, Sodger Jo stayed up on the bar, beating the rhythm with his tankard, working the crowd into a fine frenzy.

"What a disgraceful display!" said Malcolm scornfully to the Prince. "These old soldiers think of nothing beyond the next mouthful of whisky- it's pitiful!"

"No, my friend- it's magnificent!" shouted the Prince, shoving the dancers in front of him roughly out of the way. "This veteran and I shall stand shoulder-to-shoulder, in the heroic struggles to come!" He jumped nimbly back up onto the bar, bowed theatrically to the crowd and then danced a shambolic can-can, arm-in-arm with Sodger Jo. The inn erupted into cheers, then fell silent as the Prince gestured for quiet.

"We stand on the very brink of greatness, my friends!" shouted the Prince, clapping Sodger Jo heartily on the back. Sodger Jo teetered for a moment, and then toppled off the bar backwards, smashing glasses and bottles into smithereens as he fell.

"It's the way he would have wanted it!" said the Prince. "The march on London starts here, *mes braves*! Follow me! Follow me! *Bas agus buaidh, ragazzi!* Death and victory!"

He threw himself down from the bar. Unlike Sodger Jo, the Prince was immediately caught in the upstretched arms of his adoring subjects. They hoisted him high on their shoulders, as Merry Andrew let rip on the pipes, filling the inn with intoxicating music once more.

"So, eh- where're we off to now then, Cherlie?" Callum shouted up at him.

"Come now, Callum!" said the Prince. "Surely there must be a house of ill repute somewhere in Ayrshire?"

They processed out, the Prince ducking his head just in time to avoid being brained on the door-frame by his over-zealous bearers, and the crowd rushed out after him.

All of a sudden, Johnnie and Tam were left alone at the bar.

CHAPTER 39

———

ALONE AT THE BAR- OR almost alone. Just as Johnnie opened his mouth to speak, King Billy blundered past him, hot on the trail of ale.

"What's that bloody animal doin' here?" said Johnnie, laughing in spite of himself.

Tam pointed at the tankard of beer in his hand.

"Right enough!" said Johnnie. "On the swally as usual, eh?" He paused for a moment before he spoke again. "You're no' comin' with us this time, are you, Tammie?"

"No' this time, Johnnie," said Tam.

"So this is it, then?"

"For now! It's like everyone keeps tellin' me," said Tam. "We all have our own paths to follow. And they're tryin' to show me where my path leads too, but when I look, it's just the one that runs alongside their own. Well, our paths have run a long way together, Johnnie- longer than many do in a lifetime- and maybe they'll cross again before the end! But now you tell me your destiny leads you into battle, by way of kings and armies, and other such grand things as that, and that's no' for me! My way is to stay wi' my land, wi' my own folk. An' anyone who wants to stay there wi' me is welcome... But I'll no' ask you to change your heart, Johnnie, for you couldn't- no more'n I could change my own!"

Johnnie threw his arms around Tam, embracing him, just as Rannoch returned to the bar.

"What are you two clowns up to now?" said Rannoch. "Charles Edward will be half way to Fort William by now!"

"Best be off then, eh, Rannoch?" said Tam drily.

"I have unfinished business here..." said Rannoch.

"Any time you want to finish it-just say the word!" said Tam, suddenly bristling. "There's no time like the present, eh?"

"Tam..." said Johnnie. "We're talkin' here, Rannoch. I'll catch you up in a second, alright?"

Rannoch nodded and slunk away, his customary smirk stealing across his face once more. He slipped out of the inn, moving swiftly through the night-shrouded side streets of Ayr, ghosting over cobbles and through dark closes. But he was not alone. Even the man of shadows himself had his own shadow, not missing a step or a turn, stalking him through the night.

"Three's a crowd, eh?" said Johnnie, and they finished their drinks in a companionable silence. Finally, Johnnie put his hand on Tam's shoulder. There were no words left to say. Johnnie shaped to leave, half-turned back and then walked out, leaving Tam standing alone at the long bar.

Almost alone.

"Tam O'Shanter! Is that you?" rasped a hoarse voice. "Over here! Help me, neighbour! I'm suffocatin' down here!"

"Hosea?" said Tam. "Is that you, Farmer Goldie? Where are you, man?"

He started to look for the voice, picking through a heap of wrecked furniture. Now devoid of people, pipers, cows and monkeys, the inn looked as though the Four Horsemen of the Apocalypse had just ridden through it.

"Over here, Tammie!" croaked Goldie. "Quickly, son!"

Finally Tam found him, still wedged in between Gregor and Ruaridh's huge bodies on the floor, gasping for breath.

"It's alright, Hosea, hang in there, pal! We'll have you out of there in a jiffy!" said Tam, straining to roll Ruaridh's unconscious body off

Goldie. He pulled the skinny farmer up to his feet, and then steadied him as he hungrily sucked the air back into his lungs. As soon as Goldie could stand upright, he grabbed Tam's shoulder. He was shaking with emotion.

"They took him, Tam! They took Wee Tam!" he cried. "I should've stopped them… But they took him!"

"Who did, Hosea? You mean Hielan' Mary?" said Tam. "It's alright, I asked her to mind the bairn for a while!"

"No! It was my daughter, Tam!" said Goldie desperately. "My poor Nannie! They're all in it together!"

"Nannie and Mary?" said Tam, a sickening feeling coming over him.

"An' that Kirkton Jean!" said Goldie. "They left together! Now Wee Tam and Nannie are both lost to us, Tam! What'll we do?"

Tam couldn't find the words within him to answer. He wrapped Goldie in his arms, as the old man broke down sobbing, sobbing as though he would never stop, muttering the same phrase over and over again in his misery.

"What is it, Hosea? What are you tryin' to tell me?"

Goldie looked up at him, blinking through his tears.

"The Auld Kirk…" said Goldie. "The Auld Kirk is where you must look for him, Tam! For both of them! For that's where they took her, all those years ago. The Auld Kirk!"

CHAPTER 40

———

CHARLES EDWARD CAREFULLY COMBED HIS lustrous locks, whilst Malcolm, Callum and Souter Johnnie waited for him impatiently outside Poosie Nansie's bawdy-house.

"Bonnie Prince Charlie, eh?" said Callum.

"Bonnie Prince Charlie! I like it, *ragazzo!*" said the Prince. "That's the kind of nick-name that could stick to a man! And let us devoutly hope that the establishment lives up to the same description..."

Poosie Nansie's bawdy-house was located directly above the hostelry of the same name, in a small two-story cottage tucked away on the southern fringe of Ayr. It had its own entrance around the back for the convenience of its patrons, and was overlooked from the rear only by the empty moor between Ayr and Alloway, allowing gentlemen who desired it to make a discreet exit. And most of them did desire it, for everyone in Ayrshire knew that Poosie Nansie's bawdy-house made the Jolly Beggars' Inn look like the General Assembly of the Church of Scotland.

Suddenly there was a loud bellow, and a huge shaggy animal loomed out of the darkness towards them, sniffing them out.

"Ah- this noble beast did us good service at the Jolly Beggars' Inn, did he not?" said the Prince, patting King Billy condescendingly on the head. "He gave that wretched monkey of Rannoch's just exactly what was coming to him- a horn in its scrawny backside! *Dio mio,* I would give a good deal to see that again! What is his name, Stupid Johnnie?"

Johnnie scratched his head awkwardly.

"Och, he's just a coo', Your Highness! I dinnae' ken that he has a Christian name, as such…"

"Come now, my friend," said the Prince impatiently. "So fine a specimen must bear a noble name!"

"Well, they, er, they do call him 'King Billy'…" said Johnnie. "Him bein' orange, an' all… Just a wee joke amongst the farmers, I suppose! They're only simple folk, Your Highness…"

The Prince raised a regal eyebrow.

"He is named after that protestant oaf who deposed my royal grandfather?" he said. "That Hun, that doltish Dutchman, the so-called Prince of Orange? But this is most disturbing, Johnnie! This is nothing short of treasonous! I never heard of such a thing… Let the owner of the beast be brought before me, and he shall be clapped in irons forthwith! He shall be thrashed! He shall be bastinadoed to death!"

"In the name of Good King James, I hereby take the culprit into custody!" said Callum, neatly tying King Billy's halter rope around Poosie Nansie's gate-post. "To be hung by the neck here, until the beast shall come tae' its senses…"

The Prince nodded sternly as he saw royal justice done, and then hurried up the steps to the bawdy-house like a rat up a drainpipe. Callum was about to follow him, when Malcolm prodded a bony forefinger into his chest.

"No' you, man! What are you thinkin' of? You must stay here, as lifeguard and sentry for your one true sovereign!"

"He may need more protectin' up there…" muttered Callum. Nevertheless, he took up his own position at the bottom of the staircase, with a bottle of whisky salvaged from the wreckage of the Jolly Beggars' Inn by his side, and the naked steel of his broadsword lying across his knees.

The Prince crossed himself solemnly at the top of the stairs, and rapped on the heavy door.

"For what we are about to receive- may the Lord make us truly thank-ful!" he said piously, rubbing his hands together in anticipation. "Come on, my bonny lads, the last one in is the Elector of Hanover!"

Malcolm and Johnnie scuttled up the stairs after him.

"Don't do anythin' I wouldn't, lads!" shouted Callum after them, toasting them with a swig from his bottle of whisky. "An' don't go fallin' in love, 'Stupid Johnnie'! All souters love the lassies!"

"As do all princes, mon brave!" cried the Prince, kissing his fingers. "Here's to the prettiest girls in Christendom!"

—

CHAPTER 41

TAM AND MEG CLATTERED DOWN the High Street and onto the Old Alloway Road, heading south out of Ayr as fast as Meg's legs could carry them. Tam could still hear the last strains of song as they reached the Carrick Road:

"When the tother bag I sell and the tother bottle tell,
I could meet a troop of hell at the sound of a drum!"

And then the last lights of Ayr had died away behind them, and there was no sound but the buzzing of angry thoughts in Tam's own mind, tormenting him more than any troop of hell ever could have.

"How could I have left him- an' with them!" thought Tam, spurring Meg on afresh, as they rode hell for leather out into the open country- straight into the eye of the storm.

"Wi' witches! I shoulda' known! Oh, Meg, Meg, how could I have left my own wee boy alone wi' them! You fool, Tam O'Shanter, you stupid fool!"

The conditions on the rough road were as bad as Tam had ever seen, the rain blinding them and the mud thickening with each heavy pace they took.

"What a night, lass!" shouted Tam to Meg. "An' it's gettin' worse, the closer we get to home!" He remembered Goldie's words. "The closer we get to- the Auld Kirk…"

There was a dazzling flash of lightning. Meg snorted and reared up, terrified. Tam stopped to comfort her.

"You must run as you've never run before tonight, Meg girl!" said Tam. "I don't know where we're goin' yet- but God knows that we must get there fast, whatever may lie in our path! We must trust to each other, when all else fails us. For Wee Tam's sake!"

He pulled his blue bonnet further down over his eyes, and urged her on into the darkness.

Meg was running by instinct alone now, light and hope both left far behind them. She stumbled, but somehow managed to find her feet again before they both tumbled down onto the sodden ground. She limped on for a while, keeping the weight off one foot. Tam sensed her discomfort and pulled her up, leapt out of the saddle and lifted up the injured foot to inspect it. He could see nothing in the darkness, but fumbled around with his fingers. Something was wedged between Meg's hoof and horse-shoe.

"What is it, girl?" said Tam, as he pulled it free. He cursed and dropped it, as it cut deep into his fore-finger. "Metal..." he said, peering down at it through the gloom. "A wee pen-knife! What a thing to find out here..." He stooped to pick it up again, and as he did so, his fingers stumbled onto a soggy, fibrous lump, half-buried in the mud. Somehow it too felt man-made. Tam shook the water off it.

"A bible!" he said, opening it. There was a sudden flash of lightning, briefly illuminating the scrawl of a child's spidery handwriting inside the cover:

"COLIN DONAL MCGILLIVRAY. AGE 6."

"Mungo's boy!" said Tam in surprise. "But what in the world was he doin' out here? Why, we must be near..."

Tam peered in vain into the driving rain, and then another flash of lightning lit up a crooked cross across the moor.

"The Auld Kirk!" said Tam. "An' Wee Tam was with him- the day he went missin'." He stood for a moment staring into the blackness, still holding the tiny bible and pocket-knife in his hands. "What happened here, Meg?"

He ran back over to Meg and swung himself up onto her back.

"C'mon, girl!" he cried, spurring her on. "All roads lead to the Auld Kirk!"

CHAPTER 42

SOUTER JOHNNIE STOOD FIDGETTING BY the window of Poosie Nansie's upstairs parlour, watching the rain drive across the moor and rattle into the thick glass. A pretty, dark-haired girl stood in silence behind him, her hand resting on his shoulder in mute sympathy. Two rivulets of water ran down the pane together for a while, before separating and finding their own paths towards the slate roof of the inn below. Johnnie sighed deeply.

Charles Edward was slouching in an antique armchair in the corner of the room with a beautiful red-headed girl, Rowena, sitting on his lap. Seeing the Souter's distress, he gently eased Rowena off himself and onto the chair, and got up to join Johnnie at the window.

"Leave us a moment, Sophie, my dear!" he said to Johnnie's girl, putting his arm round the Souter's shoulder. "There are urgent affairs of state that I must discuss with Stupid Johnnie here..." Sophie curtsied, and went off to speak to Rowena, looking anxiously back at the Souter. "What's the matter, Johnnie?" said the Prince gently. "You're not yourself, *mon brave*! And what's more, you're neglecting poor Sophie terribly, which will never do... If there's one thing a true Jacobite must be, it is chivalrous to the last!"

"Aye, I'm sorry, Cherlie!" said Johnnie hopelessly. "I'm just... I'm worried sick about him! About Tam, I mean. After all we've been through together, to part in anger- and on a night like this! I never should have

206

left him like that, I don't know what came over me… What I wouldn't do to turn back the clock now!"

"Ah, that we can never do, *ragazzo*…" said the Prince sympathetically. "We must live and die in the here and now- you, me and Tam alike!"

He beckoned towards Sophie to come and join them by the window.

"Sometimes it's not easy to let go of the past, *mon brave!*" the Prince said. "To leave home behind. The places and people that we know- however unsatisfactory they may really be! In my case, to give up the exotic pleasures of Versailles for…" The Prince gestured towards the bleak, wind-swept moor outside. "This! But this is my destiny. We soldiers have to move on from our defeats, and march towards the victories that the future holds. And we have to make friends whenever we can, for tomorrow may never come…"

Sophie took Johnnie by the hand.

"Come wi' me, Johnnie…" she said, leading him into the next room after her.

"You really care about him, don't you, Cherlie?" said Rowena admiringly. "About all your brave men!"

"*Madonna mia*, heaven knows I am no saint!" said the Prince, lifting Rowena gallantly back onto his lap. "But never let it be said that I forgot my troops!" He stroked her cheek. "Now, where were we, *ma chérie?*"

CHAPTER 43

———◆———

THE AULD KIRK LOOMED LARGE in front of Wee Tam and the witches. Lit up by great flashes of lightning every few seconds now, it was wreathed in an eery glow that seemed to be spreading through the kirkyard. Wee Tam shuddered at the vivid memories that it brought back. He had felt it even before he saw it. He realised now that it had never really left him, like an aching numbness that had entered his very bones.

"Where are you, Colin?" he thought. "Why did they take you? And why was I spared?"

"Oh, you know where we're goin' now, don't you, my pretty?" said Hielan' Mary. "You know the way, right enough! For you've been here before, haven't you? We saw you! We were here when the other little bird was trapped in our net..."

Wee Tam nodded reluctantly, and suddenly Kirkton Jean's face loomed right up to his.

"It should have been you, too! But there's no one to save you this time, changeling!" she hissed. "We ken what you are!"

Wee Tam shrank back from the anger in her face. The anger, and the hate. But there was something else there too. He suddenly realised that she was afraid of him. He wondered why; and how he could feel it so clearly. What they wanted with him now. But there was no time, no energy, to spare for wonder. He was freezing, soaking wet and exhausted from the disorienting, forced march with the witches, more than two miles from Ayr, straight into the very teeth of the storm.

Kirkton Jean and Hielan' Mary hurried Wee Tam along the path to the Auld Kirk between them, half-leading him and half-carrying him, as though their own master himself were pursuing them. His steps faltered, and Kirkton Jean gave him a rough shove forward. He lost his footing on the muddy ground, sliding down onto his knees. But Hielan' Mary just dragged him back to his feet, and on they went.

The lightning was coming thick and fast, illuminating the serrated tops of the trees, bent double by the wind. The weather-cock on top of the steeple of the Auld Kirk whirled around, faster and faster, and then suddenly changed direction and started rotating in the opposite direction. It struck a chill deep into Wee Tam's heart.

"It's happenin', Jeanie! Just as he told Nannie it would!" Hielan' Mary said excitedly to Kirkton Jean, pointing up at the weather vane when the next bolt of lightning lit it up again. "Rannoch was right all along! The father, givin' up his son of his own free will. Somethin' so unnatural that it will break the old order of things altogether... An' this is it, it must be! It's already begun!"

"C'mon then, Mary!" said Kirkton Jean anxiously. "Right or wrong, he'll no' have got any more patient wi' old age! An' he'll be waitin' for us... We've no time for chatter now!"

As they passed the screen of trees in front of the Auld Kirk, Wee Tam saw that the glow lighting it up came from a ring of great bonfires all around it. Shadowy figures could be seen clustered around the flames. As they approached the Kirk itself, the kirkyard gates slowly ground open before Wee Tam. He tried to dig his heels into the ground, remembering all the horrors of his arrival here with Wee Colin, but his feet just slipped on the wet mud of the path. The gargoyles and the *Cat Sìth* were still now, as though subdued in the presence of a far greater power. Or had the Goldie gargoyle somehow leered at him again as they passed?

"Anythin' is possible here, boy!" said Kirkton Jean, as though reading his thoughts. "Your worst fears can all come true... For the worlds are very close together here- an' they are doin' battle tonight! Forces much greater than you can possibly imagine are at play here..."

Wee Tam could feel them wracking his body- and all the futility of resistance. He let Mary and Jean drag him through the horrible iron gates, up the path towards the door of the Auld Kirk itself. He was inside. The gates closed again behind them, with a hideous grind of metal on metal. Wee Tam shuddered. The studded wooden doors of the kirk creaked open. For a moment there was silence, and then a great cloud of bats rushed out. Hielan' Mary screamed in spite of herself, and then gasped as the doors opened further to reveal a dark figure, alone in the darkness within. He stood by the altar, his back to them, toying with something in his hands. The witches instinctively knelt before him.

"One foot in each world!" said Rannoch, without turning around. "It gives you powers you can't even guess at! I've spent- lifetimes- trying to harness them for myself. But now I know that the only way is…"

He turned to face Wee Tam. For the first time it was clear what he held in his hands- a grim, black-bladed dagger. Tam stared at it, fascinated by the play of the light on its shiny, obsidian surface.

"To send you back!" said Rannoch, pointing the knife towards Tam's heart.

Wee Tam shrunk away from the blade, but his arms were held firmly by his sides by Kirkton Jean and Hielan' Mary, who were gripping him as though their own lives depended on it.

"Take him to Hecate's Table!" commanded Rannoch, and the witches dragged Wee Tam back outside, to a huge flat-topped stone tomb in the kirkyard.

A circle of cloaked witches closed around them, as though drawn in irresistibly by the potent magic unfolding in their midst. Wee Tam could sense their excitement, as four witches stepped forward and lashed him tightly by his wrists and ankles onto the top of the tomb. He struggled for a moment, then subsided again, his eyes dilated, his small body going limp. Wicked forks of lightning flashed overhead, hitting the spire of the Auld Kirk again and again.

The whispering witches hushed their chatter, as a dark figure approached the tomb.

"He is ready, my Lord!" said Hielan' Mary eagerly. "He is ready for the knife…"

"Not so impatient, witchling!" said Rannoch. "You have the piper, my dear?"

Nannie stepped forward out of the shadows and led another cloaked figure towards the altar, his face hidden by his hood. Rannoch tossed a clanking bag of coins to him, and he caught it in a skinny, pale hand.

"Play, play as you never played before, Master Piper!" cried Rannoch. "The devil has all the best tunes! So play fit to raise the dead- and to damn the living…"

The piper pulled his hood back. Wee Tam stared wildly at him. Merry Andrew looked blankly back at Wee Tam, face completely devoid of expression, and then raised his pipe-chanter to his lips.

"Play, piper! Play!" shouted Rannoch. "Play as though the world were ending! For at last, the three changelings are come together! You, Master Piper, from the Wayward Sisters; Young Tam O'Shanter from the Still Folk; and my beautiful Nannie, from Man! And you are all slaves to my magic- to the magic of the three changelings!"

Merry Andrew smiled, and coaxed his bagpipes into life. The drones set up their humming din, and then his fingers flashed up and down the chanter, sending mischievous, magical notes capering around the gravestones and swirling around the spire of the Auld Kirk.

CHAPTER 44

———▸———

PEACE REIGNED SERENE AT POOSIE Nansie's bawdy-house. Malcolm was fast asleep, stretched out on a chaise longue, sporting an antiquated, tassled night-cap that he had somehow equipped himself with. Poosie Nansie prided herself on maintaining clothing on the premises to suit any taste. The tassles of the night-cap swung gently to the rhythm of Malcom's snoring. One of Poosie Nansie's girls was discreetly rifling through his pockets for valuables. On a sofa by the window, Johnnie was stroking Sophie's hair lovingly.

"We could get married- after the war, I mean!" he said. "The Prince would give us a place 'o our own- maybe a wee bit of land! We could even raise some bairns- just like Tam an' Kate! Just think of it, Sophie, a wee apprentice souter, to learn the trade in my foot-steps!"

Sophie giggled at his naïveté, hugging him affectionately.

"Ye're no' like the other men who come in here, John Davidson, I'll gie' ye that much!"

The Prince was fast asleep on the armchair, with Rowena curled up on his lap. She snored lightly. Suddenly he started to cough and splutter, and then began to choke. Rowena awoke with a start, sat up and stared at him. She gave a shriek of alarm. He was bright red in the face, and gasping stertorously for breath.

"Cherlie! Cherlie, my darlin'!" she cried. "Why, whatever's the matter wi' you, my love?" She dragged him upright and put her hand to his forehead. "He's burnin' alive, Johnnie! Do somethin', Souter!"

Johnnie leapt up and ran over to the Prince. He was crimson now, the sweat pouring off his forehead. Johnnie loosened his shirt, and then tore one of Nansie's best sheets into shreds to mop his brow. He ran over to Malcolm, and shook him awake.

"The Prince, Chevalier!" Johnnie cried. "It's the Prince- Prince Cherlie has been taken terribly ill!"

"Prince!" said Rowena. "I thought he was just a foreign merchant!"

"Never mind a' that now, hen!" said Johnnie. "The lad's at death's door, you can see it for yourself!"

Malcolm rubbed his eyes sleepily, looking vacantly at the Prince.

"Is there a doctor nearby, Sophie love?" said Johnnie.

"He left but half an hour ago," said Sophie doubtfully. "He was still wearin' my mistress' best silk stockings- an' clutchin' a bottle of port in each hand, for balance!"

"No' that bampot! Hell's teeth!" cried Johnnie. "He was in a worse state than the Prince himsel'! But can we no' catch him on the road? It could be the death o' Cherlie here if we don't!"

"It'll be the death of him for sure if we do!" said Sophie. "You saw the state o' the good Doctor Farqhuarson for yourself, Johnnie! We'd dae' far better to waken my mistress herself- for she is skilled in remedies. An' she has a wiser heid on her than any drunken country apothecary!"

"Then run and get her, Sophie love, as you value his precious life!" said Johnnie. "I swear he's gettin' worse by the minute! Callum! Where's Callum Stewart?"

Johnnie and Rowena propped the Prince up on the chaise longue with cushions. He was drenched in sweat now, and convulsing violently, incapable even of speech. Rowena held his limp hand in hers, pressing it to her lips over and over again, as if she could sooth his fever with kisses.

"Oh, my darlin' Cherlie!" she whispered. "My Prince! Whatever can be afflictin' you?"

"What's been goin' on here?" said Callum, bursting into the room, dirk in hand. "Show me the bass who's laid a hand on Royal Cherlie!"

CHAPTER 45

TAM AND MEG PICKED THEIR way carefully through the gnarled roots and clutching branches of the Kirk Wood. Meg pulled fitfully at her reins, instinctively ill at ease in the eery wood.

"C'mon, easy, girl!" said Tam. "Calm yourself, lass, it's nothin' we havenae' seen before…"

The weird glow from the Auld Kirk was spreading now, lighting up the trees around them. Lightning flashed down continually, hitting the cross on top of the Auld Kirk repeatedly, until there was a hideous crunching, tearing, splintering sound and then the top of the spire, cross and all, broke off and slid down the roof of the Kirk. Tam watched through the trees in amazement as the cross dashed itself on the ground with an almighty crash, sending a plume of dust high up into the night. The unearthly howl of Merry Andrew's pipes carried over it on the wind.

"Alright, so I havenae' seen that before!" whispered Tam. "But at least we know which direction we're headin' in now, eh?"

Suddenly Tam froze. Hag-like, shuffling shapes were creeping through the wood all around them, stealing between trees towards the Auld Kirk. Tam paused to let them pass, holding Meg back and whispering calming words to her. As the last of the shadows slunk by, Tam tethered Meg to a branch.

"Stay here, Maggie- an' no' a sound, for all our lives depend on it!"

He followed the mysterious shapes to the wall of the kirkyard, peered over it and then immediately dropped back down behind the wall. He crossed himself, and then slowly lifted himself up again for a better look. Then he felt a heavy hand on his shoulder pulling him back down. It was followed in rapid succession by another hand that clamped over his mouth, to stop him from shouting out. Tam turned his head slowly round, forcing himself to confront whoever- whatever- it was.

"Haud your wheesht, pal!" hissed Big Eck. "Before ye get us both killed! We're in mortal peril here, I can tell ye…"

"Big Eck!" whispered Tam. "What are you doin' here?"

"Ah'm a friend!" said Big Eck. "I mean, assumin' you're no' on the side of the forces o' darkness yoursel'?"

"How do I know that?" said Tam.

"Well, if I was in league wi' the devil himself- or whatever the hell yon Rannoch is- I'd probably be on the other side of this wall, would you no' say?" said Big Eck.

"Rannoch's here then?" said Tam.

"Aye, an' that's no' all…" said Big Eck. "So can ye promise me that ye can stay calm and coingerated, Tam?"

"What d'you mean?" said Tam.

"I mean what I say!" said Big Eck. "We can work together here, lad, in fact we're gonnae' have to- but I'm no' tellin' you everythin' I know, until I'm sure you can keep the heid, alright?"

"Alright then, Eck!" said Tam eagerly. "What have you seen?"

"I've seen a lot of crazy things in the last few hours, believe me!" said Big Eck, wiping his brow. "Ye're liable to do that when you follow Rannoch around for a while… But the important thing from your point o' view- and Prince Cherlie's- is that he's got your wee lad in there!"

"Wee Tam!" said Tam. "My son! Where is he? Have you seen him?"

"Shush!" said Eck, physically restraining Tam from jumping up to look. "Crivvens, that's what I'm talkin' about- keep the heid, man! Now if I let ye go- if, hypothetically speakin', I were to do that- can I trust you to look up, very, very slowly? Canny-like?"

Tam nodded.

"Well then," said Big Eck, releasing him from his bear-like grasp. "Let's take a chance, an' gie' it a go! But easy does it, pal! For I've my own business to take care of here, this is no' just a family matter any more..."

Tam gradually lifted his head above the wall. It took his eyes a moment to acclimatise to the light, but even then he could hardly believe what they showed him. Witches and warlocks were whirling like dervishes around the fire, in varying degrees of undress. Tam groaned involuntarily at the withered body of one elderly witch, and then clapped his own hand to his mouth. Each of the witches paused by the altar to drink deeply from an ornate quaich that sat upon it, then reeled ecstatically back away in their circle. Then a beautiful young witch, in a skimpy green garment that barely covered her body, moved to the centre of the circle, dancing gracefully through the flames. She threw a handful of powder into the fire, and it flared up high in a riot of colour. A cloud of huge night-moths danced like fireflies around her.

Tam watched entranced, obsessed, unable to tear his eyes away from her enchanting beauty. Suddenly she gave a toss of her dark hair, and he could restrain himself no longer.

"Nannie!" he shouted out, in spite of himself. "Cutty Sark!"

He stood up and gazed at her.

"Ah, for Christ's sake!" said Big Eck, cocking his pistols and scrambling for cover. "Now we're really for it, ye bloody eedjit! Every man for himsel'!"

CHAPTER 46

POOSIE NANSIE EXAMINED THE STRICKEN Prince, her kindly brows knit tight with concern. She may have been the most notorious bawdy-house keeper in the West of Scotland, but she was also a mother- and a tender-hearted one at that. She rested her hand gently on Johnnie's arm.

"He's desperate far gone already, son," she murmured to Souter Johnnie. "He is fadin' away fast now..."

"Oh, whatever can be the matter with him?" gasped Rowena.

"You say he was sound but hours ago?" said Poosie Nansie.

"Aye, an' wi' the vigour of two men!" said Rowena.

"She's right, Mistress Nansie!" said Souter Johnnie, almost beside himself with concern for the Prince. "As fit as you or I! It came upon him as sudden as..."

"As this storm itself?" said Nansie, looking at him keenly.

"Aye!" said Johnnie. "That's exactly what I was goin' to say..."

Poosie Nansie put her finger to her lips, drew the curtains and then lowered her voice as she spoke.

"Then it is witchcraft for sure, sirs!"

"Witches!" said Callum, spitting on the floor. "I feared it from the first!"

"Och, c'mon!" said Johnnie. "Really, Callum? Witches? There's no such thing, man! This is Ayrshire in 1745, no' ancient Cawdor! Nothin' ever happens here..."

Poosie Nansie turned to him.

"There are many things in this world that we look upon, but that we do not see, Souter…" she said quietly. "The other side is closer to the surface here than you may think! It is just that there is normally no window open to it. For like the very elements of nature, the three worlds- the new world of men, and the old worlds of the witches and fairy-folk- they fit together seamlessly. Until sometimes somethin'- or someone- makes those elements drift oot o' their natural order…" She held up a handsome gold pocket-watch and counted out the beats of the Prince's pulse for a minute. She shook her head sorrowfully, and then nodded towards the time-piece. "Just like the tiny misalignments in a watch. We dinnae' notice them at all until, over time, they gradually start to grind and jar against each other. And then…" She gestured out of the window, to the electric storm battering the Auld Kirk in the distance.

"An' then the worlds come intae' conflict!" said Callum. "There's been a dark cloud over him frae' the moment he landed on these shores, I could feel it in my bones!" He looked over at the Highlanders, who had now clustered anxiously around the Prince's chaise longue, speaking Gaelic in low voices. "It's no' a thing to discuss in English, but I told the boys in the Old Tongue- I told them I felt the breath o' *Dòmhnall Dubh* on him…"

"Oh, stuff and nonsense, Callum!" said Malcolm impatiently.

"What does he mean, Chevalier?" asked Rowena, nearly hysterical with fear for the Prince.

"In Lowland Scots- the, eh- the breath of Black Donald…" said Malcolm. "'Tis their heathen name for Lucifer, ye see." He glared at Callum. "But no more of this Gaelic mumbo-jumbo, for goodness' sake, man! Where is the real surgeon? The Prince of Wales needs to be treated with modern science! To be bled; leeched; blistered- not fussed over by a gaggle of old hens!"

"Sophie, child, pass me your necklace," said Nansie, interrupting the Chevalier's diatribe.

Sophie passed her the silver crucifix from around her neck, and Nansie touched the Prince's fevered brow with it. He sighed as it brought him immediate relief, cooling him down and taking some of the fire from his cheeks.

"It's workin'!" shouted Johnnie. "The fever's dyin' down! Put it around his neck, Mistress Nansie..."

Nansie shook her head slowly.

"Oh, this won't save him, son. An' the very force o' the conflict could kill him, before it cured him. The most we can do is suppress the symptoms for a while. For this shows that the poor laddie is afflicted wi' a potent spell- a killin' charm..."

"Then what can be done for him? For Prince Cherlie?" said Souter Johnnie desperately. "You who are so wise, Mistress Nansie- can you no' help him?"

"This is far beyond my arts, son," said Poosie Nansie. "There is only one who lives among men who might help him now- one who is much wiser than me. Much older. I can send you to her, to plead for her help on a mission o' mercy. But I must warn ye first that she answers to no man- and that her ways are no' always easy to follow..."

"Do it, Mistress Nansie, I beg you!" cried Souter Johnnie. "His very life may depend upon it! Where may I find her?"

"Oh, but ye already have found me, Souter Johnnie!" said a voice from the doorway. "Or rather- ah've found you! For this is our third meetin', is it no'? Third time lucky, eh? Mebbe someone up above's tryin' to tell me that I do need some new shoes, after all!"

"You!" said Souter Johnnie. "Christ! You're no' tellin' me you're the wise woman?"

———

CHAPTER 47

KATE KNELT BESIDE HER BED, saying her prayers devoutly. The intensity of her praying increased as the thunder rumbled overhead, and the storm raged on outside. Repeated flashes of lightning lit up the room, the downpour sending a steady trickle of rainwater dripping down the wall in the far corner. It was only too easy to believe in super-natural powers on a night like this one. Kate prayed aloud, as her own mother had taught her to pray against evil spirits:

> *"Saint Michael the Archangel an' all our guardian angels,*
> *Defend this family against the evil ones that roam this earth!"*

"Oh, Wee Tam!" she cried, breaking off from the prayer. "I remember the night when you first came to us! It was a night just like- just like this one... But you lay so still on our door-step. The more the storm raged, the deeper you slept! I'd never seen a child like it. Oh, just come back to me again this night, my darlin' boy, my precious blessin' from heaven!"

Suddenly there was a knocking on the door, at first hesitant and then more insistent. Kate sprang up from her knees and rushed to answer it.

"Tam! Is it you?" she cried, flinging the door open. "Where's my wee boy?"

There was a man in a cloak standing outside.

"Tam?" said Kate.

"May I come in, Mistress O'Shanter?" said Goldie, not even troubling to wipe away the rainwater that was streaming down his face.

"You don't need to wait for an invitation here, Hosea!" said Kate.

"Oh, but I do!" said Goldie. "I do now, I fear!"

"Well then, come in, come on in out of the rain!" said Kate. "Whatever's the matter wi' you? What can be troublin' ye so? Come in an' tell me, right away! I'm sorry to welcome you so, but I've had no word from Tam or Wee Tam, and the night is drawin' in..."

"That's just it, Mistress O'Shanter!" said Goldie, choking back a sob. "Your son has gone- he's been taken! Jist like my Nannie before him. Only- only- this time it was different. This time it was Nannie who took him..."

"Nannie?" said Kate. "Wee Nannie, you say? But she's... How could she?"

"She's come back, Kate!" said Goldie. "She's come back, but she's no' the same! She's changed! An' I let her- I let take Wee Tam! I'm so..." He broke down in tears. "I can never..."

"Where's Tam, Hosea?" said Kate, interrupting him. "Tell me, for the love of God! For surely he didnae' just leave Wee Tam alone back there?"

"They distracted him- the witches..." said Goldie. "I fear it was part of their plot all along!"

"Witches!" said Kate. "So whatever has become of Tam? Is he with Wee Tam?"

"He's gone tae' look for them! At the Auld Kirk..." said Goldie. "I told him tae' wait while we looked for help, but he jist took off on Meg, an' I've no' seen either o' them since. I'm- I'm so sorry, Kate..."

"How could he! How could he do this, the drunken fool!" said Kate furiously. "For all his drinkin'- his sinnin'- he's always been a good father to Wee Tam! Until now, when it matters most! Never trust a drunkard!"

"I'm no' sure it was- that it was really his fault this time, Mistress O'Shanter..." said Goldie hesitantly. "I've always been quicker to judge Tam O'Shanter than tae' praise him- but there are dark forces stirrin' tonight. Forces greater than any of us… I mean, for Nannie- for Nannie to show up like this! It's no' canny!"

"Well, canny or no', I'm goin' straight to the Auld Kirk myself, to look for the both o' them!" said Kate with determination, putting a woollen shawl around her shoulders. "I'm no' stayin' at home a moment longer, no' while my wee boy's lost oot there! An' on such a night!"

"No, no, Mistress O'Shanter!" said Goldie. "You must stay, you must be here, in case the wee lad somehow finds his way back here, and needs your protection! Ye mind that he did so once before, when Mungo's lad- when Wee Colin- was taken?" Kate nodded. "You must stay here, an' let me go in your place- me who is to blame for all this!"

"You? How can you be to blame, Hosea?" said Kate. "You are no' responsible for what Tam's done- or for what poor Nannie may have done…"

"Oh, but I let her go, Kate!" cried Goldie. "I could have stopped them, an' I just let her go! In my poor foolish weakness- I ruined everything, for my lost daughter's sake… So let me take your place- let me go to the Auld Kirk, if it be the death o' me! I have nothin' left to fear…"

Kate looked deep into Goldie's eyes, and then put her hand on his shoulder.

"Go, Hosea!" said Kate. "Go and find my boy, an' I will pray for you- for you all!" said Kate. "Aye, and for Wee Nannie too! For no one is past salvation, an' our Lord will no' stand by and watch in our hour of need. An' it is her hour of need too, I feel it." She took his hand, and they knelt down together. "Stay a moment, an' pray with me, Hosea:

'Saint Michael the Archangel defend us in our hour of need.
Be our safeguard against the devil's traps and snares.
Cast Satan down to hell, and with him all the wicked spirits;
Who wander through our world for the ruin of souls.'"

"Amen!" said Goldie. "It's- it's the first time I've prayed, since Nannie disappeared…" he said to Kate. "I havenae' had the heart since I lost her.

The faith! But I'll pray tae' him every day- I'll become a better man- if he'll just bring your Wee Tam back to you! An' whatever God may dae', I won't stand by and let any harm come to Wee Tam again while I live- I swear it."

CHAPTER 48

———

"Aye, Poosie Nansie has it spot on, lads!" said Doxy Mary, holding her hand up to the Prince's brow. The Highlanders were all gathered around to hear her verdict. "She usually does, when it comes tae' advice aboot men! We dinnae' have long to save poor Cherlie. It'll take desperate medicine now..."

"Is it poison, Mistress Mary?" said Callum. "Or are they close to us, even now?"

"Could they have taken somethin' o' the Prince's, *Calum Mór*?" said Doxy Mary, studying the Prince closely. "A ring or a trinket he keeps about him? A lock o' hair, or even a wee scrap o' clothin'? For they have long since learned to work their mischief without leavin' their lair!"

"Quite impossible, my dear lady!" said Malcolm. "My men and I have been his constant sentinels. No one could have breached the ring of steel that we have maintained about his royal person, ever since he landed on these shores!"

"What about yon lassie at the inn, Chevalier?" broke in Callum. "Ye mind the one in the cutty sark? He didnae' seem to want much guardin' from her!"

"Aye... An' his neckerchief!" said Johnnie. "She took it off him, Callum! She danced right off wi' it!"

"Someone took his neck-cloth?" said Doxy Mary. "An' it was a woman?" She looked at Poosie Nansie meaningfully.

"A pretty young thing- fair crazed wi' defiance!" said Johnnie. "I thought it was just for a keepsake... To tell her grandchildren she'd danced wi' Royal Cherlie, you know?"

"She may yet do more than dance with him, son- for this has been worked by the most fell of all their magic..." said Doxy Mary.

"Sacrificin' an innocent, Mistress?" said Callum.

Doxy Mary nodded gravely.

"First they would need a bairn though, eh, Mary?" said Poosie Nansie.

"Or a change... Or someone out of the ordinary run o' men, that is," said Doxy Mary carefully. "But mair than that: the victim must have gone willingly, or have been given up by his friends, for so fearful a spell to bind. Such black magic is no' just whipped up in a jiffy, wi' yer eye of newt, an' toe of frog..."

"Aye- that is the hardest part for them to work!" said Poosie Nansie. "Although sometimes in the Highlands a simple family will reject a poor changeling bairn, no understandin' the great gift the fair folk have chosen to give to them- by bringin' a fairy child to a couple wi' no bairns o' their own. An' that makes for dreadful magic..."

Souter Johnnie groaned in anguish, holding his head in his hands.

"What is it, Johnnie?" asked Callum. "Are you afflicted too?"

"No- no..." moaned Johnnie. "It's Tam's lad- Wee Tam! I thought he'd be safe wi' Jean an' Mary... Wi' a pair of lassies from our village. But I saw them- I saw them takin' him away!"

"Witches!" said Callum.

"No! They can't be!" cried Johnnie. "They can't be! For we just handed him over to them..."

Poosie Nansie put a comforting hand on the Souter's shoulder, but there was concern etched across her face too.

"Just a wee lad..." said Johnnie disconsolately. "He cannae' even speak!"

"Because he's so young?" said Nansie.

"No..." said Doxy Mary.

"No, Ma'am- he's a mute," said Johnnie, looking at Mary curiously. "He's been that way ever since- ever since he first arrived on Tam and Kate's doorstep that night, wrapped up in a beautiful plaid…"

Poosie Nansie crossed herself, and looked across at Doxy Mary. Mary caught her eye, and nodded slowly.

"A night such as this one?" said Nansie gently.

"Aye!" said Johnnie. "The rain was pure lashin' down, but it didnae' trouble him. No' Wee Tam! He didnae' make a sound…"

"*O mo chreach…*" said Callum. "Then it's even worse than I feared! There's powerful magic afoot now…"

"Aye! But dinnae' despair just yet, *Calum Mór!*" said Doxy Mary. "Your master is still in the early stages of the fever. An' so Wee Tam lives yet. But he's in terrible danger, poor lad…"

"How do we stop them, Mistress Mary?" said Johnnie.

"Wi' cold steel, Souter!" said Doxy Mary.

Johnnie leapt to his feet, and seized his dirk.

"Then tell me how ta' find them!" he cried.

"The trick is no' to find them," said Nansie gently, "for they hold their infernal rites at Auld Kirk-Alloway, as they always have. But first you need men staunch enough to face them in their wrath. A killin' charm means a whole coven of witches- an' a powerful warlock too…"

"We'll leave right away!" shouted Johnnie. "Who's with me?"

"We will do no such thing, my man!" said Malcolm, his face white. "Have ye lost all grip on your senses, sir? Plainly the Prince has a chill, a severe head cold- and no madcap chase over the moors will cure him of that! And as for your friend's child- why, he has his sovereign's profoundest sympathies, of course, but we cannot risk any delay to our great venture on account of one peasant laddie…"

The Prince lifted his head from the pillow, with an agony of effort.

"Madame is right…" he croaked. "I- I am bewitched! You must hunt them down, Chevalier, whatever they may be, before they drain the very life out of me…"

"We will, Cherlie- whatever it takes!" shouted Johnnie.

"Your zeal is commendable, Souter," said Malcolm patronisingly, once he was sure the Prince's eyes had closed again. "You'll make a good corporal, one day perhaps even a competent sergeant. But you're a country cobbler, not a general! To the man of war- the strategist- planning is everything. We must determine the strength we face. The terrain the enemy occupies. Reconnaissance- reconnoitring- that is what modern warfare demands…"

"There's no time for a' that balls, Chevalier!" said Doxy Mary impatiently. "Did you no' hear me right, ya great bawbag? They have this precious laddie in their power, an' the blow may fall at any time now!"

"I heard you loud and clear, madam!" said Malcolm. "But I am not accustomed to take counsel of war from elderly female drunkards! And I am certainly not accustomed to talk 'balls', as you see fit to put it…"

"Well, if you're no' accustomed tae' talkin' balls, you're daein' it awfu' well for a beginner!" said Doxy Mary. "Ye need to get oot there an' kill these bloody witches- I cannae' put it any more clearly for ye!"

"In the name of God, let us go this instant then, Chevalier!" said Johnnie. "Who's with me?"

"To face the devil and his cohorts in their own backyard?" said Malcolm scornfully. "On a night like this? I want no part in it. Death and damnation- that's young man's business!"

"How about you, Callum?" said Johnnie. "For my part, I swore to serve Prince Cherlie- swore it on the edge o' my dirk!"

"Don't venture your life on an oath, Souter," said Callum quietly. "For you'll find it's easy enough to lose! You should make your choice in the quiet o' your own counsel. Because you dinnae' need any baggage when you're standin' on the brink…"

Johnnie didn't reply. He just looked Callum straight in the eye, and buckled on his dirk. Callum nodded.

"Then I'm with you, man!" said Callum. "*Iosa Crìosd*, I've no' taken such care o' my soul that I'm feared to risk it now!"

"This is a fool's errand, Callum- surely you must know that!" spluttered Malcolm.

"I know I didnae' come a hundred and fifty miles on foot, just to run away from a wifie in a pointy hat!" said Callum. He buckled on his own broadsword and clapped his woollen bonnet onto his head. "Besides, I've a score to settle with this Black Donald- he took my auld father before his time!"

"Aye, an' he marked your own card a long time ago, *Calum Mór*!" laughed Gregor. "Nae' need to wrap up where we're off to, *co-oghan*! We might as well show up at Auld Hornie's great hall wi' our own drinkin' cups... For I'm wi' you!"

"Count me in too, *laochain*!" said Ruaridh. "I'm no' havin' the folk back in Argyll sayin' that a Maclachlan of Dunoon would go where a Stewart of Appin wouldnae' dare!"

"Och, of course we're all goin', aren't we boys?" said Callum. "Who'd want to miss this?"

The Highlanders cheered as they put their bonnets on.

"Are you all gone insane, you great loons?" said Malcolm incredulously. "We're talkin' about your immortal souls here, no' the price of cattle at Crieff Market!"

"Auld Hornie will be takin' Wee Willie Winkie here an' all, before too long!" said Johnnie scornfully, nodding toward Malcolm in his nightcap. "The devil takes care of his own, so they say!"

"Callum!" said Malcolm petulantly, stamping his foot until his tassels shook. "Are you going to stand there and hear your Clan Chieftain so vilely abused?"

"We've no time for such trifles as matters of honour now, Chevalier!" said Callum, looking out of the window as he checked the strap of his scabbard. "For we've black business on our hands the night. We must put our faith in plain words- an' Spanish steel..."

Callum looked around at the battle-ready Highlanders, and then nodded to Johnnie.

"On your word then, Souter!" he cried.

"Noo' haud on just a mo', lads!" said Doxy Mary, pulling her own cloak around her. "Ah'm comin' wi' you, ya bawbags! Ye'll get yourselves in a fearful pickle, withoot a lassie to tell ye what's what!"

"Are you sure you can keep up wi' us, Mistress Mary?" said Johnnie. "We've a long walk over broken country, and we've no time for waitin'!"

"Dinnae' you worry about me, Sunny Jim!" said Doxy Mary. She picked up her broom, twisted its handle and drew out a razor-sharp, copper-gold coloured sword-stick. Callum let out a low whistle.

"Ye dinnae' go to a bitch-fight wi' a powder-puff in yer mitt, son!" she said, sliding the sword-stick back into the broom-handle. "Ye get tooled up! Cos' it's gonnae' get pretty tasty when we find they witches, *Calum Mór*, believe you me!"

"Aye, I can see that!" said Callum. "What's it made of?"

"Bronze!" said Doxy Mary. "Ah dinnae' care much for iron, ye see. Ye might call it an allergy…"

"But is it strong enough for the job?" said Callum.

"It was good enough for your ancestors, ya cheeky bam!" said Doxy Mary. "An' they had a damn sight mair witches tae' deal with than you soft lot have today, ah can tell ye that… The Bronze Age was just hoachin' wi' witches! An' the Bronze Age would've ended pretty damn quickly here in Scotland, if ye couldnae' slay a witch wi' the stuff!"

"Bronze it is, then!" said Callum with a smile. "Like the lady said: We're all tooled up, Souter Johnnie!"

"Then let's go!" said Johnnie. He kissed Sophie long and hard, and then turned and clattered down the stairs without a backward glance.

"I'll wait for you, John Davidson!" called Sophie after him, wiping her eyes. "Just you make sure you come back for me, you hear me? Stay safe, Souter Johnnie! Stay safe, all of you!"

One by one, the Highlanders filed wordlessly out after him into the night. Doxy Mary threw her broomstick over her shoulder and followed them down the stairs. Once outside, she untied King Billy the Highland Cow, idly grazing on the fringe of the moor, swung herself up onto his back with a whoop and then urged him on after the disappearing Highlanders. King Billy bellowed, and then lumbered off into the darkness. Poosie Nansie wrapped her arm around Sophie, who buried her face in her mistress' shoulder, sobbing quietly. When all the others had gone, Callum turned back to Poosie Nansie.

"This boy of Tam's- you think he's a..."

Poosie Nansie nodded slowly.

"A changeling," she said.

"An' Doxy Mary?" said Callum.

"She is a Watcher," said Poosie Nansie. "*Coimhead*, in their tongue- and your own, of course... And faithfully watch him she has, through all these long years."

"But she's here wi' us!" said Callum.

"Aye!" said Poosie Nansie. "The paths are all convergin' now..."

"So who's watchin' Wee Tam, then?" said Callum.

Poosie Nansie smiled.

"That is why there are two of them, Callum," she said gently. "Each fairy changeling has two Watchers on this side, to help guide its path- to keep it from harm. They are no' novices in the ways of this world. And there is somethin' else you should know of Mary..."

"What is it, Mistress Nansie?" said Callum, leaning closer towards her.

"She was no' born of the fair folk..." said Poosie Nansie.

"What d'ye mean?" said Callum quickly.

"Her mother was of the Wayward Sisters, and her mother's mothers before that!" said Poosie Nansie. "All the way back to Macbeth's time, when the witches directed the very course of Scotland's history. An' yet Mary left that dark path, when she was just a lass."

"How is it possible?" said Callum. "I never heard of such a thing!"

"The witches have never held sway in the West Highlands as they do here, *Calum Mór*..." said Poosie Nansie. "Whatever they are, it is some- thin' more than men- somethin' far closer to the fair folk."

"But how could she make such a change?" said Callum.

"How do any of the changelings shift between the three peoples?" said Nansie. "It is magic far beyond my ken. But in Mary's case, there was somethin' else- somethin' that changed everythin' forever..."

"What?" breathed Callum.

"Love, Callum!" said Nansie with a smile. "The oldest magic o' them all! She met a young lad from the still folk, and somehow they talked, and- well, who can say how? They fell in love! An' so Mary became one of them."

"But they are from different worlds!" said Callum. "How could they ever have been together?"

"They made great sacrifices!" said Nansie. "Sacrifices that we can hardly imagine, livin' our simple human lives! They both left their own worlds forever, to meet in the only place where they could be together. The only common ground they have…"

"The world of men!" said Callum.

Poosie Nansie nodded.

"They left everythin'- everyone- behind them, to live wi' those who scorned and hated them, just for bein' different. They had to assume characters that bore no resemblance to their true selves, to hide in plain sight. But… But it meant that they could snatch precious moments, fleetin' days, together."

"An' was it worth it?" said Callum. "Worth all that great sacrifice?"

"Ye must ask Mary!" said Nansie with a smile. "I am no' the one to read the mind o' the fair folk! An' a changeling at that…"

"There seem to be an awful lot o' changelings comin' together all at once!" said Callum. "I'm too old now to believe in coincidences…"

"I have thought the same thing, *Calum Mór*!" said Poosie Nansie. "And about the prophecies of old. The answers are written in the stormy sky. But alas, I cannae' read them for you- that is the witches' business…"

"You know somethin' o' the still folk though, Mistress Nansie? The fairies?" said Callum.

"A little…" said Poosie Nansie. "But then a lifetime of learnin' is still little enough to know of them! For they play a long game. An' there is no knowin' what they mean to do, when once they take such a hand in the lives of men."

"Aye, a long game it is- an' a deep one too…" said Callum. "But what they start, they will finish. And so we'll find out the night- for better, or for worse! We'll win, or we'll lose, but either way, we'll find out."

He pulled a *sgian dubh* from out of his stocking and slammed it into the door-frame, where it lodged deep into the wood.

"They call it the black knife," he said. "But it is true steel. That'll keep the witches frae' your door at least, Mistress Nansie! *Dia leat!*"

Nansie squeezed his hand.

"*Dia leat!* God with you too, my son!"

Callum crossed himself, touched the blade of the *sgian dubh* for luck and then padded softly down the stairs after the others.

"*Tapadh leat mo mhàthair!*" he called back quietly. "But somethin' tells me there's no God where we're headed…"

He stepped out onto the moor, and plunged on into the darkness, until it swallowed him too.

CHAPTER 49

GOD SEEMED TO HAVE DESERTED the Auld Kirk a long time since. Nannie danced slowly towards Tam, a mocking smile playing across her blood red lips. In spite of everything he had learned about her at such a cost, in spite of all his misgivings, all he could do was watch her approach, spell-bound. He was transported straight back to Mungo's Inn- and to the old school-yard at Tarbolton School, where they had played together as children so many years before. And he could hardly breathe. Before he could even see them, he could feel the witches rushing to cut off his retreat. But still he couldn't move a muscle. Then he felt the bony fingers digging into his arms, as a group of witches pinioned him and marched him through the gates into the kirkyard. Tam looked on in horror as the bonfire flared up blood-red, and then died down. For now he could see that Wee Tam was lashed to Hecate's Table behind it, and Rannoch was in the act of raising the black sacrificial dagger high above his head. There was a white silk neck-cloth incongruously draped over the altar.

"Is that Prince Cherlie's?" Tam asked himself.

Then the chanting by the witches all around them seemed to deepen and intensify, and Rannoch paused to savour his moment of glory.

"A plague on the House of Stuart!" he hissed. "An end to the line of Banquo! Let chaos reign forever in Scotland!"

"No!" shouted Tam. "Tam! Tam, my son! I never meant to let you go, I swear it! I swear it to God!"

"Wait!" shouted Nannie to Rannoch, who looked over at them, black anger clouding his face. Nannie pointed at Tam and Rannoch lowered the dagger, glaring furiously at them both.

"Him!" spat Rannoch. "What is that rustic dolt doing here?" He slashed the air wildly with the sacrificial knife in his rage, sending the witches around him diving for cover. "You told me he had given the boy up, of his own free will! Is there no end to your bungling? Don't you understand that the spell will not bind, if he has recanted?"

Tam ran over to Wee Tam, leaped onto the altar and hugged him, great tears rolling down his cheek and onto Wee Tam's face. The witches seized Tam, but Wee Tam beamed back at him. He stretched the fingers of his fettered hand out towards his father, as the witches hauled Tam away.

"Your human father must have told him where to find us!" Rannoch spat furiously at Nannie. "This drunken sot would never have worked it out for himself! He hardly knew his own name... And yet you told me that, after everything, your father would grant you this one night's grace! Better to have slain him where he stood, than to have taken such a mad risk!"

"For the last time- let's no' forget that the plan was of your devisin', no' mine, Rannoch," said Nannie calmly. "I never wished to set foot in that filthy village, nor speak to my so-called father again! An' havin' done so, I could hardly have knifed him in a back-street- for fear of unleashin' all the crazy, unpredictable black magic of patricide upon our venture! Yet for some reason you seem to have ventured everythin' on Farmer Goldie- and on the fickle fancies of this Tam O'Shanter..."

"He would not be so inconstant, had you turned him as I planned!" Rannoch shouted. "It seems that his passions weren't quite so- enflamed- as you thought. You witches and your ridiculous vanity! At least your foremothers had no illusions on that score, bearded old hags that they were! Have a care lest I change my mind, and choose instead to favour Charles Edward as my agent for chaos for Scotland..." He examined the knife in his hand. "But never mind that now! I shall bathe in all of their blood before this night is through, come hell or high water! And I think it shall be both…"

Tam reached out to Wee Tam, straining against the witches as they dragged him bodily away from the altar, ragged finger-nails scratching through his skin and pulling at his hair.

"Let him go! What d'ye want with him, you monsters?" he shouted. "He's just a boy! He's my son!"

"Do you still no' understand? Even now, do you still no' understand?" said Nannie, looking at him curiously. "He's no' your son, Tam! Of course he's no' your son! What possible difference do you think any son of yours- any true son of yours- could make?" She laughed out loud. "Let us be honest wi' each other, at the last! You're a nobody, Tam- you've never made any difference to anybody. This is all about him, it always has been! You must have suspected the truth for years- must have locked it away in your heart of hearts!"

"He's my son!" shouted Tam.

"You must have seen how different he is," said Nannie. "How ill he fits in with the other bairns in the village! His frailty- his weakness- his sickliness… The look of the other world in his eyes, so close to the surface! But more than anythin', his real age… He is as old as these hills, did you know that, Tam? He was here when King Duncan ruled Scotland! He is older than any of us!" She laughed, taking the dagger from Rannoch, rolling it in her hand and stroking Wee Tam's neck with the point. "Come, Tam! Let the boy speak out for himself! If I'm lyin', let him say so!" Suddenly she tightened her grip on the knife and held the blade hard against Wee Tam's throat, pressing it into the skin, torturing him out of pure malice. "No, I didn't think so! Speak up, *seann fhear*, old one! What's the matter, *balach beag*? Cat got your tongue, boy?"

"No!" shouted Tam, stretching out his hand to Wee Tam, who was staring at him in terror now, desperately trying not to look at the blade so cruelly pricking his throat. "I don't care what he is! I know him, Nannie- what's in his heart! I won't let him go!"

"He's a parasite- a changeling!" cried the Cutty Sark. "*Sìthiche...* His love is like the fairy gold you see in the bed of the burn: Put it in your pocket, an' it will have melted away to nothin' by the time you get home!"

"He's my son- my precious son! Just let him go!" begged Tam. "Let him go, an' I'll do anythin' you want, Nannie!"

"Of course you will!" said Nannie, face as hard as the vitrified obsidian of the knife. "What choice have you? But you've made your sacrifice already, Tam... An' now this- this creature- must die! He is all we need to rid Scotland of another tyrant! Open your eyes, and take your revenge on them! For all the years they've deceived you... Crush the vile cuckoo in your nest! Free yourself from their curse, at long last!"

"Nothin'- nothin' is worth a wee boy's life..." said Tam, sobbing.

"Fool!" shouted Rannoch contemptuously. "We would kill every brat in Christendom to bury this Pretender! For what is he but a changeling too? We have cast the Stuarts out from Scotland once, and we will see them damned, before we see their foul brood creep back onto the throne again!"

"Leave this to me, Rannoch!" cried Nannie, pushing him away. "We could have broken his body months ago, if all we wanted to do was destroy him! It is his will we must destroy, if we want to work the killin' spell. He must give the changeling up of his own free will!"

CHAPTER 50

———◆———

"C'MON NOW, SOUTER JOHNNIE, STOP your guddlin' there! Ye're like a naughty wee boy makin' mud pies! Up wi' you and get a move on, ya bawbag!" said Doxy Mary unsympathetically, as Johnnie slipped on the wet track for the twentieth time and stumbled back down onto the rain-sodden ground again. "We're no' off tae' Kilmarnock Fair here, *laochain...*"

The sure-footed Highlanders were coursing effortlessly ahead through the driving rain, without a backward glance at the Lowland stragglers. Doxy Mary wheeled King Billy back round, holding her broomstick out to the languishing Souter. Johnnie grabbed hold of it, and with a Herculean effort pulled himself up out of the slippery mud. Every muscle in his body was screaming for rest, making glib excuses for him to give up on this desperate cross-country chase, but still he forced himself back up onto his feet once more.

"I won't desert you again, Tam!" he muttered to himself between gritted teeth. "No' if it kills me!"

"You must keep goin', Johnnie!" said Doxy Mary, more kindly this time. "For it is nearly day-break! Their rites will be reachin' their climax soon. It is now, or never, if we are to save them!"

"Then it must be now!" said Johnnie, forcing his aching body into a run once more.

"Gie' us a marchin' song, Mistress Mary!" shouted Callum from out of the twilight ahead. "An' sing it boldly, for some of us may never live to hear another one!"

"Very well, son!" shouted Doxy Mary, adroitly holding the broomstick out to Johnnie, as he tripped on a gorse-root and careered down into another muddy pot-hole. She bellowed out her song, as they thundered pell-mell into the breaking day:

> *"O Thou! Whatever title suit thee!*
> *Auld Hornie, Satan, Nick, or Clootie!*
> *Wha' in yon cavern grim an' sooty,*
> *Closed under hatches,*
> *Ladles about the fire and brimstone,*
> *To scald poor wretches!"*

"If hell's worse than this, ah dinnae' want to see it!" panted Johnnie to himself.

> *"Hear me, auld Hangie, for a wee,*
> *An' let poor damned bodies be!*
> *I'm sure small pleasure it can gie',*
> *Even to a devil,*
> *To skelp an' scald poor dogs like me,*
> *An' hear us squeal!"*

"Amen to that, Mistress Mary!" came back Callum's voice.

He hardly even sounded out of breath, Johnnie thought bitterly, as he took another fearful tumble down onto the soaking, scratchy heather. Once again, Doxy Mary scooped him up with her broomstick and urged King Billy onwards into the night. She sang on:

> *"An' now, auld 'Cloots', I ken ye're thinkin',*
> *A certain Souter's rantin', drinkin'!*
> *Some luckless hour will send him linkin'*

To your black pit!
But faith! He'll turn a corner jinkin'
An' cheat you yet!"

Johnnie smiled in spite of himself, and set his face into the storm.

"Aye, I'll cheat you yet, Rannoch!" he vowed.

CHAPTER 51

———◆———

NANNIE TOOK TAM BY THE hands, her eyes gazing hypnotically into his. He pulled away from her in a moment of futile resistance, before his will failed him again. They were only a couple of paces away from the dreadful altar, but Tam felt as though they were in a world all of their own, the only two beings in existence.

"I thought you of all people would understand, Tam!" said Nannie. "We have to go back to somethin' real- to somethin' natural! To somethin' that comes from the land..."

"So that we can be ruled frae' England instead?" said Tam.

"England!" said Nannie scornfully. "They know nothin' of our country- of our lives- in their great, man-made city of smoke and machines! But so long as there is no government here in Scotland, we will still be free- free to make our own reality! That's what this is really about, Tam- what it's always been about. No gods, no masters! Freedom!"

"What about Rannoch, then?" said Tam. "Does he no' plan on bein' our master? Or even our god?"

"Perhaps he does!" said Nannie with a laugh. "But he is a master of chaos, and that is somethin' very different!"

She let go of his hands and proffered the quaich from the altar towards him, cupping it in both hands. It was brimming with a pungent, aromatic liquid. Tam turned his head away instinctively.

"Freedom to make our own reality- together, Tam!" said Nannie. "Isn't that what you really want? For you and I to be together? Everythin' you want can come to pass, if you only join us! Drink, Tam, and seal the compact between us forever!"

Tam tried to shake his head, but her spell lay heavily on him now. He just stood motionless as the witches bound his hands tightly behind his back. He struggled for a moment, but couldn't free himself.

"But you're- you're evil..." he whispered. He looked at her fearfully, but she just laughed out loud.

"Who's to say what good and evil really are, Tam?" she said. "They're just words that make-believe religions use to control people! Is one rock good, and another one bad? Is the wind good when it dries your clothes on washin' day, and evil when it blows them off the line into the mud?"

"I never heard anyone say that..." said Tam uncertainly.

"No! Even the most cantin' hypocrites of the Kirk don't say that- for they know they can't control the wind and rain wi' their words!" cried Nannie. "What they don't understand is that they cannae' control the real Scotland either- our Scotland! All these words they dream up or glean from ancient, foreign tales in dusty bibles, these far-fetched concepts o' right and wrong, o' good and evil, o' blessed and damned- they're all just different choices!" She paused as a gust of wind caught her dark hair, and carelessly swept it back out of her eyes with the back of her hand. "An' the difference between the witching way and the Kirk's way is just that we do give folk a choice! It's no coincidence that the Scriptures are packed with sheep and shepherds... We're all born as shepherds, until we choose to give that up and sleep-walk through life. Do you want to be a sheep, Tam? Is that what you really want? For your-self an'... and your son?"

"I don't know what tae' think!" said Tam. "There's truth in what you say, right enough, but deep down you're just as desperate to force people down your road as the rest of them! In the end, are you no' just the same as the very popes and priests that you'd have us reject? When all is said and done, what you really want is the same thing- power over the rest of us!"

She laughed again.

"Perhaps you're not really so simple as you think, Tam O'Shanter!" she said. "As Rannoch thought... An' what if we do- what's so wrong with that, after all? For power is part of nature too- just look at the lightnin' above our heads!"

"It's part o' nature, right enough," said Tam. "But- but, och, I'm no' sure how to say it right... What I mean is, when you're a farmer, you see some bloody awful things in nature! Cruelty- pain. Sufferin'. They're part o' nature, right enough. But sometimes you have to reach for- for somethin' better, somethin' higher, whether you can touch it or no'..."

"Good, better, best!" said Nannie mockingly. "They all mean different things to different people! Wouldn't everyone take power if they could- if they only dared?"

"Maybe some would," said Tam doubtfully. "But I think I'd just settle for my farm and my family, and the odd dram on market day..."

"And that's why you're so important!" said Nannie, touching his face. "That's why we all need you... Offer people that, and the whole world is yours!"

"But I'm no' of any importance to anyone!" said Tam. "You even said so yourself..."

"No' to Rannoch!" said Nannie. "He just wants to kill the change-ling, and harness his magic to kill the Prince! He wants to rip the heart and soul out of Scotland..."

"An' what do you want then?" said Tam.

"I want to win them for myself, of course!" cried the Cutty Sark. "For the witches. For our way of life. For centuries we have been hunted and persecuted, by the very people who are our natural followers! Our own flock! I'm no' like Rannoch, Tam- I can make the people's life better, take away the burden o' the parasitic priests and princes who have preyed upon them for generations!"

"I don't think either of you really understand Scotland..." said Tam. "The people dinnae' care about your grand plots or your mysterious spells! They want a bellyful of bannock, and a good, sound roof over their heads. They want to give their bairns a better life than they had themselves, an'- an' they want hope…"

"And you really think that's what the brave new world of the Stuarts offers you?" said Nannie, lips curling scornfully. "They dream of a return to the dark days of King James! To barbarism, and witch-huntin'… To the Middle Ages!"

"I don't know," said Tam. "That's sort of the thing about hope, is it no'? If you knew for sure, then it'd be somethin' else again! Guaranteed happiness! It'd be like the life of the rich folk- the easy life…"

"Oh, so that's what you really want is it, Tam?" said Nannie with disgust. "The good life! A life of plenty!"

Now it was Tam's turn to look at her curiously.

"Want it or no', I'm certainly no' very likely to get it…" he said. "But I wonder whether- whether you really live in the same world as I do at all! For all you say about folk wantin' different things, you make it sound as though every path you can choose has a great sign-post above it: good, bad, happy, sad. But that's no' really how it works. No' in my life. There probably isn't a straight route to perfect happiness for someone like me- or even for someone like Royal Cherlie, if it comes tae' that! We just have to do what seems right at the time, hope for the best an' no' look back too much at the things we cannae' change… That's the one thing I've learnt from all of this."

"What is?" said Nannie.

"Well, I wasn't even tryin' to do what seemed right- I wasn't happy with my life, an' so I thought everythin' had to change. But all that meant was that I was just goin' with the flow, wherever the wind blew, you know? Nothin' changed," said Tam. "An' the more it wasn't right, the worse I felt- and the less able I felt to do anything about it. Kinda' vicious circle… But now I think I was just- just makin' it all too complicated! Like you lot still are, wi' your schemes and your stratagems…"

"It will be simple enough soon, Tam!" said Nannie, pointing to Wee Tam on the altar. "The last hope of the Stuarts will be dead! Already he is a broken man, lollin' red-faced in an Ayrshire bawdy-house- a fittin' end for a degenerate dynasty"

"But there is another- Prince Cherlie's father..." said Tam, desperately playing for time.

"Did you really think we had forgotten about the Old Pretender, hillbilly boy?" interrupted Rannoch, running his finger along the blade of the dagger. "The old fool will never leave Rome again! His body is now as broken as his dithering mind... We could not waste a killing-spell on so feeble a foe, but we found a way to break him forever!"

"Colin!" said Tam, remembering the bible and pocket-knife. "Poor Wee Colin!"

"Yes, he was a poor enough specimen- but quite enough to undo geriatric James Stuart!" said Rannoch, smirking.

"You- you monsters!" shouted Tam.

"Why, Farmer O'Shanter- who would you have had me kill first?" said Rannoch. "The wretched Colin? Or your so-called son?"

Tam bowed his head, unable to answer.

"I thought so!" said Rannoch. "You see, the difference between us is just a matter of- priorities..." He turned to Nannie. "My patience is over, witchling! It's time to end this now. If you can't win this country's heart, then let me cut it out!"

"Very well..." said Nannie, a smile playing slowly over her beautiful mouth. But it wasn't a beautiful smile, it was something far deeper, more powerful than that. And even as he watched her face, Tam could feel himself drifting out of his own body, watching himself from the outside- as though in a dream.

"At last, after everythin', you are finally beginnin' to know yourself, Tam..." said Nannie. "That is the gift of Rannoch- and his curse. As soon as you started to dream of cutty sarks, your path was always leadin' you straight to this altar! For it's more complicated than you think, Tam O'Shanter- harder than you could ever imagine- to turn back once you've started. The ability to choose our own destiny is the rarest gift of all..."

Tam gazed at her, and as he looked into her eyes he felt his will sinking like a stone under her spell. She proffered the quaich to his lips once more, and this time it was not an invitation. She put her hand on Tam's cheek, and gently lifted the quaich up to his lips. If any man in the world could have resisted her then, it was beyond Tam. He took a deep drink, and the liquor burned his mouth like fire. It was something like whisky, but like no whisky that Tam had ever tasted. It tasted like the wind and the rain and the burns and the mountains, like the spray of the sea and the pale sun creeping through the mist. He staggered and bowed his head, his shoulders slumping in submission. Nannie gave a silvery peal of triumphant laughter.

"You've found the darkness inside you, Tam!" she said exultantly. "The darkness I always sensed there... And now it's time for you to embrace it! Let the changeling go... And join us! No gods, no masters!"

Rannoch smiled, and raised the fearful obsidian dagger high over Wee Tam's head. Merry Andrew, pipes resting on his shoulder, looked on without a flicker of emotion.

CHAPTER 52

BACK IN THE NEAT PARLOUR of Poosie Nansie's bawdy-house, Malcolm, Sophie, Rowena and Nansie herself watched in silence as a red-faced priest, Father MacFarlane, administered the Last Rites to the Prince. The priest didn't seem wholly comfortable with his surroundings, but nonetheless he solemnly made the sign of the cross on the Prince's hand with Holy Oil.

"By this Holy Unch-shion and by His own most graaacious Mercy, may the guid Lord pardon ye whatever, eh, misdeed, ye've committed by thought, word or deed…" intoned Father MacFarlane. He had to raise his voice to make himself heard over the lashing of the rain against the window-panes.

The Prince gave a great shudder at these words. His face was still bright red, burning up. Rowena sobbed quietly, and Sophie hugged her.

"Stop you, my son, I'm sure there's nothin' so bad as aaall that to speak of!" said Father MacFarlane kindly, taking Charles Edward's hand.

Malcolm took the opportunity to lead Poosie Nansie to one side.

"My dear lady! A moment of your time, if I may…" he said smoothly. "I may perhaps have judged this case a little over-hastily- for indeed there is nothing natural, in this sudden demise of our dear Prince!"

"I fear you're right, Chevalier," said Poosie Nansie quietly. "I sensed witchcraft from the first. And Mary would no' lightly have gone out into such a night wi' your men…"

"Well, indeed, indeed!" said Malcolm, wringing his hands. "But is there really nothing to be done about these damned witches of yours?" he said, raising his voice in his vexation.

"Hush, Chevalier," said Nansie under her breath. "It's a sin tae' interrupt the Last Rites, and in such profane language, surely ye ken that! The poor lad stands on the very threshold between this world and the next..."

Malcolm crossed himself piously.

"Oh, indeed, indeed- a mortal sin," he said. "But a sin is just what it is to watch him- expire- prematurely like this, when I've put so much into this uprising of his..." He cracked his knuckles pensively, drawing a frown from Father MacFarlane. "And I'm not just talking about the financial side of things, either! *Mac Cailein Mór*- the Duke of Argyll, that is- will be furious if he should ever happen to hear that... Och, you know- that we had happened to travel a while in the Lowlands, at the same time as the late Prince... For it has been no more than that, when you really come to think of it!"

"For shame, Chevalier! Prince Cherlie is still alive!" said Poosie Nansie, looking at him askance. "An' besides, I was under the impression that you and the Duke of Argyll were ancient, implacable foes?"

"And so we are, my dear Mistress Nansie, so we are!" said Malcolm. "But sometimes there is a fine line between pillaging a man's property, and forming a political alliance with him. For you must see that the case was rather different, when it seemed that we would be shortly putting the Campbell lands to the fire and sword, in a second Battle of Inverlochy. If we cannot, in fact, sack Inveraray and loot Argyll's crops and cattle to the last grain, then a policy of conciliation may yet prove more prudent... For the Prince was to be a second Marquis of Montrose in his wrath, but now it seems that he may be sadly indisposed from playing such a role!"

"It certainly looks that way, doesn't it, Chevalier?" said Poosie Nansie, looking at the Prince in concern. He was deathly pale now, despite the blankets that Rowena and Sophie were heaping on top of him. He was convulsing so hard that it was all they could do to keep them on him. His arms were involuntarily raised above his body, like a prone sleep-walker. "The poor young laddie!"

"God rest his soul!" said Father MacFarlane. "It cannae' be long now, my children... We must move on wi' the Rites: 'Naaaked came I out of my mother's womb, and naaaked shall I return thither: the Lord gave, and the Lord hath taken away; blessed be the name of the Lord...'"

"I just thought- as one business person to another- it was prudent to explore all the possibilities?" Malcolm whispered to Nansie. "If you have any suggestions as to how to mitigate this dreadful loss, you will not find me ungrateful, I assure ye!"

"What on earth do you mean, Chevalier?" said Poosie Nansie.

"Well, take these witches- surely they cannot be completely invincible?" said Malcolm. "Or perhaps there is some sort of understanding that we could reach with them- short of actual physical confrontation?"

"They are dread foes!" said Nansie. "For they are cursed already, and fear none but their own master... An' I believe he is guidin' them in person tonight."

"There must be something that can be done though, my dear lady?" said Malcolm warmly. "Your friend- Mistress Mary- seemed quite set upon it!"

"If any livin' beings can foil them tonight, it will be Mary- and her fellow Watcher," said Nansie. "I don't know what else to tell you, Chevalier, for I have not a tenth o' their learnin'- nor their power. But what I can say is that the witches have but one weakness, by night or day- they darena' cross a runnin' stream, unless they first renounce their sins in the presence of the Lord..."

There was a great flash of lightning, followed by a rumbling volley of thunder, as though the earth itself was being rent asunder.

"Far greater adversaries than the likes o' you and *Mac Cailein Mór* are doin' battle here tonight, Chevalier!" said Poosie Nansie, looking out of the window. "Whilst you scramble for Scotland's land, the powerful ones of the world are wagin' war for its very soul! We can do nothin' now but watch- and wait!"

CHAPTER 53

"THIS IS IT!" SCREECHED NANNIE exultantly. "This is the moment- when chaos finally triumphs! Be true to Scotland, Tam!"

Rannoch plunged the dagger down towards Wee Tam's unprotected chest. Wee Tam could do nothing but screw up his eyes in silent terror, and await the dreadful blow. Suddenly there was a sharp crack, and Rannoch dropped the dagger to the ground, holding his hand in pain and cursing vilely.

"Bull's-eye!" shouted Big Eck, reloading his pistol. "Now get the hell oot o' there, Tammie!"

"Be true to Scotland!" screamed the Cutty Sark.

Finally aroused from his stupor by the gun-shot, Tam spat out the mouthful of liquor from the quaich that he had been holding in his cheeks.

"Scotland forever, ya bass!" he spluttered.

He rocked back and landed the perfect head-butt on Rannoch's nose. Rannoch went down like a sack of bricks, clutching his face in agony, and pulled Nannie down after him. The obsidian dagger was still lying edge-up on the ground where Rannoch had dropped it, and Tam fell to his knees and cut the ropes binding his hands on its razor-sharp edge. A swarm of witches tried to rush him before could get back to his feet, but a brace of shots rang out, and the two closest witches crumpled down to the ground. The others scattered in confusion, and Tam lunged for the knife, snatched it up and brandished it all around him.

To his astonishment, the witches melted away before the spell-infused blade, and two more of them were dropped where they stood by Eck's deadly accurate pistol fire.

"Scotland forever!" shouted Big Eck, picking off another witch with a head-shot, before ducking down behind the kirkyard wall to reload again.

Tam scrambled towards the altar and cut Wee Tam free with the sacrificial dagger, but just as he was lifting him off the altar Nannie made a lunging grab and caught Wee Tam by the ankle. Tam tried to pull him free, but she clung on with an iron grip. For the next few seconds there was a desperate tug-of-war between Nannie and Tam for Wee Tam, which Tam was winning until Wee Tam's frayed tunic came away in his hands, leaving Wee Tam in the witch's clutches.

"Johnnie!" said Tam, cursing the ancient tunic.

Big Eck lined up a shot at Nannie, but cursed and lowered his pistol, afraid of hitting the boy. Then Tam lunged forward and kissed Nannie full on the lips. Stunned, she let go of Wee Tam, and Tam hurried him towards the gate in the kirkyard wall, covered by another volley of pistol-shots from Big Eck. Passing Merry Andrew by the altar, Tam tossed the sacrificial knife to him. Paid in kind in accordance with the ancient code of pipers, Andrew immediately dropped the bag of coins that Rannoch had given him, scattering them carelessly onto the altar. Now he skirled his pipes anew, and this time it was a different tune that he charmed out of them. An ancient one, an ancestral call that rang through Kirk Wood, to where Meg stood tied up, waiting skittishly for Tam. At the sound of the fairy music, she pulled her reins free and trotted towards it, summoned inexorably by the ageless animal magic of the *mnathan-shìdh*.

"Get them, you idiots!" screamed Rannoch, still holding his nose. "Kill them all!"

"But the spell?" said Nannie.

"Just kill them!" spat Rannoch. "Can't you see that Merry Andrew is not the third changeling, after all? They would all be dead already, had we brought the three changelings together here! The spell has not bound... And so you were wrong about that, too!"

"An' what about Merry Andrew?" said Nannie calmly.

"Someone bring me that damned piper's spleen!" said Rannoch furiously. "He who pays the piper, calls the tune! A plague on these rebellious Scots... By Hecate, they are more trouble than the rest of Europe put together!"

The wild bagpipe music surged around the grim old kirkyard, reverberating back off bells and spire, racing along the stone walls. Tam whistled loudly, and Meg came thundering out of the wood and into the kirkyard, rearing up on her hind legs to scatter the seething mass of witches before her. Tam swung Wee Tam up onto the saddle and then jumped up behind him, seizing her reins.

"Run, girl! Like you never ran before!" he cried to Meg, who whinnied back. "Aye, I know I keep sayin' that, but this time nothin' else will do!"

A witch swung a burning torch at them, but Wee Tam somehow managed to duck and then seize it out of her hands. He whirled it around to hold off the swarming witches behind them, whilst Meg used her hooves to clear a path.

"Stand up to them, you idiots!" screamed Nannie. "These feeble mortals can't harm you! Don't let them escape the kirkyard! Drive them back, and then tear them to pieces! Rip their eyes out!"

Wave after wave of snarling witches closed in on them, faces etched with hatred and hunger, clawing at them, blocking all exits from the walled pen of the kirkyard, corralling them inexorably back towards Rannoch and the Cutty Sark. For every witch that Wee Tam could singe with his torch or Meg could dash with her hooves, more seemed to come stealing out of the very night, the sheer weight of numbers penning them in- and always there was a clutching of fingers and nails on their clothes and skin. Big Eck had long since taken to his heels, and was nowhere to be seen.

"We're trapped!" said Tam desperately. "Where do we go now?"

Wee Tam clutched at his shoulder, and then pointed his finger towards the deserted church building itself. It was the only way that wasn't completely blocked by teeming hosts of witches.

"The Auld Kirk? You're jokin', son!" said Tam. "There's no way out of there! It's a death-trap!"

But they couldn't stay where they were either. The kirkyard was mobbed with witches, and already Tam could feel Wee Tam gradually being pulled off Meg's back behind him, the grabbing hands gaining ever more purchase on him.

"Christ, I hope you're right about this, lad!" said Tam. "C'mon girl, I ken this seems, eh- completely insane- but head for the Kirk! Into the Kirk, lass!"

Tam spurred Meg hard towards the Auld Kirk. At first she shied away reluctantly, but she seemed to sense that there was nowhere else left to run to. She built up a head of speed, smashing any witch who tried to stop them out of her way, and then crashed straight through the worm-eaten wooden doors of the church.

"The fool! We have them now…" said Rannoch triumphantly. "Follow me!"

Inside the Kirk, Tam whooped, and opened his eyes.

"We made it!" he shouted.

Wee Tam squeezed his father's waist to tell him he was alright.

They clattered down the aisle of the church, witches pouring in after them, bats flying crazily around their heads. And then the witches parted, and Rannoch himself strode silently down the aisle towards them. The doors of the Kirk swung shut behind him.

"Right then! Plan B, son?" whispered Tam to Wee Tam, behind him. "'Cos I'm no' entirely sure this one is workin' out for us…"

Wee Tam shrugged his shoulders. Tam slowly circled Meg at the altar at the end of the aisle, trotting back towards the door and straight towards the advancing Rannoch. The witches behind Rannoch were steadily torching the pews as they went, so that the exit behind them was now completely blocked. The pews slowly roared into flame, like fire-demons in some infernal congregation, eagerly awaiting Rannoch's Satanic sermon. Tam turned Meg around again, desperately searching for a way out, until they faced the low stained glass window above the altar, their backs towards Rannoch.

"You're trapped this time, Farmer O'Shanter!" shouted Rannoch triumphantly, his eyes blazing brighter than the burning pews. "Hand the changeling over and you can still walk free! I can wait a little longer for your soul... But first give me the fairy-child! Your part in this is over!"

Tam rubbed Meg's head.

"It's now or never, old girl!" he urged her. "You'll just have tae' trust me on this one..."

He touched his feet to Meg's flanks and she sped down the aisle, a baying pack of witches hot on her heels. Tam whispered in her ear, and she leapt up onto the altar and used it as a springboard to vault straight out through the stained glass window. The old glass shattered into a shower of rainbow fragments, raining down onto the ancient flagstones of the church. For an endless moment they plummeted into the darkness, until finally Meg landed on solid ground outside, stumbled, regained her footing and then sped away from the Kirk.

"Christ, I didnae' really think that was goin' to work!" said Tam, as Wee Tam squeezed his waist again. "We were nearly roasted like herrings there, son! Just dinnae' tell your mother about that window, for ye mind she contributed three shillin' to the restoration fund- she'd be black affronted to see it now..."

The witches rushed up to the shattered window, but all they could see was the last swish of Meg's tail as she galloped hard for Kirk Wood. Too late, they turned to see the fire gutting the Kirk. And then it enveloped them completely. Merry Andrew's pipe tune reached a demented crescendo, drowning out the hideous shrieks as the fire swallowed up the witches trapped inside the Kirk.

Rannoch looked up, only to see the slate roof of the Auld Kirk crumpling like a collapsing house of cards, and then tumble straight down onto his head.

"Curse you, Tam O'Shanter!" he screamed.

CHAPTER 54

———

TAM LOOKED BACK OVER HIS shoulder at the Kirk for as long as he dared, as Meg weaved between the trees of the Kirk Wood. Behind them the old stone walls shook and smouldered, and then there was another great rumble as they slowly collapsed inwards. The screams and curses of the buried witches carried out to them over the night air, and then fell silent.

"That one's for you, Colin!" said Tam, feeling his head clear as they left the Cutty Sark behind them. "Rest in peace, son! An' you'll maybe rest a little easier this night, for bein' revenged... For your fire's still burnin' in this world!"

He showed Wee Tam Colin's bible and pocket-knife.

"From now on we'll carry this burden together, son," he said.

"The two of us. It must have sat awful heavy on your wee shoulders, bearin' it all alone these past few months..."

Suddenly Meg gave a loud whinny of warning, and Tam ducked under a low branch that had threatened to take his head off, holding onto Meg's reins for dear life.

"Christ!" said Tam. "Let's get home first though, eh!"

They hurtled out of the Kirk Wood and onto the edge of the moor. Tam laughed aloud with exhilaration, urging Meg on.

"Tam O'Shanter!" cried a deep voice, from out of nowhere.

Tam pulled up sharply.

"Who is it?" said Tam. "Speak your name!"

"It's your new best pal, Tammie!" said Big Eck, stepping out from be-hind a tree. "D'ye think any o' your fancy Highland friends could shoot like that on a wet night? Did ye no' see me take the knife clean oot o' his hand, from thirty paces! Eat your heart oot, William Tell, ya bass!"

"You saved our lives back there, man!" said Tam. "Thank you! But why did you come back?"

Big Eck laughed.

"I've been wonderin' that very thing myself!" he said. "You have no idea what yon Rannoch is like, Tam- what he's capable of…"

"Well, I'm startin' to get the gist o' it…" said Tam. "An' nae' of-fence, but ye didnae' exactly seem the hero type, back there at the Jolly Beggars'!"

"No' exactly!" said Eck. "But somehow I just knew that this was my moment. What I was born for. Finally, it all seemed tae' make sense! I've lived long enough now to ken that it's a strange old world, but I've never known a night like this one…"

"Right enough, Eck!" said Wullie, stepping out from Kirk Wood. "You chaps willnae' believe what I saw in the toon, the night…"

"Nor me!" said Farmer Goldie, following him out of the shadows. "My Nannie's come home, Tam! An' this time- this time we'll have tae' send her away for good… To save Wee Tam."

"Wullie!" said Tam. "An' Hosea! You too? Are you lads gonna' tell me what in the world you're doin' here?"

Big Eck was carefully loading a shiny bullet into each of his pistols. Wee Tam stared at them in horror, as Eck methodically primed the flash pans.

"I think we're all here on the same business, Tammie…" said Big Eck. "Young Callum Stewart sent me to follow Rannoch, ye see. On pain of death- tae' start with!" He squinted down the length of each pistol barrel. "But then I couldae' slipped away easily enough, in my own country. Of course I couldae'! After all, two garrisons o' English redcoats have no' found it so easy to follow my trail here, these forty years past." He tucked the pistols into his belt. "Primed and loaded! Aye, well, I wondered at the time how Callum could have been so Hielan' as to trust me to carry oot his biddin'. He didnae' even bother to send one o' his clansmen along with me! But then I started to realise what Callum had already jaloused- that I'd never cared about anythin' before. No' like- no' like ah care about Prince Cherlie, an' his cause!" Tam stared at the burly smuggler in astonishment. "It's his father's throne, Tammie!" continued Big Eck. "An' I just couldnae' allow him to be murdered in cold blood like this- tae' be cut off in his prime, by these bloody witches! I realised that this time I couldnae' stand by. It wis time to draw a line in the sand!"

"Right enough, Eck!" said Wullie. "He's a crackin' lad, Cherlie, he is that!"

"So I did follow Rannoch- and I watched him, and I listened tae' him," said Eck. "Now, I'm no' what ye'd call a fretful fellow…"

"Right enough!" said Wullie. "Nothin' can fash Big Eck! Nerves o' steel is what he has!"

"But what I saw of this Rannoch fair made my blood run cold, lads…" said Eck. "I'd no' care to repeat it in front of the bairn here- an' I'd no' even believe it myself, if I'd no' seen it wi' my own eyes!"

Tam felt a tug at his shoulder from Wee Tam.

"What is it, son?" said Tam. "I'm just thankin' the big man here for savin' our lives back there!"

Wee Tam tugged even more vigorously at Tam's shirt until Tam looked round.

"Christ!" he said.

"Not exactly, Farmer O'Shanter…" said Rannoch, wiping a smear of dust from his face as he stepped out of Kirk Wood. "Although I suppose you could say that we're rivals in the same trade!" Behind him the moon was blacked out by a cloud of winged creatures and witches on broomsticks, flooding towards them out of the Kirk Wood. "The damnation trade…"

CHAPTER 55

―◆―

SOUTER JOHNNIE AND CALLUM SCRAMBLED up to the top of the hill overlooking the Auld Brig o' Doon, just as the sun finally hit the horizon. For better or for worse, the long night was nearly over. Johnnie was panting hard after his night's exertions, whisky sweat beaded on his forehead, clothes ragged and tattered from the countless falls and tangles. And yet there was a grim resolution in his eyes that the folk of Alloway would hardly have recognised in their happy-go-lucky, lacksadaisical souter. Despite his fatigue, he refused to rest for a moment, desperately scanning the moor stretching out in front of them below for any sign of Tam. It was a view he'd seen thousands of times in summer and winter, rain and shine, and yet something about it just didn't seem quite right to him.

"Half a minute- where's the Auld Kirk?" he said. "Och, there it is, of course it is- but look! The roof has collapsed, Callum!" He stared at it again. "An' the great cross- the cross is gone!"

"Well, I'm certainly no' a priest," said Callum. "But that doesnae' seem a particularly encouragin' omen..."

He scanned the moor with a hunter's eye.

"Look, Souter!" he shouted, grabbing Johnnie's arm and pointing up at the swarming mass of flying creatures emerging from the Kirk Wood. "Is that what I think it is?"

"What- what'n the world is that?" said Johnnie in astonishment.

"Nothin' from this world!" said Callum crossing himself. "*Iosa Crìosd!*"

"That there's witches, son!" said Doxy Mary, coaxing the exhausted King Billy up onto the crest of the hill. She drew her sword-stick, tested the keen blade with her finger and then let the morning light play along it. "It's time to get it on, laddies! Ah'm goin' to fillet me some witches like Finnan haddies…"

CHAPTER 56

—

"THIS CHARADE HAS GONE ON long enough!" said Rannoch. "Does anyone have any last words, before I damn your wretched souls to torment for all eternity?"

"Aye!" said Big Eck. "How's your monkey?"

"Absalom?" said Rannoch. "You will all pay dearly if any harm has befallen one hair on his flea-bitten head! Where is he?"

"Why don't ye tell the man, Wullie..." said Eck, hands drifting imperceptibly to the handles of his pistols.

"Right enough, Eck..." said Wullie, clearing his throat. "So I wis' just strollin' through the Market Square..."

"Get to the point, you dolt!" shouted Rannoch. "We're about to disembowel you alive!"

"Well, the truth is that it went hard wi' the furry wee bugger, sir!" said Wullie. "Tae' cut a long story short, he's, eh, he's been hung as a spy at the Mercat Cross..."

"What!" shouted Rannoch.

"Hung by the neck until deid..." said Farmer Goldie.

"I know what hanging is!" screamed Rannoch. "But he was a monkey!"

"Aye, right enough..." said Wullie. "I ken that- you ken that- but unfortunately the Kirkmichael farmer lads didnae' ken that... They hadnae' seen a monkey before, an' they thought it must hae' been a Frenchman, what wi' his fancy wee clothes an' all. Speakin' o' which, it's no' a' bad news..." He delved into the pocket of his breeks and pulled out a tiny

259

garment. "I did manage to save his wee waistcoat for ye, at least!" He held Absalom's waistcoat out to Rannoch, who dashed it out of his hand impatiently. He seized Wullie and shook him by the shirt collar until his bones rattled. Taking advantage of Rannoch's momentary distraction, Big Eck lunged over towards Meg and slapped her on the rear.

"Ride, Tam!" he shouted. "You must save the bairn, tae' save Prince Cherlie!"

"Ride hard, for runnin' water!" said Goldie. "We'll hold them off for as long as we can..."

"Come with us, lads!" said Tam. "We cannae' leave you now!"

"We'll no' make it on one horse!" said Eck. "Go now, or it'll all have been for nothin'- an' that's no way for an old smuggler to die! I never took a bargain price for my crop, an' I'll certainly no' take one for my life!"

"Ye're a brave man, Eck McIver!" said Tam.

"I'm a bloody fool, is what I am!" said Eck, laughing. "But a bloody fool wi' a cause, an' that's somethin'..."

"Right enough, Eck!" said Wullie, standing four-square beside him, brandishing a cudgel resolutely.

"What about you, Hosea?" said Tam urgently. "You're light enough..."

"Maybe so, Tam- but I'm deid already," said Goldie. "I have been since my Nannie went- my true Nannie... An' besides, I promised your Katie that I'd no' just stand by, an' see any harm come to Wee Tam again, no' while I live! I'm gonnae' keep that promise."

Wullie passed Goldie a spare cudgel, and he gripped it resolutely.

"God bless you all then!" cried Tam, spurring Meg on. "And thank you! Thank you!"

"God speed, son!" said Big Eck.

He, Wullie and Goldie hitched up their breeks and set their shoulders towards Rannoch and the witches.

"Now go, Tam!" shouted Eck. "Go! Before they cut you off! We'll deal wi' this little lot!"

"I think you'll find that it is we who shall deal with you, smuggler!" said Rannoch.

"Oh aye? You and whose army?" said Eck defiantly.

Rannoch smiled and gestured back at the infernal hordes massed behind him at the edge of the Kirk Wood, awaiting his word.

"Oh- that army..." said Eck. "Aye, well you'll have to get through us first!"

"Right enough, Eck!" said Wullie. "Same rules apply!"

"Let's see whit ye've got, Beelzebub!" said Goldie. "For I hear ye've a glass jaw on ye, son!"

Rannoch laughed long and loud, as Meg sprinted off behind Big Eck. Then he stepped towards Eck, eyes blazing.

"Have it your own way!" he said. "Perhaps ignorance really is bliss... For it beggars belief that after everything you've seen, you could still dare to dream of thwarting my will!"

Eck levelled his long pistols coolly at Rannoch.

"No' so much me- as my two wee pals here..." he said. "I'm gonnae' light you up, Black Donald!"

Rannoch laughed again.

"Bullets can't hurt me!" he said scornfully.

"Is that a fact?" said Big Eck. "No' even if they're made of good old church silver?"

Rannoch stared at him in horror, his face suddenly showing every one of his countless years, in all of their bottomless malice. Big Eck smiled slowly.

"Despair thy charm, ya bass!" he said, and let Rannoch have it in the chest with both pistols. For a moment Rannoch stood defiantly, staring back at Eck, and then he put his hands up to his mouth in horror. His teeth were crumbling away, leaving hideous toothless gums that were sinking into his head. His ancient body writhed, twisted and then dissolved into dust.

"Aye, I thought so!" said Big Eck. "How art thou fallen from heaven, O Lucifer, son of the mornin'! Ye dinnae' work the Ayrshire coast all these years, withoot knowin' how to deal wi' a wee witch or two! An' when ye're shootin' wi' silver bullets- ye jist load it, cock it and dump it..."

"Right enough, Eck!" said Wullie.

"Kill them!" screamed Nannie, rushing through the ranks to the front of the group of witches. "Kill them! Smash in their skulls, and drink their blood!"

Suddenly she recognised Farmer Goldie and pulled up short, holding back the tide of witches for a precious moment, as Meg galloped across the open moor behind them.

"You shouldn't have come here..." she breathed. "Even I can't save you now, father!"

"God save you, Nannie!" cried Goldie. "I love you!"

And then the witches seethed towards Eck, Wullie and Goldie, with murder in their eyes.

"Let's sing a song, lads, to keep oor spirits up!" cried Eck. "Altogether now!" And he sang out loud, as Wullie and Goldie battered the witches back with their cudgels, breaking arms and fracturing skulls, desperately trying to buy as much time as possible for the Tams to escape.

"The devil came fiddlin' thro' the town,
And danced awa' wi' the Exciseman!
And every wife cries, 'Auld Satan,
I wish you luck o' the prize, man!'"

Big Eck blazed away with his pistols, and then pistol-whipped any witch in range with the stocks, singing a lusty chorus all the while.

"The devil's awa', the devil's awa',
The devil's awa wi' the Exciseman!
He's danced awa', he's danced awa',
He's danced awa' wi' the Exciseman!"

"It's been a pleasure workin' wi' you, lads!" shouted Eck, as the witches finally wrestled away his last pistol and dragged him to the ground, through sheer weight of numbers. "Scotland forever!"

"Right enough, Eck!" said Wullie. "Scotland forever!"

"Scotland forever!" cried Farmer Goldie.

And then the wave of hatred broke over their heads, and they were all lost together, beneath a storm of tearing nails and teeth. There was one last snatch of song from Big Eck:

"We'll make our malt, and we'll brew our drink,
We'll laugh, sing, and rejoice, man!
And many braw thanks to the great black devil,
That danced awa' wi' the Exciseman…"

And then his voice fell silent forever.

CHAPTER 57

———◆———

As FIRST LIGHT CREPT OVER the horizon, Callum and Johnnie could just about make out the shape of the running horse. It was hurtling towards the Brig o' Doon at full tilt, skipping sure-footedly over tussocks and bumps.

"You see that, Johnnie lad?" said Callum.

"It's him! It's really him, Callum!" shouted Johnnie, leaping up and waving his arms wildly. "Tam- Tam! And that's Wee Tam, sat up there behind him! They're alive! They're alive! An' they're comin' this way!"

"Aye- an' see what's behind them!" said Callum. "Ye never saw the likes o' that, comin' down the old Crieff drove-road!"

Johnnie and Callum stared in amazement at the black cloud of witches, fanning out to fill the sky behind the tiny figures of the horse and its riders. Meg was galloping flat out, but even so the host of swarming witches was gaining on her fast. Some wore the form of seagulls; some of grimacing gargoyles and imps; others were in human guise, atop broomsticks- but all were ferocious, implacable, relentless.

"They're hot on Tam's heels!" said Johnnie. "He cannae' hold them off for long! What do we do, Callum?"

"Hurry, lads, we must get to him before they do!" shouted Callum, already swinging into action. "Now, now, now, now, now! Prince Cherlie's life depends on it too! On me, Clan Stewart! On me!"

Callum sprinted down the hill towards the Brig o' Doon below, without waiting to see who was following him. Johnnie, Ruaridh, Gregor and the rest of the Highlanders coursed after him. King Billy brought up the rear, lolloping over the broken ground, with Doxy Mary bouncing along on his back, holding on to his horns for dear life.

"Wait for me, ya bawbags!" she cried. "I'm gonna' slay me some witches!"

"So what do you, eh, normally do in this situation?" panted Johnnie, eyes glued to the desperate chase beyond the humped bridge.

"Charge them, by God!" shouted Callum. "Charge them! Though Auld Hornie himself should be leadin' their line!"

"I think he's actually the one wi' the sonsie face at the back there!" said Johnnie. "But I'm no' feared- they say the devil loves a cobbler!"

"Och no, ye're on the wrong track there, Lowlander!" said Gregor, unslinging his own broadsword as he caught up with Callum and Johnnie. "The devil loves a tailor- souters he's nae' sae' fond of..."

"Bugger!" said Johnnie. "I always suspected it, for I've never had any luck at the cards... But there's nothin' for it now, I suppose!"

Ruaridh caught up with them too, and put a friendly hand on Johnnie's shoulder as he loped along behind him.

"Ye mind that wee wager from the Inn, where ye lifted my purse, Souter?" he shouted. "Ye fancy goin' double or quits on who gets killed first now?"

"Brothers-in-arms, eh?" said Johnnie.

"Hist, stop your jabberin', Souter!" shouted Callum. "Stop, all of you, and form up! Form a line! Form a line!"

They halted on the military crest of the hill, and Callum hastily formed them into a single rank.

"Clan Stewart!" he cried. "I'll no' speak to you 'ay truth an' honour, for we've a Maclachlan wi' us, and he'd need a translator! You'll fight because you've a wee bit o' breath in your lungs, and a drop o' blood in your veins. And when that's all spent- you'll maybe have earned the rest!"

The Highlanders roared and drummed their broadswords on their bucklers. Callum threw away his scabbard and shouted the ancient Highland battle-cry: "Claymore!"

The other Highlanders and Souter Johnnie took up the wild cry, working themselves into a frenzy, until the moor was ringing with their voices. As the sun rose high up over the hill, the Highlanders charged down it towards the Brig o' Doon, a tide of tartan plaids and glinting steel.

"*Creag an Sgairbh! Creag an Sgairbh!*" rang out the clear Stewart voices across the Valley of Doon. "The Rock of the Cormorants!"

"Tam O'Shanter!" cried Souter Johnnie, drawing his father's dirk. "The Brig o' Doon or bust!"

"*Mnathan-shìdh* forever!" cried Doxy Mary, laughing wildly as she slashed the air with her bronze blade. "*Buaidh nó bás! Buaidh nó bás!* Victory or death, ya bass! Yaaaah!" She drove her heels into King Billy's side. "Ride like the wind, Billy, ye old Hun, ye!"

King Billy bellowed, shook his great horns aloft and charged for the bridge.

"*Buaidh nó bás!*"

CHAPTER 58

———◆———

"THE WHOLE DAMNED HIVE O' witches is comin' down upon us!" shouted Tam, giving spur to Meg once more. "Home, Meg, darling, home! You must run for all of our lives now!"

Tam could feel the rushing wind of the host of witches behind them now. Unearthly voices wailed curses and screamed hideous, blood-curdling threats. He peered back over his shoulder, and then quickly turned back. They were only yards away, inexorably closing the gap, blocking out the light. And of all the monstrous forms and grotesque expressions that Tam saw in that shadow-world, none of them was so terrifying as the lovely Cutty Sark herself. The cloud of witches parted to let her through, and she surged right up to the front of the chasing pack, flying in human form, cutty sark flapping in the wind.

"No gods, no masters!" she screamed, her beautiful face etched with a blazing, killing fury. "We have them now! Kill them! Tear them to pieces!"

Tam could feel Wee Tam shuddering with fear behind him, and he knew that he had to try something- anything- before they were overtaken. He cut off the track to head cross-country, shaving off precious yards, sending Meg leaping nimbly over bogs and fences. She was running as she never had before, but she was also tiring quickly now. She stumbled and nearly lost her footing, somehow managing to steady herself just in time to clear a gorse bush. But over the uneven ground they were already losing time to the airborne hordes racing behind them. The witches were nearly upon them.

"They're tirin', girl!" Tam shouted, crossing his fingers on the reins as he spoke. For they were desperately close. "They're nearly spent! An' I can see the Brig o' Doon! Runnin' water, girl!"

That gave Tam an idea, and sometimes an idea is the closest thing to hope that you're likely to get.

"I've no' done much prayin' in my time, Lord..." he said. "But Wee Tam never harmed anyone, an' I reckon you owe me one for puttin' John Calvin into the world! So maybe you'll gie' me a wee hand in my hour o' need, Big Man? An' forgive me this- for it's needs must, when the devil drives!"

He turned and threw Wee Colin's bible back at the onrushing witches. A few of them sheered off their course to avoid the Holy Book, shrieking with rage, but the rest just plunged on after him, faster than ever.

"Looks like we're on our own wi' this one!" said Tam. "So don't let me down now, Maggie, darling! Fifty yards tae' the Brig o' Doon, and then we're home and dry..."

It might as well have been fifty miles as fifty yards though, thought Tam. Nannie was only half a length behind now, and she was still gaining ground on them, inch by precious inch. She stretched out her hand towards Wee Tam, willing him within her grasp, but Meg sensed her coming and drained her own reserves of energy to the dregs. She put on a desperate spurt of speed, instinctively straining to keep Wee Tam out of Nannie's clutches.

"Give me the changeling, Tam!" screamed the Cutty Sark. "Give him to me, and I'll spare you!"

"Never!" shouted Tam, spurring Meg on once more.

Wee Tam shied away from her finger-tips, but he only just eluded her this time. The witches were coming thick and fast now, and no sooner did Nannie fall back a few inches than another gnarled, bony hand reached out to seize Wee Tam in her place. Tam slashed wildly at them with Wee Colin's pocket-knife, ignoring Wee Tam's shudder at the proximity of the metal, and the latest marauding hand came away with nothing but another clump of Wee Tam's rapidly disintegrating tunic. But now pale, skeletal hands were multiplying, clawing and grabbing at Wee Tam. The knife was snatched out of Tam's hand, and then dropped to the ground as the metal burnt the witch's fingers. There were still ten yards to go to the Brig o'Doon when Meg finally faltered, and the chasing pack of witches caught up with them.

"There is no escape this time!" cried the Cutty Sark triumphantly. "Show them no mercy! You should have given up the changeling while you still could, Tam O'Shanter!"

The sky grew dark as the Tams and Meg were gradually engulfed by their enraged pursuers. Tam urged Meg on desperately to one last effort, but this time she had nothing left to give. Now Nannie came storming through the baying pack of witches.

"Destroy them!" she shrieked in a fury. "Pluck out their eyes!"

CHAPTER 59

———

THE HIGHLANDERS SWEPT AFTER CALLUM and Johnnie onto the bridge approach on the far side of the Brig o' Doon. They were screaming like berserkers, brandishing broadswords and dirks high above their heads as they ran.

"Tam O'Shanter!" cried Souter Johnnie.

"Johnnie!" shouted Tam, seeing him on the other side of the bridge for the first time. For a moment the two friends locked eyes across the Water of Doon. The leading rank of witches halted dead in their tracks as they saw the Highlanders and King Billy surging towards them, caught unawares by the sheer sound and fury of the Highland charge. Nannie wheeled around in a fury, rallying her witches on again.

"On, on, you fools!" she screamed. "No mortal soldier dare stand against us!"

"*Buaidh nó bás!*" shouted Doxy Mary, drowning out her voice, and still the Highlanders kept coming, up onto the far approach to the bridge. And all the time Meg was stealing precious yards to safety. She too had seen the familiar face of Souter Johnnie on the other side and, taking full advantage of the witches' hesitation, she gave one last spring forward towards him. Now they were within inches of the keystone of the bridge, and safety. Meg stretched her front leg out to step past it, but just as she did so, Nannie threw out her hand and managed to seize her tail. Meg kicked and struggled, but the Cutty Sark was holding her back with superhuman strength, clamping her tail in a remorseless, vice-like grip. The witches rushed up on them triumphantly, pouring onto the bridge in scores, shrieking horribly in their lust to maim and destroy. Dozens of hands reached out now, dirty, broken fingernails clawing mercilessly at Tam and Wee Tam.

At the back of the Highland charge, Doxy Mary lifted up her hands and chanted.

"*Ag àrdachadh uisge! Ag àrdachadh uisge!*"

The Water of Doon started to bubble and rage, but only on Mary's side of the river.

"Tam!" she shouted. "Tam! I'm no' powerful enough... You must raise the river yourself! It's the only way now, son! Remember Merry Andrew! Remember Merry Andrew! You must use the ways o' the *mna-than-shìdh*! Only they can save you now!"

"What's she shoutin'?" said Tam. "Raise the river? How could I do that?"

And then he realised that she wasn't speaking to him.

"Wee Tam!" he shouted, spinning around in his saddle. "Can you do it? Can you raise the river?"

Wee Tam started to shake his head, sobbing as the witches dragged him bodily off Meg's back, gouging and scratching his skin with their rough, serrated nails.

"I think you can!" shouted Tam, desperately trying to pry their hands off him. "I think I've always known it!"

Now Tam was being dragged out of the saddle himself, but he thrashed and struggled, and finally fought his way out of the witches' clutches. Just long enough to shout once more:

"I know you can do it, Tam!"

And then Wee Tam realised what Doxy Mary had been trying to tell him. He closed his eyes and stopped struggling, sinking to the ground as he surrendered himself to the elements.

"It's all over now, Tam!" screamed Nannie, as Tam was finally hauled out of his saddle, battered and clawed at by the furious witches. "It's just as I told you! Now the changeling has been destroyed, and he has destroyed you too! He's your enemy! He always has been!"

"No!" shouted Tam, rolling over the stones of the bridge to Wee Tam and hugging him to his chest. "He's my son! And Kate's son. And we love him!"

Suddenly a great swell of bagpipe music rippled over the water and the River Doon rose up in a fury, enveloping Tam, Wee Tam, Meg and the witches altogether in surging, foaming water.

Nannie grimly held onto Meg as the wave of water crashed over her, and then she staggered back, Meg's tail in her hand, and the Doon swept her and everything on the bridge away in the torrent. All except for Meg, who whinnied in pain and then finally flew, riderless and tail-less, past the keystone of the bridge.

CHAPTER 60

SOUTER JOHNNIE, CALLUM AND THE Highlanders watched in amazement from the far side of the bridge, as the River Doon swept all before it in its anger. The normally placid river smashed witches against the great rocks of its bed like rag-dolls, sweeping their broken bodies away in the current, and then subsided back into its usual course. Johnnie looked in vain for Tam and Wee Tam in the carnage, and then sank down to his knees in misery.

"After everythin' that they've been through!" he said. "To get so close- and then to lose them now..."

Callum put a consoling hand on his shoulder, but there were no words he could find to say. As the water died down, a plume of smoke rose up from Meg's tail, curling high above the Brig o' Doon. Suddenly Meg leaped and bucked, and a hand shot out above the foaming water, still clinging onto her reins. Tam's head struggled its way above the surface, coughing and spluttering. Meg bent her back to pulling him out of the water, and Tam dragged Wee Tam out of the water after him.

"Pull, Meg, pull! What're ye waitin' for, girl?" shouted Tam. "It's no' the Sabbath day yet!"

Meg whinnied, energised once more, straining and struggling to drag her sodden master out of the river.

"Pull, Meg!" shouted Tam, hauling himself and Wee Tam out onto the bank. They lay there for a minute, coughing and spluttering in the shallows, and then Meg bent her head again and pulled Tam gently up to his feet. She licked his face and then Wee Tam's, rubbing her mane against their freezing heads. Tam hugged her neck, shivering violently.

"That's another one I owe you, auld lass!" he stuttered through his shudders. "That's a lot of oats!"

Johnnie and Callum hurried down to them, wrapping them in long tartan plaids against the cold.

"An' they say Lowlanders are borin'!" said Callum. "Ye've more lives than the King o' the Cats, Tam! But what's happened to her tail?" he said, pointing to the steam rising from poor Meg's singed stump of a tail.

"I think that's what ye'd call a close shave, Callum!" said Tam. He patted Meg's face again. "You left it pretty late there, Meg, you old drama queen! And as for you, Johnnie-come-lately... Thanks for coming back, brother!"

Tam and Wee Tam embraced Johnnie, only for Tam to leap back in alarm as he caught sight of a cloaked figure in a black hat over his shoulder.

"Christ, who's that!" said Tam.

"Och, it's just Gregor, Tammie!" said Johnnie.

The Highlanders were picking carefully through the debris on the bridge in the traditional fashion, separating the booty from the wreckage.

"It's no' exactly the bountiful spoils o' war!" said Ruaridh, trying on a discarded witch's hat. "But it'll maybe do the missus for church on Sundays?"

———

CHAPTER 61

THE PRINCE'S EYES FLASHED WIDE open, the old fire burning brighter than ever. He lifted up his sheet to check that everything was intact, and then looked jauntily around him. Malcolm and Poosie Nansie didn't even notice him stir, so deeply engrossed were they in poring over Poosie Nansie's neat book of accounts.

"Holy Oil, forsooth!" said Malcolm. "Surely the Church should defray all ecclesiastical costs? What do we pay our tithes for?"

"Father MacFarlane had no idea he'd be called upon to administer the Last Rites so swiftly, Chevalier," said Poosie Nansie. "I had to provide the Holy Oil from my own supplies. That wis best Italian olive oil!"

"Ye should've used lard..." grumbled Malcolm. "An' let's be clear on one thing from the very outset, Madame- I'm not paying a penny for the- late- Prince's high-jinks in this house! Ye must know that a contract for immoral conduct is not enforceable in a court of law in Scotland!"

"Really, Chevalier!" said Poosie Nansie. "The poor lad is still alive! And besides, the balance is clearly for services rendered, no' on account. 'Twould only be equitable for you to settle the Prince's affairs like a gentleman now..."

"Fie, Madam, there are no courts of equity in Scotland!" said Malcolm. "And if it comes to that, you should have satisfied yourself he had the stamina for it before you let him loose in a house like this! I have half a mind to bring a suit against ye for delict myself, in the person of the Crown of Scotland... I believe that Rowena creature was too saucy for the lad!"

Rowena flew at Malcolm, incensed. Poosie Nansie and Sophie dragged her off the cowering nobleman, but not before she had inflicted a livid red mark on his bald pate with the heel of her shoe.

"Compose yourself, madam, I beg ye!" spluttered Malcolm. "We must all bear up with dignity at such a time! 'Tis the very least that we can do for his royal memory..."

The Prince cleared his throat loudly, waking up Father MacFarlane who was still dozing away next to him. The jovial priest sat up in surprise.

"God be praaaised! I thought we'd lost you there, my son!" he said. "I had performed the Last Rites!"

Malcolm turned around hastily and hurried to the Prince's side.

"Your Highness- thank goodness!" he said. "I've been worried sick about you!"

"And your books of account, it would seem, Chevalier!" said the Prince, ignoring Malcolm as he looked around the room. "But where is Stupid Johnnie- and my bonny Highlanders?"

"They've been to the gates of hell for you this night, Your Highness!" said Poosie Nansie. "That much is clear, from the speed of your recovery... For even knowin' that there was witchcraft at work, they hurried to the heart of the coven to root it out!"

"Did they, by God!" said the Prince heartily. "Stout fellows! We must feast them like heroes!"

"Aye, well, I'll speak to cookie..." said Nansie.

"Speak to your girls, Madame!" said the Prince. "Man cannot live by bread alone, eh, padre?"

He winked at Father MacFarlane, who smiled uncomfortably.

"Is there any other comfort we can procure for you now, Your Highness?" said Malcolm solicitously.

"Perhaps some privacy, Chevalier..." said the Prince, kissing Rowena and pulling her down onto the chaise longue with him.

"I always knew that some day soon my prince would come!" said Rowena happily.

"Well then, my work is done here, my son!" said Father MacFarlane, gathering his cassock around him and bustling out of the door. "Glory be to God!"

The others hastily withdrew after him.

"Amen to that, *padre mio*!" called the Prince after Father MacFarlane. "Amen to that!"

CHAPTER 62

———◆———

TAM AND WEE TAM LED Meg back to their little croft, enjoying the feeling of the pale sunshine on the backs of their necks. Wee Tam petted Meg's face and made a fuss of her.

"Home, Tam!" said Tam. "It never felt so good to be here! I cannae' believe that I- that I just took it for granted, for all these years…"

Wee Tam swung open the rickety door of the byre, and Tam led Meg in and tied her up. He ladled a generous portion of plump oats into her feed-trough, and she ate hungrily, only pausing to nuzzle his hand in gratitude.

"Enjoy it! For you've certainly earned it the night, girl!" said Tam. "We should be enterin' you into the Ayr Races- all you'd need is a troop of witches behind you, bayin' for blood, an' you couldnae' lose! Now you get some rest while you can, for who knows what'll we'll run into today…"

Wee Tam smiled, and they walked across to the cottage. Tam turned to Wee Tam, ruffling his hair.

"No, dinnae' mention it, Tam! Only too happy to save you from a pack of demented harpies, wantin' to sacrifice you wi' a magic black dagger! Really, it was my pleasure- any time…"

Tam opened the door to the croft, and was immediately drenched by another bucket of icy water. It sucked the air out of his lungs, and he stood spluttering.

"You can control the water now, Tam!" he said. "Could you no' have diverted that somewhere else?"

"So ye've finally decided to come home have ye, Tam O'Shanter?" said Kate, hugging Wee Tam to her chest as if she'd never let him go. She put her hand up to Tam's cheek, and then wrapped him up in a dry blanket. "Well then- it's better late than never, I suppose! Ye brought my wee boy back, and yourself, and that's all I've prayed for this night!"

Tam wrapped his arms around the two of them. He was about to tell them that things were going to be different, but somehow there was no need.

"Our wee boy!" said Kate. "Our blessin'! You're back home wi' us now!"

"Changeling no more!" whispered Tam. "You belong here. You're our son!"

CHAPTER 63

FROM THE HILL ABOVE THE O'Shanter croft, two black-cloaked figures looked down upon Tam, Kate and Wee Tam. A man and a woman, to all appearances. The man was leisurely filling a pipe, packing Big Eck's French baccy down with the end of the witches' obsidian dagger. He lit the pipe in the face of the morning breeze and got the tobacco drawing gently, no trace of fear or fatigue on his unlined face. Only when he had completed the task, wreaths of smoke drifting peacefully through the morning air, did he start to sing quietly:

"Now, all who this tale of truth shall see,
Each man and mother's son take heed:
When e'er to drink you are inclined,
Or cutty sarks run in your mind,
Think! ye may buy the joys o'er dear;
Remember Tam O'Shanter's mare!"

"Ye earned yourself a pretty souvenir there, Andrew!" said Doxy Mary, pointing at the sacrificial knife. "Well, why not? Ye may no' say much, but ye did well enough in the time of need! We have watched to the end, *coimhead*, an' it has been the great pleasure o' my life to watch wi' you!"

She looked very different in her own world, the years stripped away from her face, and the bloom of nature taking its place in her cheeks.

"*Gràdh geal mo chridh!*" she called to Merry Andrew, with love in her eyes.

He smiled crookedly back at her, but his own eyes sparkled all the same. He tapped out the bowl of his pipe, cleaning out the ashes with the point of the black knife. And then he girded his bagpipes, and slowly raised the chanter up to his lips.

"Tae' think they ever thought you were the changeling, my love!" laughed Mary. "Whoever heard of a witch playin' the bagpipes! Now I'm the only one left- for poor Nannie was too brittle for this world, too much of water after all, and Wee Tam has found his own place here at last!"

Merry Andrew shook his head gently. He tapped his forefinger against his ear, and then he started to play.

And finally Mary understood everything. For the music, as it wound its way through that quiet countryside, scampering and chuckling gleefully along the pebbled shores of the River Doon, sweeping up hill and over moor, dancing in the wind over the purple-fringed sea-shore, told the ancient story of Scotland. It told of the first great magic that had taken root so many millennia ago, and of the younger powers that had come along afterwards to vie with it. It told the deep secrets that Rannoch had spent so many lifetimes searching for, and would never guess at now, as though they were the passing gossip of a market-day. It told tales of great wrongs, of unbearable suffering- and of endless forgiveness and rebirth.

"Changeling no more!" said Mary. "And so I have found my home too! I belong here at last."

A great tear rolled down her smooth cheek, and she rested her head on Andrew's shoulder and listened, spell-bound, to the pipes. The music was for all the world, and of all the world, but no one was listening except for Merry Andrew and Doxy Mary- and Wee Tam, snug at home in his mother's arms. Wee Tam heard it in his heart, and he smiled, for all the fairy-folk love music.

About the Author

GUY WINTER GREW UP IN Edinburgh before studying law at the University of Oxford. He is now an energy partner at a City law firm, but still recites *Tam O'Shanter* badly and drinks a dram too many on Burns Nights.

In addition to *Tam*, Winter is the author of *Watchdog: A Credit Crunch Fairytale* under the name Robert Anderson. He lives with his wife and two daughters in southwest London.